Damned, Delicious, and Dangerous

Damned, Delicious and Dangerous

Delilah Devlin
Lisa Renee Jones
Megan Kearns

APHRODISIA

KENSINGTON BOOKS
http://www.kensingtonbooks.com

APHRODISIA BOOKS are published by

Kensington Publishing Corp.
850 Third Avenue
New York, NY 10022

All Kensington Titles, Imprints, and Distributed Lines are available at special quantity discounts for bulk purchases for sales promotion premiums, fund-raising, and educational or institutional use.

Special book excerpts or customized printings can also be created to fit specific needs. For details, write or phone the office of the Kensington special sales manager: Kensington Publishing Corp., 850 Third Avenue, New York, NY, 10022, attn: Special Sales Department, Phone: 1-800-221-2647.

Aphrodisia and the A logo Reg. U.S. Pat. & TM Off

ISBN-13: 978-0-7582-2250-4
ISBN-10: 0-7582-2250-4

First Trade Paperback Printing: June 2008

10 9 8 7 6 5 4 3 2 1

Printed in the United States of America

CONTENTS

The Demon Lord's Cloak 1
Delilah Devlin

Night Sins 81
Lisa Renee Jones

The Devil's Paradise 155
Megan Kearns

The Demon Lord's Cloak

Delilah Devlin

Prologue

"We'll all be dead by morning." Martin's voice quavered as he emptied another glass of Frau Sophie's precious peach schnapps.

"Who'd have guessed it'd be nigh onto impossible to find a virgin in this valley?" his companion said.

"Pah! Even my own daughter," Martin moaned. "What's the world coming to, Edgard? Young women giving themselves like barmaids . . ."

Edgard's shoulders slumped. "I tell you it was the last May Day celebration. The bürgermeister should never have let Sophie provide the drink."

"We should have locked every last one of the unmarried maidens in a cellar. Well, no use grousing." Martin set down his glass. "We have a problem. Now's the time for clear thinking."

"There's no solution. The village will disappear, swallowed by Hell itself when we fail to provide *his* bride." Edgard's reddened eyes widened. "Couldn't we mount a raid on Fulkenstein down the valley . . . take a girl or two . . ."

"There's no time left. We only had the new moon to give

that devil his due. It ends tomorrow night. We'd never be back in time."

Edgard shook his head, sighing. "We've failed. Daemonberg will be no more. Best get the women packing tonight so we can flee come morning. A thousand years of prosperity and health—gone for the lack of a single maidenhead."

"We're doomed, I tell you." Martin lifted the schnapps bottle and tilted it over his glass. He gave it a shake, and then slammed it down on the table. Turning toward the bar, he shouted, "Sophie, *liebchen*, bring us another bottle, will you?"

As he turned back to his friend, he saw a woman step through the doorway of the inn. Her beauty arrested him: far prettier than any of the strapping blond women of the village, this one was slender and delicate, with deep reddish hair that glinted like fire in the torchlight, reminding him of the bay he'd bid on and lost at an auction in early spring.

He elbowed Edgard beside him. "Look there."

Both men turned to stare at the young woman.

"Where's her escort?" Edgard whispered.

"She looks wary. I'd wager she's on her own."

They shared a charged glance, shoulders straightening.

"What do you suppose the chances are she's a virgin?" Edgard asked softly.

"She's beyond fair. What man would care whether he was her first just so long as he's her last? Besides, what other options have we?"

Sophie slammed another bottle in the center of the table and gave them a scathing glance. "If you go home to your wives legless with drink, I'll not take the blame."

"We'll have just one more glass," Martin assured her, reaching around to pat her rump. "For the road. We've business to attend."

Sophie rolled her eyes and turned, her ample hips rolling as she walked across the room to greet the young woman, who waved her away.

"If they only knew the solemn duty we perform," Martin whispered. "They'd call us heroes."

Only, Martin and Edgard could never tell a soul. That, too, was part of their sacred oath, handed down from father to son.

Edgard poured them both another drink, then lifted his glass. "To another hundred years of peace and wealth."

Martin lifted his glass with one hand and crossed himself with the other. "To the fair maiden with the red hair—God rest her soul."

1
_____

Voletta felt faint with alarm; her stomach was in knots. *I can't have lost it. Someone must know where it is!*

But what were the chances anyone here would just give it back to her? She didn't have any gold to offer as a reward for its return. She'd already had to steal the voluminous cloak she wore so she wouldn't walk naked into their midst.

She stepped farther into the entryway.

"Hullo, Miss," an elderly gentleman said as he approached, his avid gaze sliding over her hair.

She clutched the edges of the cloak, only too aware its thick folds hid her nudity. "Good evening, sir."

"You're a stranger here."

Her nose twitched at the sour smell of liquor and unwashed skin that emanated from him. Not many men believed in the value of a thorough cleansing.

If only she hadn't been so fastidious herself, she might never have paused beside the gurgling brook, then noted the thick green curtain of foliage that rendered the glade an irresistible temptation.

"Miss, are you looking for someone?" he asked, his gaze looking beyond her shoulder furtively.

She took a deep breath. How to explain? "I lost something."

"Yes?" he said quickly. "Perhaps we can help you find it. Why don't you come have a seat? Can I take your cloak?"

"No! I'm chilled. And I won't be staying long. I've just come to make an inquiry."

"Come along, now," he cajoled. "You must join my friend, Edgard, and myself. I am Martin, by the way. I promise we are as harmless as we are hospitable. We might even be able to help."

The old fellow seemed a friendly sort, although she didn't feel quite comfortable with the way his gaze kept searching her face.

"Come, come. You seem overset. Have a wee drink with us—just to warm you up. Then we'll help you find whatever you've lost."

Unused to talking to men, to anyone for any length, really, she tried to demur. "I shouldn't. I must keep looking."

A frown drew his thick peppered brows together, then quickly faded as he smiled once again. "What is it you've lost?"

She nibbled her bottom lip, then blurted, "My fur. I've lost my fox fur."

"A fox fur, you say?" His glance slid away, and his gnarled fingers scratched his head. "Was it part of a garment?"

"No . . . not yet. It was . . . a gift. I need it back."

"Come along. Edgard purchases furs. Although one fur is hardly distinguishable from another."

"Oh, mine was unique," she murmured.

She let him lead her to a table at the rear of the establishment. Another man stood, younger than his companion, with a large, round belly and ruddy cheeks. He drew up a chair and indicated that she should sit.

"No," Voletta said, holding out a hand. "I really should be on my way."

"But your fur . . ." the elderly man began.

Each passing moment deepened her unease. "I'm sure I just missed it in the darkness. I'll retrace my steps."

"A fur, did you say?" the fat man said, giving a pointed glare at his companion. "Where did you leave it?"

"Beside a brook. I put it down for only a moment."

"Today?"

"Yes, just before dark."

His gaze sharpened. "A fine fur, was it? Unblemished by any trap's teeth?"

"Of course!" she said, feeling hope at the man's brightening expression.

"And red as your hair, miss?"

"Yes, as a matter of fact, it is."

"I saw just such a fur. The bürgermeister brought it to me. My wife is even now sewing it onto a fine cloak."

"Sewing it?" she asked, pressing her hand to her belly.

"Yes, as part of the dowry for a nobleman's bride."

Voletta reached for the man's arm. "I must have it back."

The heavy man dropped his gaze to her hand, then reached up slowly to pat it. "And you shall. We will go to my shop in a moment. Would you have a drink with us first?"

Relief made her lightheaded, and she nodded. "But quickly, please."

"Of course. Don't fret yourself."

Voletta accepted the beaker the older man handed her and took only a sip, then set her glass on the table. "Sir, I apologize for rushing you, but could we please go retrieve my fur?"

"Of course." He stared expectantly. "How are you feeling?"

Voletta shook her head. "Fine, can we go now?" Only she didn't feel fine. Her head swam. The men before her seemed to teeter and stretch. "How odd," she said, her voice sounding to her own ears as though it rose from the bottom of a deep well.

"Best get her out of here, Edgard, before she topples."

"Come, miss. You wanted to see my shop?"

She tugged at the collar of her cloak. "S'warm."

"Catch her!"

"Seems a shame. A beautiful girl like her."

The voice, Edgard's, she remembered, came from right beside her.

"Just get the trunk off the cart," Martin whispered harshly.

Voletta tried to lift her head, but the movement made her nauseous. She pried open her eyelids and found herself looking down at a rutted track. Graying daylight stabbed like tiny daggers at the backs of her eyes.

The air around her was damp and cold. Her skin prickled—she was naked! A fog had rolled in, droplets catching on her breasts and cheeks. The bastards had taken her cloak!

She forced up her head and stared after the men riding atop a cart rolling down a long, steep trail. Then she noticed other things: her hands were tied behind her; a rope was wound around her waist to keep her upright against a pole.

She pulled at the ropes around her wrists, to no avail. Should she call out? Naked, she felt terribly vulnerable . . . *human*.

Then she heard a sound . . . soft, measured footfalls.

In front of her a shadowy form appeared beyond a dark iron gate at the end of the trail. The outline of the figure shimmered, then solidified before her widening gaze. She blinked. Maybe the apparition had just been a floating tendril of fog that had given her that impression.

The fog cleared for a moment to reveal the imposing figure of a man.

Voletta's breath caught. The man stood still, only feet away, his hard-edged face devoid of emotion, his lips drawn into a thin line.

He was tall, his shoulders broad, his hair and eyes black as midnight. The cotte and chausses he wore were equally dark, unrelieved by any embroidery or a bright cuff. He lifted his hands, pushed open the gate, and stepped through it.

"Please," she whispered, "untie me."

"I shall," he replied, his voice deep and ragged, as though rusty from disuse.

He stepped behind her, and his fingers glanced against her wrists. The ropes fell away.

Voletta turned, ready to flee down the rough trail, but his hand snagged her wrist. Alarmed, she gazed back.

"You don't understand," he said slowly. "I know you are frightened, but you must come with me. You are mine, now."

She tugged her hand, hard, but his fingers wrapped tighter around her wrist, and he started to walk back through the gate.

Digging her heels into the ground, she said, "You must release me. Those men kidnapped me. I'm not supposed to be here. I can't belong to you."

Silence greeted her outcry, and he forged onward, forcing her to walk behind him or fall to her knees.

"I'm expected. My family will be looking for me," she lied, shortening her steps only to stumble when he walked faster. He was strong; his fingers banded her wrist like steel. She tried to pry them away, but his grip bit into her flesh, and she gasped.

"You only harm yourself," he said, his voice as devoid of softness as his clothing and his face.

"I beg your pardon, but you are the one dragging me, sir," she bit out.

He shot a glance over his shoulder. His eyes peered at her, curiosity easing his dour expression. "Don't you fear me?"

"Of course not," she said automatically, but then realized it was true. She didn't fear him, *exactly*, but she was wary, and growing increasingly so the further into his demesne they went.

The man grunted and turned away, tugging her behind him.

They continued along, lush grass giving way to slick cobblestones. Above her stretched a tall, imposing keep made of large gray stones. Two menacing towers stood watch at the ends of a long wall. A portcullis, its gate raised, loomed like a great, toothed maw.

Voletta shivered, and her alarm caused her heart to thud loudly in her chest the closer they approached. Despite her creeping trepidation, details began to niggle. No heads appeared above the crenellated curtain wall. No gatekeeper greeted them inside the portcullis. In fact, no one appeared to be inside the bailey as they entered.

And yet, everything was perfectly attended. The cobblestones were clear of falling leaves; the grass beyond the cobblestone was perfectly manicured; the iron chain that lifted the portcullis gleamed with oil. As she stared behind her, the gear that lowered the gate began to move and creak, and yet no one stood beside it to work the mechanism.

Again the fog licked in front of her, and, in the mist, she saw the outline of a ghostly figure leaning over the lever he turned.

Cold, afraid now, Voletta quivered, her knees shaking so badly she stumbled behind him and landed on her knees at last.

The dark man halted, his back to her, his hand still clasping her wrist. A sigh escaped him, and he turned. Bending over her, he pushed away her outstretched hands and lifted her into his arms.

Voletta had been close to a man a time or two—had felt the hardness of their muscular bodies pressed to hers, had breathed their hot breath and inhaled the musky scent of them. They'd been pleasant to touch, delicious to kiss.

They'd also been easy to evade when their caresses grew too intimate, too unnerving.

With this one, however, she sensed strength beyond the tensile muscles that held her easily to his chest. His square jaw and straight lips spoke of an inner will that would brook no arguments.

He held her naked, completely vulnerable to his will. That

she wasn't squirming, fighting tooth and nail for her freedom, shocked her—and deepened the shivers that pricked her nipples into tight buds.

She had to find the cloak with her special fur, and quickly. This man tempted her to linger and discover just what belonging to him entailed. Voletta guessed his possession would be a carnal form of enslavement. For what woman wouldn't be drawn by his rugged form and fierce, enigmatic gaze?

However, she'd managed to escape manly lures for a very long time. No matter the fascinating package, she'd just as soon flee before she saw him fully unwrapped!

She'd heard the men talking. Her fox's fur had been sewn onto a cloak for a nobleman. This nobleman, she had no doubt. It must rest in the trunk they'd dropped on the trail outside the gate.

"You've left the trunk behind," she said, in a small voice, not wanting to let him see how much it meant, and certainly not wanting to draw his gaze downward. The thought of him staring closely at her body heated her skin.

"The trunk does not concern you," he murmured, sounding not the least winded by carrying her so far.

"But it contains things that belong to me."

"I will provide all that you need."

Her legs squeezed together. He hadn't purred, hadn't injected a hint of heat into his voice, but his low, growling words still scraped her nerves raw. "That's so arrogant! What if there is something that means the world to me inside that trunk?"

He halted on the steps leading into the keep and stared into her eyes. "From this day, I will be your world, your only companion, your only lover."

A shudder racked her body. He'd said it so intently, as though making her a promise.

A sudden fullness choked her throat. She read steely determination in his eyes, yet at the same time, she detected a hint of vulnerability beneath that hard gaze. The yearning she sensed pulled her, and she drew back. This man could make her question her need to escape.

Voletta knew in that moment he would never willingly let her go—and part of her, the weak and feminine dimension of her being, was grateful he intended to remove the choice.

2

Damien—Lord Malphas—watched, fascinated, while bright color flooded the woman's cheeks and crept slowly down her neck to stain the tops of her round breasts.

Since the moment he'd spotted her tied to the post awaiting his arrival, he'd tried not to stare. For a thousand years he'd retrieved his "gifts" from the town of Daemonberg—only to be disappointed.

His previous brides had ranged from blond to brunette, sturdy and strapping women who'd nevertheless cried and wailed at the sight of him and his enchanted castle. When the crying had finally calmed, he'd done his best to keep the women happy, seeing to their comfort and making sure all their needs were met. Some had become friends—over time. Most had shared his bed, but, in the end, not one of them had been the one he'd needed.

This woman was different—a fascinating and fey sort of creature. Her gentle, slight curves appealed to him after having had so many large, buxom women. However, not being a small man, he worried he might hurt her the first time they came together. He vowed he'd be gentle, although he knew instinctively his will would be tested.

When he'd untied her, he'd noted the long, auburn hair—such a rich, warm color—that hung in a tumble of curling waves to the tops of her firm buttocks. The gentle swell of her hips, the turn of her narrow waist, the apple shape of her small breasts: there wasn't any part of her that didn't tempt him to follow its shape with his lips and tongue.

Close up, her eyes flashed gold with a quiet defiance and were framed by sooty lashes. Her skin was unmarred by a single freckle or mole and was the color of sweet, fresh milk. Her feminine parts . . .

Well, he would look closely soon enough, but the glimpse he'd allowed himself of the auburn thatch between her legs and her strawberry nipples made his mouth water with a thirst for her cries.

He took a deep breath and stepped with steady deliberation up the stone steps to the door of the keep, trying to control the riot of excitement flooding his body. It filled his loins with a quickening thrum that pulsed through his cock at the thought that just maybe this woman was the one who could end his imprisonment.

For, if not, he was doomed to another century within these wretched walls—and she would grow to hate him. Kept from her family and friends, with only him for company, she would surely go mad or become hopelessly morose.

This time, however, he'd do everything right. He'd woo her gently, learning her passions while he sated himself on her pretty flesh.

Please let the woman be interesting and amusing, he prayed. Or he'd spend his days roaming the rooms apart from her, riding his horse until the dawn as he'd done for a millennium.

The nights, with this one, would be a delight. If he approached her as women dreamed, with gifts, soft words, and caring caresses, she'd open to him like a rose.

If he failed, they were doomed to live in misery until her death, then, once again, he'd wait until the day the gate allowed him to open it so that he could bring inside another bride.

So many women. He'd forgotten all but the first and the last. None had filled the emptiness of his days. Gabriel had promised him a reprieve if he could learn to love. Only the Fallen Ones seemed doomed to spend their long lives alone—a curse by The Father for their betrayal.

Damien held the woman close, breathed in her fresh, woodsy scent, and prayed that this time he'd learn the meaning of love. For, this woman with the fiery hair and cautious gaze stirred him as no other ever had.

Damien paused as the door to the keep opened silently. He waited for a gasp, but noted from the corner of his eyes that her only reaction was a narrowing of her gaze. What should he tell her about the odd things she would witness over the coming days? Part of him wanted to watch her, to silently gauge her courage. Another wished to ease her past any fears she might have.

However, unused to talking to another being, he remained silent, knowing he'd only say the wrong thing. He had no gift for honeyed words.

The woman shifted in his arms and stared around his home. He wondered what she saw . . . wondered whether she recognized that the bleakness of the place mirrored the emptiness of his soul.

"Please, sir," she said softly, "I can walk on my own. You should put me down."

More likely she wanted another chance to escape, to run across his bailey and slip between the gates. If she was successful, she would win her freedom. He could not go after her, and the townspeople were not obliged to replace her. They'd done their duty.

He remained silent, crossed the hall to the stone staircase and walked steadily upward, the scrape of his footsteps and her soft, quickening breaths the only sounds between them.

"Will you rape me, sir?" she asked, her voice small, so feminine that his belly clenched.

"I will not," he ground out, although he didn't know if that was true. The closer he drew to his chambers, the more his thoughts clung to the fact that his great oak bed filled the center of the room. A soft, down-filled mattress with thick, silken covers awaited their comfort, the corners turned down in invitation by his retainers.

How he would love to lay her across its surface and follow her down to press his body against hers. But he would take her slowly, he promised himself.

"'Tis madness, this," she whispered.

Indeed it was. His body was wound tightly, ready to pounce. He'd drop her into her bath and leave quickly before his need made it impossible for him to restrain himself. It had been so long since he'd touched another.

He pushed through the door of his chamber. The bath awaited, steam rising from the tub. The scent of the roses floating on the surface of the water nearly made him stumble.

Without warning her he lowered her into the water, regretting that the swirling petals hid her body from his view. "I'll leave you to your bath," he said gruffly.

"Please, sir," she said, her small fingers wrapping around the scrolled edge of the large copper tub. "The trunk?"

He'd expected her to ask again for her freedom. "I'll see to it," he said, although no effort on his part would be required for it to be retrieved.

Her lips trembled, but she quickly glanced away. "Thank you."

Yes, this one was different. She hadn't flailed until the waters had washed over the edge of the bath and flooded the floor. She hadn't pleaded incessantly for him to release her. Hadn't even asked him his name.

"You may call me Damien," he said, and walked quietly out of the room.

Voletta watched the door close behind *Damien* and sighed her relief. Freed now from his embrace, she could finally breathe without dragging in his scent with each inhalation.

However, clean, male musk—his own unique aroma—lingered in the room. She sank deep in the tub and breathed the scent of the roses swimming thick upon the surface of the water, wanting to replace his smell—letting the water cleanse away the feel of his arms and chest against her skin.

She turned her troubled thoughts from the man to this mysterious keep. His home was perfect, but also cold and remote. Nothing was out of place. Notable only for an absence of clutter, an absence of color, an absence of people—but all this perfection had to be maintained. There had to be servants, but where were they? Or were they all like that ghostly apparition turning the gear to drop the portcullis gate into place?

Not that she'd spent much time in any keep or even a humble abode. Still, she did think it a very odd place.

Candles burning in iron wall sconces bathed the paneled walls with a golden light. The flooring was gray slate, a tad bluer than the rock of the outer walls. There were no rugs or rushes on the floor, nor tapestries on the walls to hold the warmth inside the room, yet the air was a pleasant temperature and dry.

Voletta lay her head against the edge of the tub and let the warmth of the water drain away the tension that had gripped her body since she'd awoken. A faint ache remained behind her eyes from the potion she'd been given, but the pain was dissipating quickly. Soon, she'd plan her escape, but first she had to retrieve her fur.

A slight breeze drifted over her shoulder, and she opened her eyes. The door remained shut, and yet she sensed a presence in the room.

Her gaze darted into the dark corners, but she found no one there. From the corner of her eye, she caught sight of a large wooden trunk.

Her heart leapt, pounding faster. How had it arrived without her noticing?

No matter, the means of her escape lay inside. She stood, letting the water sluice down her skin, and stepped over the edge of the tub onto the floor. She hurried to the trunk, unbuckled the leather straps that held it closed and lifted the lid.

She sifted through clothing, embroidered linens, beeswax candles tied in bundles and small stoppered bottles with liquid that sloshed when she jumbled them to the side.

At the bottom of the trunk, her hand slid across soft, warm fur and she dragged out the cloak. Tears of relief filled her eyes as she held it to her cheek and breathed in the scent of the precious fur, now attached to the collar of a black cloak.

"I see you've helped yourself."

She jumped, holding the cloak in front of her to shield herself from Damien's gaze.

His lips curved in a slight smile. "But I think it's intended for me to wear. The hem's far too long for you."

Voletta lifted her chin. "I like the softness of the fur against my cheek," she murmured.

"Perhaps, I'll have it tailored for you. Cut down to size." His gaze swept down to rest on her toes peeking from beneath the cloak. "You're quite a bit smaller than I am. For now, if you'd like, wrap it around your shoulders to ward off a chill. Dinner has arrived."

Her head turned, following the aroma of roasted chicken. A small table was set before an open brazier, a fire burning on the grate. She shook her head. "More magic?"

"Magic?" His lips twitched. "Maybe you were distracted and didn't notice when it came."

"I wouldn't have missed servants entering the room. I saw you arrive. Please, tell me what is happening."

"I think it would be more amusing for you to guess."

Unwilling to plead for him to appease her curiosity, she shrugged. "It hardly matters."

"Still hoping I will release you?" he said, his words coming more easily now, more quickly.

"I know you will not."

"Think you can escape me?"

She felt a smile tug at her lips, and quickly let her gaze slide to the table. "I must keep up my strength. Shall we eat?"

His breath caught and held. "Am I invited?" he asked slowly. Did she really want him to linger in this room, with her?

"This is your room, *non?*" she said, with a shrug.

"Yes, how did you know?"

"Well, it wasn't due to any masculine clutter you left lying around."

"Then how?"

She gazed up from beneath her lashes. "I think you should guess."

A smile slowly stretched his lips, and Voletta's heart began to thump harder again. The smile eased the harshness of his features, making him even more appealing.

"You should put on the cloak."

Only she couldn't. Not with him watching. "Is there something else I might wear? You're right, it's far too large."

"A robe is behind you."

No longer surprised by how things appeared whenever

needed, she glanced behind her shoulder to find a belted robe hanging from a hook on the wall. Holding the cloak to her chest, she wrestled the robe clumsily onto one arm, switched hands, slid another arm into the garment, then closed the edges, letting the cloak slither to the floor.

His amusement glittered in his eyes, but he didn't mention the fact that her modesty came a little late. She was grateful for his restraint, needing no reminder he'd held her naked in his arms.

He waited patiently as she approached the small table and slid into one of the chairs. Then he seated himself and reached for a knife to carve slivers of meat from the bird, which he slid onto silver plates. He added sliced apples, and leafy greens, then pushed one plate across the table. "Eat."

Unused to being served by a man, she knew it was customary for a gentleman to serve, even feed the woman beside him. "May I have a knife?" she asked, hoping to forestall him performing the intimate duty.

"And a fork," he replied, reaching beyond the bird to hand her both.

She'd have wagered neither had existed before she'd asked for them, but she didn't acknowledge this further proof of magic. "This is a fork?" she said, staring at the odd implement with its dual tines. She watched as he speared a piece of chicken with his fork and raised it to his lips.

"They came in a trunk . . . some time ago. The person who arrived with them explained their function. Quite useful, don't you think?"

She didn't reply, simply stabbed a leaf. Only the piece was too large for her to put into her mouth without seeming rude. She understood the rudiments of manners, even if she'd rarely seen a need for them. However, she didn't like the thought of embarrassing herself in front of him.

From beneath her lashes, she watched him fold a leaf against the fork using his knife and copied his movements as best she could.

"What is your name?"

As she chewed, she lifted her gaze slowly, reluctant to increase the intimacy between them. Every part of herself she relinquished drew them closer. "Voletta."

"Lovely," he murmured. "Would you like to tell me about yourself?"

She shook her head and lowered her gaze to the plate and stabbed a large piece of chicken. She stuffed it quickly into her mouth, less concerned now to display a lack of manners than she was to share information.

"No matter. We have time to learn everything about each other." His tone was suspiciously glib and cheerful.

Strange, he'd been so quiet when he'd first captured her. "And I thought you weren't very talkative," she said around the food, then swallowed hard.

"I was concerned before that we wouldn't suit."

"Something's changed I'm unaware of?" she asked sharply.

Again, his lips twitched.

Voletta set down her knife and fork. His quiet, gloomy demeanor had been so much easier to resist. Him teasing and amused unsettled her.

"Are you finished?" he asked quietly.

Unsure how she should answer and what he planned next, she nodded slowly.

"Would you like to rest?"

Did he mean he wanted to bed her now? For she knew that was why she was here. "Will you rest with me?" she asked, wanting to know, tired of waiting for him to pounce.

"Would you like me to?"

She lifted her chin. "Do I have a choice?"

His eyelids dropped for a moment, then lifted, his gaze locking with hers. "You may deny me, but I wish that you wouldn't. I promise you pleasure, Voletta."

Her mouth suddenly dry, she swallowed. She could say no. She probably should. Yet, he'd handled her gently. Given her privacy when she'd needed to regroup her thoughts. He'd seen to her every need, so far.

Alone for so long, she wondered what it would be like to take him inside her. Would she feel joined, somehow changed by the experience?

Besides, she was only delaying the inevitable. Better to surrender now than have him force the issue later. The tension apparent in his tightly curled fingers told her he held himself back.

If she were smart, she'd let him have his way and wait until a more opportune moment, when he eased his watchfulness, to escape.

"I think I'm ready," she whispered.

Damien sat still as a stone statue for a long moment, then his chest rose, his breath dragging slowly to fill his lungs.

Was his heart racing like hers?

He rose from his chair, so tall he blocked out the light from the candle in the sconce behind him. The shadow stretched to cover her, just as he soon would.

Such a fanciful thought, but she held on to it, even relishing the element of dangerous portent that spurred her heartbeat and her breaths faster.

He reached out a hand, and she placed hers inside his large, warm palm. "May I have candlelight?" he asked.

So that he could watch her, she knew. Blushing, she nodded. "May I have a moment to slip into bed . . . ?"

"Without me watching?"

Again, she nodded, relieved when he turned his back.

She walked toward the bed, her knees shaking, and slowly

drew off the still damp bedrobe and dropped it at the end of the mattress.

Then she saw the cloak, lying in a heap on the floor, the red fur looking mussed, abandoned.

Only for a night, she silently promised, then climbed onto the bed.

3

Damien turned slowly, then fought hard to mask a grin.

Voletta had pulled up the coverlet to hide her breasts and was tugging it higher still. He wondered if she was considering pulling it over her head altogether.

He pretended indifference to the fact that she lay naked in his bed and covered their dishes, even though it wasn't necessary. As soon as he walked away, they'd vanish.

He strode toward her, pausing in a pool of light, and then, starting with his cotte and undertunic, he untied the knots holding them together and dropped them on the floor before glancing at Voletta.

Her gaze darted away from his naked chest. Rosy color flooded her cheeks.

Her interest in his body deepened the thudding of his heart and reaffirmed his decision not to wait. When his hands began to work at the ties of his chausses, she squeezed her eyes shut.

He chuckled softly. "You may as well look, love," he murmured. "As it is, I have the advantage over you."

"Because you've seen all of me?" she bit out.

"There are some views I've only caught glimpses of."

Her brows drew together in a fierce frown, then one eyelid peeked open as he began to slide the rest of his clothing down his thighs.

The other eye opened and both widened as his cock was freed and bounded upward toward his belly. Her innocence was proven by her expression of astonishment.

He hadn't realized until then how much he cared he'd be her first. The townspeople had sworn to provide only virgins, but he'd found several who had hidden their indiscretions well, although he hadn't really cared.

Again, everything about this one was different. A primal, fierce satisfaction filled his chest, and blood rushed south to thicken his already swelling cock.

No other man had taken his pleasure with her.

Watching her cheeks reddening and her mouth parting around shallow breaths, he approached her cautiously, slowly, letting her look her fill. "You have no need to fear me, Voletta. 'Tis only flesh."

"I know," she said breathlessly. "But I'm thinking about where that flesh must fit."

"Don't worry that it won't."

Her wide eyes filled her small face, but she scooted to the center of the bed, and lifted the edge of the covers.

Damien accepted her invitation and slid beneath them, noting her body had already warmed the sheets. In no hurry to press for more intimacy, he rose on an elbow to look down on her.

She was lovely, her face almost elfish with its small pointed chin and high cheekbones. Her eyes, slightly slanted and tipped upward, blinked warily back.

He lifted his hand, careful to move slowly so he wouldn't startle her, and stroked her cheek with the backs of his fingers, enjoying her womanly softness.

"You're very beautiful," he murmured.

"You think so?" she asked, sounding surprised.

He almost asked if no one had ever told her that before, but didn't want to hear about any other men.

Cupping her cheek with his palm, he slowly rasped his thumb across her full lower lip, and then slid his hand down to grip the coverlet. "May I dispense with this?"

"If you must," she said, but gripped it tighter to her chest.

"You won't be chilled, I promise," he said, giving it a tug.

"I'm already shivering."

The hint of defiance in her tone pleased him. She didn't fear him, only the act to come. He'd thought he would be days, maybe weeks from this moment. Triumph filled him with heat, drawing his balls close to his groin, tightening his belly, readying his sex to join with her.

He drew the coverlet from her fingers and tossed it to the end of the bed, baring them both.

Voletta's hands covered her breasts.

"Are your nipples cold?" he asked, teasing her.

"I think they are," she whispered.

"Do they tighten?"

Her breath caught. "Why are you toying with me? You know they are sensitive."

"To the chill in the air?" he asked, noting the air was warm.

"To your presence," she admitted, her eyes filling with tears, her bottom lip trembling.

Another sort of warmth crept inside his chest, lodging next to his heart. "Then we are blessed," he said, teasing her lower lip again, and earning a pouting moue that kissed his thumb.

"Why?" she asked, her voice so soft he had to lean closer.

"Your body already knows its master."

"I have no master."

"Shall I prove you wrong?"

Her eyes closed, and she swallowed. "Please."

Voletta couldn't look into his black eyes. They seemed to cast a spell over her, draw responses she'd never dreamed of giving. Something in the darkness of them spoke of loneliness—a feeling she understood all too well—but she didn't want to empathize with this dark, powerful man.

"Shall I tell you what I want to do?" he asked, swirling his thumb across her lips.

The movement, slow and sensual, seemed to drug her. She felt the rasp across her tight nipples where they sprang hard and alert beneath her palms. Feeling like a coward for hiding, she forced her eyes open to meet his intense gaze. "I want to know what you intend to do."

His long body nestled closer to her side, his cock brushing her thigh, then resting there, heavy and hard. Its presence disturbed her more than she cared to admit. A promise lay in the thick, satiny flesh that throbbed slower than her racing heart.

"My hands will cup you here and here," he whispered, moving his palms from her face to press the backs of her hands, then resting heavily upon her belly. "My lips will follow to suckle them gently until you clasp the back of my head to deepen my caress."

Voletta shook her head. "I'd never do that."

His lips curved at the corners. "Oh, you will. Heat will travel fast as lightning to dampen your woman's flesh, and you'll begin to writhe."

She wrinkled her nose, pretending disgust when her woman's flesh was already becoming embarrassingly wet. "I cannot believe I'll writhe," she lied.

"You'll be so overcome by your passion," he said, so close his breath tickled her ear, "you'll spread your legs eagerly and beg me to kiss you there. You'll demand I use my tongue to tease and lap—"

"Never!" she said, scowling at his crudeness. "The very thought—"

"Excites you, doesn't it?" When she opened her mouth to voice another protest, his finger pressed her lips closed. "Doesn't it?"

When he lifted his hand, she whispered, "Yes," with more longing than she wanted to reveal.

His eyes searched her face. "Are you still frightened?"

"I never really was."

"Shall I begin?"

"What must I do?"

"Not a thing. Let this be my gift to you." Then he came over her, his body settling atop hers, pressing her deep into the mattress. "Can you breathe?"

Of course she couldn't, but not because he squeezed the air from his lungs. He rested on his elbows, supporting the weight of his broad chest.

"I'm fine," she said, her words clipped due to the shortness of her breaths.

"I can see that. Do you gasp often?"

Had he only crawled atop her to torment her into submission? "Will you touch me now?" she asked, mortified as soon as she blurted out the words.

"Are you already begging?" he asked, a lopsided grin stretching his mouth.

"No! Only wondering if you are keeping with your plan."

"I'm thinking of changing my direction," he said, staring at her mouth.

"If you veer, how will I be prepared?"

His gaze narrowed, sending her heart racing faster. "Are you going to argue with me the entire time I make love to you?"

Voletta swallowed, then rolled her eyes. "Probably." At his soft laughter, she felt a smile tug at her lips.

"Is this helping?"

"Helping?"

"To settle your unease."

She nodded, fearing another word from her might send him into gales of laughter at her pride's expense.

"Good." The amusement in his expression faded and he swooped down, pressing his lips to hers.

Voletta murmured, wanting to speak to end the torment tightening her body, needing to move against him as his kiss deepened.

His face slanted to better align their noses. His lips nipped at her lips, tender little bites that fueled her ardor. When his tongue swept into her mouth, she grew silent beneath him at last, touching his tongue with hers, then thrusting it into his mouth so their kiss melded, just as their bodies soon would.

She had no fear he'd harm her. Felt no reluctance to venture deeper into this passion. With her heart beating as loud as a drum inside her head, she lifted her hands and clasped the back of his head, threading her fingers deep into his dark hair to hold him there.

When he drew away, she moaned, gasping for breath as he moved down her body, his lips and tongue tracing a path along her neck and down her chest until he was fulfilling his vow to ravage her breasts.

His lips drew on the hard little buds, his tongue swirling on the tips, and her hips did indeed rise and fall, *writhing* against his belly and his chest. He moved lower, his fingers slipping between her dampened folds to part them.

When his mouth sucked on her nether lips, Voletta's eyes shot open, and her hands twisted in the bedding. Her hips rocked up and down, seeking a deeper caress . . . until finally, his wicked tongue stroked into her opening, laving upward, touching on the hardened little kernel at the top of her sex that seemed to swell larger the more he touched it.

Suddenly, Voletta screamed. She was outside herself, exploding upward, the light narrowing as darkness enfolded her, wrapping her in a delightful, boneless lethargy as she fell back against the covers. She closed her eyes, dragging in deep breaths, feeling as though she'd run miles across a meadow.

"What have you done to me?" she gasped.

"Given you pleasure, little one."

Voletta's hands fell on the pillow beside her head, and she didn't care that her legs were splayed wide, her knees arched, or that his shoulders were clasped tightly between her quivering thighs.

As the last rapturous pulses faded from inside her, and her knees opened to fall languorously apart, she wondered if he'd killed her.

Damien's hands slid beneath her buttocks to cup the soft globes, ready to take her again. He'd tasted her passion, felt it slide onto his tongue in a creamy trickle. He'd have her again, feast on her flavor. He just needed her to wake up so he could begin again.

However, she lay with her mouth still agape, her hands tucked like little birds within the tangle of her hair. He bent over her and rolled his face against her moist folds, coating his chin and mouth with her essence. Lord, how he'd missed the taste of a woman.

Somehow, he didn't think any before her had ever been as sweet or fresh of scent. Her cries when she'd surrendered to her release still rang in his ears: sharp, enthusiastic, howling, nearly yipping at the end.

Would she awaken embarrassed by her enjoyment? Damien pressed a kiss to the red little button that peaked from beneath its hood. Still, she didn't stir.

Sighing, he crawled up her body and once again hovered over her, waiting for her to open her eyes.

His cock surged against her soft belly, and he gritted his teeth. He was old enough, experienced enough, to withhold his own pleasure. His hips ground once, just to relieve the ache building in his balls, and he moaned.

Voletta stirred, and she widened her legs, her thighs moving restlessly alongside his.

"Don't move," he whispered.

Her inner thighs tightened, just a light, aimless squeeze, and Damien lifted his buttocks, settling his cock between her legs. The length of him rested along the furrow of her sex, which was still wet and steamy from his efforts.

A little tentative glide and he knew he wasn't in control, wasn't able to even wait until she roused.

His cock pulsed against her, and his belly jumped.

He pressed his face into the corner of her shoulder and gathered up her thighs, hooking his arms beneath them. Then, centering his cock at her entrance, he slowly pushed inward.

Voletta came awake, her eyes rounding as he pressed into her. "Oh God! Stop!"

Her opening constricted around the head of his cock as her body resisted his intrusion. Damien's teeth ground together. "You must let me ease inside."

"I must? You said you wouldn't cause me pain."

"Damnation!" he growled, and eased out, then rolled to his back beside her. His balls ached for release, and he gripped his cock, determined to give himself release before he lost control completely and frightened the woman to death.

"Are you in pain?"

"Yes," he ground out. He dropped his hand from his cock and splayed his legs to ease the pressure in his ballocks. "No," he amended. "I only ache."

A sniff beside him drew his attention from his own distress. "Are you crying?" Had he hurt her?

"Of course not. Your scent is ripening."

"You have a keen nose," he muttered.

"You're aroused."

"And keen insight," he growled.

"I'm sorry," she said softly.

Damien drew a deep breath and forced himself to relax. "No, I should have waited until you were ready. It's my fault."

"This whole experience is very enlightening."

Damien grunted, trying to concentrate on breathing, inhaling slowly, exhaling even more slowly to lengthen his heartbeats and ease the fullness in his cock.

"If I was to be completely honest, I'd have to say that was the most . . . curious experience of my life."

The woman obviously liked to talk in the afterglow of her release. Sighing, Damien put an arm beneath his head, determined to listen closely to what she said. Perhaps, following the meanderings of her mind would take his own thoughts off his dilemma. "I take it you've never felt passion?"

"Oh no. I'm a virgin." Her head turned toward him, her brows drawing into a worried frown. "I am still, aren't I?"

"Decidedly so," he said, with wry amusement.

"And yet, I feel changed somehow. Lighter of spirit."

"I gave you pleasure."

"Pleasure," she wrinkled her nose. "Well, it wasn't quite like rolling in a field of flowers or tasting a particularly sweet strawberry. I'm not sure pleasure is the right word."

"How would you describe it?" he asked, starting to enjoy the silly conversation.

"Well, parts of it were uncomfortable."

"Which ones?"

She shrugged, the movement lifting her breasts. "Should we be talking about it?"

"We can say anything to each other. We're lovers now."

"Well, perhaps you're mine, but I would think I don't qualify until I've participated."

He liked her logic. "You have a point. But go on. Which parts were uncomfortable?"

"Most of it actually. My body was wound so tightly, I felt almost ill—until that last moment, that is."

"You felt ill? Sickened?"

"More like everything inside me was constricting, and I couldn't breathe easily. My heart raced so fast I thought it would stop." She turned her face on the pillow, looking directly into his eyes. "Actually, I believe it did."

"For that last moment?" he asked, smiling.

"I suppose you think I'm terribly stupid."

"No. Sweet."

"The thing is," she said, pausing to take a deep breath, "even though it was terribly confusing . . . and almost frightening . . . I want to do it again."

Damien felt more of his tension ease. He'd truly pleased her. He lifted his hand and traced a finger along the side of her cheek. "Perhaps you'd like to try something different this time," he said, trying to keep his tone casual.

"Oh no!" she said, enthusiasm brightening her gaze. "I'd like *exactly* the same thing again."

Perhaps he'd pleased her too well. "If I tell you I can produce the same sensations any of a hundred different ways, would you be willing to experiment?"

Her golden eyes widened. "A hundred different ways?" she breathed.

He nodded, enjoying the way her teeth nibbled on her lower lip as she considered his proposition. What would it feel like to have those teeth nibble on the soft skin at the head of his cock?

"Will you kiss me again?"

"Of course," he said, then added slyly, "but which set of lips would you prefer?"

Her mouth gaped. Violent color flooded her cheeks. "Sir, you shouldn't say such things!"

"If I am to know what pleases you, you must tell me."

Voletta's chin lifted in the air. "I think our experiment will be cut short," she said, her tone prim.

With a soft laugh, he clasped her wrist and pulled her onto

her side so they faced each other, chests and knees coming to-gether. She smiled shyly as they arranged their legs more com-fortably, her thigh slipping between his.

He cupped her stubborn chin, forcing up her gaze. "Will you trust me, then, to guide you? Will you allow me to do any-thing I wish?"

Voletta's smile dimmed and her eyelids dipped, cutting off his window into her thoughts. "In this bed," she said, her words measured, "I will let you lead."

4

Damien stared at Voletta, thinking about how she'd worded her consent. The woman still hoped to escape. Although disappointing, her continued resistance served as a gauntlet thrown down to spur his efforts to woo her. "Kiss me."

She blinked, and her tongue darted out to wet her lips. "I thought you were leading."

"I am. I just ordered you to kiss me."

A ragged little breath escaped her lips as she leaned toward him. Her nipples touched his chest. Her mouth an inch from his, she halted.

Damien lifted one eyebrow. "It's just a kiss."

"Somehow . . ." she said, her voice breathless, "it's become so much more intimate."

"As it should, between lovers."

"I'm participating now?"

"Kiss me," he said, closing his eyes.

Her mouth touched his, lightly at first. Then her soft, wet lips opened and she mouthed his lower lip, moving it beneath hers, as though discovering its texture.

Damien didn't move, holding his breath while she moved her mouth then circled her head to deepen her kiss. He didn't open his eyes until she drew back.

"You aren't helping," she complained.

"You were doing the kissing. Why should I?"

She wrinkled her nose. "Because I'm obviously not very good at it."

With their faces close together, sharing the same pillow, he'd never felt this content to simply talk with a woman. "You were wonderful," he said quietly.

"I was?"

"Try using your tongue now."

"I didn't think of that."

"I could hardly think of anything else."

"You like my tongue?"

He lifted an eyebrow. "Did you like mine?"

She frowned at him while color once again brightened her cheeks.

"You liked it a little too much, hmmm?"

She went for his lips, likely to halt the embarrassing conversation, and kissed him again, this time opening her lips and prodding his with her tongue.

Laughing softly into her mouth, he let her take her time to explore, enjoying the touch of her hot tongue as it lapped along his, then trailed the roof of his mouth and the edges of his teeth, until she grew breathless and leaned away.

"You should breathe through your nose."

"I'll remember that next time," she said, gasping.

Next time. A slip, he was sure.

"What shall we do now?"

"Must you always know what's coming? Don't you like surprises?"

She shrugged. "Most surprises hold more than a hint of danger."

"What dangers are there here? I hold no weapons."

Her gaze slid down his body, then slowly back up.

Her pointed gaze made his lips twitch. "It is a weapon of pleasure. What other dangers?"

Her expression saddened, then she jutted out her chin. "I might lose my breath."

"Do you fear losing yourself?"

"I don't like giving over control . . . forgetting what I am about."

"Is that a danger here . . . with me?"

She nodded, revealing a raw vulnerability in her gaze that drew him to her.

He lifted his hand and smoothed over the indention of her waist to her hip and back again, then he slowly brought it to her chest and caressed her. Her pink nipple dragged across his palm, and he paused to give her breast a gentle squeeze.

Her eyes closed as she sucked air between her teeth. "Again?"

He caressed the soft globe, rubbing his thumb over the distended tip, teasing it, working her flesh until her breaths came faster. "Would you like more?"

"Please."

He liked that word coming from her, and swept his arm around her to pull her higher and nuzzle her tender breast with his nose and mouth.

Slowly her fingers combed through his hair, and he deepened his caresses, opening his mouth to swallow as much of her small breast as he could.

"Yes, like that."

He moved his hand from her hip to place it between them, sliding a finger between the folds of her moist sex, seeking the nubbin that bloomed hard and throbbing. He circled it as he circled his mouth, using his tongue to rasp her nipple and his thumb to scrape her clitoris. Then he thrust a finger inside her narrow channel.

"Oh dear God," she gasped, but didn't move her hips away. They stilled, and she lifted her uppermost thigh, giving him greater access to her sex.

Damien stroked in and out, swirling his fingers in her liquid heat, rolling his knuckles against her inner walls to increase the friction.

Soon, her hips were rocking forward and back as she moaned softly, forgetting herself at last.

Damien's own body reacted harshly to her growing pleasure; his balls drew so close and tight to his groin he, too, had to lift his own thigh to give them space. His cock, tucked against her thigh, throbbed in time to his quickening heart.

He had to have her, had to bury himself inside her heat, slide into the cream he'd drawn from deep inside her. His mouth still filled with her soft breast, he removed his finger from inside her and drew one of her small hands from his hair to carry it downward, coaxing her to wrap it tightly around his shaft.

With his hand guiding hers, he moved it up and down, showing her how he needed to be touched. When her grip tightened around him, he left her to explore while he raked through the curling hairs covering her mons and thrust two fingers inside her.

While he rocked his hips to glide his cock inside her grasp, he stroked his fingers into her, again and again, until they both strained toward each other.

He came off her breast, keeping only the nipple between his teeth, and chewed it softly, tugging and pulling at it until she whimpered sweetly above him.

Soon, it wasn't enough. Damien rolled them until he settled on top of her.

Voletta's mouth was slackened, her cheeks a fiery red, her eyes slightly glazed with passion.

"I will enter you, now," he said, remembering to give her warning. "Raise your knees."

Voletta didn't question, didn't demur, she simply bent her quivering thighs, bringing them up to frame his hips.

He bent over her and kissed her, then reached between them to guide his cock into her entrance. When the head nudged inside her, he spread her folds with his fingers and began to circle his hips, slowly screwing into her, pulsing softly, entering her a fraction of an inch at a time.

Her hands gripped the bedding, and she started to constrict around him again.

"Love, breathe deeply. Don't be afraid."

She drew in deep, ragged breaths, releasing them in mewling sighs as he pushed inside.

Damien knew he'd never felt anything in his entire existence so wonderful, so powerful, as the warm, melting heat of her. Her trembling lips, her trustful gaze, gave him the strength to hold back from plunging as deep as his cock insisted. For a time at least . . .

When he tapped the tender barrier deep inside her, he stopped. His arms and thighs shook with need, but he waited until her gaze locked with his.

"Why did you stop?"

"I'm afraid I can no longer be gentle."

Her eyes rounded. "Oh!"

Once more, he gathered her thighs beneath his arms, tilting her hips to receive him. Planting his hands on the mattress, he rose over her.

When he'd arranged them both to his liking, he breathed deeply. "Are you ready? Shall I stop?" He prayed she wouldn't say yes, because he knew he couldn't.

"Will there be much pain?"

"'Tis slight, and soon over."

"How do you know?"

"Experience." He wouldn't mention the nearly hundred maidenheads he'd pierced.

"I think you should hurry."

"Why?"

"The more time you waste talking, the more worried I'm becoming."

Damien closed his eyes and drew back his hips, then plunged forward, tearing the thin membrane as he drove deep into Voletta's body.

She gave a sharp, strangled scream and clawed at his back.

But Damien couldn't stop now. His hips lunged, thrusting deeper each time, tunneling down until his groin met hers and he couldn't reach any farther. Her moist, tight cunt enveloped him, clenching tightly around his shaft.

He was lost in sensation, gliding forward and back, past all thoughts of the woman beneath him or her mewling, desperate cries.

Voletta dug her fingernails into Damien's back, trying to hold on to his wildly heaving body, the first sharp pain of penetration forgotten as friction built inside her with each deep thrust. With his thick cock crammed deep into her passage, he consumed her breath and mind.

The gentle teasing man was gone, replaced by a fierce, straining warrior bent on ravaging her body.

She'd seen the moment he'd lost himself. His black eyes closed, his body tensing as he'd poised inside her then backed out and slammed deep.

After she'd gotten over the shock of it, the ferocity of his taking, she'd thought the worst was over. The pain, although considerable, had faded instantly beneath the violent, pounding thrusts that followed. Her whole body jolted with each stroke, her back sliding up the mattress.

This raw, fierce pummeling frightened her—

and thrilled her beyond anything she'd ever known.

Holding on to Damien was like riding out a thunderstorm with the rain lashing at her body in gales.

Sure she couldn't take a moment more without fainting, she gasped for air as he drew out of her abruptly.

Before she could voice a protest, he flipped her onto her belly, dragged her hips up, and, once again, worked his way inside her from behind with short, hard bursts.

Voletta came up on her hands, pressing backwards, countering his thrusts with pushes of her own, helping him sink deeper, reveling in the way he stretched her and burned her inner passage.

She threw back her head, arching her back, finding she could take him all the way to her womb. As his cock stroked inward, the hard, quick thrusts slapped her bottom, her flesh warming inside and out.

When his fingers dug deep into her bottom, she strained along with him, recognizing the journey's end. When it caught her, she yelped and grew rigid, unable to move as the exquisite tension burst and she was hurled headlong beyond herself.

As she crumpled to the bed, Damien following her down, she wondered if she'd ever have the strength to loosen the bond he'd slipped around her heart.

Struggling to regain his breath and his unraveled mind, Damien blew hot against the back of Voletta's damp neck. Their bodies still connected, their flesh sharing the sweat of their efforts, he felt weak, seared by the brilliant blaze of passion that had swept them both away.

The waning pulses that rippled along his cock felt like the gentle stroke of her fingers, soothing away the last of the storm that had overtaken him.

Damnation! He'd wanted to be gentle.

Determined to do the right thing now, he began to roll away

from her, but she squeezed her legs together, trapping his cock inside her.

"I'm crushing you," he said.

"You aren't. Now, hush until I can catch my breath."

Bemused, Damien settled over her and slipped an arm beneath her belly to cradle her closer.

After a time, her breaths evened, and she drew deeply, sighing on the exhalation. "How remarkable! I find I am still alive."

Damien grinned behind her. "You doubted?"

"I thought the first time that my heart had stopped. This time I hurtled outside myself. I'm quite done in." A yawn followed, and she nestled her bottom closer to his groin. "S'nice."

It was indeed nice . . . and disturbing. Things were moving quickly between them. As a man who'd had centuries to ponder the slightest changes in his life, this little red-haired whirlwind had unsettled him in only half a day.

He nuzzled her neck, breathing in the strengthened scent of her. An unusual musk—like grass and rain . . . and furred animal. "You should rest. When you waken, I'll take you for a walk."

"Mmmm . . . will you stay with me?" she said, sleepily.

"For a while . . ."

She sighed and soon drifted off to sleep, her breaths deepening.

Damien rolled to his side, bringing her with him, his cock still lodged inside her. Spooned together, his arm around her narrow waist, he was content to lie beside her. Now that she didn't distract him with conversation, and his own desire was sated for a time, he thought back upon the morning.

Voletta. Not a German name at all. French. He wondered if she could be a product of the plain villagers who'd served him buxom women all these years.

Perhaps she was a changeling among them. He could well

imagine how she would stand out. Had they offered her because she was so different from them? The women he'd had before were plain-looking and plain-spoken, almost coarse in their appearance and language. Simple folk.

Beyond her appearance, Voletta's actions and words also set her apart. Although he'd been without a human companion for decades, his conversations with them had been remarkable only in how unmemorable they had been.

However, Voletta's sweet innocence and amusing insights lingered.

I'd like exactly the same thing again! He smiled, remembering the intensity of her excitement when she was ready to embark on their second round of lovemaking.

Damien pressed a kiss against her shoulder, intending to leave her to her rest. Instead, he dragged his lips along her soft skin and glided his hand upward from her belly to cup her breast.

Small, round, and softer than any peach he could wish for, it filled his palm. He traced his forefinger around the velvety areola, noting the difference in texture between it and the skin surrounding it. He realized he could spend hours touching and exploring her sweet body.

The nipple beaded, and he rolled it between his fingers. Hot, silken fluid bathed his cock, still tucked within her body. Even asleep she responded to him.

Not the least tired, his body roused. His cock filled her slowly, nudging deeper, stretching her walls.

He should pull out. He'd used her sorely. She required time to recover. There were other acts he could perform to assuage the heaviness settling in his loins.

Instead, bastard that he was, he rutted against her, softly at first, trying not to disturb her sleep, but needing to feel her walls clench around him again.

And they did. As well, her legs scissored together and apart, small movements that nonetheless dragged on the part of his shaft not embedded in her sweet flesh.

"Voletta," he whispered.

She murmured sleepily, but didn't waken.

Cursing himself and his wayward cock, he tried to hold himself still, but her cunt closed and relaxed, milking him softly.

Too softly. He needed to move, needed to thrust himself against her. He buried his face in the corner of her neck and gritted his teeth. His hand squeezed the breast he palmed harder.

"Ummmmm," she moaned, and slowly awoke. He knew the moment she realized what was happening, because she covered his hand with hers.

"I wanted to leave you alone," he said, trying to stir up a little regret. "To let you rest."

"I'm glad you didn't."

"Are you sore?"

She gasped, then softly replied, "Yes, but I think you'd cause me greater discomfort if you didn't continue."

"Lift your thigh onto mine."

She did, immediately.

He reached between her legs and slid his fingers around her sex, pulling apart the lips framing his cock to ease the friction. Then he brought his fingers to his mouth and wet them before returning them to play with the little button at the top of her lips.

He swirled his fingers over it, listening to her hissing breath to gauge how hard to rub. Soon, he got it just right because she moaned and moved her hips, inviting him to deepen his shallow strokes inside her.

"You should play with your breasts," he whispered in her ear.

"I should?"

"Pinch them for me." He flicked her earlobe with his tongue.

"The tips?"

"Yes."

Although he couldn't see her do it, the catch of her breath and the deeper roll of her hips told him she obeyed.

"Do you think you can take more of me?" he asked.

"I think I'll die if I can not."

5

What a delicious way to awaken: enveloped in warmth; Damien's wide chest blanketing her back; his strong arm resting heavily on her waist; his fingers rubbing the nubbin between her legs just hard enough to make the pleasant ache between her thighs throb again.

She murmured and nestled her bottom closer, moaning when his sex slipped deeper inside her.

Voletta held her breath until he started rocking softly against her, stroking her gently with his cock. She let loose a ragged moan and her nipples hardened, pressing into her palms as she cupped herself.

Soon, she couldn't help but pulse backward to meet his thrusts, luxuriating in the drag and push that heated her channel. She felt consumed by the heat he built—and connected to the man in more than just a physical way. Damien seemed to understand precisely what she needed.

The joyful experience of being with him tempered her impatience to quit the place in haste. But, of course, remaining there was still out of the question.

There was a part of her she would never be able to share. He might live in an enchanted castle where everything he wished for appeared, but he expected a *human* bride, a woman, as his companion.

However selfish it might seem, she was willing to linger there a little while longer and explore their budding relationship. She knew exactly where her pelt was and could escape at any time. So why not enjoy this interlude and leave them both with memories to savor?

She gave her nipples a final tweak, then reached behind her to cup the back of his head as she arched her back to press her buttocks tighter against his groin. "Deeper," she moaned, "I need you to move deeper."

"It may be how we're positioned," he whispered in her ear. "I'll have to pull out."

"No, I couldn't bear that," she whimpered. "Just please, *more*."

He groaned and shifted behind her, his torso moving away from her back while his cock remained embedded inside her. Then his hand was on her leg, lifting it higher, and he slid a thick, muscled thigh between hers, opening her wide so he could buck deeper between her legs . . . and it was enough. More than enough.

With his fingers still swirling, pressing, rolling on the knot of bundled sensations, she crept closer to the precipice. Tension curled low in her belly. Her breaths shortened until she panted. She couldn't move, couldn't help him, could only *feel* as he held her splayed open and pounded inside her.

She felt only twinges of discomfort from their previous joining. She burned inside, her tissues stretched and abused by the girth of him and his quickening movements as he dragged his cock in and out of her, pushing ever deeper, yearning toward her womb.

When he plucked her clitoris, she hurtled toward the darkness, light dimming at the edges of her vision, narrowing her focus.

Toward the end, she knew she screamed. She thought she might have howled.

However, Damien was relentless. He didn't let her escape gracefully into the rapture. He continued to move inside her, spurring the tension impossibly higher, until it swirled and coiled, and she felt as though she would never return to herself. She hovered beyond the edge, her body shuddering.

His hoarse shout rang in her ears as he jerked against her. Hot, fiery liquid jetted deep inside her. Only when the last clumsy pulses ended and he snuggled against her back, closing her legs to hold his cock firmly inside her again, did the coil within her fully unwind.

When her breath returned to her, she whispered, "Is there anything more beautiful?"

"I've never had the likes of this before," he said softly.

She smiled, hoping it was true. She wanted to see his face. "I wish I could turn, but I don't want to let you go."

"I think I should come out of you, my dear. You need time to recover." He pulled away, leaving her empty, her liquid gushing from her channel to wet her thighs.

"I'm sticky."

"I have a cloth." And without moving from the bed, he produced a warm, wet cloth and scooped it between her legs, washing her gently, the heat easing her aching flesh.

When he'd finished, he turned her onto her back and stretched alongside her. He laid his chest across hers and looked down, cupping her face and rasping his thumb across her bottom lip.

Gazing at his dark hair tumbling around his face and his darker gaze locking with hers, she knew part of her already belonged to him.

While she knew she had to leave, she began to think that perhaps he wouldn't mind if once in a while she returned to renew their acquaintance. Their reunions would be joyous, something to be anticipated. She wouldn't think about their many partings.

She lifted a hand to his cheek. "Kiss me," she said, surprised she felt like crying.

When his lips brushed hers softly, she knew she was falling in love, because she couldn't imagine ever tasting another kiss as sweet.

"What are you thinking now?" he asked.

Rather than give him an awkward truth, she quipped, "I'm thinking how good you look without your clothes."

He snorted laughter, and his eyes filled with merriment. "I think I'm supposed to say that."

She grinned. "I will never lie to you."

"Will you ever tell me the full truth?"

She kept silent, knowing he read the regret in her expression.

Thankfully, his smile dimmed only slightly. "I suppose I have my secrets, too. You should rest."

"I'm really not tired, and I think I probably need to move around a bit or I'll ache worse later," she said wrinkling her nose.

Damien's brows lifted and settled, a mischievous look settled over his face. "Come for a walk with me?"

She nodded, eager to put some distance from this bed, where she was tempted to linger.

After she'd dressed in clothing hanging conveniently from another hook on the wall, Damien brought her outside the keep, taking a dirt path into a wooded area. Mist still hovered close to the ground, blotting out the sunshine, but the day was warm. As they entered deeper into the copse, Voletta gave Damien curious glances, wondering what he seemed so determined to show her.

His glance stayed on the path in front of them, and his hand cupped her elbow, guiding her as though she was precious.

When he halted, she dragged her gaze from his face to look around her, and her breath caught. He'd brought her to a tiny paradise. A pond lay in the center of a clearing with a willow that draped over one side, fronds dipping into the water like lazy fingers gliding on the surface. Lacy ferns and delicate orchids blanketed the ground surrounding the path, all the way up to the bank of short grass that ringed the pond and stopped at the water's edge.

Voletta was tempted once again. A breeze tugged at her hair and pulled at her gown, urging her closer to the water.

Damien lifted a hand to the ties at the side of her bliaut. At her nod, he undid them and swept the fabric over her head. Before he could reach for her again, she danced away and pulled her undergown off, then stepped into the shallows.

The water was surprisingly warm and felt like silk as it lapped around her ankles.

"It's deep enough for a swim," Damien said, his gaze sweeping over her nude body.

"Join me?" she asked, already turning away to walk deeper into the water.

"I'll watch."

She glanced over her shoulder to find his stare resting on her body. "Afraid you'll melt?"

"I'm afraid I won't be able to stop myself from taking you again."

"In the water?" The thought tantalized. Would she ever tire of exploring the many ways they could make love? "Is that one of those hundred different ways?"

One side of his mouth rose in a smirk. "I can think of at least a half dozen acts we could accomplish quite nicely."

She bit her lip, wanting to ask him to explain, but he shook his head and lowered himself to the grass. "I'll be here when you come out."

Voletta dove toward the center of the pond, pushing deep beneath the surface, twisting over and over as she glided through the water. As she came up for air, she tossed back her hair and gasped, letting out a little laugh.

When she caught sight of Damien, he was lowering himself to the ground again.

"Did you think I'd drowned?" she asked, treading water.

"I was calling myself a fool for not making sure you knew how to swim."

"Of course, I know how." She lay back, floating on the surface, letting the water fan her hair around her. "I could spend hours in the water."

"The pond is to your liking?" he asked, his voice muffled by the water.

"It's beautiful," she said, staring up into the willow. "Almost perfect."

"Almost? What's missing? I'll change it."

She turned her face toward him. "You're too far away."

"You could come here."

"Then I'd have to leave the water. I'd be cold."

"I'd warm you."

She stared back up at the willow, smiling at the deepening rumble of his voice. He was becoming aroused. "Then you'd have to show me one of those 'acts.' "

Warm water lapped along her body as she floated, lulling her into drowsiness. When a hand smoothed over her ankle, she was too at ease to startle. "I like this," she said, opening her eyes to find him naked and standing in the water beside her.

"Thought you might."

She let her body drift upright and treaded closer to him.

When she was within arms' reach, he snagged her waist and pulled her close. "Wind your legs around my waist."

She dipped her chin and smiled, then complied. Her body

drifted against his, her breasts skimming his slick chest. When she wound her legs around him, her sex opened, scraping against the silky hairs on his lower abdomen. Voletta grabbed his shoulders and rubbed her body against him.

His cock bobbed against her bottom and she guessed what new 'act' they would explore before his hands closed around her soft cheeks. He lifted her high enough to position his cock at her entrance.

She drew a deep breath and snuggled her face into the crook of his neck as he guided her down his shaft and back up. "Does one ever tire of this?" she groaned.

"Never, if one does it right."

"I think you have the knack of it," she said, squeezing her inner muscles around him.

"And I'm blessed," he gasped, moving her up and down faster. "You're gifted, love."

She threw back her head and groaned. "I think you're just easily pleased."

His grunt, so masculine and amused, encouraged her to move, to take him. She gripped his shoulders hard and pulled herself up, then released, countering the movements of his hips as he plunged into her.

The water churned between them, splashing around them as they strained against each other. Voletta couldn't look away from him. His jaw tightened, giving him a fierce, hungry expression. His cheeks darkened; his eyes narrowed. When his fingers dug hard into her bottom, she moaned, knowing she'd sport two rows of crescent bruises.

When at last their passion crested, they stayed wrapped in each other's arms, swaying together in the water.

"We're in the open," Voletta said. "Anyone could have seen us."

"What a silly thing to say. You know there's no one here but us."

"And the ghosts."

His hand paused its soothing motion on her back. "You've seen them?"

She nodded.

"You aren't frightened of them?"

"They haven't tried to harm me. They seem to serve your needs."

"Our needs." His lips brushed her forehead.

"Should I fear them?"

"No." His gaze locked on hers. "Come, let's leave the water."

Although reluctant to break the connection, she unhooked her feet and let her legs drift down. Before she could bob beneath the surface, he picked her up and strode to the grassy bank.

Towels lay beside their clothing, and Voletta stood silently while he patted her dry.

"Do the ghosts ever leave this place?" she asked, when he'd finished and tossed the towels to the side.

"Never," he said, his voice clipped. "They serve this keep. They are enslaved to it."

Voletta shivered and drew on her chemise. "And what about you?"

The towel he scrubbed across his chest stilled. "I am imprisoned here." He said it matter-of-factly, without inflection, which told her how much emotion lay beneath the bald words.

Even though she knew it caused him pain, she persisted, wanting to understand. "But you've been outside the gates. You brought me inside."

"I can only go as far as the post." His gaze met hers, empty, emotionless. "And only once every hundred years."

"Once every hundred years . . . ?" A chill prickled her skin. "What are you?" she whispered.

He grimaced. "Most women prefer not to know. They prefer to believe I'm a human trapped inside this castle. They pretend not to notice I never age."

"I'm not most women. I know there's something special about you, as there is about this place."

He turned away, stepping into his chausses, then pulled his undertunic over his head.

She reached out and placed her hand on his arm. "Please, I really want to know."

His head fell back, and he closed his eyes. "My name is Damien, Lord Malphas. Is that name familiar to you?"

Of course it was. She'd been raised a Catholic before she'd come into her skin. "Malphas was one of the angels who descended from heaven. One of the fallen angels."

He turned to spear her with his hard, black gaze. "Yes, I was."

Her head canted, her gaze trying to discern whether he was telling the truth. "Malphas was Hell's builder. He constructed fortifications."

He raised his hands, staring at his palms. "I built extraordinary things, magical things, but when my brother and I fell out, I was imprisoned here."

Her eyes widened, and then her jaw dropped open. "Is this one of your own creations?" At his nod, she said, "That's diabolical!"

The corners of his lips twitched. "My brother's known for his imagination, among other things."

"So, you're a . . . devil?"

"Not a very precise term."

"Lucifer is your brother? That's who you're talking about, isn't it?"

"We all share the same Father, Voletta. This doesn't alarm you?"

Alarm her? She'd been told the fallen angels were evil, bent on tempting mankind into betraying its faith so that it could be drawn into Hell. Her legs quivered, but she lifted her chin, refusing to let him see her fear. "Where are your wings?"

"Taken. When I was banished here."

"Why were you banished?"

"Because I grew bored with the depravity around me. I dared to criticize and was cast out for my efforts. You didn't answer my question. Are you afraid now that you know the truth?"

Voletta sighed, letting the tension leave her body. Her answer mattered to him. Could he be so evil if he cared what she thought? "Well," she said slowly, not entirely sure what she thought. "You've been kind to me . . ."

"I've kept you here against your will."

"Are you trying to remind me why I should be frightened?"

His smile didn't reach his eyes, which were dark and watchful. "You promised to speak only the truth."

"If I choose not to speak, will you let me be or hound me to death?"

"Is that even possible?"

"I don't know." She couldn't restrain her humor. "I'm arguing with a demon. Doesn't that tell you something about me?"

"It only tells me you may be addled, which I'm beginning to suspect is true."

She snorted. "I'm not mad. Just curious. But I will tell you, I don't fear you'll grow horns and devour me." She gave him a glance from under her lashes when she realized she didn't know for sure that wasn't true. "Will you?"

His laughter, full throated and hearty, warmed her. "Voletta, I sport no horns, other than the one that rises to your goading."

Her gaze dropped down his body, then flew back up when she got his meaning. She sniffed and turned her back to hide the heat rising in her cheeks. "I'm glad my ignorance amuses you."

"Your *innocence* pleases me." His arms came around her, drawing her back against his chest. "I would know that I don't frighten you."

At the soft intensity of his tone, she let the stiffness of her posture melt away and leaned against him. "Perhaps I'm just a bit worn out, but I'm not frightened. Nor am I truly surprised. I'm not sure any surprises can exceed the ones you've already shown me."

She slid her hands over the arms crossed on her belly and hugged him. "So, you are trapped inside here, and yet, how do the things come? The ones you wish for. Do they move from one place to another, or are they created from thin air?"

"That bit of magic I'm not sure of," he said, his breath gusting softly against her neck. "I hired a mage to create it. Those kind are notoriously secretive about their methods."

"You have a castle where all your needs are met. Beautiful gardens to walk inside—"

"—a horse to ride—"

"You have a horse?" So he wasn't entirely alone. "And then you've had women, like me, provided by the village. How often?"

"Once every hundred years."

"And when they die?"

"Then I am alone."

"How long since your last companion?"

"Nearly sixty years."

Sixty years since he'd had anyone to speak to or to touch. Now she understood the stark loneliness in his gaze. "What I don't understand is how you had the patience to be so gentle with me. You must have been desperate."

He laughed.

"Well, now you will have me," she said, squeezing his arms, "and I can make trips outside the gate and bring you back wonderful things no mage's magic can bring you."

His body stiffened behind her, and his arms fell away. When she turned to stare up at him, his smile had slipped away. The alertness entering his expression alarmed her.

"What haven't you told me?" she asked, her heart tripping.

"The gate is only open for three days."

"Three days . . . and then what?"

"The path beyond it disappears."

"I'll be trapped with you?"

"A moment ago that hardly seemed a terrible thought, did it?"

Voletta noted the tension evident in the thinning of his lips and the wistful expression in his eyes. She didn't want to feel empathy for him, didn't want to worry about how lonely he must have been—would be again when she was gone. Had he wooed her only to ensure her submission?

Or did he truly care about her? Could she handle the possibility that he'd only been kind to ensure her cooperation?

His hand reached out, but she pulled back before he could touch her face.

She stared at him, accusing him.

His hand slowly dropped to his side, and his shoulders straightened. "I'll leave you to your thoughts," he said. "I'm going to ride my horse."

She walked away from him, following the path out of the woods until it intersected the road that led away from the keep to the iron gate. Her gaze went to the tall stone walls that stretched as far as her eyes could see.

"You'll never get over it," he said, from just behind her. "And the gate won't open unless I command it to."

Tightness filled her chest as though a hand clutched her heart and a band encircled her ribs. She couldn't catch a deep enough breath. It might already be too late, but she had to try to escape. "I have to go back inside. I have to rest," she said, not looking at him.

"I understand. I'll see you later."

She gave him a jerking nod, swept up her skirts, and began to walk toward the keep, but the urgency that filled her had her breaking into a run. By the time she reached the steps leading into the keep, she was crying.

6

Damien didn't go to the stables. Instead, he slipped through the cellar door and up a narrow staircase to a secret passage behind his room. There, he watched through a spy hole as Voletta rushed into the room, leaving the door ajar, and flung herself on his bed and cried.

His heart ached, and he wished that he could go to her, but he didn't want to see the accusation in her eyes. He knew she doubted him; and he could understand that because he did intend to keep her there even if she didn't want to stay.

He had no doubt that, with her soft heart, she would come around eventually.

Damien wished he could lie down beside her and pull her into his arms to soothe away her worries. Her little fists pounded the pillow, and she cried harder, her sobs shaking her shoulders.

His fingers dug into the stone of the passage wall. He couldn't tear himself away. Instead, he watched, each sob deepening his remorse and strengthening his resolve to make her happy.

Her cries lessened, and she lifted her head. Her tear-filled gaze narrowed on the trunk. She slipped off the bed and walked toward it, hiccoughing softly. She lifted the lid and pulled out the black cloak that his retainers had returned when they'd tidied the room.

What was it with the cloak?

She walked back to the bed and sat cross-legged, then began to tear the pelt from the collar of the cloak, using her teeth to bite the stitches.

Wondering what she was about, he stayed stock-still, because something in her expression was so intent, so focused, he knew he was about to learn something very important.

When the last of the stitches had been removed, she laid the cloak to the side and stripped off her clothing. Then she lifted the pelt, smoothed a hand over it lovingly, and swung it back to cover her shoulders.

From one moment to the next, her head jerked forward, her hands came down on the mattress, and the pelt seemed to creep across her skin, flowing down her arms and legs to cover her pale skin in glossy, red fur. Her body shrank until in its place on the bed stood a small red fox.

At last he understood what had been so different about her. She wasn't from the village, and she wasn't even human.

And he knew his little were-fox intended to bolt.

"Lock the doors," he said aloud, knowing all the latches would instantly be in place.

Damien watched the fox jump from the bed and run toward the door just as it slammed closed. She yipped, pacing in front of the door, then scratched and used her teeth to try to bite the wood to shred it.

When it became obvious her route of escape was closed, she circled the room, her tail straightening behind her as she ran around and around.

He watched her for a very long time until she'd exhausted herself. Then, her narrow chest heaving, she leapt back up to the bed, reached behind her shoulder with her snout, and bit into her fur, tugging it away from her skin, sweeping it away, the action pulling and stretching her skin and body, until she was transformed.

Voletta curled into a ball in the center of the mattress, panting softly.

He pushed a lever to open the wall and stepped inside the room, walking quickly toward the bed.

Reaching over Voletta, he plucked the fur from her fingers.

She lifted her head, tears streaming down her face, exhaustion lending purple shadows beneath her eyes. "You cannot keep me here," she said, her voice ragged. "I can't be caged."

Damien rolled the fox fur into a small bundle.

Her gaze darted toward it, widening. "Please give it back."

He shook his head, his jaw clenching. "You'll stay with me. In whatever form I wish."

She came up on her knees, her hands outstretched toward the fur. "I don't belong to you. I'm not an object—I'm a person. If you keep me here, trap me, I'll come to hate you."

"Nevertheless," he said coldly, "you'll remain with me. I'll have the use of you." He walked from the room, shutting the door behind him, pausing only long enough to hear the dull click as the wooden latch fell into place on the outside of the door.

Within the room, Voletta threw back her head and howled, knowing she'd made a horrible mistake, knowing time was fleeting, and soon she would indeed be trapped with him for an eternity. No mere sixty years of existence. As a were-creature, she'd be condemned within these walls for her—eternal—life. She'd never run through the forest again with pine needles prickling the pads of her feet. She'd never smell the rich, deep scents of a wild forest—warm, musty resin, lush greenery, pine needles releasing their scent as they were crushed beneath her running feet.

The smells would be replaced by the heavy, cloying perfumes of the flowers in his garden.

She'd thought she was falling in love with him and that he was coming to care for her, but his affection had been a lie, a ruse. He couldn't love her and do this to her.

She pulled the edges of the blankets around her, snuffling, sobbing softly. She burrowed her face into the down pillow and, eventually, fell asleep.

Damien rode until dusk fell, around and around the far edges of the outer curtain wall, until both he and his horse were bored with the view and had spent themselves. However, no matter how far or fast or hard he pushed the horse and himself he couldn't escape the memory of her expression as she'd faced him.

She would come to hate him. Slowly, he came to the realization that he would come to hate himself as well.

He didn't know if he could bear to see the wonder and affection leach from her expression over time. But could he give her up? He'd be alone for another one hundred years, and, even then, would he have the heart to let another woman inside after having had Voletta?

He turned his horse toward the keep. Together, their bodies trembling from exertion, they headed back to face her. Once inside the portcullis, he spied a small figure huddled on the steps of the keep. She'd remembered she could command the servants inside to release her.

He brought his horse to a halt in front of her, and looked down at Voletta, who sat with her arms wrapped around her knees. She looked small and forlorn as her eyes rested on him, sweeping over his body and his horse before sliding away.

He dismounted and flung away the reins. "Take him to his stall and rub him down. Feed him," he commanded his invisible retainers.

Then he drew a deep breath and approached Voletta. He held out his hand to her.

She stared at it for a long time, then looked up at him. Her expression was devoid of anger. Only a deep melancholy dragged the corners of her lips downward and shadowed her eyes.

He thought he would have preferred if she spit and clawed at him. This quiet sadness made his stomach knot, caused a pain in his chest that he suspected was regret.

She placed her palm inside his, and he pulled her to her feet. Together they walked inside the keep and up the stairs to his chamber. She didn't demur, didn't try to draw away. Her leaden footsteps told him she'd not fight him.

Damien slowly grew angry the closer they drew to his chamber door. Where was her fire? Why wasn't she fighting him? Pleading with him? Her dampened mood fed a quiet fury that built inside him. His anger was directed at himself, he recognized, but that didn't help melt the cold resolve freezing hard inside his chest.

At the open door, she glanced at the bed and her chin came up.

Maybe there was a little defiance left in her. *Good.* He would use it.

"Bring a pillow from the bed," he said, quietly but firmly.

Her gaze swung toward him, and her lips thinned.

"A pillow," he bit out. "Bring it." He flung away her hand and began to strip away his clothing.

She stared at him. With his legs braced apart and his hands on his naked hips, every muscle tensed, he knew he intimidated her. Again, he felt a deep satisfaction as her eyes widened. "As long as you are stubborn, this is how it will be between us. Now, bring the pillow. I'm thinking only of your comfort, love."

Her gaze narrowed and an angry wash flamed across her cheeks. She turned on her heels and stomped toward the bed, grabbing a fat pillow and tossing it at his head.

He caught it easily and smiled, then dropped it to the floor between his feet. "You know what I demand."

"I'm afraid I don't," she murmured, tossing back her hair.

"Then let me explain. You will come to me and take my cock between your hands and into your mouth."

"I won't do it."

"You will, because you know what I will give you in return."

"You think you can tempt me with your lovemaking?" she said, her voice even and tight. "Well, there is no love, and this isn't what I want."

"I will make you crave the taste of me, because each time you submit, I'll reciprocate, giving you many more times the pleasure you give me."

Her chest rose and fell quickly, her breaths shortening. "I will hate you."

"So be it, but you will still come, howling my name."

Tears shimmered in her eyes, but she stepped woodenly toward him when he lifted his hand to beckon her closer. When she stood in front of him, he grasped her shoulders and forced her to her knees on the pillow.

"I don't know what to do," she said, so softly he had to strain to hear the words.

"You've held me before. Stroke me with your hands. Take the tip of me into your mouth and suckle."

She closed her eyes for a moment, then reached up and grasped his thickened shaft.

Damien fought to control his own breaths as she rubbed her hands up and down his length and leaned close. Her tongue wet her lips and he nearly groaned, then couldn't help but let one loose when her mouth opened wide and engulfed the crown of his cock in moist heat.

His fingers combed through her red hair, encouraging her to take more of him as she glided her mouth forward and back, letting his cock ride the length of her tongue and push deeper into her throat.

She didn't gag and didn't pull away. She swallowed around him, her throat working to caress him as he stroked in and out. One small hand gripped his shaft, working down and up, gliding in the moisture from her mouth, while the other reached down to gently cup his ballocks.

Damien stared at her, drinking in the sight of her mouth working his flesh, storing memories even while he let his anger consume him. He'd fuck her mouth, fuck her body in ways she couldn't yet imagine. She'd remember him always, as he'd remember her for an eternity.

When his balls tightened, drawing close to his groin, and his thighs tensed, he knew he was close to release. He'd wanted to drench her throat with his seed, but he changed his mind, wanting her body beneath his, her thighs wrapped tightly around his hips when he came. He wanted to hold her close, drink in her scent, sink into her silken depths.

Damien tugged her hair, drawing her off his cock, and bent to pick her up.

Voletta lay inside his arms, her wide, golden eyes never leaving his face, her nostrils flaring, catching his heightened scent.

In three strides he reached the bed and laid her on it; then he grabbed the neck of her bliaut, ripping it away along with her snowy-white chemise. Watching her legs splayed wide and her arms lying limply on the mattress, he knew she'd surrendered to the passion but wouldn't give him everything he wanted. She'd withhold her participation.

Fine. He had her where he needed her. Soon, he'd press past her silent resistance. He'd find the fire burning inside her and make the flames lick higher. Maybe, he could even convince her she couldn't live without this, without him.

He crawled onto the bed between her legs and paused over her, resting on his hands as he rooted with his cock between her legs, finding her slick folds and sliding through them and into her in a single, easy glide.

He'd already done that, stretched her to accommodate his size, breached her innocence to claim her. As he stroked inside, slowly at first, he reminded her with his steady thrusts who had taught her about love, who had been the first to enter her body and her heart.

Voletta clutched the bedding beneath her, fighting the urge to reach up and glide her hands over his sweat-slicked skin. She didn't want to give him anything, wanted him to know that even while he moved inside her, she held back a part of herself.

While she'd sucked his sex deep into her mouth, she'd fought the urge to moan around him. The taste of his musk, the scent of his warm skin, had been too delicious.

When his body had tightened, she'd felt elation that she'd been able to rouse him so. She'd been tempted to explore beyond the confines of his command to see him tremble, see him lose control.

Instead, he'd pulled her away and carried her to his bed, once again asserting his dominance by rising over her, stroking inside her. She clutched the bedding to prevent herself from giving him more. Never did she want him to know how close she'd come to surrendering completely to his will.

She loved him and knew it would be so easy for him to consume her. She had no experience with men, had built no defenses against this dark allure.

Again, he stroked inside her, rooting deeper, filling her inside, overwhelming her outside. When his arms thrust beneath her thighs to lift her bottom from the bed, her heart leapt at yet another proof of his power. He could take her, force her body to accept him, make passion blossom inside her, without her consent.

Even now, his cock stroked her walls, swelling her sex to clasp him tighter. Wet, succulent sounds betrayed the excitement building in her core.

On his knees, he wrestled her hips higher, pulling her up to meet his quickening thrusts. Unable to hold back her response a moment longer, her back arched off the mattress, her hips circled on his cock, and a ragged moan slipped between her lips.

A satisfied smile curved his lips, and he halted his movements.

Her sex clenched around him, urging him silently to continue, but he leaned over her, pushing her thighs higher into her chest. Then he reached along her arms and pried her fingers from the bedding. "Hold your legs close to yourself and do not let go," he urged her.

With her breaths rasping, she did as he asked. He sat back on his haunches and smoothed his hands down the backs of her thighs until his fingers glided along the sides of her folds.

Her sex opened and clasped, embarrassing proof of her arousal, but he didn't smile. His eyelids dropped halfway as he stared down at her and rimmed her opening with his fingers. Then he leaned over her. His mouth drew on her folds as his fingers penetrated, dipping in and out while she bit her bottom lip to stop from crying out.

When his fingers left her opening and stroked downward, her breath caught. He circled her tiny forbidden hole, then dipped one thick fingertip inside.

"No!"

"Yes," he soothed. "You'll like this. I promise. Don't fight me."

She couldn't. Not while she held her thighs high against her chest, a position which curved her sex upward toward his questing lips and fingers.

She stared down at his dark head as he stroked his tongue between her folds and worked his finger into her dark passage.

Her body tightened around him, rejecting him even as fresh liquid spilled from inside her to greet his kisses.

His dark, amused laughter gusted against her, and she couldn't help the way her sex continued to open and close, trying to draw him deeper inside.

When his finger was inserted past the second knuckle, he rolled his hand around, tugging at the tight ring, easing the constriction until he could slip another finger inside her.

Although her tender tissues burned, another sort of fire licked at her core, and she pulled her legs higher, wider, straining upward to find the release she knew hovered just beyond her reach.

When his tongue lapped lower, trailing toward her back entrance, she grew restless and simultaneously appalled at her eagerness. Surely he wouldn't lick her there!

But he did, pulling out his fingers and rimming her with his tongue. His thumbs pressed on either side of the small hole and opened her. He dipped his tongue into her, tickling her with short, teasing flutters, then causing her to cry out when the hardened tip plunged into her.

"Damien! Please stop!"

He did—abruptly—and her eyes flew open.

He spit onto his fingers and rubbed the moisture on the glistening tip of his sex, then held himself as he directed the head of his cock to the tiny hole.

"God, no!" she cried out as he pushed against her, the burning pressure causing tears to fill her eyes.

"Don't fight me," he bit out, his jaw clenching as he pushed into her.

Suddenly, the constriction of the tiny ring eased and he was inside her.

He halted, his chest heaving, his gaze locking with hers. One hand curved under her bottom, lifting her higher; the other hand glided over her wet cleft, two fingers clamping around her hardened nubbin while his thumb plunged inside her channel.

"Think you can resist me? Think you can ever tell me no?"

Voletta couldn't breathe, couldn't look away from the dark promise in his gaze. He could draw her like a moth flying too closely to an open flame. He'd burn her, consume her like a raging fire. If he never came to care for her, she'd never survive. But she couldn't tell him to stop. "Please," she sobbed.

His hips brushed forward and back, a gentle glide that tugged at her inner tissues. His fingers swirled on the hard, swollen button. He eased in and out again, slowly, and her belly tightened, knowing that soon he wouldn't be able to control himself.

His cheeks reddened; his mouth opened to drag air into his lungs. Then he gave her deeper, faster strokes, all the while circling on her, his fingers plunging into her channel.

Voletta's breaths shortened to jagged gasps, and her eyelids fluttered closed.

He moved faster, thrust deeper, and plunged in and out, stroking both entrances. The moist sounds of them moving together, the slap of his belly and groin against her flesh, only heightened the excitement building a thrumming tension that pounded against her chest and temples.

A low, deep groan escaped him and then his movements quickened. He pounded faster, his body slamming into hers, scooting her up the bed with each hard stroke.

Voletta felt the tension burst inside her head, unraveling inside her womb. She screamed, pitching headlong over the crest of a wave of heat that had her whole body shaking and spasming wildly.

Above her, Damien's eyes squeezed tightly and he shouted, barreling into her, his movements jerking as his seed spilled inside her.

When she came back to herself, he lay against the backs of her thighs, his chest heaving. Her hands clutched his hair, and she pulled him down to kiss his mouth, his chin, his nose, anything she could reach.

Until she remembered what he planned to do.

She sank against the mattress and let her arms fall away, waiting for him to move off her. No longer in the throes of a passion that robbed her mind and will, she couldn't let him comfort her. Couldn't let herself give him comfort.

This was all they would ever have. She would never forgive him for taking away her freedom.

"I was orphaned as a child. Raised by a witch," she whispered. "Near Fulkenstein, farther down the valley from here."

Damien shook his head, trying to gather his scattered wits. He lay sprawled over her, crushing her legs against her body.

Carefully, he pulled out his cock from the heat of her tightest passage and rolled to his back. "A cloth," he rasped.

When one appeared in his hand, he rolled to his side and began to gently bathe Voletta. Her legs had eased down to the bed, but her hands fluttered as though she wanted to ask him for the linen. He pushed away her hands and continued.

The least he could do was give her ease, clean her after he'd taken her so harshly.

A virgin yesterday, already she'd been forced past her maidenly inhibitions. This act should have been months in the making. He should have wooed her, teased her, prepared her gently. Instead he'd commanded it, taken her.

His hands shook as he finished his task; then he requested a clean cloth to take care of his cock.

"Did you know you weren't human?" he asked quietly,

hoping she'd continue the story so he could learn another secret he might use to hold her there.

She turned away from him, rolling to her side. "I never quite fit in," she said, in an eerily calm voice. "I thought it was because I was raised by Hilde, and because my parents had come from across the border . . . from France. I looked different from everyone else. I spoke with an accent. Even after I'd learned their manner of speech, I still felt . . . outside them."

"When did you find out?"

"At the time of my first menses. I fell asleep that first night on my pallet, but woke up miles from home, naked, in the woods. When I returned to the hut, Hilde explained what had happened. That I'd transformed and run like a wild creature into the forest."

"She wasn't frightened of you?"

"She'd always known. My mother warned her before she disappeared."

"She vanished?"

"Hilde suspected she and my father were trapped. Killed by poachers."

"How did you come here?"

She turned back to him, a sad smile on her face. "After Hilde died, I burned her hut and entered the forest. It's the only place I belong."

He cupped her face, smoothing his thumb over her lush lower lip. "You can belong here. With me."

"Inside these walls?" She shook her head. "I'll wither inside." Her lip trembled beneath his thumb.

Time stood still for Damien.

Already, he missed her smiles and the funny things she said. Missed the innocence that had curved her lips.

He rolled over her, stretched out on top of her, and then bent down to kiss her mouth.

She turned her face away.

He didn't force her. Instead, he trailed his lips along her jaw, then worked his way lower, feeding the passion he knew was inside her, pausing at her breasts to suckle until her breaths shortened and her belly quivered.

He nudged apart her legs, and she opened them willingly. He settled between them, content for now to feast on her skin as he worked his way down her body, determined to taste every inch of her.

His hand plumped up a small breast while his tongue followed the sweet curve beneath it. She was soft as a ripe peach; he'd never forget her flavor, never forget the feeling of her nipple scraping across his tongue. When he sucked it into his mouth, she mewled and, at last, clawed at his back.

Damien smiled around her breast and bit her, nipping her playfully as he moved lower, sucking her skin, leaving dark love bites on her belly and lower abdomen.

When at last he hovered above her feminine mound, he breathed in her scent, lapped her sweet, musky flavor into his mouth, loving her with his tongue and lips while she moved restlessly beneath him, her hips lifting into his kisses.

When she came, sighing softly, her fingers tightening in his hair, he kissed her inner thighs and moved up to hold her but didn't take his own pleasure.

As she drifted downward, she snuggled her face against his chest. "It's not that I don't want to be with you," she said, her voice breaking.

"I know."

"I want to hate you. Anger would be easier." She sighed. "I wish you hadn't made me love you."

He lay frozen beside her, squeezing his eyes shut. "Go to sleep, love."

She nodded, her cheek sliding along his skin.

Long after her breaths had deepened and the candles burned low, he held her, not wanting to miss a single moment with her.

* * *

The next morning, the table stood once again at the end of the bed, laden with steaming, silver plates of meat. Voletta realized she was starving. As she speared slices of beef and roast pork with her fork, her heart felt lighter than it had the night before.

The reason was obvious. She was in love. But the man who'd managed to slip into her heart was nowhere around. She picked at her food long after she'd satisfied her appetite, half hoping for him to appear.

This morning, the thought of an eternity spent with Damien wasn't quite so dark, not nearly as frightening. Panic didn't make her heart beat wildly; her breaths didn't catch in her chest.

If she had to give up her freedom, would it be such a terrible thing to spend her days with him? Her nights she knew would be wondrous.

Even her anger at his high-handed insistence had waned. She could empathize with him. He'd been alone and lonely for so long, and she knew he cared about her. Perhaps that would be enough.

Setting down her fork, she covered the dishes and dressed in a fresh gown, thanking the servants who hovered around her out of sight. Then she left the room, trailing a finger along the walls and down the staircase, leaving the castle for the misty morning that awaited her outside.

Sunshine was something she'd miss. She guessed the constant mist was just one more punishment heaped upon Damien. Did he even remember how it felt to have sunlight warm his skin?

The bailey was empty, swept clean of leaves; any grass that might have crept between the cobblestones had been plucked to leave a pristine path to the gate. The portcullis stood open and she followed the sounds of a horse's hooves pounding in the distance.

The sight that greeted her stole her breath. Seated on his

magnificent black horse, Damien rode like the wind, his hard-edged face set, his jaw clamped tight, his expression remote.

Man and horse flowed together. It was a magnificent sight—both looked so dark and powerful.

He spotted her, urged his horse away from the worn grass path beside the curtain wall, and rode toward her. At the bottom of the steps, he pulled back on his reins, halting in front of her.

He stared down, his gaze sweeping from head to toe, his expression giving away none of his thoughts.

A chill filled her. Something about him seemed different, removed. The look on his face was the same he'd worn when he'd found her tied to the post.

Had yesterday and last night meant nothing to him? Was he not as changed as she was?

After a long moment, he extended his hand and unhooked his foot from his stirrup. She placed her slippered foot atop his and let him pull her up in front of him, glad to be close to him again.

He gave a gentle kick to the side of his horse and they started out, heading down the path—away from the keep.

"Are you feeling well this morning?" she asked, nervous and unsure how to open a conversation with him.

"I am. Did you sleep well?" he asked politely.

Sitting crossways on the saddle in front of him, her unease grew at their stilted words. Yesterday, they'd teased each other. She'd even have settled for angry words, but the distance seemed to stretch between them despite the fact that her hip rode the juncture of his thighs.

Could he already be bored with her?

As they neared the iron gate, her heart tripped, thudding dully in her chest. "Why are we here?" she asked, looking up to meet his gaze.

His black eyes gave away none of his thoughts. He halted in

front of the gate and dismounted, then reached up to grip her waist and set her on the ground.

Her legs trembled, and she held his arms for a moment to steady herself. "What's wrong? Why have we returned here?" she asked again.

He held out his hand in front of him. "Voletta's fur," he said.

The red pelt shimmered into existence, tightly rolled and tied with a leather cord. Then he held it out to her.

She understood now. He was saying good-bye. Giving her back her fox's fur and her freedom.

She opened her mouth to speak but didn't know what to say. So, she stood silently as he transferred the fur to her hand and leaned down to give her a chaste kiss on the lips.

With a final, sweeping glance at her hair, he met her eyes for a charged moment, and then turned on his heels, grabbed his horse's reins, and walked away without looking back.

She stared after him, hoping he'd look back and give her a hint what he felt for her, because she wasn't sure now.

He never glanced back. Her gaze dropped to the rolled up fur in her hand and she turned to the gate. She put her hands against it and pushed.

It opened easily. Beyond it stretched the long, rutted path down the mountain with wild forest on either side. The fog hid all but the post, the ropes that had bound her still circling its base.

All she had to do was tear off her clothes and settle the fur around her shoulders, and she could run free again.

Somehow, the thought didn't incite elation in her heart. She glanced over her shoulder, her gaze clinging to Damien's tall frame growing smaller in the distance as he approached the inner wall surrounding the keep.

He walked so stiffly, straight, as though holding himself rigid. Was he tempted to turn and hurry back to her? Did he want to beg her to stay?

Because she would. If only he'd ask.

In that moment, she knew he loved her. Truly, deeply.

He hadn't wanted to influence her choice by letting her see his despair—because she would have been moved by it.

Voletta closed her eyes and said a prayer, hoping she was right. She bent toward the ground and set her fur upon the path, then closed the gate.

The thing that had set her apart from others wouldn't come between her and Damien. Not ever. She'd gladly lose her freedom to roam if she could share her days with him. She'd wear her human skin so long as his hands were the ones to roam her body.

Turning, she saw that he approached the portcullis and would soon disappear from sight. She picked up the hem of her gown and ran.

Damien heard the sounds of feet running up the hill behind him. His heart leapt, but he was afraid to look back. He slowed his steps, dropped the reins of his horse, and waited.

When Voletta's arms came around his waist, his knees nearly buckled.

They stood for a long moment, her with her arms around his waist and her face pressed to his back as she sobbed softly, him with tears of joy filling his eyes.

He closed his eyes for a moment, fighting for composure, then he turned within her arms to cup her sweet face.

Her hand reached up and a fingertip picked up the track of his tear. Her eyes held a glistening wonder. "You love me, don't you?"

He didn't trust his voice and nodded.

A smile tipped the corners of her lips. "I knew it."

He cleared his throat. "Why didn't you go?" he asked, his throat tight.

"I discovered freedom isn't what I want most in this world."

"What do you want? I'll give it to you."

A warm smile curved her mouth. "You already have." Then, standing on tip-toe, she reached up and kissed him.

A sudden wind whipped up around them as they held each other close. Tendrils of fog began to dissipate, blending back and forth before they disappeared. Sunlight broke through the mist.

Damien turned his face upward and felt the warmth on his skin and thought he might have heard the flutter of wings in the distance. "Yes, Gabriel," he whispered. "I have learned my lesson."

"What's happening?" she asked.

"I think I've been paroled," he said, smiling down at her.

His horse nickered nearby, reminding him he needed tending. "Take my horse," he said aloud.

Footsteps shuffled behind him, and he turned to see a man standing behind him, his face beaming. "Yes, milord. Shall I give him a rubdown?"

Damien stared at the man. Had his reprieve earned his retainers theirs as well? "You've been here all along?"

The man's grin stretched wide, revealing a gap-toothed smile. "We're all glad you found your true love, sir."

Voletta tugged his hand. "They're not ghosts anymore?" she hissed. "Does that mean they've been here all along?" Her cheeks grew rosy, and a fierce scowl drew her brows together.

"Beg yer pardon, ma'am," the man said, "but I promise we didn't see much."

The man's broad smile did little to ease Voletta's embarrassment. She groaned beside Damien.

Damien didn't want to meet the staff just yet. He couldn't wait to discover if he was truly free. He grabbed Voletta's hand and walked down the manicured trail toward the iron gate.

He paused in front of it, holding his breath as he pushed against it. The gate swung wide. The path was clear of any cloying mist, and he could see far beyond the post.

Excitement filled him as hand-in-hand they walked outside the curtain wall. "Where would you like to go?" he asked, staring around him at the lush green forest.

Voletta squeezed his hand, laughing softly. "How about we pay a visit to the village at the bottom of the mountain? I think I would like to introduce you to two gentlemen I know. I think you will become fast friends."

Night Sins

Lisa Renee Jones

Prologue

Within Our Imagination Lies the Truth

We've all heard stories. Tales told around camp fires and at slumber parties. Urban legends, myths, and, yes, ghost stories. We go to the movies, yearning for a dark thrill. We buy the newest horror novel the minute it hits the shelves. We *beg* to be scared. Wanting fear. Needing it. Getting a high off the adrenaline rush of spine-tingling terror. Convincing ourselves these dark things live only in the imagination . . . but that's what evil wants us to think. It thrives on our ignorance. Drinking innocence like fine wine. Waiting. Planning. Lurking in the shadows of existence with the poison of its presence and then targeting the souls of the defenseless for attack. Preying on the weak and using them to stalk those that are stronger.

And only one force stands between the hunted and the hunter.

Born with a beauty meant to disguise the potency of their skills from those they hunt, they are the Chosen Seven. Women born into their destiny as part of magical genetic lines. These gifted seven are overseen by the Council of Lords, who represent the law over all things paranormal.

These seven women not only protect humans from the paranormal beings who exist in this realm, but also from those who wish to enter from beyond. From Purgatory.

Each woman guards a portal that opens with the full moon and must be sealed with her magic. Without these women's skills, their duties, life as humans know it would never be the same.

For, in Purgatory, there is darkness beyond human comprehension. Sinister beings demanding to be seen and known, yearning to take control of the living. Preying on those who believe them non-existent. There is only one way to stop their malicious intent to claim good for evil.

The Circle of Seven.

Supporting the Chosen Seven, placed in surrounding cities without portals around the world, are magical women of the same bloodline, called Watchers. These Watchers not only protect humans, but also protect the secrets of their world.

Upon the death of a Chosen One, higher powers are unleashed to one of the Watchers, making her one of the Chosen Ones. Though, no one ever knows who this will be.

The war rages onward.

1

Kayla Ward shivered as she stepped inside the chilled lobby of Night Sins Hotel Casino. *His* hotel. *His* territory. One of numerous hotels and bars he owned in Las Vegas. A dangerously hot vampire who dripped money and sex and affluence, Ethan could damn near make a woman wet by merely existing.

In the year since she'd been awarded her post as the Watcher in charge of the Vegas area, she'd had several encounters with Ethan, all at his instigation. Encounters the Council of Lords would consider forbidden. Vampires didn't follow the Council's laws and that made them the enemy.

Kayla knew all of this. She knew he was off limits. Yet, Ethan was good at enticing her into his world, dangling secret little tidbits of information—about helping protect innocents—as bait. Always using that bait to lure her deeper under his spell, deeper into his seductive game of cat and mouse. A game she yearned to play but didn't dare. To act on such a desire would only lead to trouble. Trouble she couldn't afford.

Already, The Council of Lords felt she walked the line. They felt she pushed their rules to the limit, beyond what they found acceptable. She'd barely managed to land her post thanks to that reputation. If the Council knew of her association with Ethan, she might just find herself packing. If she dared act on the sizzling attraction between herself and the vampire, she might never see another post again.

On the other hand, they expected her to handle her duties, and handle them well. So what was a girl to do but to go straight to the place she knew would bring answers? Especially now, when innocents were dying and Ethan might well know who was responsible.

She headed for the elevators, tuning out the sound of slot machines and excited guests, cataloging her surroundings. Not that she expected to make an emergency departure, but one could never be too prepared.

Continuing her inspection, she noted exit routes. West exit behind the quarter machines. East exit behind the cluster of roulette tables. Stairs to the right of the east doorway. One, two . . . three security guards trying to blend into the crowd, wearing all black and looking like professional wrestlers. Right. Real discreet. They might not be wearing identification, but it was clear they were the muscle of the place.

She arrived at a set of six elevators just as a pair of shiny gold double doors opened, revealing an empty compartment. As she stepped inside, red velvet-covered walls surrounded her, enveloping her in the bold color predominant within the hotel. Red . . . blood red. No doubt Ethan found it amusing to surround people in something so symbolic of his existence. Of his true self. He might claim he no longer craved the taste of blood, but his crimson obsession screamed otherwise.

Tucking a strand of long, raven-colored hair behind her ear, Kayla let her eyes drift upward. She scanned the mirrors overhead, seeing no obvious surveillance equipment but sensing she was being watched. Sensing *him*.

Glancing down at her black v-cut T-shirt, she checked for

cleavage, satisfied to find herself well covered. She'd dressed in all black, preparing for a night patrolling for nasty spirits, not dodging cameras with a ceiling vantage. Certainly, she didn't need to send the wrong messages to Ethan. As it was, she melted on contact with him, and, for the life of her, Kayla didn't know why.

She didn't melt for anyone . . . well, no one but *him*. Damn it to hell. Truth be told, just his name drew a reaction. Ethan and sex were synonymous. He simply oozed sensuality.

"I know you're there," she murmured under her breath, eyeing the mirror again, promising herself she'd walk away from the temptation he represented. From the offer of pleasure he never failed to deliver in his oh-so-convincing way with every encounter.

A moment later, a *ding* signaled her arrival on the twenty-fifth floor, and Kayla was greeted by yet another wrestler-esque security guard. With a curt nod, he led her to another set of elevators, clearly already aware of her identity and destination.

The thirtieth floor . . . Ethan's private quarters.

Traveling to that higher floor, to his lair—or so the tightly secured high rise location felt—Kayla began to experience doubt over her choice to approach Ethan. By the time the security guard opened oak double doors to allow her entry into Ethan's private study, she found herself beyond ready to get the meeting underway. No. Over. She wanted it over.

Ignoring the sleek black leather couches and the dozen or so televisions lining the far right wall, all with various images of the casino playing on them, she focused on only one thing . . . him. Ethan.

The doors closed behind her, shutting her inside the room—inside the small quarters of the vampire hiding beneath a deliciously male, deceptively harmless-looking, human exterior.

"Hello, Kayla," he said, his sensual mouth hinting at a smile. Kayla stared across the mahogany bar he stood behind, feeling the heat of his attention, the impact of his presence no less intense, no less potent, than on their previous meetings. The man—no, she reminded herself—the *vampire*, stood a good six-foot four, and possessed the kind of hair that begged for a woman's fingers. A mixture of auburn and brown, it was sleek on the side and fell near his collar.

He wore a perfectly fitted dress shirt, the top two buttons undone to display just a hint of a broad chest with a light sprinkle of hair. The deep blue color of the expensive material matched his eyes to absolute perfection. Dark brows framed eyes filled with seduction, almost mystical in their ability to pull her under their spell.

"Hello, Ethan," Kayla said, sensing they were about to go into the cat and mouse game they always played together.

"Finally you come to me," he said, his tone hinting at the conquest he felt he'd achieved.

"Not by choice," she told him, holding her ground, feet solidly planted, keeping the safety of distance between them. She knew how her senses were impacted when she got close the Ethan.

"There is always a choice," he said, his tone soft and sensual.

She didn't like those words, perhaps because they held far more truth than she wanted to face. No matter how good her intentions, her decision to come here would hold repercussions if discovered.

"That might be true," she countered, forcing herself to walk toward him, doing her best to ignore the way his gaze touched her from head to toe "But don't kid yourself, Ethan. If I felt I had another choice, I wouldn't be here." She stopped behind a bar stool, her hands settling on its sleek silver back.

He poured a glass of brandy and slid it in front of her. "Sit down and have a drink." His head tilted ever so slightly, his gaze sharpening. "Then maybe you'll admit how much you wanted an excuse to see me. You, my sweet, might not ever admit it, but you get high off danger." His voice lowered. "You *enjoy* the forbidden."

She rolled her eyes and slid onto the barstool. Ignoring the little voice inside that screamed with the truth of his words. With the excitement she felt over every encounter with Ethan.

"I *enjoy* getting my job done," she said, her tone sharp as she tried to get them focused on business, not on her unnerving attraction to Ethan. "Which is why I'm here. I understand the police have three dead bodies, all female staff members from your clubs, all with bite marks on their necks."

His brow inched upward. "I'm impressed," he said. "Very resourceful, Kayla, considering that information is not public knowledge."

"You're not the only one with resources," she reminded him. "The police think it's a serial killer of some sort. I think it's vampires—The Blood Brothers." Her hands settled on the wooden surface before her, hoping Ethan would tell her she was wrong. The Brothers used blood like a drug, drinking it for the high long replaced by injections to curb the craving.

"Yes," he said after a long pause. "It's the Brothers. And it's being dealt with . . . my way."

It didn't surprise Kayla he meant to dismiss her. Ethan liked control. "I can't take that answer, and you know it. This is as much my business as it is yours. I protect this city. The Council is going to find out and they'll expect me to handle this."

"Yet you haven't shared your suspicions with them?" He studied her a moment. "Why is that?"

The Council made her follow rules. Rules that didn't allow her to seek out Ethan, the one contact who might end this without more killing. It's why she'd risked so much coming here.

But she wasn't about to admit that to Ethan. "My job is to solve problems, not report them."

Without warning, he moved and leaned on the bar, his palms settling beside hers, their fingers touching. A charge of electricity shot through her, but somehow she managed to hide it. His eyes held hers, his nearness unnerving. She felt the connection damn near to her toes: intimate, yet, tense.

"Do you know how the Watcher before you died?" he questioned.

The question shocked her, mostly because she'd often wondered about the answer. The Council had told her it was of no consequence to her duty. But as much as she wanted to know, she wasn't going to be led wherever Ethan was trying to take her. "What does that have to do with anything?"

"Do you know how she died?" he demanded, his voice low and curt. He didn't give her time to respond. "Of course not. Your Council tells you nothing but expects everything. She died fighting The Brothers, just as you will if you don't leave this alone."

The words hung in the air, heavy with implication, for several long seconds before he added, "She died after I told your precious Council to get her the hell out of here. They expected her to solve a problem she wasn't equipped to solve . . . just as they will expect of you."

Kayla swallowed hard, a bit shocked by the news. Had the Council sent her to Vegas, their troublemaking Watcher, because they felt she was disposable? The thought didn't sit well, and she found herself becoming defensive.

"She couldn't leave," Kayla argued. "Watchers have a job to do. And that job demands we protect our cities at all costs."

His brow inched upward. "Including death?"

She swallowed. "Yes. Including death."

"Very noble, Kayla, but sometimes noble isn't enough. As much as your Council likes to believe it can control the paranormal world, this city needs support it can't give. Support you can't give. Why do you think I'm here?"

She hated his coded words. "What are you talking about, Ethan?"

"Two years ago, the Brothers vowed to take over one city at a time. When they made a presence here I followed."

"You're saying you're here to stop them."

"Exactly. Which is why they're targeting my clubs."

She'd heard of the battles between the Brothers and their own kind. Everyone knew. The Brothers had become a problem for more than the vampires. Kayla had long believed the divide between the Council and the vampires hurt the war against the Brothers.

Which was why she would work with Ethan if it meant victory. And why she hadn't told the Council of these murders or of her visit here today. "Let me help."

Ethan's rejection was instant. "A Watcher is no match for a vampire high on blood."

She knew little of the vampires, but Kayla doubted Ethan knew as much about Watchers as he thought he did. "Don't underestimate me," she argued. "Besides." Her teeth slid together. "A vampire is no match for a demon or a spirit. This city needs me." And it did. Each night, the Council transmitted at least five reports of paranormal activity. And though only a few of her monthly investigations represented a serious threat needing extermination, it was more than enough to be a real threat to innocents. She repeated her words. "This city needs me. You have no idea how much."

Before she knew his intention, Ethan leaned toward her, across the bar, his cheek touching hers, the slight stubble of his jaw scraping against her softer skin. Unexpected, the contact left her stunned into aroused stillness. His warm breath tickled her ear.

"You have no idea what you are dealing with, little one," he said, his voice low, seductive. "No idea how alive the vampires' senses are. How they can feel your fears and use them against you. How they burn for the taste of blood."

Teeth scraped her neck, erotic and far too arousing for her sanity. Kayla's hands went to his shoulders, intending to push him away. Somehow, she didn't. Somehow, she could only manage a verbal protest. "Stop, Ethan."

He ignored her words. "Did you know I can smell your desire, Kayla? That no matter how hard you try to pretend otherwise, I know you are slick and ready for me." She tried to jerk away from him, but his hands went to her arms, holding her in place. "And do you know what it makes me want? It makes me want to taste that arousal on my tongue, Kayla. I want to lick you all over until you scream my name. To feel you quiver and shake beneath my hands and mouth. But that wouldn't be enough. I'd have to drink of you, Kayla. To taste the crimson sweetness of you on my lips and tongue as I bury myself deep in the wet heat of your body."

When she would have used force to escape, Ethan seemed to know he'd pushed her beyond her limit and released her, leaving her both stunned and shaken. Kayla leaned back in her chair, her heart beating a million miles an hour. And good lord, she was aroused. Her nipples ached and her panties were wet with want.

"We crave blood by nature," Ethan said. "I'd never take what wasn't offered, but the Brothers would and they do. Stay out of this, Kayla. This is my war."

She was reeling from his touch, her body warm and tingling all over. Lust had always consumed her in ways it didn't other Watchers. Or maybe it did all of them, and no one talked about it.

Part of her wanted to scream a rebuttal at Ethan, to remind him she had senses above and beyond human ones as well. Senses that told her of malice and aided her in battle. But he already knew this and obviously didn't care. Besides, she was beyond words. She simply wanted out of there. Away from a man who both infuriated and enticed at the same moment. A man who confused her senses, setting them on fire, heating her inside out.

"You know what?" she said, pushing out of her seat, needing space to think. "This was a mistake. I should have just dealt with this myself."

She turned around and started walking, still rattled from what had just happened, not surprised that Ethan had rejected her assistance, or even that he had used her desire against her. At least she knew what to expect from the Brothers. She could expect the same methods Ethan himself used.

She punched the elevator button and silently vowed to never return there again. To never see the vampire who tempted her to cross the line she normally walked.

"Kayla."

Ethan spoke from behind her. Close. His voice was a sultry seduction, his agility and speed a dangerous weapon.

Slowly, she turned, facing him, hating the way she had to look up to make eye contact. Hating the way it seemed to give him the power. She arched a brow, offering an expectant look, acting unaffected by all that had just happened. Trying not to react to those deep blue eyes full of passion.

After several potent seconds, he broke the silence. "I simply must demand you stay out of this, Kayla." His voice held a command, as if she were one of the many of his followers who did as he bid.

A short burst of disbelieving laughter escaped her lips. Was he joking? "You have no control over my actions." The elevator dinged and as the doors slid open, she backed inside the empty car, never showing him her back. "I have a job to do and I intend to do it well."

And that job didn't include taking orders from Ethan. Unfortunately, it didn't include taking pleasure from him either.

2

The corner booth was hidden in shadows, the tiny bar a perfect meeting spot for Jac Martine to hand over the name of the next victim to the Brothers. He was more than eager to help take down Ethan. Hungry to cause him pain. To force him out of the city. Because Ethan would leave before he'd allow innocents to die on his behalf. Another victim, and Ethan would know that all the women dying were linked to him. Ethan would know, without a shadow of a doubt, that his lovers had become targets.

Jac had come to Vegas knowing Ethan preferred to hire his own kind within his inner circle. For a year now, he'd worked as Head of Security for Ethan, feigning loyalty when all he wanted was the opportunity to cause him pain. He, himself, might not be a Brother, but his father had been. And his father had died at Ethan's hand.

Jac watched as one of the Brothers slid into the seat across from him. "You got it?"

With a nod, Jac slid an envelope toward him. The Brother

inspected the contents and then smiled. "Our leader will reward you well."

Jac let the words fill him with pleasure. Once Ethan was gone, Jac would take over his financial empire. He could almost taste the power it would give him. He reveled in the bitterness he knew Ethan would feel to know someone so close to him had taken what was his.

Death was too good for Ethan. Jac wanted him brought to his knees. Ethan would be given an option. Give up the city to the Brothers or more will die. But not yet. First, Ethan needed to feel some pain. He needed to know they meant business.

He needed to know he had caused the death of innocents.

Two days after her encounter with Ethan, Kayla eased her way past the entrance of Secret Sins—one of seven men's clubs Ethan owned. And this one happened to be where the last murder victim had worked.

Coming there had been a tough decision, but a fourth woman had died the night before, and she couldn't hide the situation from the Council much longer. The police had kept this under wraps, but there were those in the paranormal world that knew who was responsible. It's how Kayla had found out. And if the Council found out she knew about this and didn't tell them, she'd be in hot water. Yet, she still felt her best path for solving this was Ethan. The Council would work against him, not with him.

But she couldn't hold out forever in silence. She had to stop the Brothers or request help from the Council. That meant she had to enlist Ethan's help and do it fast. So she had come up with a plan. And that plan had led her to Secret Sins.

Kayla had been prepared for how the club would affect her. Already, she could feel the lust around her: pressing on her mental barriers; burning for recognition and attention; burning to take control she wasn't willing to give. Absorbing and controlling the emotions around her were part of being a Watcher. Often, in battle, the malice of those around her became fuel for her own blows, for her own ability to defend against that which would destroy her.

And though she knew coming there, being surrounded by so much lust, would beat on her defenses, she also knew she had no choice. Her first meeting with Ethan had gotten her nowhere fast, and after working her underground resources, she was quite certain one of his two top security men had betrayed him to the Brothers, intending to help them take down Ethan.

If she got up close and personal with Ethan's security staff, she'd know which one was bad. She'd feel the malice. Then, she could go to Ethan and they could use that person to lead them to the Brothers' main operation.

A wall of mirrors behind the cash register captured her eyes, and she barely recognized herself. Dressed in a short black skirt and a skintight tank with a deep V, she'd completed the outfit with "fuck me" spike heels, a long blond wig, smoky eyes, and glossy red lips. She looked like a walking invitation.

Kayla smiled flirtatiously at the brawny male taking her money and looking at her with more than a little interest, noting the lack of malice in him. He wasn't who she sought. She'd know the enemy when she found him. She'd sense the danger, sense the bad intentions.

And she'd find him, whoever he was.

No doubt, a female alone in a men's club would draw attention. Which was what she was counting on; the more the better. That would make it easier to find who she sought.

Rounding the corner, Kayla entered the main club, dim lights and sultry music closing in around her, waves of lust and desire rushing at her like a wave crashing into her body and mind. Kayla worked to block out the emotions flogging her from every direction. She drew on her training, on her discipline.

Her eyes went to the stage as heat rushed through her limbs, lust becoming a second skin. Topless women worked the horseshoe-shaped stage, moving to the beat of the sexy song, teasing the men who gathered nearby. And Lord help her, she could feel the power they felt. Feel the arousal of knowing those men were hard and hot because of the way the woman looked, the way they moved.

Kayla forced herself to inhale and focus on blocking out the environment, exhaling as she regained a bit of her composure. Again, she repeated her actions. Inhaling. Exhaling. Drawing on her well-practiced mental control.

Though she wasn't a drinker, one seemed in order now. Kayla needed to dull the impact of the heat pounding at her. She eyed a bar in the back corner, gladly taking the retreat into the shadows. The bartender, a young blond hunk of a guy, set a napkin in front of her. "What can I do you for?"

"Cosmopolitan," she said, noting the way his gaze swept over her breasts, lingering like a touch, making her nipples tighten beneath her silk top.

She eased around to rest her elbows on the bar, giving him her back as she fought the urge to reach up and touch her aching nipples to ease the pain. She focused on her next move and noted an empty table in the center of two rather rowdy groups of men who would make good targets for her attention.

Kayla's drink appeared and she downed it, avoiding the gaze of her hunky attendant, desperate to dull her senses. Though she needed to be sharp to sense danger, she needed to calm the lust enough to feel anything but fire.

"Another one?" the bartender asked.

She nodded, scooting the empty glass across the bar. One more and she'd get this party started. She'd sit smack in the middle of those men and draw enough attention to create a stir. Then, she'd scream for help and security would come. And the security team was her target.

It wasn't the best plan, but it was all she had.

Four women who'd seen his bed had died. Not even recent bedmates, but all women who, at some point, had found their way between his sheets. He knew what was going on. The Brothers wanted him gone, so they were making him feel pain.

If he stayed, people died. But if he left . . . if he left, the city would be taken over by the Brothers. A reality that would be far worse than a few deaths. And Kayla. Kayla would fall to the Brothers. She would stand alone and she would die.

"Damn it." Ethan cursed under his breath, the sound echoing in the small video room in the back corner of his personal suite. For the fifth time, he hit REPLAY, watching the video of the most recent victim of the Brothers departing his club, Secret Sins, and going to her death. He was looking for a clue as to who might have followed her, to which one of his trusted staff members had turned on him.

Because someone had. Without a doubt, someone from his inner circle had become the enemy. That he didn't know who ate at Ethan in a huge way. Few knew Ethan's personal matters. Few were allowed inside his personal affairs.

Which meant only a handful of suspects existed, all men Ethan considered loyal staff members . . . until now. Someone close to him had betrayed him.

A knock sounded on the door behind him, and Ethan turned to wave Rigo V. forward, noting the urgent look on his face. At well over six feet tall, he was broad and muscular, a true warrior of their race's Secret Services Agency. Unable to trust his staff, Ethan had called upon the SSA for added support, asking for Rigo and several others by name.

Though Ethan had long ago left his position inside the government of his people, disagreeing with some of their king's ways, he still respected his leader, and he'd remained a part of the SSA. And though most believed he'd fled to Vegas, turning his back on his people, the opposite was true. He'd come to protect it from the Brothers. They would not take this city as long as he owned it.

And that would be a long damn time.

"We have a problem," Rigo said, entering the room and shutting the door firmly behind him. "You were right about the Watcher getting into trouble. Our man just followed her into Secret Sins."

Ethan cursed under his breath, knowing his reasons for having her monitored had been proven correct. Kayla wasn't going to let this thing with the Brothers alone, and if she wasn't careful, she'd get herself killed, an outcome Ethan wasn't willing to entertain.

Since the first moment he'd laid eyes on Kayla, he'd felt protective, even a bit possessive, a dangerous combination in his race. To desire a female was part of a vampire's richly sexual nature. To feel possessiveness came only when a male began to bond with a female, which was crazy because Kayla wasn't even one of his kind.

"I know I don't have to tell you this," Rigo said, breaking into Ethan's reverie. "But if anything happens to her inside that club—"

Ethan finished for him. "The Council would blame the vampire world, and we'd be in deep shit. Yeah, I know."

Rigo fixed him in a hard stare. "We should call the king."

"No," Ethan said sharply. "You and I both know how he feels about me."

Ethan had dared to do what no other had. He'd confronted the king on his handling of the Brothers. The king had walked away from a chance at victory one too many times. Why? Because one of his twin sons, jealous of his brother's role in the vampire government, had left their world and formed the Brothers. The worst enemy the vampire world faced came from one of its leader's offspring. And their king would do anything for his people . . . anything but destroy his son. It was times like this that he was glad he had no family. He'd take the emptiness over the pain the king's son had caused him and so many others.

"He respects you," Rigo said, sitting on the arm of the sofa. "You chose to walk away."

Ethan laughed, bitter. The king had been quick to approve his Vegas post. He cut a hand through the air. "We aren't calling the king. I can handle Kayla." He turned back to the matter at hand. "What the hell is she doing at Secret Sins in the first place?" A female inside a men's club was like a walking invitation, and Ethan felt the rise of anger. Surely, he misunderstood. Surely, Kayla wouldn't put herself in such a position. "Are you sure she's inside the club and not simply nosing around?"

Rigo snorted. "Oh, she's inside all right, and from what I understand, looking to be a part of the show. She's wearing a long blond wig and not a whole lot else."

Ethan ground his teeth. What the hell was she trying to prove? "Well, if it's attention she wants, she just got it." He pushed to his feet. "But I doubt I'm what she had in mind."

This was where he put his foot down. Kayla had no business digging around inside his club. If she wanted to know about his world, he'd be happy to give her a guided tour. She'd already put herself in the line of fire. The Brothers wouldn't hesitate to take her out if she became a problem. Her present actions considered, someone would figure out she had indeed become that and more.

There seemed only one way to keep her safe and that would be to keep her close to him. A slow smile slid onto his lips. Yes. He'd keep her safe and close. Real close. And he'd deal with the slow burn she'd created in the process as well. Ethan was going to taste temptation once and for all.

Thirty minutes later, Ethan walked through his private entrance to Secret Sins, and he knew Kayla was present. He knew because he could feel her desire, knew because of the primal mating call roaring inside his limbs. Though he'd suspected his primal reaction to Kayla many times, tonight he knew it was true. Somehow, some way, her body called to his. It called beyond race, beyond what should have been natural to him.

Out of respect for his manager, Michael White, Ethan decided to do a quick stop by his office. He took the small hall to the right and stopped in the open doorway, surprised to find his Head of Security, Jac Martine, leaning against a far wall. With the dark, foreboding looks of their race—long dark hair and dark eyes—Jac was obviously a full-blooded vampire.

"Didn't expect you tonight, boss," Jac said, crossing his arms in front of his broad chest.

Ethan didn't miss the defensive body language. Though he had no tangible reason for distrusting Jac, as of late his instincts had bred caution. And when his instincts flared, they were typically on target.

He wasn't pleased with Jac's unexplained presence. Ethan had made it clear on more than one occasion he wanted Jac at the casinos on weekend nights. "I could say the same of you," Ethan commented dryly, resting a shoulder against the door jam.

"I asked him to stop by," Michael interjected. Short and stout with fair hair, his bulldog features took on a harsher than normal frown, his brows dipping with a deep V. "Some of the girls are on edge and, frankly, Ethan, so am I."

As with all humans, Michael was easy to read. His concern for his girls was genuine, which was why Ethan liked the man.

The last victim of the Brothers had worked at Secret Sins, so that concern had merit.

"We all are," Ethan assured him. "I trust Jac has shared our plan to add extra security?"

"He has," Michael acknowledged, "but the girls aren't satisfied. The murders didn't happen on the job. They happened after hours."

If Ethan was right and the women he'd slept with had become the targets, very few of the girls had anything to worry about. None of Michael's staff would qualify. Still, the Brothers were unpredictable. There seemed only one solution to protect everyone.

"I'll provide rooms at Night Sins for anyone who wants one," Ethan offered. "That gives the girls the chance to stay in a protected environment."

Surprise registered in Michael's eyes. "How long can they stay?"

"Until we know it's safe again," Ethan said. "Spread the word." He eyed Jac, his agitation cutting through the air like an electric charge. "You have a problem with this, I take it?"

"Yeah," Jac said. "Actually, I do. We're turning my team into babysitters. There's no way we can manage that many women and not have things suffer."

"Then hire more staff," Ethan said, cutting off any further objections. He found it quite curious that Jac didn't want the girls inside the hotel, well guarded. "Call over to Night Sins and clear a floor for the girls. Two to a room." He smiled and let his attention move between the two men. "Now, if you gentlemen will excuse me. I came by for . . ." *Kayla* ". . . pleasure and I intend to have it."

Kayla finished off another Cosmopolitan, feeling the dimly familiar buzz of alcohol, not at all liking it. It reminded her why she didn't indulge all that often. Her idea that doing so now would dull her response to the lust in the air hadn't worked. In fact—it was just the opposite. If anything, she felt more willing to melt into her surroundings than before. Right when she'd felt she had herself under control, a new wave of heat had sideswiped her. And this time, for some reason, she couldn't quite funnel out the extra emotions. Normally, she took what she needed and discarded the rest. But not tonight. Not now.

Perhaps coming to a place like this when she'd ignored her sexual needs for well over a year had been a mistake. This club, this room, reminded her of the needs she'd ignored far too long. And it reminded her of Ethan. For some reason, she couldn't stop thinking about him, about what it would be like to finally be with him. And it made her wish he was there so she could fuck Ethan out of her system once and for all. Clearly, he was driving her insane.

She laughed without humor. Good thing he wasn't there.

Eyeing the stage, she noted the way the blonde bombshell on it worked the males watching her. The way she squatted, legs wide, inviting them into her world of pleasure. Why couldn't it be that easy for her? But she had lives depending on her to focus, depending on her to do her job. To escape into the world of pleasure, to get lost in a place that distracted her from her duty, was dangerous.

She watched one of the men slide a bill up the dancer's leg as the woman's tongue ran along her lower lip. Kayla moaned at the sight, forgetting her self control as she explored the lust shared by the dancer and her admirer. She told herself it was to get into the mood for what had to happen, denying it was for her own pleasure, her own needs. But the dampness forming between her legs, clinging to the slit of silk she wore, said otherwise.

Kayla was sadly in need of an orgasm. No amount of reason, or even alcohol, would change that fact.

There was no use stalling. She had to do this. Pushing off the bar, Kayla began a slow strut toward the free table she'd set her sight on—the one near so many male candidates. Surely one of them would get a bit rowdy if she toyed with him.

She enjoyed, far too much, the way heads turned to watch her, the way men wanted her. She told herself she embraced the male admiration as part of the act, all part of convincing everyone she was on the prowl when she was simply becoming the bait for a trap.

But she felt on the prowl, with excitement flowing through her limbs, spreading warmth, heat, desire.

Walking past several velvet-covered doorways, she remembered seeing several dancers lead men behind them, no doubt to offer them private encounters. Her imagination went wild with thoughts of what might happen behind those curtains, with images of the females pressing close to the men, breasts in their faces, teasing them with their nipples, tempting them to touch and taste.

And as if those thoughts willed her into their reality, suddenly Kayla found herself pulled behind one of those curtains, found herself pressed tight against a hard body, her back to the wall, a familiar sensual scent she knew all too well wrapping around her. Ethan's smell. Ethan's hard body.

As she felt the thick ridge of his cock press against her stomach, she drew in a breath, barely resisting the urge to arch her hips into him. Her wish had come true. Ethan was not only there, but he was also hot and hard, just the way she wanted him.

But did she dare make her fantasy a reality? Her body screamed with a loud, demanding "yes!" All the heat burning her up seemed to increase tenfold.

Kayla stared up at Ethan, the look in his eyes potent, but no more so than the desire building inside her. Her body's demands were overcoming her. She wanted to get lost in the moment, lost in Ethan. The time felt right. The room was intimate and secluded. Candlelight flickered on the walls, the music from the club muffled by the velvet curtain.

"What are you doing here?" she whispered, her voice barely finding life.

The warmth of his hand slid over her backside before firmly pulling her tight against him, molding her hips against his. "Apparently, saving you from a room full of men."

She sucked in a breath as she felt warmth rush through her body. In some far corner of her mind, she reached for common sense, reached for right over wrong. *Push away. Leave.* But Kayla couldn't fight the cry of her body begging to stay, begging to finally feel Ethan in all ways possible. She'd wanted this, wanted him, for so very long.

"I don't need saving. I need . . ." *You.* "I came for answers." She inhaled and exhaled, clearing her head enough to focus on her real purpose, which wasn't Ethan. "Someone close to you is working for the Brothers."

His fingers trailed her cheek. "You think I don't know that? I told you I have this under control. You shouldn't have come here."

A chill raced down her spine at his touch, but she shoved aside the burning in her body. Her hands were on his chest, fingers curled so they wouldn't move, wouldn't explore.

"You don't know who it is," she stated. It wasn't a question and she didn't give him time to counter with a reply. "Like it or not, Ethan, you need me. You might know what a human thinks or feels but a vampire is another story. I can sense malice in living beings. I can figure out who it is. I need to go back out there."

He leaned close and inhaled. "You are . . . aroused. If you go back out there like this, no telling what will happen."

The minute Ethan had touched her, the control she'd had over her desire had begun to fade. And Lord help her, it only seemed to excite her more that he knew. She fought through the thickening fog. "I . . . need to go out there, Ethan. I can find out who is doing this."

"Your body demands pleasure." Somehow his hand found its way under her skirt, his palm covering her ass, fingers tracing the lace between her cheeks. "All you know right now is the demand for release." He leaned closer, even, his warm breath trickling on her neck. "Let me help you ease the pain." The words lingered as his fingers slid beneath the silk, brushing her sensitive skin. "We've wanted for far too long, Kayla. It's our time."

Pushing him away wasn't an option. She might need to find answers but, right now, she needed this more. She needed him. But . . . no. The Council. The rules.

"Something is happening to me," she said. "Ethan, I . . . I don't know what's wrong with me."

He stared down at her, his dark eyes inscrutable. "I can help."

She fought for willpower. "You know I can't do this."

A slow, sexy smile slid onto his lips. "Because I'm a vampire."

"Yes," she whispered, her fingers uncurling, spreading on his muscular chest, her will to resist slipping away. "Because you're a vampire."

"No one will know." His mouth lingered above hers, teasing her with a long-awaited taste. "It will be our little secret."

She wanted to kiss him, but she didn't dare. Somehow, she knew that would end her resistance. Yet, it would be so easy to lean forward, to feel his mouth against hers. She bit her bottom lip, fighting her urge, fighting the heat spreading through her body. Why was she so hot? Her skin felt hot. She had to get out of there but the idea of leaving this moment, of ending the contact with Ethan, felt unbearable.

In a minute.

In a minute she would move.

In a minute she would leave.

"I can't do this," she said in a barely there voice. "I can't. I have to get out of this club." Fire seemed to spread over her skin and she felt almost as if she was melting into invisible flames. "Have . . . to leave this place."

"I won't let you walk into a room of men in your current condition. It's simply not an option."

She needed out of this building. But Ethan was right. Kayla didn't even want to think about what might happen if she left this room. Her hands slid over her arms, her skin begging for contact. God. She hated how out of control she felt.

As if he sensed her struggle, Ethan responded, offering comfort without words. His lips brushed her cheek and trailed over her jaw: not a kiss, just a caress with his mouth, a caress that left her breathless and needy yet somehow soothed her needs at the same time. Yet, at the same time, his touch made the rage inside bearable.

Her nipples tightened and tingled, and she barely contained the urge to press his hand to one of her breasts. They ached. She ached. And she was wet, so very wet. She wanted him inside her, like she never remembered wanting anything before.

"The way I see it," he said, his voice low, near her ear. "You must find a way to take the edge off before you attempt to leave." He let his words linger in the air a moment. "You have two choices." He pulled back and fixed her in a hot stare. "You can pleasure yourself."

She laughed, but not with humor. "While you watch," Kayla said, far too aroused by that idea for her own good.

She ran her hand on the back of her neck, her head spinning a bit. This damn fire inside was killing her, so much so she could barely stand the touch of her clothes. It was all she could do to keep from ripping them from her body.

"Yes," Ethan agreed. "Watching has definite appeal." He arched his hips into hers, pressing his erection into the V of her body. "But I'd much rather you take option two. Allow me to do it for you."

She was fading fast and she knew it. In a damnable situation, Kayla was faced with both her biggest nemesis and her most naughty of fantasies. If she had to hand over control, she at least wanted it to be on her terms.

Ethan's people and her own shared opposite agendas in many things. Even with the absence of malice, those differences could feed dangers. But from day one, instinctively, Kayla had trusted Ethan. To date, his actions had proven her right. So she had to gamble on that trust now.

She grabbed his arms, holding on with a tight grip, fixing him in as steady a gaze as she could manage. "I'm not myself, Ethan. I'm trusting you to get me the hell out of here." She swallowed hard. "And don't let anyone else touch me. Please. Just you."

His eyes darkened. "Rest assured, no one else will dare touch you. You are safe with me. You have my word."

A sigh of relief seemed to explode from her lungs. She believed him. She hadn't missed the hint of possessiveness in his voice, and, Lord help her, for the first time in her life, Kayla wanted to be possessed.

And for the first time in her life, she was handing herself over to someone else. She was giving Ethan control.

3

Ethan felt the roar of passion and possessiveness build inside like a fire, raging wild and hot. It hadn't taken long for Ethan to surmise how rarely Kayla handed over trust and control. Yet, she'd given both to him.

Ethan lifted her leg to his waist, opening her to his touch. She stared up at him, desire ripe in her beautiful eyes. In that moment, he wanted all of her like he never had before. He reached forward and ripped her panties from her body. A gasp slid from her parted lips: full, sensual lips meant to taste and tempt. But he didn't kiss her. Not yet. When he made love to her, he'd do it with slow perfection. Right now, she needed the edge taken off. She needed relief.

Guilt bit at him as he recognized he might well be causing her pain. As impossible as it should be, his mating instincts were on fire. And that fire must be mixing with the lust of this place, overwhelming Kayla.

Regardless of the cause, they both knew what had to happen, what had been destined to happen from the moment they'd first met. Their physical need for one another had to be fed. He might not be able to claim her, but he could enjoy her.

Ethan slid his fingers into the silky wetness of her body, stroking her sensitive flesh. Kayla rewarded him with a soft moan, her head falling back against the wall, her hands sliding over her body, cupping her breasts through her clothes.

"Easy, little one," he murmured, thumbing her swollen clit. He caressed her, his fingers exploring her slick heat before he slid one inside her.

Kayla moaned again, her teeth finding her bottom lip, her chest rising and falling. "God, Ethan," she whispered, tilted her chin down to give him a heavy-lidded look. "I don't know what's happening to me." Then her hands went to his face, her mouth finding his, her tongue sliding against his, hungry and hot.

She tasted like sugar and spice, as perfect as he had expected, and his body roared with desire, screamed to be inside her. But there was no time to act, no time to press the hard length of his cock inside her.

Kayla tore her mouth from his, her breathing ragged. "I . . . I think I might . . . I . . . already . . ." She leaned forward, resting on his shoulder, clinging to his arms with a vice grip.

"Let it happen," he murmured, pressing a second finger inside her and stroking her inner wall, feeling her hips pump against him.

She clung to him, wildly moving with him, rubbing her clit against his palm, until, abruptly, she stiffened. A second later, the spasms of her orgasm began, long and hard. He held her close, steadying her as he felt her knees start to buckle.

Then slowly, her body eased. Several seconds passed before she lifted her head, her eyes locking with his, passion still burning red hot in her gaze. "It's already starting again. I don't know what's happening to me." She didn't give him time to answer. "I'm hot. I'm so hot."

She reached for her shirt, tugging the hem upward. Ethan eased it over her head and tossed it aside, his gaze fixed on her high breasts and rosy red nipples. He filled his hands with them, devouring them first with his eyes and then his mouth, lapping at one ripe peak with his tongue and teeth. She arched her back, soft sounds of pleasure flowing from her lips, her hands sliding into his hair.

Driven by her cries for more, Ethan repeated his actions on the other nipple, suckling harder as she moaned with pleasure, urging him onward with her actions, with her obvious pleasure.

She released a shuddering breath. "I need more," she said. "You, Ethan. I need you inside me." Her hand found the front of his trousers, tracing the ridge of his erection. "You need that, too."

He moaned at the touch, pressing into her hand even as his mouth found hers. Hungrily he kissed her, his fingers working on the clasp on her skirt, pushing the fabric down her hips until it pooled at her feet. She kicked it aside and one of her calves wrapped around his, her hips pressing into his.

Kayla tugged his shirt from his pants, her soft palms pushing beneath the material, exploring and teasing, setting him on edge, pressing him to forget everything but the moment.

She yanked at his shirt again. "Take it off." Her voice held an order, her eyes passionate, dark, and compelling. "Everything. Take everything off."

He'd never let any woman, not even in the midst of pleasure, issue him an order. In their ancient world, females did their males' bidding. But Kayla's demand both aroused and pleasured him.

"As you wish," he murmured, starting to work on his buttons.

Showing her impatience, Kayla reached forward, ripping the shirt apart. Before he could act, her palms splayed over his chest, pushing the shirt off his shoulders, her nipples brushing his skin with delicious friction. He could almost taste her hunger; he most certainly could smell the female desire in her.

Heat began to fire his skin, just as it had hers. As if she fed him her emotions, her desire, Ethan burned to get out of his clothes. Burned, almost desperately. He kicked off his shoes, discarding all barriers, ready to feel skin against skin. At the same time, Kayla focused on the button of his pants and popped it free. Next, she slid down his zipper, reaching inside the front of his pants and wrapping his cock in her warm grip. His eyes slid shut, his body growing thicker, harder.

Before he knew her intent, she was on her knees, shoving his pants to his ankles. Ethan looked down to see her tongue flicker out across the head of his cock.

"Hmmm," she purred. "I've wanted to do this so many times."

He sucked in a breath and pressed one hand against the wall. To see Kayla on her knees, taking him in her mouth, was pure heaven. "Why didn't you?"

"Right now," she said, her hand cupping his balls. "I don't have a clue."

Her hand wrapped the base of his cock and she sucked the tip of him into her mouth, the wet heat of her mouth damn near shaking him to the core. Her gaze lifted to his as she took more of him, inch by inch easing down his cock, her tongue working him in the process.

He wanted to move but didn't dare, fearful of doing what he would have considered unheard of until now, fearful of losing control. As if she answered his silent pleas, her hand slid around his back side, pressing him into action.

At the same time, she began sucking him, sliding her mouth up and down his shaft, urging him to pump his hips. He moved his hand to the back of her head, relishing the silky strands of her hair between his fingers and the silky heat of her mouth around his cock. In and out. In and out. She licked, sucked, pumped. He was roaring inside, his cock throbbing, his body burning. Ethan felt his balls lift and tighten, felt the rise of release deep inside. He told himself to stop, to pull back. Not to come like this.

"Kayla," he whispered, his hand trying to steady her head. But she seemed determined to take all of him, sucking him harder, deeper. He couldn't fight much more. He couldn't stop the ache for release, the need to feel himself slide inside her mouth. Just . . . one . . . more.

Ethan exploded, his body shuddering, shaking. And Kayla was relentless in her demand for all he had to give, her tongue and lips driving him insane.

He anchored himself with both hands on the wall, weak from release. Good Lord, the woman was wickedly hot. Slowly, Kayla slid up his body, her hands trailing along his legs, along his sides.

She slid her arms around his neck and pressed her body close. "I still need you inside me."

Ethan wrapped his arm around her waist. Her eyes were dilated, almost drugged. Heat radiated off her skin against his palm. Her body was soft and yielding against his. He'd longed for Kayla's submission since the day they'd met. But this wasn't submission. She'd trusted him to take care of her. Her condition wasn't improving.

As difficult as it was to turn away from the demands of his body, to ignore her desire to have him inside her, he had to.

Ethan made his decision. "It's time to go, Kayla. We have to get you out of here."

Her eyes went wide, her hands going to his forearms, gripping him with a vice hold. "No. I can't. We both know I can't go out there. Not until they leave."

"Listen to me, Kayla," he said, his voice firm. She wasn't used to taking orders, certainly not from him. "The club won't close for hours. Waiting isn't an option. I could close the club but clearing the building will take too long. You need relief you won't get as long as we stay."

"I just need you inside me. Then ... then I think I'll be okay."

"And I want to be inside you, Kayla. So much it hurts. But not like this. Not here." He framed her face with his hands and kissed her forehead. "You said you would trust me."

"I do," she whispered. "I do trust you."

Her words pleased him and they reassured him he was doing the right thing. "Good. What we are doing isn't working. You're burning up." His hands ran up and down her arms, confirming his words. "Right now, we're in tune with one another. Our desires. Our needs. Go with that. Focus on me and I'll feed you what you need to get out of here."

She shook her head. "I don't understand."

"You will," he said a second before he kissed her. There wasn't a chance in hell he could get her out of there without bringing her down again. But once he did, he'd force himself to go blank. He had to. Because if he didn't smash his instincts, his desire, his need, Kayla would remain in pain. He'd keep feeding her desires with his own

Ethan's lips clung to hers as he backed her against the wall, tasting her, calming her, taking her past the ache he knew was building again. His hands skimmed her arms again, easing down her body as he went to his knees. He parted her legs, urging her feet to a V stance.

He was ready to taste Kayla's passion, ready to devour and please. Ready to get her the hell out of this club so he wouldn't take more than she was willing to give.

Ethan wanted all she had, all she was. But not like this, not out of desperation. He wanted Kayla to give herself to him freely.

4

Kayla gasped as Ethan's mouth closed around her in the most intimate of ways, intense pleasure spreading through her limbs. He suckled her nub and she cried out, one hand on the wall, bracing herself, the other in his thick, dark hair.

She was so in tune to Ethan's arousal, to his pleasure, she'd even had an orgasm with Ethan in her mouth. His pleasure had become hers. She could feel everything he did with more intensity than she'd ever felt anything in her life.

Her breathing grew faster as he licked and teased with tantalizing perfection. She could hear herself moaning, hear her soft sobs, and in a far corner of her mind, she knew this was wrong, knew she shouldn't be with Ethan. But somehow she couldn't be sorry. This was the fantasy she'd wished for come to life.

All thoughts turned to sensation as Ethan's tongue worked her sensitive flesh, thrusting in and out, making love to her with his lips, teeth, tongue. Kayla moved with his rhythm, arching her back to give him better access, to feel more. She couldn't get enough, couldn't stop wanting and needing. His fingers worked her nub even as his tongue worked in time with her hips.

Without warning—no build up, no hint of imminent release—Kayla shattered, shuddering with the spasms of orgasm. Ethan's tongue slowed, caressing her where it had once stroked, easing her to near completion.

But he didn't allow her to come all the way down. Already, Ethan was on his feet, turning her to face him. "Focus on me, Kayla. Clear your mind and thoughts and focus on nothing but me. Breathe with me." He inhaled and she did as he said, drawing a breath and letting it out when he let his out, reaching for his mind and finding it remarkably calming. They did this over and over. "Are you with me?" he asked.

She nodded. "Yes. Yes, I think so."

"Good." He smiled. "Let's get dressed and get out of here."

In silence, they went to work dressing. As she reached for her panties, she remembered Ethan ripping them and heat rushed over her. She threw them aside and inhaled, refocusing on Ethan, clearing her mind, trying to block out the seductive beat of the music beyond the curtain.

By the time Ethan grabbed her hand and pulled her close, she was beyond ready for escape. He was right. She needed out of there.

His palms went to her cheeks; his eyes stared into hers. "Remember. Focus on me. Ignore everything and everyone else. You're strong. You can do this."

She nodded. He was right. She was strong. "But go now," Kayla whispered. "Please. Go now."

He didn't question her demand, taking her hand in his again and moving forward, shoving aside the curtain. Kayla didn't look at the stage, didn't look at anything but the floor. They passed two more velvet curtains, and she forced blackness into her mind, refusing to consider what might be happening in those private rooms.

They turned down a narrow hallway and pushed through a door. Kayla looked up in time to see PRIVATE on its surface.

Two steps into the room, they came to an abrupt halt as a dark-haired male vampire stepped in their path.

Kayla refused to look down, to cower like some weak female who couldn't handle herself on her own. Besides, thanks to the strength and calmness Ethan was feeding her, she was feeling at least a little better.

She leveled her gaze just in time to see the stranger's eyes rake her body.

"Who do we have here?" he asked, his attention fixed on Kayla.

Ethan didn't move, didn't speak, but Kayla felt the stir of anger and possessiveness in him. And she knew trusting him had been the right move. There was no way anyone would touch her with Ethan on guard.

"She's no one of your concern," Ethan replied, his tone sharp. "Why are you still here, anyway, Jac?"

Kayla studied the man as he focused on Ethan, reaching for his intentions toward his boss, but finding nothing useful. Everything was still too foggy, too clouded by the ache in her limbs, for her to be certain of this man's intentions. Damn it. He could be *the one*, but she couldn't be sure.

Jac gave Kayla another once over. "I was just leaving," he said.

"That's not an answer," Ethan countered. "Why are you still here in the first place?"

With each passing second, Kayla felt clarity in her thinking. She watched as Jac's jaw tightened, feeling the anger beneath his surface, tucked away but not hidden. "I had to pick up one of the girls," he explained. "She wouldn't come in without an escort. I'm leaving now."

Kayla kept her attention on Jac, but she was in tune with Ethan, his distrust reaching out to her like a breath of air.

"See that you do," Ethan ordered, his tone clipped. "I expect there's much to attend to at Night Sins."

Jac gave Ethan a slow nod. "I'm on it," he said, turning on his heels and walking away.

Ethan eyed Kayla, as if checking to ensure she was okay. Seemingly satisfied with what he found, he started forward, following in Jac's footsteps, his hand still wrapped protectively around Kayla's as they exited the club.

As they pushed through the heavy steel door, stepping into the darkness of night, a covered driveway greeted them. Just beyond, a steady rain pounded the pavement, rain that seemed to wash away the haze of Kayla's drugged mind and body. Relief flooded Kayla, inside and out.

Ethan murmured something to the doorman before turning to face her, positioning his body to block her from anyone's view. Kayla had the distinct impression he was sheltering her, still in protective mode. She warmed inside with this realization.

He studied her intently. "Better?"

A smile touched her lips. "Thanks to you, yes. Not myself quite yet, but getting there." Something was bothering her, though. "That man in the hallway—"

"Jac Martine. My Head of Security."

He'd certainly be in a position to hurt Ethan if he wanted to. "You don't trust him," she stated.

"I used to or he wouldn't be in the position he is now."

"Don't," she said. "Don't trust him."

His gaze sharpened. "Are you saying he's my leak?"

"I wasn't myself enough to be one hundred percent sure, but what I got off him wasn't good." She pictured Jac and felt darkness. "No," she said. "Don't trust him."

He turned his head and looked out into the rain. "There's something you should know." He hesitated, and Kayla could feel guilt and pain eating him up before he added, "All of the women who've been murdered . . . they were all once my lovers."

Oh my God. "They've made it personal."

He gave a sharp nod. "If I leave, they'll claim the city. If I stay, they'll hurt anyone close to me." His gaze lifted, shifting to the rain, his jaw tense. Several seconds passed before he turned his attention back to her. "Only a few people would know who'd been to my bed."

"Jac," Kayla said, feeling sick as she realized the implications of what she was being told. "He gave the Brothers a list."

"Seems that way," Ethan agreed.

"Why?" she asked. "Why would he do such a thing? Does he have something against you?"

"Not that I know of. And believe me, I've tried like hell to figure it all out. It could be simple greed. I'm sure they've promised him plenty in return for his actions."

A sleek black Porsche 911 pulled up beside them. Ethan turned and opened the passenger door for Kayla. She eyed him, his dark hair wild from her fingers, his expensive black pants and shirt tailored to accent his tall, broad frame. He had a quiet danger to him, a sleek perfection, much like the expensive car he stood beside.

Kayla stepped forward, sliding into the passenger seat, allowing Ethan to shut her inside. She stared out into the rain, hearing thunder sound in the distance. For a moment, she forgot the challenges facing her, forgot the Brothers. Instead, she thought about what had happened between her and Ethan. The intimate way they'd shared each other's bodies. And she felt no regret. She should, of course. But she didn't.

A second later, Ethan settled into the driver's seat, his spicy scent insinuating itself into her senses the way it always did. She was returning to normal, but that didn't stop her reactions to Ethan. He always got to her.

Alone in the small, silent car, the stormy night closed in around them, rain pinging the windows with a seduction song.

Ethan could have driven away but he didn't. The things they had done together filled the air, a taboo that had to be dealt with.

At the same moment, they turned to each other. "Kayla—"
"Ethan—"

They laughed and Kayla spoke again. "Thank you, Ethan."

One dark brow arched. He didn't question what she referenced. "Considering the pleasure involved, I hardly think you need to thank me."

"Yes," she said, meaning it. "I do. You could have . . ." Her lashes lowered as she considered her choice of words. Every option seemed crass or overly familiar.

His voice was low, seductive. "Made love to you all night?"

That he spoke of making love registered instantly in her mind. Yet, she could feel he was still in protective mode, despite the fact she no longer needed it. His words could simply be part of the role he was still playing.

"Yes," she said. "Exactly." Before she could stop herself, she asked, "Why didn't you?"

"Don't think I didn't want to," he said, reaching for her hand and brushing his lips across her knuckles. "When I make love to you fully, Kayla—and I will—it won't be in a moment of drugged lust. It will be in a moment of truth."

Kayla felt her stomach tighten, felt her insides warm. Not with the drugged lust he mentioned, but with something else, something more alluring and sensual, something enticing.

Tasting temptation had simply fed a desire for more.

5

For several minutes, Kayla and Ethan rode in silence. With effort, Kayla pushed aside her feelings for Ethan and focused on business. She had no time for sex and sins. Her world was about saving lives and protecting innocents.

And though she was eager to get home to her computer, knowing the Council could well have sent her reports to investigate, her mind raced with the implications of all Ethan had shared about the Brothers.

"Maybe what happened tonight is a good thing," she mused out loud.

Ethan glanced in her direction and then looked back at the road. "I didn't know we questioned how good it was."

She smiled and shook her head. She wasn't talking about the sex. Clearly, he was. "I meant we have a perfect chance to set a trap. You said the Brothers are targeting women who've been with you. Now, I'm one of those women."

His rejection was instant. "They have no clue who you are, and we're keeping it that way. The other victims worked for me. They were easy to find."

"Then hire me. Let's make it easy for them to find me."

"No."

She frowned, irritated at his assumption that he alone could make this decision. "Yes," she said, her tone biting. "Better me than someone else. I was born into this world to risk my life. It's what I do."

"I said no, Kayla."

It was an order, and one she didn't intend to take. He should know by now his bossy attitude would get him nowhere with her. She didn't like fighting dirty, but he left her no choice but to hit him hard.

"You'd rather let another innocent woman die?" she asked, pushing his buttons on purpose.

"I've invited all my staff to stay at Night Sins," he said, glancing between her and the road. "They'll be safe."

Okay, so she hadn't seen that one coming. "You can't babysit them every second. And even if you do, the Brothers will change strategies, and you'll be back to square one. We have a real window of opportunity, Ethan. A chance to get to whomever is calling the punches."

"Making you bait isn't going to lead us to the Brothers."

"It might. We just need to think it through. At least we have a starting point."

"Kayla—"

She cut him off. "Nothing stops me from marching into Night Sins and announcing myself. We both know Jac will remember me. I'm doing this, Ethan. With your help or without it. It would seem to me it's in both our best interests to do this together."

Ethan eyed his mirror and cursed. "We're being followed."

"See," she said, feeling a sense of accomplishment. "It's done. I'm exposed."

"It's not done. They don't know who you are and they're not going to." He took a sharp right and shifted gears. He handled the car as if it were a part of him, taking another sudden turn.

Kayla held on to her seat as Ethan cut a sharp corner and backed into a dark ally, killing the lights. The car following sped by. Ethan smiled, his blue eyes sparkling through the darkness around them. "Let's find out who they are, shall we?"

He flipped the lights back on and eased the car back onto the road, becoming the pursuer.

Kayla smiled, impressed as always with Ethan. She'd seen him in battle a time or two, and his sharp mind was as much a weapon as his honed body and warrior skills.

He kept his distance from the black Mustang ahead, the soft hum of the Porsche making it easy to keep hidden. "Do you know the car?" Kayla asked.

"No," Ethan said dryly. "But I have a good feeling I know where it's headed."

He didn't say more and she didn't ask. Kayla figured she'd figure it all out when they got to wherever they were going. Ten minutes later, they pulled into the parking garage of Night Sins.

The Mustang pulled into a spot between two other cars and Ethan hid the Porsche within the cover of two trucks. When he reached for his door, so did she.

He paused and glanced over at her. "I don't suppose telling you to stay in the car would do me any good." It wasn't a question.

"You suppose right."

"That's what I thought," he murmured and reached for his door.

As quietly as possible, Kayla eased outside the car and around the back bumper to come up beside Ethan. And she saw what he did. Jac walking toward the hotel.

"I guess we just confirmed our suspicions," Kayla said when she knew Jac was out of hearing range.

Ethan didn't respond, reaching for his cell instead and hitting a speed button before saying to her, "I'm taking you home."

She didn't get a chance to argue because he was already on the phone and getting back into the car. Kayla slid into the passenger side again just in time to hear his short conversation.

"Rigo. It's Ethan. Our leak is Jac." There was silence for a moment. Then, "Don't let him so much as breathe without me knowing about it. I'll be back to the casino as soon as I can."

He ended the call and put the car into drive. "Are you sure you can trust this Rigo person?" Kayla asked, not comfortable trusting anyone at this point.

"I trust Rigo," he said, pulling out of the garage. "When I began having suspicions about my staff, I called for help. Rigo and I served together in my government's Secret Services."

"Really?" She'd researched Ethan when she'd learned he was in her city and the Council had told her he'd once held a high position in his government. Even getting them to tell her that had been like pulling teeth. "I had no idea you were once SSA."

"Not was," he said, maneuvering the car out of the garage. "Am. I am still a member of the SSA. I told you I was assigned this city just as you were by your Council."

"The casinos and clubs are all just covers?"

"Being a big part of this city's economic structure allows me added resources." He gave her a sideways look. "How do you think I get the leads I give you? Or show up at just the right moment when you need help? I could do more if you'd let me."

The Council didn't allow such things. They considered a low profile the best way to avoid exposing the paranormal world. "You know my restrictions."

"I understand the Council's philosophies all too well. I also know times have changed. With the Brothers present, we have a new playing field with new rules."

"Maybe you should listen to your own words. The Brothers are endangering innocents and the secrets of our world. Even if our governments can't work together, we can."

He gave her another sideways look. "It's not about that."

"Then how is it, Ethan?" she challenged. "Because that's how it seems. Why would you risk innocent lives rather than let me help?"

Ethan pulled to a side street several blocks away from Kayla's apartment, obviously trying to throw off anyone who might follow them. He killed the ignition and turned to her, his arm going behind her seat. The small space shrunk, turning intimate.

His voice was low, intense. "Did it ever occur to you that I don't want you to end up like the Watcher before you?"

There was a charge in the air, electric and hard to ignore. Why did he care? She wanted to ask but held her tongue.

It was Ethan who ended the silence between them. "I need to get back to the hotel." He reached for his car door and got out. She did the same. Before she could move toward him, he started walking toward her apartment, obviously expecting her to follow.

She threw her hands up in frustration, but she didn't waste time standing there. Instead, she darted after him, catching up with a double step and grabbing his arm. "Ethan." He turned to face her. "I don't need an escort to my door. I patrol the streets every night."

"Humor me. I'm walking you to the door."

Enough of this crazy debate. She firmed her jaw and gave him a hard stare. "And I'm packing a bag and coming to the hotel with you."

He didn't blink, didn't move. For several seconds, he just stood there, looking at her. Finally, he said, "There will be conditions."

She felt a rush of relief. Finally. Progress. Still, a bite of irritation ate at her. She didn't like the way Ethan demanded control. "What conditions?"

He narrowed his gaze on her. "You stay in my room with me."

A fizzle of heat rushed through her limbs at the prospect. But she was in work mode, solid about her motives for pretending to be one of his women. And those motives said she needed to be close to the other girls to dig for information. She opened her mouth to say as much and Ethan grabbed her and pulled her into his arms, his hand holding her close.

"That's condition one, Kayla. Take it or leave it."

Intimate memories of their bodies pressed together flashed in her mind, making it hard to think, let alone find her voice.

"First," she said, suspicious about where this was headed, "Tell me the other conditions."

"We're hunting my race so we do things my way."

"Only if I agree with your way," she countered.

He stared at her a moment and then laughed. His hand slid across her lower back, molding her curves to his hard body. "I'm sure you remember how convincing I can be."

Oh, she remembered. She remembered all too well. "As long as you understand I might need convincing, then I guess we have a deal."

Jac stood outside room 1313 inside the Night Sins hotel corridor and knocked once, hard. Paused. Knocked twice. It was their code, the one he and Rigo had come up with so they'd know one another.

A second passed and the door flew open, displaying Rigo, a glass of bourbon in hand. Rigo motioned Jac inside, turning back to the executive suite he'd occupied since his arrival. Ethan took good care of those he trusted. Too bad for him he trusted the wrong people.

Leaning against the well-stocked corner bar, Rigo gave a nod. "I was right, wasn't I?"

"Oh yeah," Jac said, grabbing the crystal decanter on the bar and filling a glass with the caramel-colored liquid. "Ethan has it bad for that Watcher chick. It's perfect. We can deal with them both at once."

Rigo laughed evilly. "I can't wait to see Ethan's face when he finds out he's defeated."

Jac took a sip from his glass and studied Rigo, surprised at how much the man hated Ethan. He hated him out of nothing but jealousy; he'd wanted Ethan's role in their government and he'd been overlooked. Now he wanted power wherever he could get it.

Jac certainly would never give the man his back, nor would he keep him around when this was over. For now, he'd let Rigo believe otherwise, though. "The question is," Jac pondered, "do we kill her or simply capture her and use her for ammunition?"

"A shame to waste such a fine piece of ass," Rigo commented, finishing off his drink.

Jac had to agree with that one. The Watcher was a fine woman, for sure. And judging from the possessive way Ethan guarded her, he'd go nuts knowing she was being used for another's pleasure.

A slow smile slid onto Jac's lips. Oh yeah. He liked that idea. This was going to be fun. He'd have a little taste of the Watcher and he might even make Ethan the audience.

"If he brings her here, we'll need a way to get out of his reach."

"Easy enough," Jac said. "She's a Watcher, protector of innocents. Let's give her some innocents to protect. And the way I see it, the sooner the better."

Rigo refilled his glass. "That can be arranged."

Jac had already figured out that Rigo had connections, connections he planned to make his soon. "Meaning what?"

"The Council has a leak or two of their own," Rigo offered. "I've got an insider who will guarantee Kayla gets called to duty. Tonight, if you like. That way, Ethan never gets her inside the hotel where he can protect her."

Jac considered that a moment, an evil smile playing on his lips. "Yes." He gave Rigo a nod. "Make the call."

Tonight was the night Ethan would pay for his sins.

6

Ethan followed Kayla up the stairs leading to her loft-style apartment, watching as she kicked off her shoes and tossed her keys onto a tiny table to the right of her front door. A second later, the room was flooded with lights, displaying a cozy room with wood-paneled walls and hardwood floors. The room was given a warm feeling by the presence of throw rugs, an over-stuffed couch, and a corner fireplace. But much like his own apartment, he saw no pictures, no connection to family. Perhaps that was one of the things that had always drawn him to Kayla. They were both without roots, without anything but duty to drive them to tomorrow.

Yet, still, they lived by different rules, in different worlds.

Kayla sat down at a corner computer desk and began to punch keys. "I just need to check in with the Council and grab a few things and we can go."

Ethan gave her a quick nod as he stepped farther into the room and settled down on the couch. He'd only agreed to take her back to the hotel for one reason, and that was to keep her safe. The more he had considered the risks of her exposure, the less he'd been willing to leave her out there on her own.

The closer she was to him, the more control he had over her exposure to the Brothers. Why that was so important to him, he didn't know. There were plenty of people who would call him a cold-hearted bastard who cared about no one but himself. He'd never cared what they said about him. It didn't matter. Fighting wars meant making tough, often unpopular, decisions. He'd made his share and earned his reputation for his ability to do so.

But could he make that kind of calculated decision if it impacted Kayla? For the first time in his life, he wasn't sure. She'd gotten to him on a deeper level than the physical. Gotten to him in a way he couldn't explain. Not unless she was indeed his mate. But how was that possible? She wasn't a vampire.

From where he sat he could see her work and he found himself wanting to see the real Kayla, not the fantasy, and wishing that damn blond wig gone. When he got her back to his room, it was the first thing he was getting rid of. Right before her clothes.

With the punch of a key, Kayla pushed to her feet. "Okay. I'm ready. Nothing new tonight I haven't already dealt with. You have a computer I can check in on, right?"

"Of course," he said, standing up. "Since when does the Council e-mail you assignments?"

"It's fairly new. We used to be flying blind, patrolling and making our own contacts. But now, The Portal Guardians are all set up under the guise of operating paranormal investigation operations. They get tons of calls from all over the country and those are funneled through to the proper Watchers for investigation." She rolled her eyes. "We get a lot of active imaginations sending us on wild goose chases, but it comes with the job."

"Interesting," Ethan said, wondering if the goose chases she mentioned might not be too much of a distraction. But then, vampires rarely agreed with the methods of The Council.

His cell phone rang and Ethan reached for it, noting the private caller ID as Rigo's. He frowned and punched the answer button. Rigo wouldn't call without cause. "Problems?"

"One of the dancers left Secret Sins to get her things. She called Michael and told him she thought someone was following her. Halfway through the call, she screamed and the line went dead."

There was only one other woman at Secret Sins he knew on an intimate level. "Who is it?"

"Carrie."

And that was her. Ethan's blood went cold. "What's her address?"

"I've got a team headed out to check on her now," Rigo said.

Ethan spoke through clenched teeth. "What's her address?"

A beeping sound from Kayla's purse drew his attention and he looked up to see her retrieving her phone. He memorized the address Rigo gave him and hung up in time to see Kayla reading a text message.

She looked up, her face pale. "We have a problem."

"Tell me something I don't know," he mumbled. "Tell me what it is on the road. I need to check on one of the dancers."

"The Council knows about the Brothers, Ethan. They want me to check on a possible victim and report back immediately." He could see her mind racing. "I need to change. I can't fight like this." She ripped the wig off and tossed it to the ground and then eyed her phone. "99 Walker Street." Her gaze went to his. "You know the address?"

Ethan cursed. "It's the same address Rigo just gave me. You have two minutes to change. I'll meet you out front with the car."

She nodded and then reached out, touching his arm. "If you leave me I'll show up anyway."

He gave her a nod. "I have no intention of leaving you." And he didn't. He planned to keep her close and safe.

"Okay then," she said, studying his face and appearing satisfied with his answer. "I'll see you out front."

Only minutes later, Ethan pulled in front of Kayla's apartment to find her standing at the curb, dressed in black from head to toe.

She yanked open the door and slid inside, tossing a small bag in the back, which he assumed contained her wig and previous get up.

"You know the victim?" she asked.

"Yeah," he said, hating the truth, feeling responsible. "I know her."

"Maybe it's not too late."

Ethan ground his teeth again. "Maybe." But he knew the chances of Carrie being alive were next to zero. If she'd been attacked when she was on the phone with Michael, too much time had passed. Yet another woman in his life had found her demise. And here he was keeping Kayla close, as if that would keep her safe.

Perhaps the best thing he could do was get the hell away from her.

99 Walker Street had a similar set up as Kayla's own neighborhood. Side by side apartments lined both sides of the road, with street-side doors leading into second floor lofts. In Carrie's case, she also had a back entrance, offering Kayla and Ethan two points of entry to consider.

Having parked the car a mile away in a small garage, careful to be discreet, they approached the apartment on foot. Exchanging a quick look, they silently agreed to approach the rear of the building. Though both Kayla and Ethan were well armed, their guns were holstered. They were both aware of their limitations.

Discretion was critical for safety reasons, but neither of them wanted attention brought to the paranormal world, either.

Kayla surveyed the dark windows, the interior as pitch black as the outside of the building. With her instincts not quite right yet, she felt more on edge than normal.

They squatted down at the edge of the wall, inspecting the door. "I have a bad feeling about this," Kayla whispered.

"You and me both," Ethan murmured softly.

A scream from inside the building put them both in motion. "I'll take the front," Ethan said, already moving.

Kayla didn't watch his departure, her attention on the ground in front of her, on the door she had to go inside. A warning screamed in her head and she started running, her hand going to the knife sheathed just inside her jacket at her ribcage.

She had reached for the doorknob when her instincts told her someone was behind her, to her right. She kicked, making hard contact, and drew her knife. Rotating around she found herself faced with not one, but three male vampires. She inhaled, absorbing their emotions, their hatred, and making it her own. Frustrated, as the task was more difficult than usual, she still managed to let their emotions fill her.

She threw a punch, and another, successfully fielding what was thrown at her. This wasn't the first time she'd been outnumbered, though it was her first time facing vampires. They were strong. So damn strong. But she didn't let herself think about it. She couldn't. She *would* survive and save that girl.

Suddenly, Ethan was there. One of her attackers was thrown aside, tossed like he was nothing. Kayla caught a glance of Ethan as he reached for another attacker, leaving her with only one to deal with, and *one* she could easily handle.

She kicked him solidly in the chest and he stumbled to the ground. Rushing forward, she straddled him, holding the knife above his chest, ready to plant it in his heart. The old fables about a stake in the heart killing a vampire were true, of course.

At least, to some degree. Shove a stake—or, in this case, a knife—in anyone's heart, and they died. She reared back and prepared to plant the knife.

A male voice roared through the air. "Do it and she dies."

Kayla froze, knife drawn back, arm lifted high. She looked up for the source of the voice. And that's when she saw the woman, her back held against the broad chest of a muscular male, a blade at her throat.

Ethan spoke then, his voice as tense as she felt. "Rigo? What the hell are you doing?"

"That's Rigo?" she asked, still poised to slam the knife into the vampire's chest, not daring to look away from the man she still held captive.

Kayla's question was ignored as the man called Rigo answered Ethan. "I'm showing you who has the real power," Rigo said. The two vampires who'd been battling Ethan moved to stand on either side of him.

"What the hell are you talking about?" Ethan demanded. "What kind of game are you playing?"

Jac rounded the corner and he wasn't alone. Two more muscle-bound vampires framed him. "No game," Jac said. "Rigo simply got smart. He was tired of fighting for a king who gives no rewards."

"This is the Rigo you trusted?" Kayla demanded of Ethan, planting her foot on the vampire's chest beneath her so she could survey the situation. At the same time, she eased her knife to the front of her body rather than poised above her head.

Ethan didn't get to respond to Kayla. Rigo did it for him. "I am indeed the Rigo he stupidly trusted."

Rigo eyed Kayla and gave her an evil smile. He touched the blade to the woman's neck. The woman whimpered. "Help me."

"I am also the Rigo who will slice her neck if you don't drop your weapon and back away."

She clenched her jaw and stared down at the vampire on the ground, fighting the urge to be done with him. "I don't mind cutting her," Rigo said, as if he sensed her resistance. "Unlike Ethan, I don't fight my nature. I like blood." He laughed, amused at himself. "Give me a reason to cut her, Watcher. *Please.*"

With a frustrated sigh, she threw the knife away and took several steps backward. "Stand beside Ethan," Jac ordered.

She did as he said, not unhappy about her new position. Together, she and Ethan would be stronger. But she didn't look at Ethan as she took her place by his side, afraid to take her eyes off their enemies.

"Turn around," Jac ordered, walking toward them, his eyes locking with Ethan's. When neither of them moved, Jac raised his voice. "Turn around or the girl dies."

Ethan glanced at Kayla and gave her a tiny nod that said they really had no choice. Slowly, they did as they were told, moving in unison.

"Put your hands on the wall," Jac ordered.

Kayla and Ethan did as they were told. They stood there, hands before them, eyes locked. She could see his mind racing with potential escape options. Hers was doing the same thing. Strategic moves played in her head.

But before a solid plan could form, Jac was there, close, his hands on her hips. "I'll need to search you for weapons."

Kayla felt herself recoil and then anger formed. She started to turn, ready to fight to the death, ready to stop this now. But she wasn't the only one who reacted violently.

She heard Ethan curse even as he turned and reached for Jac, yanking him forward. "You sorry bastard," Ethan spat at Jac. "I'll kill you."

Kayla had to get to the girl. She started running toward Rigo but it was too late. The woman she'd intended to save fell to the ground, lifeless. Kayla didn't stop. She charged forward, determined to make Rigo pay. But, suddenly, a sharp pain pinched her shoulder and dizziness rushed over her. She reached toward the pain to find a dart stuck in her skin. Kayla yanked it out and tossed it aside, knowing she was in big trouble.

She turned to find Ethan, just in time to see not one, but three, darts hit him. "Ethan!" she screamed, seeing him stumble even as she started to run toward him. But her legs were like jelly and she started to fall, slipping into darkness.

Ethan.

7

Ethan woke with a jerk, trying to sit up, only to find his hands tied above his head. He eyed his surroundings, taking in the dimly lit space and realizing he was inside a cargo van of some sort. Beside him, Kayla still slept, clearly under the influence of the drug they'd been given, her hands also tied. Thank God, she was okay and still with him.

Sedation didn't last long on a vampire with elder blood such as his own. But they'd filled him with plenty of drugs. The heaviness of his limbs left no doubt of that. The question was—why bother even trying to sedate him? Why not just kill him and be done with it?

Whatever the reason, Ethan didn't plan to find out. He yanked at the thick, corded ropes, testing their strength. Yanked again. Nothing. They were solid.

"Ethan?" Kayla jerked upward, trying to escape, only to find she couldn't budge. She eyed the restraints before fixing her gaze on him. "Where are we?"

"Nowhere good," Ethan said, rolling to his side to face her. "Are you okay?"

She blew a strand of raven hair from her eyes. She nodded. "Considering the circumstances, fine." Her head lifted as she surveyed the van. "There was a knife in my boot they might not have found."

"How exactly would you propose we get to it?"

She frowned. "I don't hear you making suggestions. We have to get free. We're outnumbered and they're stronger than us."

"They're young and weak," Ethan said. "Not even a close match for me. All except Rigo. He's of elder warrior blood like myself."

She stared at him a minute as if he were insane. "Forgive me for saying so, but we both got our asses kicked."

Ethan gave her an irritated look. In some ways, he was a typical male vampire; namely, he didn't like his ability to protect his woman questioned. He ground his teeth. Not that she was his woman. No matter how much his body screamed that she was his mate, it was impossible. Both biologically and realistically. To be together would be a crime in both their worlds. Besides, his willingness to die in battle had always been an advantage. Being alone meant no one to worry about in life or death.

Even the deaths of those women close to him hadn't affected him as Kayla did. Yes, they upset him because he felt as if he'd created the women's death sentences. But he was a warrior. He knew the evils of battle, the poison of the enemy. But Kayla was changing him. He couldn't begin to think of her death, even in a mission of war, even knowing she was born into a life of battle.

No. He wouldn't see her die. No matter what he had to do, he wouldn't let harm come to her. With that decision, he shackled her legs with his own bigger, stronger one, pulling her close even as he moved toward her.

"What are you doing?" Kayla demanded, her soft curves now pressed to his body.

"When a vampire drinks blood, he is stronger. I need to be stronger, Kayla."

Her face went pale. "What are you saying?"

He stared into her eyes, hoping she would see and feel the good intentions in his actions. But he couldn't give her time to debate his actions. Any minute, the van could stop, and the door would open.

"Forgive me, little one," he said, and he sunk his teeth into her neck. Their lives might well depend on him drinking of her. And being a Watcher, she would offer him more power than a human.

Kayla stiffened beneath his bite, a gasp escaping her lips. Ethan stroked her back, telling her without words he meant her no harm. And she didn't fight. Slowly, her body eased into his. Slowly, she gave him her trust.

And he knew then, with her blood on his tongue, that Kayla was indeed his mate. Somewhere in her bloodline, she had a vampire ancestor. He closed his eyes, losing himself to the next few seconds, tasting the truth as it flowed through his veins. He felt her connection to him in his body, in his soul. But fate had played an evil trick on them. For he didn't dare complete the three blood exchanges needed to fully mate. He could never fully claim Kayla.

Kayla whispered his name, drawing him back to the present. Ethan reminded himself to be careful, not to drink too much. Though he no longer lived with the thirst, the taste of blood revived the hunger. And the taste of one's mate set a male on fire. Ethan forced himself to pull away, to seal Kayla's wound with his tongue.

He pressed his forehead to hers. "I'm sorry," he whispered.

But she didn't yell, didn't complain. "Just tell me you can kick their asses now."

He laughed. He didn't remember anyone ever making him laugh the way she did. "Yes. Now I can kick some ass."

She smiled. "Good. Because I really want to beat some vampire ass."

Ethan laughed at her outrageous comment. "As long as it's not mine."

"Oh, we have some fighting to do, Ethan," she said, leaning back to fix him in a reprimanding stare. Her eyes darkened. "Don't take what isn't given freely ever again."

He gave her a short nod. "You have my word."

"Good," she said, seemingly satisfied. "But when this is over, there will be further conversation over what just happened."

"I certainly hope so," he said, leaning forward to claim her lips. And though he merely brushed her mouth with his own, not daring to linger, he couldn't help wondering how he would ever walk away from her.

He knew he had no other choice.

Kayla watched as Ethan yanked hard and broke the rope holding his arms over his head. "You weren't kidding about being stronger now."

He didn't respond but focused on ripping the ties from his wrists and tossing them aside. And just in time. The van pulled to a stop.

"Oh crap," Kayla murmured, her heart racing. She wanted to be free so she could fight. She didn't have any plans to die this night, or anytime soon, for that matter. "Untie me. Hurry."

But Ethan didn't do as she bid. Instead, she watched in horror as he bit his wrist, drawing blood. A second later, he was by her side, shoving his arm at her mouth. "Drink. We can't wait until we're trapped again. We need to act now."

She shook her head, curling her lips inward. What the hell was he thinking? She wasn't a vampire. "Drink, Kayla. My blood is rich with power. Power you'll need to survive this night."

She shook her head, refusing again.

Ethan made a frustrated sound. "You said you trust me," he

said. "If that's true, do as I ask now. I mean you no harm. You can sense that."

The front doors opened and shut. Kayla didn't have time to process, only to trust. And trust Ethan she did. She drank long and deep, surprised that the taste didn't make her gag. In fact, it was sweet and easy to swallow.

The sound of someone messing with the back door said they were out of time. Ethan yanked his arm away from Kayla, leaving her to her own devices to free herself—clearly more confident than she that she could do so—and he moved toward the exit, preparing to attack.

Kayla yanked at her ropes, amazed to find she could, indeed, break them, amazed to find how powerful she felt.

As she tore the restraints away, the doors burst open and Ethan charged forward. Kayla quickly made her way to the edge of the van. She could see Ethan surrounded by a group of vampires a few feet away. Though he was holding his own and then some, he needed her help and he was going to get it. But before she could exit the van, Jac appeared, blocking her way.

"Ethan's a little busy right now," he said, smiling. "But no worries. I'll take care of you myself."

"You can try," she said, grabbing a strap across the top of the van and kicking her feet at him. She slammed him in the chest and he stumbled backward.

Not about to wait until he found his footing again, she jumped out of the van and landed in a squatting position, retrieving her knife from inside her boot at the same time. She dared a quick sideways glance at Ethan, noting he now battled only two vampires, having taken down several others. Nothing but old vacant warehouses surrounded them, and Kayla couldn't place their exact location. The only positive thing about being in the middle of what appeared like nowhere was a lack of humans to worry about.

Jac started to get up and she charged at him, hand wrapped

around the handle of her weapon. Strong legs had always been a plus for Kayla, and they were even stronger now. She used them, kicking Jac again, relieved to see him land flat on his back.

She caught a look on his face, too. A look that said he was as surprised as she was with her newfound strength, strength born of Ethan's blood and of her own ability to funnel her enemy's malice. And one thing was for sure: Jac had plenty of darkness in him to use to her benefit.

Kayla dove at Jac, ready to go hand to hand with him, only to find herself lifted mid-air and pulled hard against a muscular body. "Not so fast."

Her heart skipped a beat. She knew the voice. It was Rigo. And she remembered what Ethan had said. Rigo had elder blood in him. He was the strongest enemy she had to face today. She didn't want to give him the upper hand, and as long as he held her from behind, that was what he had. Her elbow landed solidly in his ribs but he didn't budge. She followed that by planting her knife in the meat of his thigh muscle.

He laughed. "I like pain."

Damn! Kayla's blood was pumping, her adrenaline in overdrive. She had to get free. As if he sensed she was about to act, Rigo lifted her off her feet, carrying her with the ease of some-one lifting a small child.

Kayla screamed for Ethan, having no idea if he could hear her, half afraid she'd break his concentration and get him hurt. Worse, she could see Jac was getting to his feet. Now, she'd have Jac and Rigo to deal with at the same time. Jac she could take. But Jac and Rigo together, she wasn't so sure.

Ethan's blood boiled into pure rage when he saw Rigo carrying Kayla toward an old warehouse in the distance. He yanked a dagger from the waistband of the vampire he was facing off with and jammed it in the vampire's gut. A second later,

Ethan removed the dagger and watched as the enemy crumbled to the ground.

All strategic thoughts of using Jac and Rigo to find the main operation of the Blood Brothers disappeared. Ethan simply wanted this over and Kayla safe.

Ethan charged at Jac, who eagerly met him halfway. But then, Jac had no idea Ethan had fed, no idea that Ethan had the strength of Kayla's blood. Jac was young and weak, no match for Ethan. With a mere few blows exchanged, Ethan was able to bury his weapon in Jac's chest. Before bidding farewell to the traitor he'd once called a friend, Ethan gathered Jac's armory, including three silver stars.

Then Ethan took off running. When he was close enough, he fired those stars into Rigo's back with all his might. One. Rigo jerked but kept running. Two. He stumbled. Three. Rigo stopped in his tracks. Ethan raced forward, closing the distance between himself and Rigo, desperate to get to Kayla.

But Kayla proved she could fight, and fight well, on her own. She took advantage of Rigo's injuries, struggling with such fierceness that for several seconds she broke free. Ethan felt an instant of relief that was quickly smashed as Rigo grabbed her again and turned to face Ethan, Kayla as his shield.

"I'd love nothing more than to kill your woman, Ethan."

"Hurt her and I swear I'll make you beg for death."

Kayla fixed Ethan in a look and then let her gaze discreetly move to the knife in Rigo's leg, silently telling Ethan her intentions. For several seconds, Ethan and Kayla stared at one another. One. Two. Three. Kayla reached for the knife, and, at the same time, Ethan moved forward.

In a hard, fast blow, Kayla slammed the knife into Rigo's side. Rigo roared with pain, his injuries finally taking a toll on him, his grip on Kayla going slack. Instantly, Kayla skirted away, out of reach.

Ethan blasted into Rigo, taking them both down to the ground, Ethan on top. The stars were still planted in Rigo's back and Rigo screamed out as they pressed deeper into his skin. Ethan shoved Rigo's shoulders hard against the dirt, ensuring the silver made complete penetration. With that action, with the pain it delivered to Rigo, what could have been a war became another easy victory. Ethan removed the knife from Rigo's side and sent it barreling into his chest.

"That," Ethan said between clenched teeth, "was for our king." He stood up, straddling Rigo's big body, and spit down on the vampire who had been a trusted member of his government's most elite military. "Traitor." He stepped away from Rigo, disgusted that someone of Rigo's stature would behave with such evil.

Kayla appeared by Ethan's side. "Feels kind of anticlimactic."

He quirked a brow. "Meaning?"

"I thought they'd be harder to beat." She smiled. "They weren't so tough."

"They were nothing. Just a couple of greedy bastards with a private agenda. The Blood Brothers aren't so easy to defeat. Their leader wants to rule more than his own people's destiny: he wants to rule the vampire world and move on from there."

"And he's starting with Las Vegas," she said.

"No," Ethan said. "Vegas is one statement of power."

She eyed the warehouse. "Any hope this is their main operation?"

Ethan shook off the idea. "Not a chance. The Blood Brothers have money and power. This is nothing but a place where Jac planned to murder us."

Kayla hugged herself with those words. "We should check it out anyway."

He nodded. "Agreed."

Thirty minutes later they'd finished their search, and, as Ethan had expected, there were no signs of the Blood Brothers.

They did, however, find a phone and he called for help. The van's tires had been sliced sometime in the midst of battle. A car was on its way to pick them up and he'd arranged a crew to clean up evidence of their battle.

Kayla sat down on an old crate and sighed, her frustration obvious. "So we basically achieved nothing, it seems." She ran her hand through her wind-ruffled hair. "Nothing besides killing a few assholes."

Even tired and beat up, she looked beautiful. "That's not true," Ethan assured her, claiming a crate across from her. "We saved lives. The murders will end now. They were all a part of Jac's plan to drive me out of town. You can tell the Council—problem solved." He winked. "That should get you some points."

She didn't seem concerned about the council. "What about traitors inside your operation? Someone was helping Rigo."

"They'll be handled," he assured her.

"And what of the brothers?" she inquired. "Will this be enough to drive them out of town?"

Ethan laughed, but not with humor. "Not a chance in hell. They'll lie low and regroup, but they aren't going anywhere." He studied her a moment, thinking of what that meant for Kayla. She'd remain at risk, a target for the Brothers. "Which means I'm not going anywhere, either."

Their eyes locked and held, awareness rich within the air. "That makes two of us," she said, softly.

So there it was, Ethan thought. They were both there to stay. Where did that leave them? So much had happened, had changed, in such a short time.

They were bound together by the very circumstances and fate that had pressed them apart. And Ethan didn't know what the hell to do about it. And truth be told, at least for tonight, he didn't want to think about it either.

What he wanted was to take Kayla home and make love to her. To end this nightmare of a night with her in his arms. The problems, the questions needing answers, would all be there in the morning light.

But he wasn't a fool. Holding her, feeling her body surround his, would only make walking away harder. And he had to walk away, no matter how much he didn't want to. The writing on the wall was clear. They were of two different worlds. She was a Watcher. He was vampire.

A match made in hell regardless of the fact that, in his arms, she felt like heaven.

8

Kayla sat in the back of the black car with tinted windows that had arrived at the warehouse to pick them up, Ethan by her side. But they weren't touching. They weren't even speaking. The distance between them spoke of strangers, not of two people who'd shared the heat of passion and the victory of battle.

The closer they came to her apartment, the more Kayla's stomach twisted in knots. What came next for her and Ethan? By the time they drew to a stop, she was ready to come unglued.

"I'll walk you to the door," Ethan said, moving to get out of the car.

Kayla grabbed his arm and he turned back to her, a brow lifting in question, those damn blue eyes fixing her in an intense stare. "Yes?"

She didn't want him to do the gentlemanly thing and escort her to her apartment. Being a gentleman had never been what she'd wanted from Ethan. "I don't need to be walked anywhere."

"Humor me," he said, as he had hours before in a similar situation.

She'd broken rules tonight. She couldn't turn back time. The way she saw it, the damage was done. Tomorrow was a new day. No, damn it, she would not *humor* him. There was plenty more she'd be happy to do, though.

"If you want to walk to that door with me, then it better be to come inside." She paused with intent. "To stay."

Ethan stared at her a long moment. "You're sure about this?"

She wanted this. She wanted Ethan. "Very."

He gave her a short nod and then spoke to his driver. "We won't be needing your services any longer this evening."

A few seconds later, they stood at her door and Kayla handed over her keys to Ethan, per his insistence. No matter how much she didn't care about him being a gentleman, he insisted on playing the role. She stood there on her front porch, her skin tingling with awareness as she watched Ethan turn the key.

He stepped inside her apartment, turning on the lights and motioning her forward. She went ahead of him, pausing on the bottom step. Ethan flipped the locks into place and Kayla had the satisfied feeling of shutting off the rest of the world. This was her place, her comfort zone.

She realized then that Ethan had willingly come to her territory, her safe zone. Prior to this night, she'd always assumed he'd demand she go to his. But the truth was, on many occasions he'd come to her, sought her out. Offered her help where he could have turned away.

Ethan turned to her. Appearing satisfied he'd completed his task, he walked toward her, wrapping his arms around her waist. She stood on a step that put them closer to eye level, and somehow that put them on even ground, offering a more intimate more intense connection.

"You can still change your mind," he said softly. "In fact, you probably should."

She narrowed her gaze on him, surprised by his words. "Why is that?"

His tone was dry. "Surely your Council wouldn't approve."

A tiny smile played on her lips. It was late to think of such things. "I doubt they'd approve of much I've done this night." That brought her to an important subject. "Like me drinking blood."

His lips brushed hers. "My blood," he said, his voice low, almost possessive. "You drank my blood. Just as I drank yours."

The way he said the words came out incredibly erotic. It was clear it aroused him to think of them sharing as they had. It shouldn't do the same to her, yet, it did. Her nipples tightened and tingled, her body warmed.

"I need to understand," she said. "I need—" He cut her words off with a kiss. A deep, passionate kiss. Kayla melted into him, her body sizzling and ready for more. So ready. She'd wanted him forever, it seemed. She'd resisted because of what was right and what was wrong. But as his tongue slid against hers, taking her deeper and deeper into the passion that burned between them, the lines of right and wrong faded. There was only this night, only the two of them.

Ethan's fingers lightly brushed her hair from her face, his lips nipping and teasing, before he soothed her with a gentle caress of his mouth. "I swear I'll answer your questions," he finally said. "I know what you need—"

It was her turn to cut him off. Kayla kissed him again, inhaling his spicy male scent, so deliciously enticing. "If you know what I need," she whispered against his lips, "why are we still standing on the stairs?"

Ethan didn't argue, lifting her in his arms. She took his cue, wrapping her legs around his waist, letting him carry her up the stairs, eager for what came next.

At the edge of the living room, he paused, and she answered his silent question. "To the right, down the hall."

Inside her bedroom, her curtains were open, moonlight spilling into the room in a silvery gray stream. Ethan set her on her feet beside the bed and their eyes held and locked. Together they undressed, no questions, no resistance. They both knew what they wanted, what they had wanted for far too long.

When clothes were no longer an obstacle, they faced one another again. Kayla reveled in the perfection of his body. Glorious from head to toe, he was all sinewy muscle, powerful and strong. Her gaze drifted from his broad chest to his flat, rippling abdominals to the hard length of his aroused cock. She would have reached out, would have wrapped her hand around the width, but Ethan took action first.

The next thing she knew, she was flat on the bed, Ethan on top of her, his shaft settling between her legs with delicious promise of what was to come next. And he was kissing her, kissing her with such passion, such intensity, she thought she would go up in flames. This was what she'd waited for, what she had fantasized about many a time.

Desperate for more of him, Kayla wrapped one leg around his calf, arching upwards, sliding her aching core along his long, hard length. Her hands went to his face, feeling the stubble of his jaw on her sensitive skin, amazed at how arousing it was, how something so little could be so sensual and sexy with Ethan.

"I want you inside me, Ethan," she whispered hoarsely. "Like I've wanted that for a lifetime."

Ethan responded by lifting himself up on one arm and looking down at her, his lids heavy, eyes dilated with passion. Suddenly his mood seemed to shift, to darken. He squeezed his eyes shut and tilted his head back, making a frustrated sound. The next thing she knew he was on his back, arm over his face.

"What is it?" she asked, confused and lost by the sudden change. "Ethan—what is it?"

He inhaled and let it out before turning to his side to face her, his weight on one elbow. "Your mother was a Watcher. What about your father?"

She shook her head. "What?" she asked. "My father? Men aren't Watchers. He was human."

"Are you sure?" he questioned. He hesitated, then asked, "Could he have been a vampire?"

No. Why would he say such a thing? Her throat went dry, her heart beating at double time. The implications of what he suggested could make her an outcast in her world. It would certainly strip her of her post.

Ethan didn't say things without reason, which made his question all the more disturbing. "You think he was a vampire?"

He gave a short nod. "I believe you have vampire in your bloodline, and it makes sense that it was your father."

"Because I drank your blood and it made me stronger," she stated, assuming that was where he'd drawn his conclusion. Surely, her mother would have told her such a thing. Wouldn't she have? Yes. Of course. "I would know."

"It's more than that." He ran his hand down her hair, moving closer again. "From the moment we met, we were drawn to each other."

"That means nothing," she said, rejecting that as a reason to claim a vampire in her lineage.

"Tonight in that club, you were on fire," he explained. "You know why?" He let the question linger in the air for several seconds, clearly not expecting her to answer. "You were on fire because my mating instincts were on fire as well. There is only one mate for a vampire, little one, and some never find that person. Tonight I confirmed what I've suspected a long time now. Tonight everything inside me said that mate for me is you. I know it sounds impossible. I refused to believe it myself. But any doubt I had disappeared when I tasted your blood on my tongue."

She shook her head. "That can't be." Kayla sat up and moved away from him, back against the headboard, knees to her chest. "I . . . no. This can't be." A thought occurred to her and she stiffened. "Oh God. We drank from each other. Does that mean . . . is that . . . are we . . . ?"

He came to her then, his hands going to her cheeks. "I would never bind you to me without your consent."

She knew that. She did. And it comforted her to realize that. "How does a vampire mate?"

"Three blood exchanges must take place. The third must be done while making love."

Kayla digested his words, thankful that nothing could happen she didn't control. He kissed her forehead, a tender act she felt from head to toe. Then, he moved away, leaving her feeling empty and alone. He said nothing more as he pushed to his feet and reached for his pants.

"Where are you going?" she asked, unable to stop herself, though, Lord only knew, she tried.

He glanced over his shoulder before turning to face her. "I can see you need some time to process all of this and I'm going to give it to you." A muscle in his jaw tensed. "I'm asking nothing of you, Kayla. I simply thought you have the right to know what I believe to be the truth. This is our secret." He grabbed his shirt and shoved his arms into it, leaving the buttons untouched. "I'm headed out of town anyway. I need to see my king. It would be best to tell him about Rigo in person."

Her stomach twisted in knots. She should be glad he was leaving but she wasn't. She should be glad he wasn't pushing this mating thing. Yet, again, she wasn't. "I thought you were staying here to fight the Brothers?"

"Oh, I'll be back before the Brothers have time to regroup, you can count on that. I won't leave you to deal with them alone. A mate protects his woman."

The prospect of his return brought relief that lasted all of a second. Her tempter flared at his possessive macho attitude. None of this changed anything about her world or her life.

"Damn it, Ethan," she spat, glaring at him. "I am a Watcher, as much a warrior as you. I *don't* need protecting."

She crawled across the bed to the edge of the mattress and stood up, facing him, intent on getting dressed. But the instant she was within arm's reach, Ethan pulled her close, his warm body enclosing hers, creating a rush of red-hot desire.

"You argue about not needing protection," he said, "but say nothing of my claim that we are mates."

She settled her hands on his chest, the familiar banter of their relationship offering her comfort. "Because it's a crazy notion not worth arguing about. And stop twisting my words. You're infuriating."

"So you've told me often," he said, his hand sliding over her bare ass, molding her to his hips.

He was hard again, just as she was wet. There was no question they turned each other on. No amount of ice she tried to create survived the fire.

"We might be forced to deny our bond, but I *will* be close by, looking after you. I have since the day you arrived in this city and I don't plan to stop now."

Arguing was no use and she knew it. She also knew it was well past time she took control again. Kayla slid his shirt off his shoulders. "You talk too much," she said. "If you really want to take care of me, then shut up and fuck me."

His lips lingered above hers, teasing and tempting. "I won't fuck you, little one. But I will make love to you."

Hmmm. She liked that. Actually, both options sounded rather enticing. "Would you consider doing both?" she asked, her hand sliding to the front of his pants, tracing the ridge of his erection.

"Perhaps," he said. "After I've made love to you three or four times we can discuss other diversions."

She smiled, shoving his pants down his hips. "Promises, promises."

A moment later, she lay on her back, his weight on top of her, his kiss more passionate than any kiss she'd ever known. And when he slid his hard length inside her, he filled her with more than satisfaction. He filled her with certainty.

Kayla knew in that moment that whatever the future might hold for her, Ethan would be there. And, as always, he would be her biggest secret.

Once a delicious temptation, he would be an indulgence she could never turn away.

The Devil's Paradise

Megan Kearns

Thank you to Delilah, Layla, Myla, Shayla for including me on a crazy idea dreamed up at a hotel bar one spring afternoon in Dallas.

1

Dashiel Wilde had gone from Hell to Texas and couldn't tell the difference. Whether covered by a thick blanket of stars or the Earth's crust, his view remained the same: unbearable heat, rocks, and scorched hills.

He stood on the last stair of The Last Resort Hotel's entrance. He gazed out on the dark, open land. One step away lay brown, cracked Texas soil.

The gnarled oaks and sparse grass might as well have been six hundred miles away as six inches. A ragged breath escaped from his lungs. As long he remained soulless, he was bound to the hotel.

After two hundred years, he didn't care if the grass was sparse and the trees stunted. He'd give anything to walk in the open and feel the give of earth under his feet instead of hard marble. Simple pleasures he'd never valued, until he'd lost them.

His jaw tightened and he spun around. He had no one but his selfish anger to blame for becoming a devil. Eternal regret burned his throat. Of all the consequences, his loss of personal liberties was minor.

A low drone from the hotel's three brass bells echoed. He glared up at the three towers hating the sound. Their ring signaled another start of his eternal duty: providing damned souls with two days of indulgences before they paid for their sins.

"Evening, Mr. Wilde." Robert stood at the curbside podium.

He nodded in the valet's direction as he straightened his gray silk suit. "Is everything ready?"

"As much as can be." The short, dark, Italian bell captain adjusted his red and gold cap.

"Not good enough," he growled. Everything must appear normal. Another leak of the hotel's existence and there'd be hell to pay.

Dash gripped the compass in his pants pocket as he scanned the entryway. Several wrinkles marred the crimson carpet running toward the heavy wood double doors. A snapped of his fingers smoothed the material. Another snap, and the fountain beside the walkway gurgled to life.

If anyone told him years ago that he'd tire of wanton women and fine food, he'd have laughed. But, after two centuries of every culinary and carnal pleasure, he'd grown bored.

The sweep of headlights interrupted his thoughts. Golden beams snaked along the curved driveway, the first arrival in a parade of guests compelled by their mysterious invitations. A tall brunette in a short, gold gown uncurled her legs from her Mercedes Benz.

Dash leaned beside the entrance and flipped open his compass. The needle pointed to the young woman. The arm hovered between damnation and sexual freedom, and then swung hard left. Condemned by her vices.

So young. He snapped the brass lid shut. Wrongs committed and the damage done to one's soul had little to do with age. His own foolish youth was proof enough.

She sauntered toward him. In his former life, she'd never look twice at him unless to turn up her nose. Expensive perfume eclipsed the sweet scent from the hibiscus-filled planters. "Welcome to The Last Resort."

"Are you the owner?" she purred.

"Manager," he gave the required smile, "but I guarantee you'll meet my boss soon."

She leaned in closer; her copper lips hovered above his. "I like a man in charge."

Practiced fingers slipped inside his silk jacket. He grabbed her wrist. "No, you'd like a trip to Tiffany's courtesy of my Visa." He twisted her hand until she cried out and dropped his wallet.

Obsidian sparks flashed in her dead eyes.

"Find yourself another pretty boy friend," he snarled. His blood burned beneath his skin. As he tucked away his billfold, she hurried off. Her spiked heels rapped on the cream marble.

"You let her go?" Robert's black gaze narrowed to a viperous slit.

"Punishment isn't our job." Dash dropped his voice as he drew out each word. "Be thankful you only lost your soul, not destroyed it."

Robert nodded emphatically as he climbed into the car.

As the red taillights disappeared, Dash rubbed the back of his damp neck. He was responsible for all who worked at the hotel, but learning their lessons was up to them.

A snowball had a better chance in Hell than their odds of ever learning. Who could love a selfish bastard like him? But at least he had a glimmer of hope.

Justice Malloy rolled down the driver's side window. A welcome breeze blew through her platinum hair. The A/C *would* quit in the middle of a summer traffic jam.

Orange detour signs led her away from the congestion of downtown Austin and onto a dark two-lane road. She leaned back in the seat and rubbed her forehead.

Less than six weeks remained until her brother's college tuition was due. Before her parents' deaths they would have simply written a check for six thousand dollars. But, medical bills had changed everything.

A deathbed promise to her mother to raise Lawson and send him to school made the six grand her problem. She had one chance to earn the money in time: convince Charlene Dawson to hire her to coordinate her daughter's sudden wedding.

Tonight's meeting with the dame of Austin society, and Justice's mother's best friend from Junior League, had gone well. But the contract depended on finding a unique reception venue by Monday, no simple task in a town of politicians, lobbyists, and techno millionaires.

Her fingers tightened on the steering wheel. Somehow she had to come up with a unique site.

Speaking of places, where the hell was she? She scanned the dark road for the detour signs. The landscape had turned sparse, more like West Texas than subdivision-overrun Travis County.

"I must've missed a turn," she mumbled.

Her head became heavy and the empty highway grew dim. Justice switched on the radio. Country rock filled the small car.

God, she was tired. More than a long day, ten years of caring for her mother battling cancer and raising Lawson were catching up. She'd never regretted her decision.

Another three miles passed without so much as a billboard, or speed limit sign. As she fumbled for her cell, she spotted a golden light shimmering in the distance. *Whew!*

Cresting a steep hill, a sprawling, authentic Spanish mission-style building materialized, complete with red tile roof and triple bell towers. She slowed and turned into the long circular drive.

The name THE LAST RESORT glowed blue on the tall peach stucco sign. A flutter of excitement tickled her stomach. The Last Resort might just be the answer to her prayers.

She eased her sedan along the drive between the lush tropical flowerbeds and sprawling lawn. All appeared much too green for the middle-of-summer drought. She frowned and pulled up to the entrance.

A short, dark-haired man in a red and gold jacket approached. "I'll take your keys and unload your bags."

"I'm not checking in, I just need some information." She smiled. *And directions back to the highway.*

The man frowned. The gesture elongated his narrow olive-skinned face. "You don't have an invitation."

From his tone, she gathered he had orders to stop anyone not on the guest list. She called on all of her charms for signing corporate sponsors. The resort was the perfect location to seal her deal with Charlene Dawson. She had to get inside.

She glanced at the man's nametag. "Robert, I'm an event planner." She handed him her business card. "One pricing packet from banquet services and I'll be gone."

His face remained blank. Damn. She smiled and scrambled for a means to persuade him. "I'll only be a minute."

Nothing.

"I'd be happy to escort the lady," an athletic, dark-haired man in a tuxedo said as he stepped from the BMW parked behind her. He flashed his perfect white teeth, opening her car door.

Her driver's seat view was eye level with his crotch, doubtless the location of his happiness. Like others, he clearly assumed by her platinum blonde hair that she was a naïve. Too late they realized she'd played with the big boys for a long time and was immune to their charisma.

Smart money said use him to get inside and ditch him. "And where did you hope to escort me? To the lobby," she stepped out of the car, "or straight to your room?"

Mr. Smooth smiled. "I'd never take you—"

"No, you're right," she removed his sweaty hand from her arm, "you won't *take me.*"

His tanned face hardened. "Bitch."

"Yes, I am." She smiled. "But not yours."

He stormed up the red carpet.

"You could have gotten in with him." Robert stared.

Too tired and worried, she let her composure fall away. "Deception and whoring aren't how I do business." She met his dark gaze in the dim glow of the covered patio's lanterns.

Her father always said honesty was the best policy. She swallowed and went for broke. "I need this hotel to get a client or my brother will have to sit out another semester of college."

Robert glanced from her to the double doors. "Go inside." He plucked the car keys from her hand.

"Thank you." She pecked the stunned bell captain on the cheek. "You're an angel."

The heels of her sandals click-clacked as she hurried up the steps. As she stood in the doorway, the hotel's three mission bells rang. She jumped. The deep, haunting tone reverberated off the marble and high ceilings.

Ornate cream arches led into the heart of the lobby. Classically styled columns supported gilded cobalt skylights. Their reflections shined in the dark wooden floor like a mirror. Baroque carved tables and chairs covered in gold silk added to the grand opulence.

She shook off her stupor, more convinced than ever she'd found the right location. As she headed for the long walnut check-in desk, low soulful notes of old jazz rode curls of smoke.

Patrons packed the blue lobby bar. Everyone wore either a custom tuxedo or a couture gown. The über elegant guests talked as they lounged on the many settees.

Among the intimate cocktail crowd she recognized several prominent faces, including cattle baron Henry Grange. She bit back a gasp. The ornery rancher almost never left the Rio Grande Valley. She glanced around for an event sign, but found none.

Whose party had such irrestible pull? She headed for the reservation desk.

A tall, square-jawed man stood behind the counter and smiled. At first he appeared no different than the other polished men she'd passed.

But as she drew closer, she noted his ready stance and intent gaze tracking her movements as a predator did its prey. His charcoal suit appeared custom tailored for his broad shoulders. Her stomach fluttered. "Hello," she said over her dry throat.

"Welcome to The Last Resort."

His voice, a mix of a rough gravel rasp and warm, smooth whiskey, sent a shiver from the top of her spine to the tips of her toes. The man had the ultimate bedroom voice. Did he talk when he made love, or was his tongue too occupied with his lover's skin?

"T-thank you." Damn. No one flustered her professionally or personally. Business was her focus, not the rugged stubble on the man's angled cheeks. "It's a lovely place."

"Not nearly as lovely as your face." He wrapped his larger hand around hers and raised her fingers to his lips.

His warm mouth against her knuckles sent an electric jolt up her arm. Oh, he was smooth. So much so she was sorely tempted to let him charm her out of her damp silk panties.

"Checking in?" He continued holding her hand.

"No." But she could certainly stand to check him out a little more. Solid chest, straight nose, and—She hadn't come to the hotel to pick-up men.

She took a deep breath. First, came her client and her brother. Only after meeting their demands would she see about fulfilling her own *needs*. "I'd like an information packet on your banquet and catering services." She extracted her fingers, and noticed the loss of warmth immediately.

His mouth, so sexy a minute ago, thinned.

"You weren't invited?"

Honesty had worked on the first go round, so she took the same approach. "Truthfully, I was lost when I saw the hotel."

Eyebrows, a shade darker than his short blond hair, rose above blue eyes deeper than the Pacific Ocean. "Honestly, Mr.—" She pressed her palms against the cool cherry countertop and leaned toward his gold nametag. The sweet scent of campfire smoke filled her lungs and clouded her brain. "Mr. Wilde—"

"It's not possible," he muttered, "not again."

As his gaze fell, a flash of red lit up his pupils. A trick of the light. She shivered.

Crinkles pinched the corners of his eyes. The high counter blocked her view of the source of his frustration. Metal clicked, and he looked up.

"Call me Dash."

Despite his smile, his irises darkened. "Thank you. I'm Justice Malloy."

"*Justice,*" he arched an eyebrow, "an ideal myth."

"Much like polite men." She set her handbag on the desk and smiled.

He gave a sharp laugh. "Are you a lawyer?"

"No, but my father was a D.A." Old sadness clogged her throat. Ten years, and she still missed him.

Dash's hooded gaze centered on her. "Are you interested in exploring?"

Innuendo rumbled through his voice, tightening her nipples. She stepped back, but he'd likely already spotted her physical response through her white silk top. His uncommon mix of polished style over raw male power intrigued her.

What could it hurt to play along? "Exactly, what would I be *exploring?*"

"You tell me." He stepped closer.

The counter provided little protection against his over-whelming broad shoulders and muscled frame. His pupils glowed like hot coals of wicked delights. A sizzle sparked across her skin and settled deep between her legs. "I'll stick with exploring the hotel, for now."

He walked around the desk as smooth as the flow of the Colorado River. "Allow me to show you around." He held out his hand.

She studied the temptation embodied in his long fingers. "My own personal guide?"

"We aim to satisfy all of our guests' needs." The corners of his mouth curved.

Her stomach fluttered once more. "And does your itinerary include testing the room mattresses and a view of the ceiling tiles?"

"Only if you want." He laughed.

Did she ever. The realization sent a shock through her sex-deprived nerve endings. She glanced at the empty counter. "Aren't you the night man?"

"Not exactly." His deep chuckle echoed off the marble columns and high ceiling.

"Then, who are you?"

2

Dash clenched his jaw at Justice Malloy's haughty question, *Who are you?* He stared at her as she stood in the elegant lobby wearing perfectly matched cloths with her straight-as-an-arrow spine. He'd known her kind all his life: rich, beautiful, and with superiority bred into her veins.

A flash of old insecurity hit. Suddenly his gray suit felt like dirty, torn rags. Hands fisted at his sides. That poor, foolish Irish farm boy had died the day he'd sold his soul.

The knowledge he was a devil would send her cute little rich ass running. And, if the truth about The Last Resort got out again, he could kiss any chance of ever regaining his soul good bye. A chill slithered through him.

"I'm the hotel manager." He forced a polite smile.

She arched a single platinum brow. "Just the man I need."

Glass crashed. The echo cut off any questions about her *needs.* Through the spiked fan of palm leaves, he spotted jagged shards of broken mirror spread across the lobby bar. Damn it all.

She glanced from the mess to him. "Do you have time to give tours?"

No. But until he learned if she was a sinner or a sex kitten he couldn't let her out of his sight. "When it comes to the hotel I have eternity." He flashed a tight smile. "What would you like to see first?"

Ravenous hunger filled her eyes, like a starved animal. His cock filled. Every inch of Justice Malloy screamed sex, from the Marilyn Monroe curls to the red lips and curvy hips. So, why hadn't she registered on his compass as a wanton?

"Let's start with the size of your grand ballroom." She picked up her purse and monogrammed red leather notebook.

"Does size matter?" He caught the southerly dip of her gaze. The ridge of his zipper pressed farther against his hardening cock.

"Sometimes." She ran the tip of her tongue over her lower lip. "It's always better to go a little bigger at least when it comes to wedding receptions."

The molten heat speeding through his limbs froze. His focus immediately went to her left hand.

"Not mine." She waggled her empty ring finger.

The momentary tightness in his chest released. He rubbed the sore spot above his heart and frowned. Vows and gold bands meant even less within the hotel walls than outside them.

"Ladies first." He gestured to the long corridor behind him.

"Good manners or an opportunity to look at my ass." She smiled as she walked past.

"Why else do you think the custom developed?" He admired how her backside swayed with the swish of her skirt. With her back turned, he snapped his fingers and set the lobby back to rights.

"And here I thought chivalry was dead." She paused, waiting for him to join her.

Dash chuckled. "I appreciate a woman who can think on her

feet." He leaned closer and brushed his mouth against her ear. "And even more off their feet."

The tip of her tongue slid over her lower lip.

An urge to kiss her rose along with his cock. Her movements pegged her a wanton. The roll of her hips, the tight points of nipples, and her teasing all pointed to lust. One look inside the ballroom should sway her and the compass needle.

The crystal chandeliers threw a fractured pattern of light down the marble hallway.

A gray-haired man with a stern face, and a tall middle-aged cowboy in a black Stetson, approached them.

"Mr. Anders?" Justice's head snapped toward the pair. "It's good to see you. And you, too, Mr. Langtree."

"Evening, Ms. Malloy." The older man's steps faltered, but he quickly recovered and hurried away.

Dash aimed his compass at the retreating pair. Damned. He frowned. What connection did Justice have to a cheat and a blackmailer? "Friends?"

"We've done business," she said as they continued walking.

Could he have been wrong about her? Was she also damned? The uncomfortable possibility sat heavy in his gut. The old adage about birds of a feather contained more truth than most people realized.

"Those two men each wrote me a check for ten thousand dollars last year," Justice offered, as if reading his mind.

His stomach sunk lower. "Interesting associates you have."

She stopped in the center of the hallway and whirled on him. "Exactly what are you implying, Mr. Wilde?"

Voices and music from the ballroom at the far end flooded the corridor.

"I work for Austin Children's Charity. The money went to a fundraising gala I planned." She stood with her hands on her hips.

Sparks shot from her eyes. If guilty, she'd not anger so quickly.

The pressure in his stomach relaxed. "I didn't make any accusations."

She let out a breath and resumed walking. "There's a fraud investigation going on regarding both men's business and anyone who's ever met them is being questioned. I've worked too hard for my professional reputation to see it ruined."

The probability that she was one of the damned lessened with every moment. His fingers curled around the compass. Much as he didn't want her damned, her status complicated matters. Music pulsed louder the closer they got to the ballroom.

"That's some party," she half shouted over the thumping bass.

"Like you've never seen." Her reaction when the set of dark double doors opened would seal any sexual intentions.

"Oh, I bet I have." She crossed her arms over her chest.

The position squeezed her breasts together. Rounded, creamy tops peaked over the draped white silk neckline. He scraped his teeth over his tongue. "I'll take that bet."

"I didn't mean—"

"Too late." He grinned. "I win and you give me a kiss."

"Just a kiss?" Pale brows arched above her darkening gaze.

"Unless you want more." He leaned against the door and admired her shapely waist and bare arms.

"And if you lose?" She absently rubbed her collarbone.

Dash's cock jerked at her self-caress. All too easily he imagined her touching herself, fingers dipping into her pussy while he watched. "If by some miracle I lose, I'll leave you alone for the rest of your stay."

Her white teeth sunk down on her lower lip. He held himself back. Soon enough he'd have his mouth on hers.

"I accept."

The confident tone didn't fool him. "The Divine Ballroom." He pushed down the brass handle and threw both doors open.

* * *

Justice's feet stuck to the floor. Round dining tables with couples having sex atop them filled the center of the room. On the band riser, half a dozen men and women took part in an orgy. Legs tangled. Arms disappeared between sweat-slicked bodies.

Either she'd walked onto a massive porn film set or straight into Sodom and Gomorra. She swallowed hard. "Oh, fuck," Justice said as she stared.

"Literally."

She jumped at the rough voice next to her ear.

"See something that interests you?" He trailed his lips along her jaw.

Shivers wobbled her knees. Interest? So much time had passed since she'd last had sex, it'd taken her a minute to process the scene. "I can't say there's anything to hold my fascination." She held her tone even with supreme effort.

"Liar."

He paused at the corner of her lips and she felt his mouth shift into a smile.

"I win," he said.

Son of a bitch, he had bested her. She pulled back and retreated into her professional persona. "Did you run out of rooms?"

"Never."

"A shame your guests can't find them." She blinked as a dominatrix in a leather corset, thong, and thigh-high boots led a man on his hands and knees wearing a dog collar right past her. She took a closer look at the wrinkled face of the crawling man and gasped. "Is that Governor—"

"Yes."

She whipped her head toward him and his nonchalant answer, as if she'd asked about tomorrow's weather. "Is it always like this?"

"Usually." He smiled as though thoroughly enjoying her discomfort.

The tip of her tongue pressed against her top lip. "This might not work for a wedding reception."

"Really? Why?"

She ignored his feigned innocence and pointed to a naked woman lap dancing her way down the line of seated spectators. "The new version of musical chairs for starters."

He craned his neck around a lesbian couple making out to look at the floor show she'd indicated. "That's one I haven't seen."

That made two of them. She moved to the safety of the half-eaten buffet. It took all her willpower not to gawk at the crazy sex taking place all around her. The traditional missionary and sixty-nine positions she recognized, but others she couldn't fathom the name let alone how.

To her shock, moisture slipped between her legs. Had she lost her mind? The more she ignored her surroundings the wetter her pussy became. She grabbed a bottle of wine for a distraction.

"2003 Barolo Valpolicello," Dash offered.

She glanced at opposite end of the long table and the main course. "Veal chop in demi-glacé sauce?" She stretched on her tiptoes for a better look.

"Impressive." He crossed his arms over his chest. "It's served over wild truffle risotto."

"Hmmm." She set the bottle back down.

"Not to your liking?" His shoulders stiffened.

Interesting. He'd only bet her a kiss knowing damn well she'd lose. Now, on her own turf of entertaining, he presented her with the perfect opportunity to turn the tables. "The meal is an excellent choice. But I'd have chosen an Amarone Reserva Privata over the Valpolicello."

Bright red colored his cheeks. Though, by the lines creasing his forehead, the stain resulted from anger rather than any embarrassment.

Justice caught herself stepping backward, but not before she bumped into someone. Her heel turned and she flailed her arms. Dash's strong hand caught and steadied her.

"Excuse me," she said to the tall man decked out in gold chains. Something about his leering gaze prickled the hairs at the back of her neck.

Dash looped his arm around her shoulders and led her away.

Before she turned, she caught the fire-red gaze he shot the other man. The intensity was—inhuman. At the same time the tension in her shoulders disappeared.

"Who is that?" she whispered as they made their way back to the hall.

"A football player." Dash frowned. "One you don't want to meet."

Warning cut along the edge of his words. What wasn't he telling her?

"You look like you need a drink," he said as they reached the corridor, "and an orgasm."

Justice's step faltered. A buzz of hot energy filled her chest. "I agreed to a kiss."

"Which I'm happy to collect." His attention zeroed in on her mouth.

She resisted licking her lips and enticing him further. The man had gotten the better of her once. No way was she permitting him a repeat. "I don't have time for you or your games."

"Life is shorter than you think." His hard steps echoed as he led her back toward the lobby.

He'd turned colder than a blue northerner blown down from Canada in January. "It's also about more than just me," she snapped.

"You're right, it's about those who hire someone else to plan their wedding."

"I help people." She cut in front of him.

"Those too rich to do anything for themselves." He smiled.

The sentiment didn't reach his icy blue eyes. She slammed her hand against the etched glass doors of the bar and blocked his path. She'd been called a spoiled rich girl before, but never had the label rankled her more.

"Based on your demonstration in the ballroom you know an equal amount about wine, food, and by the cut of your suit, fashion." His anger to her criticism confirmed her suspicions. He wasn't born to society. He'd learned to move through society's circles, not been born into them.

"Should I assume you're a spoiled rich boy, born with a silver spoon in his mouth?"

A bark of bitter laughter had the same effect as adding vinegar to lemonade. The comment had apparently stung, but so had his. "No? Then don't assume the same of me."

A red glow, like embers, flickered in his eyes.

"Money isn't everything," she lowered her voice as a couple walked passed.

"Have you ever had to live without it?" He surged forward, pinning her between the door and his solid chest. Fury poured off him.

She refused to back down. "Yes! Right now, I have my brother's college tuition to pay by the start of fall semester. The brother I raised since he was thirteen and my parents died of cancer." She was shouting, but she didn't care.

Once the release of frustration started, she couldn't stop. "They had money. Plenty. But it didn't save them." She wiped away the tears blurring her vision. "In fact, it didn't even pay for all their medical bills. So don't tell me I don't know what it's like to live without!"

She sucked in several ragged breaths before her breathing returned to normal. Closing her eyes, she leaned against the door. Way to lose control, she sighed.

* * *

Dash stared at the silent woman before him, nothing like the volcano of anger and passion he'd watched a moment ago.

After her haughty attitude, he'd assumed she was as shallow and self-centered as everyone who entered The Last Resort.

Could he be wrong? If her claims were true, she could never learn about his past. He ran a hand through his hair.

"I'm sorry about your parents." The hardship of losing those who'd given you life and raised you was a pain he understood.

Her thick lashes rose above her moist eyes. "Thanks." She straightened. "I got a little carried away." She blushed.

The pink high in her cheeks made her appear even younger. "I hadn't noticed." He smiled.

She laughed as she stood on her tiptoes and pressed her lips to the side of his face.

Dash froze. The hard points of her breasts rubbed against his chest. His hands slipped around her waist and rested on the sweet curve of her hips.

Justice gave him a chaste kiss. "Payment for our bet."

He chuckled. "Not even close."

"You never specified what kind of kiss." She smiled.

Damn, she was smart. "Which means I can decide."

He ran his fingertips up her ribcage and along the sides of her breasts until he cupped her face. As she sucked in a breath his mouth descended on hers. He thrust his tongue inside.

A moan traveled from her mouth and into his.

Ripe and warm, he lost himself in the softness of her lips. He nibbled and dipped in and out, first with strong thrusts and then changed to a slow side of moist flesh on flesh: the same as he'd do to her pussy with his cock.

Pressing harder against him, she dug her fingers in the back of his neck dragging him closer. Her foot slid along the leg of his trousers.

He groaned and ground his cock against her softness, his only thought of burying himself inside her warm, wet pussy.

Emotions overwhelmed his senses. She not only took, but she also gave of herself. The feeling took Dash's breath away. He slid a hand over the back of her thigh and beneath the hem of her skirt. He groaned at the silkenness of her skin and at the feel of a single, firm globe of her ass cupped in his palm.

His fingers traced down the narrow silk band of the thong separating her cheeks.

A moan broke from her throat. As he stroked over the puckered rosebud of her ass, she jerked against him.

Shouts exploded inside the bar.

Dash wrenched his mouth free. Damn. Another second and he'd have taken her right there. He blew out a breath. She'd come for sex, no question.

"I think I'll have that drink." Justice turned and entered the bar on wobbly legs.

After that kiss, he needed a stiff one himself.

3

What the hell had just happened? A sizzle crackled through Justice's nerve endings. One kiss had her body hotter than an inferno. Either she'd gone far too long without sex, or Dash Wilde was that damn good.

She suspected the latter as she circumvented the maze of black tables and chairs. At the heart of the dark interior stood the bar. On the far end, a woman performed a slow striptease for a trio of men.

Warmth hissed through her veins. "Charby Vodka. Straight up." She signaled the short, gray-haired bartender.

Light gleamed off the rows of bottles packed into the two cases behind the man. The mirror reflected a dark-haired woman bent over a table, her skirt shoved above her bare ass while a hard-bodied young man fucked her from behind.

"Make it a double." She swallowed hard. The sight of sexual exhibition had turned from a shock to a turn on. Her drink arrived and she downed half. The clear liquid burned down her throat.

Scratch The Last Resort as a reception site. She was worse

off than when she'd arrived. Besides lacking a location for Charlene Dawson and therefore the source of her brother's tuition money, now her sex-starved hormones had awoken with a vengeance.

The smoky air pressed against her bare arms and legs. Without looking, she knew Dash was close by.

"I see you've passed by the requisite glass of wine to what you really want." Dash stood beside her and nodded toward the bartender.

Her mouth went dry, but she held on to her poise. "After the display of familiarity in the ball room," *and even more the kiss*, "I thought we were past formalities."

"But we aren't familiar, yet." Dash accepted a crystal tumbler with a healthy shot of Jameson Distillery Reserve. He sipped the Irish whiskey.

Mesmerized how his lips curved around the rim of the glass she stared. Muscles from his strong jaw to his throat rippled as he swallowed. An undefined raw undertone ran beneath the poised motions. She reached for a steadying shot of her drink.

"Join me." He directed her to a small covered table in a corner secluded by darkness and palm fronds.

Desire clashed with duty. Before her mind had decided, her feet followed. Annoyed with herself, she maintained her composure and slipped into the leather booth. Dash moved in behind her.

Heat radiated from his body and bathed her skin like the summer sun. Wetness collected between her legs. She shifted. "One kiss won't make me fall into bed with you."

"I don't mind giving you a second." He leaned closer.

Warm, moist breath tickled her earlobe. Trapped between his body and the deep green wall, she shivered. She'd never had a one-night stand or blown off work, both of which she was on the verge of doing. "I need to finish some work."

"What about your needs?" he whispered.

The gravelly smooth bedroom voice sent bursts of desire from the tips of her breasts to her pussy.

His solid chest pressed against her shoulder. "Your desires?"

She inhaled a quivering breath. If she tumbled from grace, Dash Wilde's bed sounded like the perfect place to land. "Are you offering *fulfillment?*"

He replied with a brush of strong fingers over her knee.

Nerves from the top of her thigh to her inner walls jerked as he slipped his hand under the hem of her skirt. She glared at Dash, who continued to slide his hand higher.

"Wandering men aren't my type."

A deep chuckle and flicker of his lips confirmed her suspicions of another side beneath his polished exterior.

"Perhaps I'm embracing the local German culture's love of wanderlust?" He stroked the edge of the panties framing her sex. "But I'd rather embrace you."

"We're in public." Her voice trembled as much as her pussy.

"Do you think anyone will notice?" He nodded toward a naked woman sitting atop the bar with a man's head buried between her spread legs, licking her cunt.

Justice shivered as he stroked the inside of her thigh. Images of Dash's tongue licking her hot, wet folds sparked in her brain.

"No one can see."

She glanced down at the long black tablecloth.

"Your needs." He slid an arm around her shoulders while his other hand brushed the silk panel over her damp curls.

Air rushed from her lungs. The aroma of whiskey and sweet campfire smoke replaced the oxygen. She had a ton of work and too much riding on Charlene Dawson's contract.

Dash wiggled a finger beneath the fabric.

Nothing would get accomplished tonight, she reasoned.

He traced the seam of her outer lips.

She gripped the table edge. A moan rolled from her core and up her throat. The bar patrons blurred.

The tip of his finger dipped inside her folds. "You're already wet." He pulled his hand away.

Before she cried out for more, he raised the digit to his mouth, eyes closed as he sucked her juices from his flesh as though sampling a gourmet meal. A burst of hot desire squeezed her walls tight. "Dash—"

"Your body knows what it wants." He returned his hand to her pussy and massaged the hood of her clit.

She couldn't stop the hard jerk of her hips against him. Sweat ran down her neck. She wanted more. Needed more.

"How long since a man brought you to orgasm?" He circled her opening. "Had his hands on your pussy?" He bit down on her earlobe.

She ground her aching cunt against the ridges of his hard knuckles, anything to relieve the pressure growing in her womb.

"Since someone's sucked your clit?" He flicked the sensitive nub.

"Ahhhhhh." Jolts rocked the tiny bundle of nerves. She gripped the table as aftershocks shook her muscles. The torment sat on the fine edge between pain and pleasure.

Her mind was too lost to answer his questions. She spread her legs wider, urging him farther in.

"How much time since a hard cock filled your tight pussy and fucked you until you screamed?"

Two long fingers plunged into her channel. Her walls clutched the long digits.

"How long?" He pulled back until only the very tips remained inside her pussy.

A wail of frustration nearly ripped free of her throat. Panting, she forced her brain to remember. "Put it this way," she twisted her neck and nipped at his jaw, "the drought's gone on so long the Red Cross setup an emergency tent."

He chuckled and thrust back inside. "No wonder you're so tight," he murmured.

"Yes." She pinched her lower lip between her teeth. Letting a man get her off in public was decadent and selfish, and at the moment she didn't care. "More."

He added a third digit. It was like being fucked with a short, thick cock. Forgotten muscles and tissues stretched accommodating his welcome intrusion.

"You came here for this." He thrust deeper. "You want freedom to explore your passion."

His words didn't make sense, but she didn't care. He could sing the ABCs so long as he used his rough bedroom voice.

"No one knows how wet you are." His free hand stroked along her neck.

She moaned. Sweat beaded on her skin. The backs of her thighs stuck to the leather seat. Each shift brought a lush sting of flesh peeling away from the material.

"No one knows I've got my fingers inside you right now making you even wetter."

The pressure around her walls tightened. She was so close.

"They can't feel your pussy squeeze with every stroke." He traced the tip of his tongue along her ear.

"Dash," she whimpered. Much more torment, and she'd cross the permanent bridge into insanity. The first fuzzy tingles of orgasm started in her belly. Still, the man beside her didn't relent.

"They can't see your hips grinding your clit against my hand."

Right then she wished she had his cock, but she couldn't find the energy to say so. Rules, composure, everything but Dash and the sensations he kindled from her body went up in smoke.

"They don't know how slick your juices feel running over my fingers."

"Close, so close," she mumbled. She rubbed the right side of her body along his solid torso. The friction of their clothing against her breast only made her need for contact with his flesh more.

"Come in my hand," he growled.

A thumb pressed on her clit. She pitched forward and gripped his forearm.

"That's right." He continued thrusting. "Pour all your sweet cream into my hand."

The spiral of heat inside her exploded. She cried out as her orgasm overtook her. Muscles clenched all at once.

Rocking against his hand, she rode the climax to its peak. Moisture poured from her channel, washing over his fingers. Red and gold sparks popped behind her closed eyes.

Justice leaned her limp body into Dash's. Slowly her mind returned. Her problems hadn't disappeared, but her tension had certainly eased. "Your customer service is first rate." She winked.

Dash smiled. "It's our pleasure."

"No, the pleasure was definitely mine." Too spent to move, she allowed him to readjust her panties and skirt.

"Fulfilling our customers' desires is our priority." He pulled a small circular case from his pocket.

The object looked like a pocket watch, but the golden lid blocked her view. Creases lined his forehead. "Problem?"

His lightning blue gaze snapped up. "Everything is back to normal."

"If *normal* is a man kneeling on the bar while a woman gives him a blow job." She sipped her abandoned drink.

A deep chuckle rumbled through his chest.

The sound sent a lush shiver down her spine. Strong arms, long, talented fingers, and a square jaw: Dash was her type of man. He had the right personality: quick wit, social poise, and a hard edge beneath. Damn if her timing in meeting him wasn't wrong.

The bell captain, Robert, approached their table. He gave her a smile before whispering in Dash's ear.

She couldn't hear the words, but by the hardness spreading over Dash's face and his narrowed eyes, the information wasn't good. He murmed a reply.

Robert snapped straight and made a beeline for the frosted bar doors.

Dash turned toward her. "It appears there's a problem—"

"I can guess—No, actually I probably can't." She took another drink. This was good. No awkward conversation and no temptation to extend her craziness and take a *tour* of one of the rooms. Still, the pull to stay tugged harder.

She couldn't. "Go." She waved her hand, using all her self discipline to do so.

Dash rose, his jaw set. "Enjoy the rest of your stay." Hard words squeezed out between his thinned lips as he wheeled.

"No, I—" *didn't mean it like that.* She sighed. "Great."

The doors swung open and golden light from the lobby invaded the shadowed interior. Her gaze slid toward the brightness, half hoping to find Dash Wilde's tall figure striding back through the swirls of smoke.

Instead, the arrogant football player from the ballroom entered and headed for her. *Oh shit.* Her pulse beat faster.

"Baby, I've been waitin' to get you all night," he drawled and slid into the booth trapping her.

"I'd hate to break your streak." She glared, ready to climb over the table if needed.

Dash snapped his fingers and the blood vanished from the lobby floor. Cleaning up others' messes heated his boiling blood. He'd gotten Justice Malloy off, controlled her body, and yet had been dismissed like a powerless servant.

Footfalls echoed across the marble floor.

He recognized his bell captain's uneven gate. "Has the *guest* been secured?"

"Yes, sir."

Another snap and the splintered table in the main hallway flew back together. "Good." Every gathering, one or more soulless went too far. Providing the damned with their final indulgences included everything except harming a wanton.

"Make sure that bloody son of a bitch stays in dungeon—" His accent had slipped out. He clenched his teeth.

"Yes, sir." Robert remained.

"Something else?" He glared in the bell captain's direction.

"Mr. Wilde, are you sure it's a good idea leaving the lady in there alone?" Robert nodded toward the bar.

Dash didn't need to ask which *lady* as he stalked to the front desk. "She's just like everyone else here," he growled.

The moral compass had indicated lust by the narrowest of margins, but her brush off showed her true colors. Rich. Spoiled. A selfish bastard, like him.

"She's different." Robert shook his head.

He stopped. Never had the man dared argue. "Since when do you like women?" His eyes burned as he stared at his female-hating bell captain.

"I don't." He bristled.

"She's here for sex." Let someone serve her wants. He clenched his fists at the thought.

What did he care what or who Justice did so long as she never learned the secret of The Last Resort.

He didn't have time to babysit. He had guests to see to, or rather see they didn't tear the hotel apart.

A piercing scream ripped from inside the bar.

He didn't need two centuries' experience to differentiate the sharp cries of pleasure and terror.

Dash's heart stopped. He knew the feminine voice without question.

Fuck.

He shot toward the bar. Once more his anger and selfish hurt had put someone innocent at risk. He just hoped this time his selfishness hadn't cost Justice her life.

Adrenaline pumped through his limbs. He had to stop the incident before the other damned descended like sharks. He slammed the bar door, shattering the glass.

In two seconds, he found Justice. The bastard football player had her trapped in a corner. She put up a hell of a fight, but her strength was no match.

Anger seared his muscles. He shot forward, shoving aside anyone in his path. "Let go," he growled and grabbed the back of the man's collar. He yanked him out of the booth.

The asshole spun around and swung.

A fist caught Dash on the jaw. Pain exploded over the right side of his face as his head snapped the opposite direction. Someone screamed.

"That's what you get." The man stuck his thick face in Dash's. "You touch me again, and I'll—"

"Wrong choice, boy-o." Dash threw a punch to his opponent's head.

The man staggered, but didn't fall.

His shirt was pulled tight as the football player jerked him forward. Rage drove his fist into his opponent's gut and sent the athlete flying backward.

The victory was short lived.

The man charged, slamming Dash into the wood paneling. Pain exploded in the back of his head and down his spine.

"Do you know who I am?" the football player shouted.

Flecks of saliva spattered Dash.

"Nobody puts their hands on me," he shouted, and reached for Justice.

Dash launched his body forward, and his shoulder into the

arrogant bastard's stomach. "Run." He spared a single quick glance at Justice.

He threw the man across the tabletops. Glass crashed. Patrons screamed. Fire spread through his insides faster than ever. A half a dozen more jabs were rewarded with a sharp crack of a nose breaking. He didn't let up.

As much as he hated the son of a bitch, he hated himself more. The compass said Justice didn't belong, but he hadn't believed it. It was his fault the motherfucker had gotten his hands on her. He threw a knuckle bruising punch to the kidney. Groaning the man doubled over.

Robert burst through the remains of the bar doors.

"Lock him up, now." Dash shoved the bloody athlete toward the bell captain.

The bar patrons remained frozen, staring.

"Everything's fine." He snapped his fingers and the broken room returned to its former state.

At the change, people returned to their drinks and sex.

As he headed out, he noted his glowing red eyes in the bar mirror. Nothing he could do about them now.

Straightening his tie, he rushed through the door into the lobby. Justice headed for the door. Damn. He ignored the pain in his back and throbbing skull. "Wait."

She glanced back and slowed a fraction.

"You can't leave!" he shouted, and quickened his pace. He had to get to her before she headed for the door.

"Just watch me." She sprinted for the entrance.

Dash stopped. Closing his eyes waited for the inevitable. Beyond the last set of columns, every step Justice Malloy took, the door drew farther and farther away.

"No!" She ran faster, never making any progress. "Let me out." She whirled on him. Tears gleamed in her brown eyes. "I want to leave!"

Knots wound his shoulders. "You can't." He limped forward. "Not until midnight on Sunday."

She shook her head. With her pale skin and curls she resembled a frightened child.

A long forgotten instinct to cradle her in his arms the way he had once soothed his two younger sisters awakened.

"No, I want to go now." Her wide gaze swung between him to the door.

"I would if I could, but no one can." He let out a breath.

"What do you mean?" She swallowed and calmed a fraction.

"This isn't any ordinary hotel."

"Where am I?" She skittered backward.

A trickle of blood dripped down his chin. He wiped it away and stared at the bright red streak on his hand. Justice's face faded into those of his long-dead siblings.

His chest squeezed. He'd killed them with his selfish desire for revenge.

He sagged against the pillar. So caught up in protecting his lost soul, he'd almost cost a woman her life. Guilt burned from his stomach up his throat.

"What is this place?" She stalked up to him, her heels snapping on the marble.

Everything in his nature shouted for him to lie. He resisted and took a deep breath. He owed her the truth, even if the revelation ended his chances to regain his soul.

"Let me get this blood off and I'll tell you."

4

Dash froze. Had he just agreed to tell Justice Malloy the truth? She deserved answers. But he still didn't know how or why the woman had arrived at The Last Resort.

Several people emerged from the lobby bar and eyed Justice. "What does the lamb say to escaping the lions?" he murmured, and wiped a fresh stream of blood from the corner of his mouth.

She glanced toward the crowd. "Am I trading one den of beasts for another?"

Fear still cast shadows in her wide brown eyes, but her calm returned. "Worried you'll be devoured, or worse, that you won't?"

"What makes you think I want it?" Her brows rose as she stepped inside the elevator.

He pressed the button for the ninth floor and leaned closer. "Oh, you want it." The smell of her curls and skin, like ripe strawberries, made his mouth water. "You proved just how much in the bar."

Her breath quickened.

The thought of his fingers splayed into her wet pussy tightened his chest and cock. "Or had you forgotten?"

A sharp jerk yanked his head downward.

"No. I haven't." She wrapped his tie around her wrist. "Nor your promise for answers."

Dash met her fierce gaze. While he admired her ballsy move, he noted her trembling hand.

"Don't play with me," she said.

He bit back a grin. Play was exactly what he wanted, but not in the manner she assumed. "You don't mean that."

"Mr. Wilde—"

"Dash, since we're already on intimate terms." The heat from her breath warmed his skin. With his mouth so close to hers, he could almost taste the vodka on her lips.

"Your hands in my pants doesn't make us intimate," she snapped as the elevator stopped and the gilt cage rose.

"But it does make us more than strangers." He unwrapped his tie from her fingers. Their steps thunked against the wood floor as they walked down the long cream hallway.

He pulled a large brass key from his coat pocket and opened the last room at the end of the long hall.

"Where are we?" She inched over the threshold, ahead of him.

Dash hesitated. He'd never brought a guest to his private suite. "My home."

He snapped his fingers and a fire sprung to life in the parlor grate.

She jumped. "How did you do that?"

A slight tremor shook her voice. The knowledge he had caused her distress tugged at gut. He dropped the key on the walnut table behind the old fashioned green settee. "Come, my child, and you shall hear."

"You'd better hope I'm over eighteen or you'll be thrown in jail."

An acid laugh broke from his lips. "What makes you think I'm not already?" Without a backward glance, he walked into the bathroom.

The first of the two granite sinks filled with hot water. Sore muscles protested as he stripped off his ruined jacket. The silk hit the marble floor as his tossed cuff links bounced along the vanity.

A purple bruise darkened his left cheek beneath the dried blood. He caught Justice's reflection in the mirror.

"Nice." Her gaze swept over the walk-in shower encompassing the entire back of the bathroom, but stopped on the oversized sunken bathtub behind him. "Bandages?" She turned toward him.

He pointed to the cabinet under the sink and unbuttoned his shirt. More than once he caught Justice stealing looks. She was still interested. He hid a gun.

"You talk and I'll doctor." She lined up a collection of gauze and antiseptic.

"Now who wants to play games?" He smiled as she gingerly sat on the vanity.

"Fine. Let's start with twenty questions." She dunked a washcloth in the sink. "Where am I and why can't I leave?"

Dash let out a slow breath. In their verbal one-upmanship, he almost forgot the promise to tell her the truth. Tightness in no way related to his injuries seized his muscles.

"What I'm about to tell you can never be repeated." He grabbed her hands and forced her to look him in the eye.

"Why?" She swallowed.

"Never," he growled. Flames burst under his skin. She jerked, but he held tight. Damn. Being honest was harder than he remembered.

He took a deep breath. "I'll die."

Her eyes widened as realization glowed.

"Do you believe in the concept of an immortal soul?" He

paused, waiting for her nod as much as to steady his voice. "Whenever the number of damned souls reaches a critical level, this hotel appears. The damned and those seeking sexual freedom are drawn here for forty-eight hours of indulgence." He waited for her nod before continuing. At the end, the wantons leave with no memory and the damned are . . ."

Justice ceased wiping the blood from his face. "*Damned*, as in Hell?"

He nodded.

The rag fell from her hand to the marble floor with a slap. She backed away, her face as pale as her hair. "You're the devil?"

"No, not *The Devil*." Her muscles relaxed. "But I am *a* devil, now."

"That's impossible." But her shrill laughter said otherwise.

"Is it?" He folded his arms in front of him. "How do you explain the door retreating?"

"Special effects." She threw up her hands.

Easy explanations didn't exist any more than the rationale she sought. "What about the lack of cars on the road driving here?"

"Wouldn't traffic jams be more your—I mean hellish?" She gave a weak smile.

"You tell me." He snapped his fingers and a vodka rocks appeared on the vanity beside her.

Seconds ticked by and with each one he expected her to bolt from the room screaming. Little by little the fear in her brown eyes lightened.

She reached for the drink grimacing as she swallowed. "But you weren't always a devil?"

"No." He shook his head and leaned against the cool mirror.

"How did you—"

He glared.

"Forget I asked." She stooped and retrieved the washcloth.

He closed his eyes. No one except The Devil knew the details of their bargain. He hated himself enough without adding Justice's. As much as she'd sacrificed for her family, she'd never understand or permit him to protect her.

"I won't hurt you."

She touched her soft fingers to the side of his face. His cock filled and he was thankful she didn't notice.

"I believe you." She caressed his cheek.

Several seconds passed before her words sunk in. He blew out a sharp breath. The water in the basin turned red as she dunked the cloth.

"How do you know who is who?" She wrung out the excess.

"Meaning, are you going to Hell or a wanton?"

A tight smile stretched her shaky lips.

He had the urge to laugh, but resisted. How could a woman, who was devoted to her dead parents, to caring for her brother, and who raised money for charities, think herself damned? "With this." He dug in his pants pocket and pulled out the compass.

"A moral compass?" She gave a small laugh.

The melody was as sweet as any he'd ever heard his mother sing as a babe. He grinned. "We have a hell of a sense of humor."

"What does it say about me?" She scooted closer until her bare shoulder brushed his chest.

Nerve endings buzzed at the contact. "Undecided with a touch of wanton." He showed her the needle so she'd see he spoke the truth.

"So in two days I can leave." Her eyes closed and the tension drained from her rigid spine. "Has this ever happened?"

"Only once." He clenched the metal device.

"What happened?"

"Nothing, if the little fucker hadn't written a hit song about it," he muttered. By sheer luck, the tune had come out in the seventies and everyone blamed too many drugs for the wild idea.

"You mean . . ." She let out a low whistle and dabbed ointment over his cuts. "How did I end up here?"

"If I knew the answer to that . . ." He patted the cut at the side of his mouth.

"Finished." She stowed the arsenal of medical supplies away. "Why didn't you just snap your fingers for this like everything else?" She glanced up from beneath the cabinet. "For that matter, why not just magic me out of here?"

He'd rather magic her to his bed. The heat in his groin flared. "I can control objects, not people."

"Free will?" She dusted off her hands.

"Yes, and unbreakable rules." He was surprised she understood, but then, Justice Malloy was a surprising woman. He stood and led her to the parlor. "But I can do something else."

"Oh." Her tongue slipped over her lower lip. "What's that?"

"Get you off." He stared at her long legs and the points of her tight nipples beneath her top.

"I think you already did that." She sauntered closer.

"Once isn't nearly enough." Already he wanted his hands stroking her soft skin.

"For whom?" She stood in front of him. "Me? Or you?"

"Maybe both." He snapped his fingers and a silver charger appeared on the narrow table beside them.

She swept her gaze over the dark green and brown antique furniture. "Not what I'd expect."

Warmth crept into his cheeks. The old fashioned style from his days as a mortal suddenly made him feel foolish. He pressed his thumb to his pinkie to change the décor. A hand wrapped around his, stopping him from snapping his fingers.

"Don't." She squeezed. "This is your home, you shouldn't change it for me."

He simply nodded. Not one of the women he'd taken to bed

had ever protested him catering to every preference. A warm, fuzzy sensation filled his stomach.

In that moment, he wanted to do something for Justice.

"How am I ever going get any work done?" She rubbed her temples and groaned.

"I can offer you Internet access, but no e-mail or phone."

"Thanks." She gazed at the dancing fire. "I can't take time for myself right now. My brother is depending on me."

"There will always be someone who needs something." He reached out and turned her face toward his. "What about you?" He stroked her delicate jaw. "You can't go anywhere."

"True." She bit her lip. "And it is late at night." Her tight shoulders dipped, relaxing.

He was making progress. He uncovered the tray, revealing fresh strawberries and a dish of dark melted chocolate. "You're not going to refuse and say you're on a diet?"

She arched an eyebrow. "Wouldn't that be against the rules of forty-eight hours of indulgence?"

"If not, I can make it one." He smiled.

Justice plucked a berry from the tray and swirled the fruit in the melted chocolate. As her teeth sank into the bright red skin, her eyes closed and she moaned. "Delicious."

Yes, she was, with her head thrown back and her neck exposed. His cock hardened.

"You should try some," she said, taking another bite.

Dash lowered his head to hers and licked the rich confection from her mouth. She gasped and put a hand to his chest. "Mmm. You're right." He lapped at the confection coating her sweet lips.

"I think I need another taste," she said.

He stared as she dunked another berry and brought the dripping delicacy to his chest. His breath hitched.

Screw waiting. He wanted her right then. He didn't question

the need. Another second and he'd knock the tray over and take her right there.

A trail of warm, thick liquid spread down his sternum as Justice dragged the fruit along his skin. His heart pounded as he waited for her next move.

"Oh, did I spill some on you?" Hungry mischief danced in her deep brown gaze.

"A little." His voice thickened.

"Let me clean up the mess." She pressed her mouth to the top of his rib cage and licked the confection from his body.

Fire ravaged his skin. Her delicate pink lips moved against him like satin. Dash grabbed her hips and pulled her pussy against his throbbing cock.

"Mmm." She smiled. "This tastes much better."

He thrust his hands beneath her skirt and along the outside of her hips. She gasped and a rush of warm, moist breath washed over his stomach. Small, blunt teeth nipped at his flesh. "Ahhh," he groaned.

"Should I stop?"

The little tease damn well knew the answer. *"Fuck no!"*

Justice giggled, a decidedly playful sound that suited her. He cupped the firm globes of her ass in his palms, massaging the pliant muscles while she feasted on him.

Breaking his hold, she traveled lower.

The closer her mouth came to his cock the harder he got. His balls pulled tight. Her innocent curls and white outfit made the sight of her wicked torment all the hotter.

She worked her way down his body. The flat of her tongue laved across his stomach.

His abs contracted. The tips of her fingers slid inside the waist of his trousers. His cock jerked. One glimpse of her lips swallowing his hard shaft and he was done.

Grabbing her beneath her arms, he hauled her up, crushing

her against him. He kissed her. Chocolate and salt from his skin flooded his taste buds.

Arms encircled his neck as Justice's tongue met his stroke for stroke. The hard pressure hurt like a bitch against his cuts, but he didn't care. Nothing did except having more of her.

"I wasn't finished," she breathed against his cheek.

"I haven't even gotten started."

5

Justice stared into Dash's burning gaze. Guilt crept like the rays of dawn through cracks in a shade. She should be searching for a reception site and securing her brother's tuition. But, logistically, she couldn't.

Since she was stuck in the hotel, why not enjoy herself, and Dash Wilde? Her gaze skimmed the muscles outlining his bare chest. "What did you have in mind?"

A slow smile curved his lips. The fireplace's orange-red glow snaked over the hard planes of his cheeks and torso.

"Wouldn't you rather I showed you?" He never took his eyes off her.

Excitement snaked along her nerve endings. She hid the effect of his statement behind a skeptical arched eyebrow. "I'd say it depends on what's on display."

"You."

Before she could reply, he swept her up in his arms and headed for the bedroom. Solid male flesh surrounded her. Even if she refused, she couldn't escape Dash. Her vulnerability heightened her anticipation.

The knot of desire in her belly pulled tighter. With a snap of Dash's fingers, the double doors to the master bedroom suite swung open.

A high post bed dominated the center of the room. The dark wood furniture and the deep green and navy décor marked it as a masculine domain. Sheer cream curtains covered French doors on the far left side of the room.

Dash didn't say a word as he moved with intense purpose. She glanced upward at the midnight blue painted plaster. "What, no mirrors on the ceiling?" she joked.

A snap broke the silence and a glass sheet appeared above them. She chuckled until she looked closer. The reflection showed Dash's strong, sleek back, muscles she'd yet to explore.

"Like to watch?" he whispered as he stopped beside the bed.

The shock of the gravelly smooth voice in her ear made her jump. She quickly recovered. "If there's something worth watching."

"Oh, there will be." He continued holding her.

"I could've walked."

"You're very capable of helping others." He buried his nose in her curls.

"Thank you—"

"When did you last help yourself?" He raised his head pinning her with his unexpected question.

For the life of her, she couldn't think of a single recent occasion.

"Uh-huh." He smiled as he set her down beside the bed. "Do you have the guts to let someone see to your needs?"

He pulled her top over her head and unzipped her skirt before she could answer. "Aren't I doing that now?" She stood clad in only her white silk thong.

Dash's nostrils flared. "No." He trailed one finger down the valley between her breasts. "Have you ever given up control?

Put your pleasure and yourself completely at someone else's mercy?"

She shivered, not from cold, but from the heat of his touch. No, she hadn't. The idea of submission had never had much appeal, but Dash's hypnotic voice had her reassessing her opinion.

"And what about you?" She licked her lower lip. "Where is your pleasure?" His blue eyes flashed wide. She unfastened his pants.

"This isn't about me." He pulled her hands away. "It is about you."

His dodging told her more than any answer. No one had. Sadness filled her chest. Although Dash was a devil, he'd shown her kindness.

He lifted her onto the bed, and gently pushed her back. With a snap of his fingers, black silk scarves appeared and bound her wrists to the headboard.

She tugged against the restraints.

"Relax," he whispered in her ear in the ragged bedroom voice she loved. "Submit." He pinched her lobe between his teeth.

She cried out and arched off the bed at the sensation of his warm mouth engulfing her ear. He claimed he didn't possess any influence over free will, but Justice swore he had magic in his voice. Why else would she agree to his demands?

"I can do anything I want to you." He cupped a breast. "With you." He released her flesh to stroke her wet pussy. "And you can't stop me." His lips hovered over hers.

Her pulse raced. He was right. Warm breath fanned her mouth and chin. Feeling vulnerable and exposed, she let her excitement eclipse her fear.

A snap, and the tray of strawberries and chocolate appeared on the nightstand. Her gaze swept from the food to Dash. Tremors rippled through her nerve endings as she lay in wait.

"How does it feel?" He brushed his thumb along her breast.

"Maddening," she said through her pinched lips.

He chuckled and stripped off the scrap of silk masquerading as her panties.

He plucked a strawberry and slid the berry along her lips. The cool skin was heaven to her parched mouth. She bit down, spilling the sweet juices on her chin and down her neck.

Dash's mouth crashed down on hers. Tart fruit, whiskey, and the taste of him mixed together. He sucked on her lower lip. She moaned as he bit at her swollen flesh.

The tip of his tongue swept up the thin line of pink juice on her chin. "So perfect." His hot, moist caress slipped down her neck. "So sweet." He lapped at the liquid in the hollow of her throat.

Her grip tightened on her black silk bindings. "Oh." She wanted her fingers in his hair urging him closer, but the scarves stopped her. Arching her head back to give him greater access to her neck was her sole means of encouragement.

Desire sank from her belly to her womb.

"Look up," he ordered, as he shed his pants and stretched out beside her.

As she raised her gaze, she saw his skin, hot and solid, against her. A long, hard cock pressed against her outer thigh. With a groan she turned in the direction, but a hand against her cheek stopped her.

Her earlier assessment of his sleek, solid muscles didn't do the physique in the reflection credit. Cords of sinew outlined his thighs and calves. She tried to reach but couldn't.

"Damn." She glared at the ties.

"Like what you see?" He trailed the half-bitten strawberry down the side of her neck closest to him.

"I'd like to touch more," she grumbled.

"In time." He blew over the wet trail of fruit juice.

She shivered. "What about you?" She dared shift her gaze from the ceiling to the man beside her.

"You're the most incredible sight I've ever seen," he breathed.

It was likely a line, but Justice couldn't help the thrill that shot through her. He sucked at her neck with his warm mouth and she forgot everything else. The simple contrast between hot and cold made her squirm.

"I see soft, pale skin." He dragged the fruit over her collarbone and suckled.

Her muscles tightened, and she arched her shoulders off the mattress. More. She needed the weight of his body atop hers.

"Tastes like strawberries." He nipped at her flesh. "Sweet and ripe."

A small mew escaped her lips. Oh, God! His voice and words had moisture coating her pussy. Her empty channel clenched.

"Such pretty, full breasts." He took a bite of fruit so the juices escaping his lips rained down over the tight nipple of her right breast.

"Ah." She came off the bed so hard and fast she feared her spine might break. "Dash?" She rolled her head toward him.

A wicked grin stretched across his face. "This is what I want." With his thumb he spread the liquid around and over the peak. "You helpless in the face of your own passion."

She couldn't find any words or make her mouth move. He'd exposed her and now she was at his mercy.

"I want you helpless before me."

The statement should have sparked her anger, but didn't. A part of her craved the freedom of allowing someone else to be in control and care for her. But, she'd never admit it to Dash.

"And you want it, too," he growled in her ear. "Don't you?"

Damn. Did the man read minds? She pressed her lips together.

"You want to be taken." He dragged his lips along her temple. "You want my mouth on your nipples." He snagged another berry and dripped more chilled juice over the stiff point.

She cried out.

"The tighter your nipples get, the more they say you want this. "But you have to depend on me to get it."

Every word was true.

"Say it." He flicked the tip of his tongue over the tormented point.

"Yes," Justice screamed. "Yes!" She expected him to laugh or somehow revel in the power, but all he did was lift her breast to his lips.

The moment his mouth made contact she gasped. Above, she stared at the line of muscles along his back as they flexed.

The same image showed his eyes closed in pleasure as his mouth moved over her breast. A surge of desire rocked her. At the same time that his tongue circled her nipple, she witnessed the bold act. The combination of sight and touch fanned an unexpected and erotic mix.

She arched toward his mouth.

His lids lifted revealing eyes bluer than the brightest Texas summer sky. Her breath caught. "More, please."

With a smile he took her throbbing nipple in his mouth. Justice gave herself over to him as he suckled the fallen fruit juice. Each pull on the bud sent shocks straight to her pussy. At this rate, she'd come long before his cock ever filled her . . .

With his other hand he pinched the opposite nipple and tugged, simulating the movements of his mouth on the other. She couldn't take much more.

"Mmm." He raised his head and licked his lips. "But it's missing something."

The only things missing as far as she was concerned were her ability to touch him and his thick, hard cock moving deep inside her pussy.

"Dash." As she struggled against her ties, he moved an overflowing spoon of dark chocolate over her.

Was he—Her gaze shot to his. Wicked torment burned in

the hot coals of his pupils. She watched in the mirror as a stream of warm chocolate drizzled over her breasts and down her belly.

"Much better," he murmured, as he smeared the chocolate on her stomach.

"Don't stop." She didn't even recognize the thin voice as her own.

"I want to taste all of you."

Her pussy quivered at the possibility of such a talented mouth focused on it. "No one's stopping you."

He laughed. "But I prefer to go slow." To emphasize his words he licked the stream of chocolate between her breasts with one long stroke.

Writhing beneath him, she couldn't argue.

"I like to savor my meal."

When was the last time anyone had *savored* her? Or had they ever? Once more, she stared upward as Dash dragged his tongue over her breasts. With each stroke, the dark, sticky sweetness he'd spilled on her disappeared.

When he'd all but lapped her top half clean, he slid down to her belly. With the tip of his finger, he smeared more sauce over her abdomen.

Her hips thrust closer. The ache in her empty pussy cried out for him.

"Not yet."

A frustrated scream built in her throat.

He trailed kisses to the edge of her curls, but, when relief appeared inevitable, he swept higher. She gripped the scarves. Her fingers had long ago gone numb, unlike the rest of her body.

His tongue circled the small pool of chocolate in her navel before drinking the liquid.

Desire pressed harder around her channel. Her toes curled into the bedding. Crawling up her body, Dash kissed her: hard, and demanding. She tasted candy, fruit, and hunger. As he pulled away, she stretched to hold on to the connection.

When she glanced at him, she saw he held another strawberry. She held her breath. Silently she pleaded for him to focus on the part of her that was wet, and had been ignored too long.

The cool, prickly skin of the berry slid over the top of her thigh. Silently she begged for him to double back. He slowly caressed the inside. She spread her legs wider and waited for relief to reach her pussy.

"So wet," he murmured. "Pink and sweet. Just like a berry."

Her channel clenched . . . fingers, tongue, she didn't care, so long as Dash filled the tortured space. "Maybe you should eat it and find out for sure."

"Perhaps I will."

She sighed.

"One day."

"What?" She jerked up against her ties.

Dash laughed and gently pressed her into the feather pillows. "Anxious for my mouth on you?"

"Yes," she groaned.

He dragged the chilled fruit over her outer lips.

She gasped at the coldness against her heat.

"This isn't enough for you." He used the tip of the berry to part her damp folds and sweep between them. "You want my tongue like this."

Unable to speak, she nodded. The swell of pressure lifted her hips. Every spot he touched tingled.

"My tongue deep inside your pussy." He pressed the narrow end of the strawberry against her opening. "Like this."

"Yes," she screamed. Sweat covered her skin and she felt as though her body was on fire. When she pried her eyes open, she noticed the tight set of Dash's jaw and the beads of perspiration dotting his forehead.

At this rate he'd drive them both insane. How could he withstand this torture?

"This is what I want." He barely dipped the fruit inside, coating the berry in her juices. "I love strawberries and cream."

She froze as he brought the fruit to his mouth and bit into the red, tender flesh. His lids fluttered closed as he savored the flavor.

A dribble of liquid landed on her pussy and oh-so-slowly slid down. All her muscles clenched simultaneously. "Dash!"

His eyes, now a dark blue, opened. "Here." He brought the treat to her mouth. "Taste what I do."

The half of a strawberry glided along her lower lip. Without thought, her tongue flicked out.

"Damn." He grunted and air rushed from his lungs. "Taste how sweet you are." He teased her mouth once more. "Know when my head is between your legs and my mouth is on your pussy what I'm drinking."

Uncontrollable tremors shook her. His touch and the sensual description in his rough voice were too much. The tension reached her teeth and they chattered as she stretched for the treat he now held between his lips.

The familiar tart flavor of the fruit along with the musk from her slick walls hit her taste buds. Dash's tongue plunged inside. Together they reveled as they shared the flavor of their desire.

She rubbed the tips of her breasts against his chest as their tongues twined and filled each other's mouths. How she wanted to touch him! She yanked her arms as hard as possible, but the silk didn't budge.

"Now, you're ready." His breath was ragged.

"I passed ready a long time ago," she whined before she could stop herself.

He smiled. "But it didn't count until I said it." He slid lower on the bed until he lay between her spread legs.

Justice stared down her naked body to where his face hovered above her pussy. After so many close calls, she held her breath, afraid a single movement would cause him to stop once again.

The flicker of the shadows and the soft breeze through the French doors faded. Nothing existed except Dash.

In slow motion, his head lowered to her pussy. At the first touch of his tongue on her deprived folds, she screamed.

"You taste better than I imagined." He breathed in her scent.

She hooked one leg over his broad shoulder and pressed the heel of her other foot to his back encouraging him to return.

"So plump and ready." He flicked his tongue clockwise around her clit and then reversed directions.

The long awaited contact was heaven and hell: heaven because the attention was exactly what she wanted, hell because the pressure and friction wasn't strong enough. "More."

Dash complied and soon the flat of his tongue parted her nether lips.

New moisture trickled along her inner walls and out onto his greedy, waiting taste buds. She wound her other leg around his side and, in the process, spread herself farther for him.

"That's it, let me have your pussy."

"Yes." She ground against the thumb massaging the hood over her clit. At this point, she'd give him any damn thing he wanted so long as he released the climax screaming for freedom.

He dipped his tongue inside her vacant walls.

She cried out at the flutter and her muscles squeezed. Frustration welled up as he drew back, but satisfaction and two thick fingers quickly replaced the feeling.

He twisted and worked them in and out of her as he circled the base of her tiny clit with his tongue.

The welcome ball of pressure coiled tight and readied for the explosion. A strong tingle rumbled low in her core. The moment he sucked her bud hard inside his mouth, she exploded.

"Dash!" His name tore from her lips. Her body jerked upward as tremors flew through her limbs all at once. His mouth and fingers didn't stop. They continued working her channel until every drop of her orgasm poured free.

On the final shudder, her muscles gave out and she collapsed on the comforter. Behind the buzz in her ears beat her rapid heart.

Beside her, Dash crawled back up her body. With him lying beside her, his hard cock pressed against her outer thigh.

She felt she should say something, thank him, but words floated away like smoke. Turning and kissing him hard was the best she could do.

"You're amazing."

A waver broke his voice and took her by surprise. Easily it was the best orgasm she'd ever had, but she hadn't thought Dash would feel similarly. The possibility gave her a strong sense of sexual power.

"Do you know what's next?" He covered her with his hard body.

"Untying me?" she tried. He chuckled and kissed her. The taste of her orgasm still clung to his mouth.

"Now, I want to know how you feel coming around my cock while I'm buried deep inside you."

The thick tip nudged her entrance. Sensitive, she jerked against him and whimpered. The man might kill her with pleasure, but what a way to go.

He balanced his weight on his forearms. In the mirror, she watched the tendons along his shoulders and back rise. She cursed the silk that prevented her from running her hands down the muscles.

"I want you inside me." She shifted her gaze back to his. Dark and light blue swirled like clouds in his eyes. "I want your cock now."

With a groan, he thrust inside her pussy.

The sudden fullness drove the air from her lungs. "Oh—" A full year had passed since she'd had any man's cock inside her. Tissue burned and stretched around his hard, thick cock.

"Damn, you're tight." A drop of sweat fell from his forehead and onto her neck.

Fullness overtook her. Once more, she wrapped her legs around his waist.

"Want more?" Wickedness gleamed in his eyes.

"Yes." She shifted her pelvis and drew him in deeper. Her muscles gripped his thick shaft, determined to hold on to him.

"Like this?" he growled. He slid back in her channel and slowly pushed forward.

"More." Hard and smooth, he moved through her wetness with ease. This time, he pulled back until only his thick tip remained inside her opening. Before she could tell him to stop, he slammed forward. "Oh, yes."

The friction from the head of his long cock bumping against her womb was exactly what she wanted. She ground her hips against him. The coarse hairs of his groin rubbed against her delicate clit.

"Harder." The fabric around her wrists twisted and tightened. She didn't care. The only feelings that mattered were those Dash created in her pussy.

He obliged and thrust into her with short, firm strokes.

The taut muscles in his ass and thighs gleamed with sweat as they contracted.

"Fuck me harder," she wailed. Tension wound tighter around her channel and she squeezed him.

"Hell." He shoved his hands under her hips and tilted them upwards. "You want me to fuck your pussy hard."

"Yes." Her head thrashed from side to side on the pillow.

Dash rose like a dark, powerful being and towered over her. Moisture ran down the ridges of his taut belly. Teeth gritted, he focused on her as he pistoned his cock.

Harder and harder, each stroke sank him farther and farther inside her. Then, with one hard slam, everything exploded. "Dash," she screamed and everything went black.

The high-pitched sound of Justice's pleasure ripped away the last of Dash's control. He buried his cock as deep as possible and launched his seed into her quivering womb before collapsing on top of her.

A few moments later, when movement returned to his body, he pulled himself up enough to check on the woman beneath him, eyes closed and kiss-swollen lips half parted, she slept. His chest tightened at the beauty and trust in her content features.

He carefully slipped from her warm, tight pussy. What the hell did he do now? He glanced around the dim, quiet room. All the times he'd fucked women before he'd gone to their rooms and left afterward.

Well, he sure as hell wasn't leaving. He could move her to another room, but her safety remained an issue . . .

He snapped his fingers and released her hands.

She rolled to her side and snuggled against him. His heart stopped. He watched in fascination as her small hand slid across his chest.

The hardness around his heart cracked. Even after she'd received her pleasure she still wanted to be near him. He didn't want her to leave.

But she would, in another twenty-four hours.

His lungs seized with a fear he hadn't felt since . . . since he became a devil. He swallowed against the strangle hold. The chaotic evening and shock of an uninvited guest was at fault. Nothing more.

6

"I see you found your bath." Dash smiled as he stood in the bathroom threshold gazing at Justice's wet skin peeking from beneath the bubbles.

"I did." She scooted lower in the sunken tub. "Thank you."

"My pleasure," he murmured, never taking his eyes off her. The fuzzy sensation of last night returned to his stomach. It was not a feeling he had any business dwelling on. He cleared his throat.

"There's a laptop with a wireless Internet connection in the parlor whenever you're ready." He nodded behind him. "I have—work to do."

"No rest for the wicked?" She arched a pale eyebrow and grinned.

He let out a genuine laugh for the first time in years, and one at his own existence, of all things. "You didn't figure that out last night?"

"Perhaps you can remind me." She crooked a finger and urged him closer.

Twelve hours ago the same gesture would have pissed him

off. Now, he recognized her playfulness. The reality knocked his legs from under him and he sat on the tub ledge.

He'd only known the names of the other women he'd fucked at the hotel. At least most of them he knew. Already he had learned about Justice's family, her work, her body.

She reached up and cupped his cheek.

At the touch of her wet flesh, he groaned. "Now who's being wicked?"

She sat up. The heat of the water had puckered her skin. Crystalline bubbles clung to her breasts. Tiny pop-pops of suds interrupted their ragged breathes. The scent of the roses scattered over the bubbles filled the room.

"You're welcome to do anything you like while I'm gone, but do not leave this suite." His voice hardened. The thought of another guest harming her turned his insides to ice. "It's not safe."

She nodded.

"If you need something, call down to Robert."

A small shiver rippled through her shoulders. "Why was I the only one attacked?"

He brushed a damp curl from her cheek. "Those who've killed their souls can sense yours and are drawn to it."

"Not for good reasons?" She glanced up.

He shook his head. "What—" he took a deep breath, "happened last night was my fault."

"No." Her wet curls threw droplets at him and across the black marble ledge.

The denial was kind, but he knew the truth. "I shouldn't have left you alone. It's a mistake I won't make it again." He had never meant a promise more in his life.

"I have no desire to go exploring, at least not as far as the hotel goes." Her hungry gaze slid down his body.

"Good." The tight knots in his muscles unwound. Until the tension left he hadn't realized the extent of his worry. "You're welcome to anything you'd like here, but *never* open the door next to the bathroom."

The corners of her mouth turned down. "Why? What's in—"

"Because you bloody can't," he roared. Justice jumped back. Water sloshed over the tub's edge, and around the backsplash. "Nothing to concern you."

A white-hot inferno swirled inside him. He couldn't stop the red glow burning in his eyes. That room contained his soul. Fucking sick punishment to see what you wanted most and not be able to do a damn thing about it. One touch by the wrong person and he'd lose his soul forever.

Sharp gusts of air fanned through his nostrils. "Don't *ever* open the door."

"All right." She swallowed. "I promise."

The heat snuffed out. He leaned his head back against the cool black granite. The lack of understanding wasn't her fault. "I didn't mean to yell," he mumbled.

"It's okay." She scooted closer and put her small hand over his along the tub rim.

He glanced down at their hands. "You forgive too easily."

"You're too hard on yourself." Her fingers tightened.

How could he not be? Nothing would change the past or return his four siblings' lives. A thick ache filled his throat. "What makes it so easy for you?" He pulled a rose from one of the crystal vases surrounding the tub.

"Everyone gets mad, Dash." She sighed. "We all do and say things we don't mean when we're upset or scared." She looked at him point blank.

He refused to meet her gaze. The woman saw more than anyone he'd crossed paths with, enough to see through him to his sins. He trailed the rosebud along her neck. "And anger means anything is forgivable?" he snorted.

"No, but intent does."

He frowned.

"You apologized, which tells me your intent wasn't mean or hurtful, and that makes all the difference." She rose up from the tub and slipped her hands around his shoulders.

Rivulets of water streamed over her breasts and down her belly. His jaw tightened at the thought of sliding against her slick flesh and then deep inside her.

But the questions she'd raised without further probing wouldn't leave. "What happens when someone hurts you," he swallowed, "badly, without intent. Can you forgive them?"

He didn't understand why he asked. The forgiveness he sought was impossible. Those whom he needed it from most had died because of him.

"Dash." She raked her fingers through his short hair. "It's harder, but not impossible."

He held back a snort. Yet, the little flame of hope he'd carried for two centuries flickered. "I've never met anyone like you." He shook his head.

"Considering the company you keep, I can see why." Her voice had taken on a teasing, rather than condemning tone.

"Which is where I should be now." But he didn't rise.

"You're still here." She undid his gray tie and tossed it aside. Steam curled from her body and slipped beneath his suit. "You might need help washing your back."

She laughed. "Oh, I do." She popped his shirt buttons free of their holes.

"Lucky for you I'm here." He drew the rose bud down her fair cheek, then along her neck and over the tops of her breasts not covered by bubbles.

"Exceedingly," she agreed.

Dash worked his way out of his black suit coat while she attacked his pants.

"I missed you this morning." She glanced up from beneath her lashes.

A thick lump blocked his throat. No one had ever missed

him. He stared, wanting to believe she spoke the truth and, at the same time, hoping she lied.

"Is that so hard to believe?" She pushed his shirt off his shoulders.

Yes, it was. He swallowed. "That was the sex."

"Are you sure?" The suds clinging to the tips of her breasts and thighs crackled as she pressed her naked body to his.

He groaned. His cock filled. Sweet mercy, what the woman did to him!

"I never refuse a challenge." He drew the rosebud between her breasts and over her flat stomach. Her knees wobbled as he neared the dark blond triangle of curls between her legs.

"Good, I like a man who knows how to bring it on," she whispered in a husky voice. She unsnapped the last fastening on his pants while he toed off his shoes.

Blood boiled in his veins. He stroked the rose back and forth along her inner thigh. Over the pungent floral scent wafted her musk. Memories of her sweet cream moistened his tongue. He rubbed his tingling taste buds against the roof of his mouth.

Stripping off the last of his clothing, he stood before her completely naked. Her brown eyes widened and her teeth scraped across her bottom lip. "Like what you see?"

"It has its high points." Her heated gaze dipped to his jutting cock.

He chuckled, "As well as it's hard ones."

"I'll be the judge of that." She grabbed his hand and pulled him closer.

His heart thumped against his chest as he waited for whatever she had in mind. The cloying steam added to his rapidly rising body temperature. Justice brushed her fingers down his thigh. By absolute will he stopped his legs from shaking.

"I never got a chance to do this last night." She cupped his hard cock in her palm.

"Why was that?" He noted the strain in his tone at the touch of her warm, wet hands.

"Well." She stroked along the underside of his cock. "I got a little tied up." A tiny, naughty smile flashed across her lips.

"You should complain to management." His lids drifted lower, but not so far that he lost sight of Justice stroking his cock.

"You're suggesting I let them have it?" She rolled his sac between her fingers.

Fire licked his insides. "Everything they have coming." He wanted to fuck her senseless right now. Hard didn't begin to describe his cock. He pushed out a breath through his nose.

She wrapped her small hands around his hard shaft and squeezed. He grunted and thrust into her wet grasp.

"I wanted this last night," she said, as her pink lips hovered above him.

"I know." He swallowed. Tightness pulled his balls high against his body. Liquid slipped from the tip of his cock.

"Are you going to stop me?" She smeared a pearl-gray drop over the thick head with her thumb.

His mouth went so dry the steamy clouds around him may as well have been sand. Every brush of her fingers made his nerve endings jump. "A determined woman like yourself? Impossible."

"Glad you recognize it." She reached around and grabbed his ass and squeezed.

"Damn." Desire weighted down his legs as she swallowed him inside her warm mouth. His head fell back as pleasure swam through him.

The taut muscles in his shaft clenched. He pumped himself farther down her throat, careful not to push too far.

The early quakes of an orgasm rippled behind his tightly drawn sac. "Damn, you're good." He ran his fingers through her silky hair. The satin of her mouth and the slight scrape of the blunt edges of her teeth raked his length.

She sucked harder and smiled around his cock.

"Fuck," he grunted, and squeezed his eyes shut. The image of her hungrily devouring his cock was too much.

"Mmm." The sound of her obvious enjoyment vibrated against his head.

He gripped her shoulders and stilled her movements. Every muscle from his belly to his knees stiffened. He dragged himself back from the ragged edge of orgasm. Slow as molasses, she pulled back and let his cock fall from her lips. "I love how you taste."

Her quiet voice echoed off the granite. "The feeling is mutual," he managed to reply. The flick of her tongue over his sensitive tip made him thrust toward her.

Her rich brown eyes, teeming with want, never strayed. No fear. Not an ounce of hesitation. Just pure want.

"Don't stop now." She licked a circular path around his girth, starting at his head and spiraling towards his base.

Where the hell had she learned that trick? His ass clenched as his hips thrust toward the wet sanctuary of her mouth.

"I won't go too far."

Too late. He was hell and gone and didn't give a damn. He gave himself over to her hands closing around his shaft. They encased him in their tight grip as the walls of her pussy had surrounded him last night. He thrust into the tunnel as she squeezed.

She laved his balls with her tongue.

"Suck," he growled. No sooner had he spoken than she drew the taut sac inside her mouth. Tingles shot down his legs.

He wrapped one hand around hers and pumped his cock in and out of their combined fists. "Justice," he moaned, when she moved to his other testical.

The burning stirrings before the pressure behind his balls exploded in orgasm flared. Her tongue and the tiny slurping sounds as she made a meal of his cock ended all his good intentions of stopping her.

Just as he was about to cross over to the inevitable, she pulled back.

Air burst from his lungs. There were several ragged breaths before he recovered. "Sweetheart, you could kill a man and make him damn happy to make the journey."

She pressed a kiss to his thigh. "A high compliment coming from a man of your experience."

Maybe, but he'd never experienced anyone quite like Justice Malloy before. An unusual combination of savvy and innocence. Lost in desire, he didn't catch her grab hold of him until his balance gave way and he fell toward the tub.

Grabbing the back ridge, he softened his fall. Water still splashed over the side, as well as his head. Her lithe body slid beneath him.

Bubbles half covered her nose and rose petals stuck to her wet curls. He couldn't stop a smile at the sight. "You're in the wrong spot." He grabbed her around the waist and flipped their positions.

Justice shrieked as more water flew up. She lay stretched out on top of him. The firm, reddened cheeks of her ass poked through the kaleidoscope of suds. "Not quite."

He turned her once more so her back aligned with his front. The position also meant his hard cock was perfectly snuggled against her ass. He slid his hands beneath her breasts, cupping them.

"Much better," she agreed and leaned farther into him.

Beads of sweat flowed over her hot skin. He pushed her wet hair aside and nuzzled her neck while he kneaded her breasts. The pads of his thumbs brushed her stiff nipples making her buck.

Dash couldn't get enough. Last night should have sated him. "You're all wet and hot."

"I wonder who got me that way." She reached her lips up to steal a kiss.

"The answer better be me," he growled, harsher than he intended.

"It is." She smiled. "Believe me, it most certainly is."

Attachment and bonds within the hotel walls meant less than nothing. That fact didn't deter his possessive instinct. He didn't want anyone else's hands on her body or another cock filling her pussy until orgasm broke her apart.

Where had those thoughts come from?

He slid his hand along her belly and through the wiry curls at the juncture of her thighs. "Are you wet everywhere?"

She shivered against him. Threading through the fine nest, he stroked the outside of her pussy. He took special care to avoid washing all of her juices away with too much water.

Carefully, he slid one finger between her folds. The difference between the bath water and cream of her pussy was unmistakable.

Hers had a silky texture that coated his fingers and eased the friction of his skin moving against hers. She lifted her ass and ground against his hand.

She was so damn ready. "Justice," he whispered in her ear, "get on top of me."

Without pause, she reversed her position and spread her thighs on either side of his. Her pussy settled over his hard cock. Breasts jutting out, skin slick and hot, she made a heavenly vision.

Little grinding rolls of her hips dragged her nether lips along his length. He grasped her around her waist.

"Ride my cock."

Teeth sunk into her lower lip as she moaned.

Without waiting for an answer, he thrust up against her. "I want to watch you while you get off on my cock."

"Oh, yes!" She lifted her bottom and, inch by inch, lowered herself down onto his hard shaft.

He hissed as the wet heat of her pussy surrounded him. "That's right," he grunted, "take all of me." Buried up to his hilt, he groaned.

"I want to fuck you." She gripped his shoulders as she moved up and down and up and down on him. The motion caused her breasts to shimmy and bounce.

He loved the sight. Each time she sank onto his cock, she swirled her hips and screwed him in deeper. In return, he slammed his hips up to meet her and drove himself farther into her womb.

The heat of her walls spread through the rest of his body. Sweat poured off him. Water slapped in his face and flew over the side as her pace increased.

"Fuck me." He grabbed her hips and held her flush. With frantic twitches she ground against him.

"Yes. Dash." Her head lolled as her back arched. Her eyes were closed, her skin was flushed with the rapture.

That was it, the fuse that touched off the growing explosion deep behind his balls. He hammered himself one more time into her before shooting a hot stream of cum inside her waiting channel.

Justice collapsed against his chest and laid her cheek on his shoulders.

The *drip-drip* of water broke the silence. Until he died the image of Justice at the height of orgasm he'd given her would stay with him.

7

Justice spent the rest of the day working. After digging through the Austin-American Statesman's online archive of wedding announcements, she pulled up the calendar of upcoming city events. With each click of the mouse, she whittled down her list of possible sites.

Without a location, she couldn't write a proposal, let alone have one ready by the close of business on Monday. She set the laptop on the coffee table and leaned forward, propping her elbows on her knees.

The shiny wood floor had as much of an answer as she did. She rubbed her sore temples. A low hovering cloud floated toward her toes.

The mini cloud rolled past the sofa and then disappeared. Smoke? She sniffed the air, but didn't smell anything burning. Curious, she stood and headed in the direction the fog had originated.

A puff hissed from beneath the door Dash had deemed off-limits. She glanced around, though she knew herself to be alone.

Biting her lip, she crept toward the door. Her heart thumped like a pounding bass in one of the 6th Street dance clubs.

She held her hand to the door. No heat. Curiosity gnawed at her, as did her promise not to enter the room. Reluctantly, she turned and forced herself back to her computer.

She still needed a location to present to Charlene Dawson and Lawson's tuition, neither answer lay inside.

Justice walked beside Dash with her hand tucked into the crook of his arm. They'd shared a wonderful gourmet dinner and afterward he'd asked if she'd like to get outside.

Lusty moans echoed down the corridors. After the attack in the bar, she kept alert for anyone overly interested. He led her around a corner into an empty hall. "Where are we going?"

"A surprise." He smiled.

"Does it come with a chance I'll be naked?" She slowed as they reached the end of the hall.

"No." He pointed to a door marked ROOF. "It's a guarantee." He snapped his fingers and a lit candle appeared. "Hold this."

She chuckled and followed him up a short flight of steps. The tap-tap of their shoes echoed in the stuffy stairwell. "You forget to pay the electric bill?" She led the way to the top.

"Too much light ruins the view."

"What view?"

Dash answered her by throwing open the door to the roof and the Texas night sky. In the wash of blackness shined not one lone star, but thousands.

"This is one of my favorite places," he said quietly.

When she turned, he looked away as if embarrassed by the sentimentality. So, Dash Wilde had a sensitive side. The substance beneath his charm and passion warmed her. What else didn't she know about him?

"It's breathtaking." She twirled around. "There's absolutely nothing but sky."

"Makes you feel like you're out in the open with nothing to hold you."

His voice held a wistful note. How long had he been trapped here? Suddenly, she wanted to know more than mere surface trivia about this fascinating man. She followed him to a pair of plush black chairs in the center of the roof.

"A drink?" He sat beside her with his fingers poised to snap. "Brandy? Espresso? Ice wine?"

"Honestly?" If she opened up, maybe he would likewise. "I love a good, hot cup of Darjeeling tea after dinner." She gave a sheepish grin.

"A fellow tea drinker?" He snapped and a complete tea service appeared.

"I have a question for you."

"Only one?" He drank deeply.

"I thought I'd go easy on you, to start." She winked as she reached for the cream.

"But you enjoy it so much more when I'm hard." Heat flared in his gaze.

"So do you." Her stomach fluttered at his rough tone.

The china cup appeared much more fragile in his large hand. The ease in which he handled the delicate porcelain further hinted at untold secrets.

In the past day, she'd told him about her father's battle with cancer, her mother's death, raising Lawson, and her job as a fund-raiser. What she'd learned in return, which wasn't much, came from deductions and the odd slip. Tonight, she wanted more.

"You're very generous." Dash shifted in his seat as Justice angled her chair towards him. "With your hospitality and passion, but not yourself."

A frown tugged down the corners of his mouth.

She looked at him point blank. "You don't share anything about yourself." The comment wasn't mean, just honest, and she wanted the same in return.

He stiffened. "I'm boring?"

"You don't really think I believe that?" She ran the arch of her foot along the back of his calf. His small smile appeared and disappeared. "I've seen you in action." She leaned forward and let her voice drop to a husky whisper.

"And you want more?" He hooked his foot around her chair's wooden leg and pulled her closer.

"I want you to tell me something about yourself, please." She held her breath. Moonlight and starlight lit his handsome face. Would he let her see anything beneath?

"Why?" His head tilted as he stared.

She'd seen this puzzled expression before, most often with new sponsors as they tried to find her personal angle in asking for money for charity. "Tell me because you want to?" Standing, she settled her hands on his chair's padded armrest, trapping him. "And because I care enough to ask."

He sat motionless except for a reflexive swallow. How long had he lived without anyone caring about him?

"I assume you have something specific in mind." He cupped her shoulders and smoothed his palms down her arms.

Despite the hot night, she shivered. "You understand food, fashion, and art, but you weren't born to it."

Red flashed in his eyes. "What gave you that idea?" He dropped his hold.

Damn, the man had a hard shell. She couldn't explain why she needed to know about him. *Gut instinct,* her father had called the feeling.

"You gave me the idea." She leaned farther, not allowing him to retreat. "Your comments about me being rich when I questioned you about wine."

"Is there a question somewhere?" His gaze dropped from her face to the low neckline of her gown. "Or do you just like being on top of me?"

Memories of straddling him in the bathtub while she rode

his cock weakened her knees. Her fingers gripped the chair tighter. "You are good at distraction," she ground out between pinched teeth.

His brows rose as a naughty grin curved his lips. "It's called being a devil."

The wicked promise in his voice tempted her to say the hell with personal details and force him to make good on his not so-subtle promises of pleasure. "And this is called I'm not giving in—yet."

They both knew she would, but—"As I said, last night I figured out you didn't grow up in society. You learned later in life. How?"

"How did you know?" He didn't look at her.

"My dad." She smiled as wrinkles creased the corners of his eyes. "Before he became a lawyer, he was raised on a poor ranch in West Texas. My mother's family had money and he learned enough to advance his career."

Dash's jaw fell open.

"I don't think anyone else saw his little hesitations, but I did." She shrugged a shoulder and sniffed against the sudden sadness she felt. He caught a falling tear she hadn't even noticed on the tip of his finger.

"You're really interested?"

Not wanting the topic to get too serious, she screwed up her face as if in deep thought. "Did I forget to mention that part?"

They both laughed.

"But first," Dash shot up and grabbed her around the waist, "let's get comfortable."

Justice shrieked as her feet left the ground. The chairs vanished and a king-sized bed covered in soft, white linen appeared on the rooftop. She hopped up on the high mattress beside Dash.

For a moment they lay in silence, staring up at the tiny twinkles lighting a path through the blackness like breadcrumbs.

"I grew up on a farm."

The words came out slowly. For all his elegant speech and quick wit, talking about himself didn't come easy. The fact he tried in spite of the difficulty touched her. She laced her fingers through his.

"A—poor one." His hand tightened. "When I got here, I started out working in the stables."

At his glance, she nodded, encouraging him to continue.

"I didn't know anything. Where I came from, the likes of me wasn't good enough to even look at nobility." His voice tightened.

Nobility? Up until now, she'd assumed Dash was older, but now she wondered exactly how many years.

"The—man in charge here then taught me."

Rolling on her side to face him, she kissed him on the lips. Pride for his accomplishments and pain for his difficult task warred in her heart. "Sounds like you've come a long way."

He nodded. "I had to learn everything." A long breath rushed from his lungs. "Including how to read."

On impulse she wrapped her arms around him and covered his mouth with hers. The strength of his will amazed her. She ravaged his lips, twining her tongue with his.

"You have nothing to be ashamed of." Emotion clogged her throat. When she asked him to share something of himself, she never imagined he'd trust her with such obviously painful memories.

Without a word he crushed her against him and let his body do the talking.

Justice stood in the doorway as the last golden rays fought the pull of the horizon. Dash had said he'd return at sundown. She smiled at the thought of the sexy devil who had quickly dominated her thoughts and her heart.

At the realization, she gripped the handle. She couldn't love him. Somewhere from inside the suite a clock chimed eight o'clock. In four hours, Dash and the hotel would disappear. The lump in her throat thickened.

How had she let this happen? She turned and headed into the parlor. She knew better than to confuse sex and love. Between tuition bills and the question of a wedding reception site, she had enough problems without adding a broken heart.

A silver pot of Darjeeling tea sat waiting for her on the buffet. Yesterday she'd mentioned the drink as her evening favorite.

The fact he'd remembered such a small preference meant more than any Hermès bauble he could conjour. It was one of the qualities she loved about him.

No one had ever put her first, except Dash. She bit her trembling lower lip. China cup in hand, she sank onto the couch.

A billowy cloud floated from the opposite side of the room, much larger than the puffs she'd noticed before. Icy fog seeped out from around the entire door. She frowned. What did he keep in a room colder than the Antarctic?

She rose. Halfway across the oriental carpet, she realized the door stood ajar. The brass handle nearly froze her fingers. Damn. She yanked her hand back and rubbed her bright pink finger tips together.

One peek and she'd get out. Her pulse quickened. She glanced around the suite. Certain she had the place to herself, she opened the door. A blast of frigid air hit her, like opening a walk-in freezer.

A thousand tiny cold needles pricked her skin. Wrapping her arms around her chest, she stepped into the thick fog. At first, she saw only solid white walls.

Then, a blurred blue-green glow caught her eye. As if magnetized, the light drew her closer. Unable to see the floor, she took small steps.

Blood pounded in her ears. As she drew closer, she realized

the far right wall contained rows of white shelves. On the center ledge sat a miniature luminescent tree.

"Wow!" A little cloud of her breath hung in the air before being swallowed by a larger one. She edged her way closer.

Smaller than a Japanese bonsai, it was the most beautiful thing she'd ever seen. Limbs, as delicate as intricate lace, fanned out and shimmered. Colors flowed from one end of the blue-green spectrum and back.

She hunched down for a better look. Within the spiderweb of thin branches flowed little bubbles of gold light. Some of the spheres appeared to have pictures floating inside, but she couldn't make out the images.

Carefully, she reached out for the tree.

"Stop!"

Justice screamed and stumbled backward. Dash stood in the doorway. His eyes glowed bright, blood red.

"I told you never to come in here," he roared.

"I—I." She swallowed hard. "The door was open." She scooted as far into the room and away from him as possible.

Steam hissed and billowed about his body. Any second, she expected him to fly at her.

"Do you know what could have happened if you'd touched it?" Nostrils flared, he paced in the narrow threshold. "Do you have any idea?" He whirled.

For the first time, Justice was truly frightened of Dash. Her heart pounded. Every horrible story she'd heard about devils flooded her mind. "I-I . . ." She couldn't make her mouth work.

"Get out!" he roared.

"Dash—"

"GET. OUT." He shot forward, grabbed her arm, and yanked her from the room.

She winced as his fingers dug into her cold flesh, but didn't fight him. Stumbling, she half fell through the doorway into the warm parlor. Chills shook frozen nerves.

He slammed the room's door shut. The force rattled picture frames, and the walls themselves. He laid his forehead against the door.

Justice stood a few feet away. What was she supposed to do? Did she go to him? Leave?

With a single deep breath, Dash straightened. "Just go."

Unlike moments ago, his voice barely broke a whisper. Moisture shined in his blue eyes as he turned and quickly walked away.

Pain unlike any she'd ever seen shone in his raw gaze. All the fear for herself disappeared. What had happened? She didn't have the answer. He might refuse to say.

But, he needed someone.

Every kindness he had shown her hit her at the same time. His sharp-tongued comments had caused her to reexamine her views. He's risked his life and job protecting her. He'd shown her physical pleasure, putting her needs before his own.

By entering the mystery room she'd broken the promise she'd made. The fact didn't excuse his behavior or hers. But it neither changed what she felt for him. She couldn't leave him alone in pain.

She followed his path into the bedroom, but found the area empty. Maybe he'd snapped his fingers and vanished. Then, she spied the open French doors. Quietly, she slipped outside and up a winding staircase into a rooftop garden.

The moon and stars gave off enough light for her to navigate the walkway. She rubbed her damp palms against her pants. Beyond the bend falling water splashed.

Licking her dry lips, she crept around the corner. Dash sat in a chair, his head tipped back and his hands pressed over his face.

Her heart squeezed.

Cautiously, she slipped out of her shoes before approaching him. She kneeled in front of his feet, laid her hands on his arms, and pulled them away from his face. "Dash."

To her surprise, he didn't fight her. Moisture glazed the confusion swirling in his blue eyes. She cupped his cheek.

"Talk to me. Tell me the truth."

8

Dash stared at the beautiful blond woman kneeling by his side. She couldn't still be there? Yet, the gentle grip on his wrists felt as real as anything he'd ever known.

He leaned into the comfort offered by the soft palm pressed against his face. Regret, shame, astonishment, and a thousand other emotions crashed into Dash's chest. He swallowed hard against the choking pressure.

"You're still here?" He'd all but thrown her out of the room after he'd insulted her. "Why?" Her lips pouted, a gesture he now recognized as uncertainty.

"I care about you." She stroked his cheek.

How could she, after his anger and insults? He'd intended to protect her. Instead . . .

"I'm sorry," she whispered.

The unexpected words and the pain behind them nearly broke him. He closed his eyes against the tears. Not since his siblings had died had he cried. But, right then, he could have wailed like a banshee.

"No," he rasped, and shook his head. "You." He drew a deep, calming breath. "You have nothing to apologize for."

"Yes." She tightened her hold on his hand. "You asked me to stay away from that room."

"More an order." He offered a weak smile.

Justice chuckled. "Either way, I went in against my word, and for that I'm sorry."

Forgiveness enfolded his battered conscience. From the safe embrace he saw the intent of his actions. Shame had burned him when he'd forbid her.

"It's not your fault." He stared up at the stars, unable to face her. "I didn't explain. I thought I was protecting you. Really, I was being selfish and protecting me."

"Then, tell me now."

With the gentle pressure of her hand, she drew his gaze toward hers. Instinct shouted a refusal, the same fear that had almost gotten her killed and lost him his soul permanently. This time he ignored it.

She might hate him afterward, but he needed to tell her the truth. "It's not pretty," he warned, half hoping she'd change her mind.

"The whole *Hell* and *devil* thing kind of clued me in." She gave a small smile.

"Here." He pulled her up and onto his lap without asking, eliminating chances of an outright refusal.

She settled her thighs perpendicular atop his. Her arms wrapped around his neck. "Much better."

He let out a tight breath and encircled her waist. Relishing her softness and warmth, he pulled her tighter against his body. The feeling went beyond skin.

"It's okay. You can tell me." She pressed a light kiss to his temple.

The tenderness was the last push he needed. He snapped his fingers and the chair transformed into a lounge.

"Nice trick." Justice scooted until she lay on her side, throwing her leg over his and her arm across his chest. "You got another magic wand somewhere, besides this one?" She rubbed her knee over his cock.

Dash managed a smile.

"There's no way to make this any easier." She sighed.

"No." He recognized her attempt at humor to relax him and would forever be grateful. He rested his chin on top of her strawberry scented curls. "The magic came with the job, and—becoming a devil."

She gave him a quick, reassuring squeeze. Sweat dripped under his collar plastering his shirt to his skin, he didn't release Justice.

"That room," he moistened his dry lips, "what you saw inside—"

"The tree?"

"Yes." He'd never told anyone he didn't have a soul so he had no clue how Justice would respond. The staff knew, but since they were like him, they didn't count.

Steeling himself, he prepared for the worst. "That wasn't a tree." Her head picked up beneath his. "It's my soul," he whispered.

Her enormous gaze shot to his. "Your actual, immortal—" She patted his heart.

He nodded.

"So, I almost touched . . ."

Another nod. Muscles tensed as he awaited her reaction.

"Now things make sense." She propped herself up on her elbow.

She wasn't screaming or trying to kill him. Had she gone into shock? "I just told you I'm soulless."

"No." She frowned.

"*No?*" He bolted up.

"The tree I saw is your soul. That means you have one. It's just not here." She tapped his chest.

Technically, she was correct, but . . .

"When you said everyone at The Last Resort had destroyed their souls or wanted only sex, you meant the guests."

He'd never quite looked at it that way.

"You rescued me, helped me, and made certain I stayed safe. Those aren't the actions of a soulless man." She pushed him back down and kissed him.

Sweet lips moved over his. Although it was the most innocent kiss he'd had since he was a young lad, the soft power of her acceptance hit him harder than the heaviest passion. He wrapped his arms around her, never wanting to let her go.

Finally, she drew back, but didn't leave his embrace. "Once I realized you weren't heartless, I thought it was all about wanton sex. But that didn't make sense either, after you showed me around and sat up half the night talking with me."

"With a lot of sex afterward." His gaze met hers. A hint of red colored her cheeks.

"Great sex. But if that's all you wanted we both know you could've had it without talking." A knowing smile pushed up the corners of her mouth.

He shook his head.

"What?" She stiffened.

"You're awfully calm about this." He held her close. "Not what I expected."

"After doors that get farther away the closer you walk, a moral compass, and you snapping you fingers to make objects appear, I can believe anything." She twisted in his arms. "No, that's wrong."

Dash's heart stopped. Realization had hit her. He let go of her. Justice moved, but not farther away; instead, she scooted closer, straddling his thighs. The intimate contact fired his lust and spun his mind.

She took his face between her hands forcing him to look her in the eyes.

"I believe in you, Dash."

Tears blurred his vision. He slammed his eyes shut. For a long time they lay holding fast to each other.

Justice was the first to speak. "What would've happened if I had touched your soul?" Her teeth sank into her lower lip.

"Feel my skin." She popped the button on his shirt and slid her hand along his chest. His cock stirred.

"Hot." She brushed his muscles with her fingertips.

He groaned and placed his hand over hers. "One touch will melt it."

"And me?"

Looking away, he shrugged. "Don't know." In all honesty, he couldn't say what the consequences of someone who didn't love him completely touching his soul were.

"So, you can see what you want, but can never take it." She sucked in a sharp breath through her teeth.

"Yes, and if I ever leave the grounds without my soul, I'll lose it forever."

"That's cruel."

"The devil isn't known for his kindness." He forced a stiff smile. "And, his punishment isn't without cause."

She sat back and swallowed. "What could you have done to deserve this?"

"I've never told anyone what happened." The fear he'd thought disappeared returned, knotting his shoulders. Hatred and revulsion for himself made any punishment from The Devil easy.

"Let me be the first."

His gaze snapped to hers.

"You said after I leave here I won't remember any—" her voice caught, "anything."

The thought of losing her laughter, their rapport, and her caring seared through him to the marrow in his bones. For all his magic, time was an element far outside his control.

"I'm damned either way." His jaw clenched.

"I don't understand."

He blew out a frustrated breath. "I'm selfish if I don't tell you to protect my ego and I'm selfish if I do and burden your consciousness to make myself feel better," he snapped.

"You let me talk about my parents and my brother. It's my turn to listen."

Was it really that simple? The light touch of her hand rubbing his chest convinced him. "I was born in Ireland." He started slowly. Most days he did his best to forget his other life. "The oldest of five children. My parents were poor farmers."

In his mind he saw the tiny cottage with its turf roof in the middle of a bright green field. "Me mum, she loved to sing. All day, no matter what she was doing, she'd be singing." The faraway lilt of her voice floated through his ears. "Drove me and my brother barmy, but my Da just smiled."

"Sounds as though they loved each other." Justice rubbed her hands up and down his arms.

"They did." He allowed himself a smile at the happy memory, but the moment didn't last. "Then the crop went bad." The simple statement didn't do justice to the reality of the endless field of withered plants as hopeless as their family's situation.

"We had no money for rent." His voice caught.

"It's okay." Justice scooted closer.

The warmth of her body went a long way to soothing the ice around his conscience. "My brothers and sisters and I were off playing when the landlord's soldiers arrived." Even now, he questioned whether his parents had known and if that was why they'd sent the five of them away. "When we got back, our cottage was burned and our parents with it." He choked out the last words.

"Oh God." Justice tightened her arms and pulled him against her.

Dash held on to her and buried his face against her soft curls. Behind clenched lids, his eyes burned as they had in the remnants of the smoke and smoldering ash.

"I'm so sorry," she whispered over and over.

Reluctantly, he eased away. He'd come to the part he'd dreaded. Up until now, everything had been easy. "I was furious." He clenched his fists. "The men who murdered my parents walked free while they lay dead."

"They should've gone to jail." Anger snapped in her voice.

"Over two poor micks?" he spat. "The crown would've rewarded the rich bastard for ridding Ireland of two more worthless poor." His muscles shook. "I didn't know what to do."

"How old were you?" She crawled up higher and pressed her cheek to his.

"Sixteen." He swallowed.

"You were a child," she said softly.

What he was was responsible for his siblings. A duty he'd failed. "I went into town. I don't know what I thought I'd do. On my way I met a man." In the rain on the dark road, the stranger had appeared to come straight out of the earth. Too late, he'd learned just how right he'd been.

"He promised me a way to make the men who'd killed my parents pay." Not a day passed that he didn't regret his decision.

"How?"

Tension stiffened her body. "Vengeance, in exchange for working for him for all eternity. I didn't realize he meant it literally." He offered a weak smile. "I agreed. He told me he'd find me in the morning after it had been done."

Justice winced.

"I didn't believe him, but the next day he appeared and the village was abuzz over six men dying in their sleep saying that it must be the work of the devil." Not once did he regret the men's deaths.

"Then he told me it was time for me to fulfill my end of the bargain." Sick dread swam in his stomach. "That's when he revealed his identity and what I'd agreed to."

"And your siblings?" Her hand came up to her mouth.

"I begged him to let them come." His voice cracked. "But, as they had their souls and it wasn't part of our bargain, they couldn't." Tears slipped out of the corners of his eyes. "They all died within six months."

"Now do you think I'm deserving of punishment?" he growled. Defenses rose and with their ascension, he lashed out.

"No, I don't." She forced his head in her direction. "Two hundred years is more than enough punishment."

He couldn't have heard her right. "You sacrificed everything for your brother and I plain sacrificed my siblings."

"You made a mistake. A horrible mistake," she agreed. "You didn't mean to."

"They still died." The stated fact was as cold as their four dead bodies.

"Your worst mistakes were being angry and young. But that's all. You didn't understand what you'd agreed to."

The more he fought to turn away, the more she wouldn't let him.

"I know what it's like to lose the people you love but nothing, not regret or punishing yourself, will bring them back."

He nodded. She was still there and she . . . understood, something he'd never expected. Unstoppable love for her took hold of his heart.

"You aren't that person." She stroked the back of her hand down the side of his face. "You haven't been for a long time."

Sharing the truth had lightened him. If not for her weight grounding him, he felt he would float away. "It's been a long time since I told anyone this, but—thank you." He smoothed his thumb over her soft cheek.

"I want you, Dash." She rose from the chair and stood in the center of the courtyard. "I want to make love to you now."

Fires of need kicked to life inside him. Their flames devoured the painful memories. He licked his dry lips.

"I want you right here." She reached behind her neck and unzipped her pink dress.

His cock hardened. The silk slipped from her shoulders and fluttered like candy snowflakes to the ground, leaving her naked. Bathed in moonlight, her fair hair and skin took on an ethereal glow.

Freed from the secrets of his past, his view of Justice changed. She remained the most physically beautiful woman he'd ever seen, but now he saw beyond her skin to her heart. His breath shook.

All his questions of how and why she could look past his sins faded. The mechanics didn't matter, only the result. Calming warmth spread through his heart.

"Justice." Her name slipped from his lips like a prayer.

She walked forward. With each step, her hips gave a slow roll and her full breasts swayed to the same tempo. The need to touch her and surround himself in her sweet, accepting warmth pulsed in his cock as much as his heart.

"Come with me." She took his hand and led him into the center of the courtyard. "No walls." She pointed to tall palms and thick flowering ferns all around them. "No limits."

"None," he rasped as she stripped off his shirt and pants. He curled his toes into the sandy soil. Waves of peace flooded him. He clenched his jaw and fought for control.

Humid dew covered the leaves, their slick green skin gleamed in the light. He traced his fingertip over Justice's collarbone.

"You're hot," he whispered. He ran the back of his hand down her sweat-slicked stomach and slipped his fingers between her legs and the satiny moist folds of her pussy. "And wet."

Groaning, she widened her stance.

Lightly, he grazed the tiny bundle of nerves at the top.

"Dash." She ground her pussy against his hand and pulled him down into a frantic kiss. "Hurry," she panted.

He ran a hand through her curls and cupped the back of her head. "No rush."

"But—" Her gaze shot to the sliver of blue light from the bell tower flooding the narrow spaces between the wide palm leaves.

"Shhhhhhh." He kissed her slowly, moving his mouth over hers and savoring the berry flavor of her lips. "I'm not going anywhere, baby."

But, in a few hours, Justice would. She'd walk out of the hotel and away from him forever. He wrapped his arms around her tighter and deepened the kiss. Until the last possible moment, he wouldn't let her go.

"There's nothing else, remember." He slid his mouth along her smooth, soft cheek to her ear.

Her hands worked their way down his chest. "Our own private paradise."

"Yes." He smiled at the lunatic thought, something two days ago he'd have found impossible.

Tropical orange and yellow flowers bloomed. Their large, curved petals gave off a heady perfume, sweet and lush.

"And, does this Eden have any amenities?" She broke off a speckled sherbet-colored bud and tucked the stem behind her ear.

With a snap of his finger, a hammock appeared between two of the palm trees on his left. "Anything you want."

"That's a dangerous offer." She pressed her lush body against his and rubbed against him so the tight points of her nipples scraped up and down his chest. "I only like the very best. Therefore, I choose you."

Dash let her words wash over him. Hot desire jolted his muscles. Other women had wanted him sexually, like he'd wanted them. With Justice, his want was to fulfill all of hers.

He swung her up into the hammock and followed. She climbed on top and straddled his thighs as the fabric bed rocked. With a forward tug on her waist he brought her wet pussy in line with his cock.

Warm brown eyes stared into his as she slid her body back and forth: care, desire, and understanding, as naked as her skin. "You're wonderful."

She smiled. "So are you."

His shaft slid between her nether lips and against the tight entrance to her pussy. He groaned as her juices bathed him until he moved with total ease.

"Need you inside me." Sweat beaded on her flat stomach.

Leaning up, he licked the drops rolling between her full breasts. The taste of salt and strawberries made him thirsty for more. "I can't get enough of you."

He took her breasts in his palms as he ran his tongue over her rounded flesh.

"I want more." She ground down harder on his cock.

The tight pressure of her pussy stoked the fire inside him. "Anything you want." He laved her nipple, flicking the point until she writhed. Massaging the rest of her breast, he bit and sucked the tip with his mouth while working the opposite bud in a similar manner with his fingers.

"You make me want to come," she moaned. Her spine arched and curved her body closer and closer.

"Then, come." He pinched the rosy tip harder. "Come all over me." He didn't care if he ever got relief. Sharing Justice's pleasure was enough.

Her body seized and trembled.

"That's right, baby. Let it all go." At his words, a rush of warm liquid rushed from her pussy and all over his cock.

"Dash." Head thrown back, she shouted toward the stars.

He found himself shaking in awe at the force of her climax. After making certain she'd spent herself, he released her breasts.

"I've never . . ." She gasped for breath.

"I know." He pushed the wet curls back from her flushed face. The intensity was new for him, too.

"Thank you." She kissed him.

"Nothing to thank me for." And he meant it. Giving her pleasure seemed a small token compared to the caring she'd given him. But given the chance, he'd gladly continue to repay her for the rest of his days.

"That's a shame, because I had such big plans."

Teeth nipped at his neck. "Need any help?"

Dense force, raised from need, pressed behind his balls. He gritted his teeth and fought the urge to drive himself into her ready pussy.

"Funny you asked . . ."

From the movement of her mouth against his skin, he could tell she smiled. "Where should I start?" He laid his palms on her thighs and pushed his hands higher an inch at a time. She wiggled, trying to escape and get closer at the same time.

"Sensitive?" He stroked the long, smooth inner curve of her thigh. In the back of his mind, he memorized the exact line and feel of her skin.

"A little." She shifted so the head of his cock poised on the lip of her entrance.

All he wanted was within one thrust. With a growl he locked his hands around Justice and rolled her beneath him. The hammock swung wildly as he pinned her between his body and the fabric.

Laughing, she brought her legs around his waist. "I want your cock inside me." She bit his shoulder. "I need to feel you inside me."

All his plans to wait vanished. He couldn't deny her anything. "Like this?" He plunged inside her waiting channel. Wet heat surrounded him. Her nails dug into his biceps, but he didn't mind.

He remained still within the hold of her channel. Its tightness gripping his shaft took him to the verge of release. Her legs locked and drew him in deeper.

"Justice," he gasped. The head of his cock bumped the tender wall of her womb.

"Yes," she breathed. Her eyes drifted closed in a portrait of bliss.

"Look at me," he said. All her emotions showed in her sable eyes. "I want to watch you when I come."

Her lids lifted as he moved inside her, first, with short, shallow strokes. The slow pace didn't last long. They both needed more.

Sweat ran down his arms as he balanced himself above her on the wobbly fabric. The muscles in his ass and at the top of his legs clenched as he pulled out and just as quickly drove himself inside.

All the while his gaze never broke from Justice's; flecks of gold sparked in the narrow ring of her irises not consumed by her pupils. She was close. He wanted so fucking bad to come, but he wouldn't let himself, not until after Justice did.

"Deeper." Her hips thrust up. "Almost," she panted, clawing at his arms and back. "Go with me."

"I am." The last of his restraint snapped. He thrust into her one final time.

She keened.

Her cry was the most glorious sound he had ever heard. Her channel squeezed, rippling around his cock. Burst of gold, copper, and bronze in her eyes sent him over the edge.

He poured his body and himself into her when a jet of hot cum streaked from his balls and deep into her pussy. Empty and spent, he collapsed beside her.

9

Justice stared at her watch as the elevator sped downward. Five minutes to midnight, and until she left Dash forever.

She sniffed back her tears. In the garden, he hadn't just given her pleasure, he'd made love and given himself. The mistakes in his past only made her love him more.

How could she abandon him here? He'd changed. She was certain.

As the elevator cage opened, she wiped her eyes before Dash noticed her crying. She spotted him in the middle of a heated exchange with Robert outside the elevator bank. A fern provided the perfect cover and she ducked behind it.

"This is your chance," Robert half shouted. "If she loves you she can take your soul and free you."

She covered her mouth, muffling her sharp gasp. What did the bell captain mean, *free him*?

"No!" Dash jerked his head. "I won't ask her."

"Why?" Robert whipped off his red and gold cap.

Dash loosened his clenched fists. "Everyone in her life has burdened her. I won't—I can't add more."

Her teeth sunk into her trembling lower lip. The sacrifice confirmed her belief, Dash had changed.

"Why?" Robert's muscles twitched, as if in a struggle between wanting to hit his boss and resisting the urge.

"I love her," Dash said quietly.

The tears she'd fought spilled down her cheeks. He really loved her. A smile formed on her lips. She'd waited so long for someone to love her and, more, who understood her. No way would she leave him.

Her gaze caught Robert's. She frantically waved him off. Dash would try and stop her from freeing his soul. She pointed upstairs, hoping the bell captain understood.

He nodded.

The elevator behind her dinged. The second the doors opened she dove into the car, and stabbed the button for the ninth floor.

Lights blinked across the numbered cutout above the door. She alternated between watching the car's progress and the second hand on her watch.

Less than two minutes until midnight. Finally the car slowed. She kicked off her heels and bolted down the cream and gold hallway to Dash's suite. Adrenaline pushed her legs faster.

She flung open the door, slamming it against the wall. But, she didn't stop.

Icy clouds puffed over the threshold from the sacred room. She grabbed the handle and pulled. The brass knob turned, but the door didn't move.

"No! No! No!" She had to get inside. "Open." She rammed her shoulder into the cold wood.

The first of twelve strikes sounded from the hotel's triple bells.

"I love him!" she shouted.

Suddenly, the lock gave way. She didn't stop to wonder why. The fifth chime rang out as she plunged into the cold fog.

Thick clouds filled the small space. She focused on locating Dash's soul. Throwing all caution aside, she ran toward the glimmer of blue-green light. By the time she made out the shape of the tree, the tenth bell had struck.

A quick prayer her actions wouldn't kill Dash, and she grabbed his soul as the final stroke reverberated shock through the building.

Heart beating wildly, she cracked open her eyes. Neither she nor the hotel had disappeared. Keeping a tight grip on Dash's soul, she dumped out the contents of her purse except for her wallet and keys. Ever so carefully, she placed the luminescent plant in her bag.

Hands shaking, she walked out into the hall. Glassy-eyed, half-dressed guests stumbled out of their rooms. As if called by a piper, they proceeded lemming style downstairs.

This must be when the wantons' memories turned to dreams. She held her breath. Why didn't she feel forgetful? No answer jumped out, but until she was outside, she decided to follow along.

The final stroke of midnight faded and, with it, Justice Malloy's memories of him. But, Dash wouldn't forget. Not ever. A deep ache spread through his chest.

His single regret was never saying good-bye. A stream of wanton guests traipsed through the lobby. He snapped his fingers and the front double doors swung open.

Among the blank faces, he searched for Justice. Her blond curls stood out on the outside of the column. She trudged past, without a look.

He'd known she wouldn't, but the ache in his chest still hurt.

The mass exodus surged out into the warm Texas night. He fell in at the tail end. Step after step, he never took his eyes off

Justice. He drank in her legs, the sway of her hips and the tilt of her neck, not wanting to forget a single detail.

Every fiber ached to pull her back. He didn't give in.

Justice was right. He'd changed from the foolish, angry boy who gave into selfish emotions. The knowledge brought a small comfort.

Dash followed the final guest all the way to the last step. He swallowed hard and waited for the flash as the hotel disappeared. Without warning, something slammed into his back shoving forward.

Panicked thoughts flew through his mind as his body went airborne. He landed facedown in the dirt.

He lay motionless, waiting for death. The pain promised him never came. How had he left the hotel? Twisting around, The Last Resort was gone, along with his soul. Dark, empty land stood where the building had sat only seconds ago.

"Dash." Justice appeared at his side.

He stared. How did she recognize him?

"It's okay." She crouched down and opened her purse.

"No, I can't—" The blue-green glow left him speechless. "My soul." His gaze snapped from the bright tree to her. She had saved him. "Why?"

"I'm selfish." She brushed his hair back from his forehead. "I love you and I don't want to live without you." She smiled and kissed him.

Dash grabbed her, wrapped his arms around her, and kissed her with everything he had. Love for her flowed through him.

Finally their mouths parted. "I love you, Justice Malloy."

Her smile, brighter than any star, beamed back. "Here." She lifted his soul from her bag and handed it to him.

Dash hesitated. Two hundred years spent resisting the very same action was a hard habit to break.

"Thank you." His throat narrowed. The moment his fingers

touched the small tree, its light flowed into his chest. The raging fire forever burning his veins cooled.

"Are you okay?" Justice glanced at the now rather ordinary plant.

"Better." He smiled. "Much better."

"What would you like to do first?"

"Besides make love to you until dawn and then again until noon?"

"Anything else?" Her eyes widened.

"Walk." He took her hand and they set out across the hard ground. Bright moonlight shined down on open ground, free from walls, stretching toward the horizon.

"I never thought I'd get to do this," he rasped.

She gave his fingers a gentle squeeze.

When they stopped, he set the small tree at his feet.

Suddenly, the ground rumbled and they scrambled backward. The single plant multiplied into a long arbor whose curved branches formed a corridor of hearts.

They both stared unable to speak.

Finally, Justice broke the silence. "This solves my problem of a reception site."

"You think your society client will like the rustic setting?" He wrapped his arms around her and pulled her back snugly against his chest.

"When I tell her the legend of how it grew of true love and share my ideas for the wedding she will." She placed her hands atop his.

"That takes care of your client and brother's college money. But there's still one problem."

Lips pursed, she swiveled to face him. "What?"

"I don't have a place to live." He nodded to where the hotel had once stood.

Her mouth relaxed back into a grin. "Easy, you took me in, so now it's my turn."

"With one difference."

"We won't be locked in or attacked by the soulless?" She leaned into his touch.

"Several differences, then," he laughed. Happiness filled him until he felt ready to burst. "I'm not leaving, ever."

Here's a taste of "Hot Pepper,"
by P.F. Kozak!

Appearing in TRIO,
on sale from Aphrodisia!

1

Pepper grabbed her purse and went out the back door, slamming it shut behind her. Her sister had really crossed the line this time. If it wasn't bad enough that she had come crawling back home and asked for help, Lois wouldn't let her forget how she had disappointed everyone by leaving. This time, she had actually called her a failure, to her face.

She got into her car, which she hoped would start. It needed work. But that took money, which she didn't have. Damned if she would ask her sister for it. She would walk first.

When the motor turned over and started to hum, Pepper breathed a sigh of relief. She didn't know where the hell she would go, but she did know she wouldn't spend another night sleeping on her sister's couch.

Almost out of habit, she headed downtown. Maybe she would run into someone she knew. She smacked the steering wheel with her hand. And what if she did? What would she say? "Oh, and by the way, can I sleep on your couch until I can afford my own place?" Yeah, right.

She drove around for about half an hour, checking out some

of her old haunts. The high school looked the same on the outside. Not having been in it for over ten years, she didn't know if she would recognize anything inside. The public library had already closed for the day, or she would have stopped to check her e-mail.

A new mall had opened on the edge of town. She didn't bother stopping there, either, since what little money she had should stay in her wallet. Then she drove down Elm Street, and saw the sign for Buck's Bar and Grill. Lois told her only a few nights before that Ted owned the place now, since his father passed away. She smiled knowing she might have just found another sofa.

Pepper parked in the gravel parking lot between two pickup trucks. Obviously, some things never change. Buck's had always been popular with the after-work crowd, the guys stopping for a beer before going home. Later, anyone looking for some company for the evening would drop by, or couples would come in for a drink.

Everything inside looked the same as she remembered, except for the addition of white Christmas lights strung across the room, and the pictures. Paintings she recognized as Ted's hung over the bar, as well as on the walls by the tables. She knew his father would never have allowed the lights, or his artwork, in here. Evidently, Ted really did run the place now.

Lois told her Ted would sometimes tend bar in the evenings, but the guy behind the bar tonight wasn't Ted. She didn't recognize him. Making her way past the men in work clothes and baseball caps, she managed to squeeze in at the end of the bar.

"Excuse me, is Ted here, please?"

The bartender gave her the once-over before he answered. "Yeah, he's in the office. What's your name?"

"Could you tell him Pepper would like to speak to him?"

"Sure will, sweetheart."

He disappeared through a side door for a few minutes. When he came back, Ted followed.

"Pepper? What the hell are you doing here? I thought you were still in Pittsburgh."

"Not anymore. I got laid off and ran out of money. I'm staying with my sister right now."

"Hey, kid. I'm sorry to hear that. Run over there and grab that table in the corner. I'll buy you a beer." Ted went behind the bar. He grabbed two bottles of Iron City and two glasses, and then came back to the table.

"Thanks, Ted. I can use a beer."

"Tell me what happened. I thought you were doing okay in Pittsburgh."

"I was. When my bank offered me the transfer to their headquarters, you know I jumped at it. I had no reason to stay here. I did okay, too. I learned the ropes, they made me a loan officer and sent me to school."

"Lois told me you got a promotion. I didn't know they made you an officer."

"Yeah, well, big f'ing deal. I got promoted, and went to school. My last review was a good one. My supervisor told me I'd probably get promoted again within the next year. Then a bigger bank swallowed us up. They handed me my pink slip and told me not to let the door hit me in the ass. So much for making a better life for myself."

"You couldn't find anything else?"

"No. It's really bad right now. There aren't many jobs to be had, anywhere."

"What are you going to do?"

"Don't know." Pepper poured the rest of her beer into her glass. Screwing up her courage, she plunged in. "I have a favor to ask, actually maybe a couple of favors."

"Tell me what."

"I need a job and a place to stay for a while. I don't suppose you could use a waitress here and maybe have a sofa I can sleep on?" Pepper raised her glass and took a sip. Her hand shook a little. She hoped Ted hadn't noticed.

"What about your sister? She doesn't have room for you?"

"I'm sleeping on her sofa, have been for almost a week. Every day, I hear the lecture of how I should have been a beautician like her. Today, she told me if I weren't so stuck up, I wouldn't be such a failure."

"She said that to you?"

"She sure as hell did. That's when I left and came here. I drove around awhile, and ended up on your doorstep."

"Jesus Christ, Pepper. You'd think after all this time, she would have softened a little."

"Not a chance. You know, once a bitch, always a bitch. I had no place else to go. I thought I could put up with it until I could find a job, and save enough for my own place. But, after today, I'd rather sleep in my car than hear her mouth off to me again."

Ted flagged the bartender to bring them two more beers. "If you want a job here, it's yours. As you can see, business is good. You could fill in on the floor when I need extra help, but I think it would make more sense if you help me with the books. With your banking experience, you'll probably handle the accounting better than I ever could."

"God, thank you, Ted. You've always been a good friend."

Ted nervously tapped his fingers on the table. Pepper remembered he always did that when he felt uncomfortable. He confirmed her suspicion when he said, "We have to talk about the other."

The disappointment welled up in her throat. She tried to swallow it. "It's all right. I understand I can't intrude on your life."

"Pepper, it's not that, not at all. This is more about you than about me."

"I don't understand."

"Butch is staying with me right now, has been for several months."

"He is? What about Sandy?"

"They finally called it quits. Sandy agreed to a no-fault divorce if Butch gave her custody of Stacy. It's over."

"Lois didn't tell me."

"Probably because everyone sides with Sandy. Butch left her."

"Why? I know he loves their kid."

"Yes, but he doesn't love Sandy. He never has."

"He should have thought of that before he knocked her up." She took a good swig of Iron City.

"You're still pissed at him, aren't you?"

"Why the hell shouldn't I be? He fucked up both our lives by getting her pregnant. You know damn well I thought we'd get married."

"Yes, and I also know he still talks about you."

"He does? How do you know that?"

"I live with him, remember?"

"Yeah, you told me that. Shit, if I stay with you, I'll be living with him, too!"

"That's my point. I have the space. My dad left me everything. That big old house is all mine. When Butch asked if I'd rent him a room, I thought, what the hell, why not?"

"That's how he ended up with you?"

"You know my house is close to his garage. That's good for him, and I like having the company. Can you handle living in the same house with him?"

"Ted, I don't have many options right now. If you have a place for me to sleep, and a shower I can use, I'll deal with it."

"Well, in all fairness, I can't offer that to you until I talk to Butch. He has dibs."

"Yeah, I remember. Dibs is sacred."

"You know, he still does that. He'll call dibs on a piece of cold pizza in the damn refrigerator." Ted took his cell phone out of his pocket. "Let me call him. If he's home, it'll only take him a few minutes to get here."

While Ted called Butch, Pepper went to the ladies' room. She put on some lipstick and checked her hair. She hadn't seen Butch since she left Willows Point. The last time she saw him, he'd come into the bank to make a deposit. He'd heard she planned to move to Pittsburgh, and asked if she wanted to have a good-bye drink with him. She said no. There had been no contact between them since.

When she came back, she saw Ted behind the bar talking to the bartender. She waited for him at their table. He came back carrying another bottle of Iron City and a glass. "I got him. He'll be here in about ten minutes."

"Did you tell him I'm here?"

"I told him you're back in Willows Point. I didn't say anything about your moving in with us." Ted grabbed another chair from the next table and put it between them. "I figure we'll ask him together. Let him say no to your face. I bet he can't."

Pepper pressed her cool glass against her cheek. Her face felt hot. "Ted, before he gets here, I want to know for sure that you're all right with this. I don't know if you're involved with anyone. Will my being around be a problem?"

"I'm not involved with anyone, and your being around won't be a problem."

"What happened to John?"

"It didn't work out. We went different directions."

"When Lois told me you moved back home, I wondered what happened."

"The next promising art student came along and that, as they say, was that."

"I'm sorry, Ted. I didn't know. God, I really didn't mean to lose track of you guys. It just happened."

"This feels like no time has passed since I saw you last." Ted put his hand over hers. "You know, Pepper, Butch isn't the only one who's thought of you over the years. I still remember our wild days."

"So do I." Pepper squeezed his hand. "The three of us really had something special in high school. You were the only one who really understood when Butch dumped me."

He didn't want to. With his parents and Sandy's family pressuring him to do the right thing . . . he caved. He married her because he had to, not because he wanted to."

"Yeah, right. That, and my E-Z Pass, will get me on the Turnpike."

"Look, Pepper, I know he hurt you. I also know one of the reasons you took the job in Pittsburgh was to get away from him. But that's water under the bridge now. You're right. We did have something special together. That's why I think it could work if you moved in with us."

"Do you mind if I ask you something?"

"What?"

"Have you and Butch done anything together since he's moved in?"

"Absolutely nothing."

Pepper scratched Ted's wrist with her fingernails. "So, you've both become monks?"

"More or less."

"That really sucks."

"As I recall, so do you, very well."

"Okay, I'll pay my share of the rent with blow jobs. Is that the deal?"

Ted smiled. "It could work. There aren't many women that can give me a hard-on. You're one of the very few. In fact, you're giving me one now. There's something to be said for that."

Pepper glanced at the locals sitting at the bar. "Do they know you swing both ways?"

"Not really. If I make jokes about big tits a few times a week, they're all satisfied I'm one of them."

"Even with your painting?"

Ted pointed to the far end of the bar. "See that guy down there, the one with the Pirates ball cap?"

"Yeah, what about him?"

"He bought one of my landscapes for his wife's birthday. Says she really likes what I do and surprised her with it."

"No kidding!"

"No kidding. Because I went to school there, I also got an exhibit at Indiana University. I sold about half a dozen from that show, flowers and landscapes mostly. I've even sold a few right here." He gestured to the wall behind them. "All these are for sale, except for that one."

Pepper looked at the painting that wasn't for sale. "Is that the field where you, me, and Butch had our picnics?"

"Same one. That's why it isn't for sale." A few moments of uncomfortable silence followed, as Pepper struggled with the memory. Ted kept the conversation going. "Yeah, between painting and the bar, I've been busy."

Pepper tried her best to keep things light. "Glad things are good for you. How's Butch doing?"

"Butch is doing okay, too, even with the divorce. He's running the garage now. His uncle retired."

"Think he'll fix my car for a blow job?"

"Why don't you ask him? He just came in the door."

Pepper looked toward the door. Butch hadn't yet seen them sitting in the corner. He had his head turned, looking for them at the bar. Her heart thumped in her chest as she stared at his profile. His Roman nose and curly black hair were just as she remembered. He had a suntan, making his olive skin even darker. In his jeans and T-shirt, he still looked every bit the hot Italian stud.

She jumped when Ted put his hand on her arm. "Steady, Pepper, you're shaking."

"Shit!" She took a deep breath and shook her hands, hoping to dry her sweating palms. "Ted, I might need something stronger than a beer."

"You got it, kiddo. I'll get us a bottle." Before going behind the bar, he stopped and spoke to Butch. Pepper saw Ted point back to the corner table and Butch nodded. When Butch turned and came toward her, she put her hands in her lap so he wouldn't see them shaking.

"Hello, Pepper. It's been a long time." He bent over and kissed her cheek.

"Hi, Butch. You're looking good."

"So are you." Butch sat down in the chair next to her. "How've you been?"

"Not too bad. And you?"

"I'm doing all right."

Fortunately, Ted returned at that moment and interrupted the banal conversation. He put a bottle of Jim Beam and three shot glasses on the table. He glanced at Pepper. "Everything okay here?"

"Fine." Pepper hoped that sounded believable. "Could you pour me a shot?"

Butch picked up an empty shot glass. "Me, too."

"Shots all around." Ted opened the bottle of whiskey and poured them each a drink. Pepper concentrated on keeping her hand still and picked up her glass. Ted picked up his and raised it to his companions. "To friends reunited."

Butch raised his and toasted in Italian. *"Cin Cin."*

Pepper offered a weak "Cheers," then bolted back her shot. She held out her glass for a refill.

Ted poured another one. "Have you had any dinner, Pepper? You don't want this to knock you on your ass."

"No, I haven't eaten anything. I left before Lois finished cooking dinner."

"You'd better eat something, so you don't get shitfaced." Ted flagged down the waitress. "Butch, you want a burger?"

"Sure, and a side of your greasy fries, too."

"Fuck you! You're not paying, so quit complaining."

"Well, hell, if it's on the house, throw in an order of wings, too." His typical Butch wisecrack didn't hide his concern. "What the hell happened, Pepper? Why aren't you in Pittsburgh?"

The urge to cry nearly overcame Pepper. She drank her second shot before she answered. "I lost my job." That's all she could say. The waitress came just then to take their order, giving her a chance to get it together.

After Ted ordered them some food, he told Butch what Pepper had told him, sparing her the ordeal of having to tell her story again. While Butch listened, he focused on Ted, but held Pepper's hand. The familiar feel of his fingers wrapped around hers calmed her. Ted stopped just short of asking Butch about her staying with them.

Ted picked up the bottle and poured Pepper another shot. "I'll let Pepper ask you what she asked me."

"Ask me what?"

With Butch still holding her hand, and with his dark eyes fixed solely on her, Pepper plunged in. "I asked Ted if I can stay with him for a while, until I get on my feet. He's already said I can work here at the bar, but told me you have dibs on the house."

"You know about me and Sandy? We got divorced?"

"Ted just told me. I didn't know when I asked to stay with him, and I didn't know you had moved in with him."

"What the fuck difference does that make?" Butch turned to Ted. "You got a problem with her staying in your house if I'm there?"

"Not at all. But I thought you might."

"Why?" Butch never had been one to pull any punches. His shoot-from-the-hip style had survived his failed marriage. "Do you think Sandy put me off women?"

"If she had, at least I'd be getting some. We both know that's not the case."

"Then, why do you think I'd have a problem with Pepper staying with us?"

"If you're asking me that, I guess there isn't one. If you both can handle it, then let's try it. Who knows? It just might work."

Butch squeezed Pepper's hand. "Do you think you can handle it, Pearl?"

"Don't you start that already! You know I hate that name. My name is Pepper."

"You can't bullshit me, Pearl. I know that's your real name. Your mama told my mama she named you after Minnie Pearl. I remember when your grandmother gave you a straw hat with flowers and a price tag hanging from it on your sixteenth birthday."

"Fuck you!"

"I also remember that." He tilted his head toward Ted. "I think that's what Rembrandt here is talking about. We have history, Pepper. Can you live with that every day?"

Pepper stuck her chin out defiantly. "I can if you can, Robert."

Ted interrupted. "All right, boys and girls. Play nice."

Butch shot Ted a look that curled Pepper's toes. "You mean the way we used to play?"

"Maybe." He grinned at Pepper. "Chances are good you'll get your car fixed."

"What's her car got to do with it?"

"Her car needs work. Just before you came in, she mentioned asking you if she could arrange a barter. Tell him, Pepper."

"Ted, for Christ's sake!"

"Pepper, what the hell is he taking about? What kind of barter?"

"Since I don't have enough money to get my car fixed, I wondered if you'd work on it for a blow job. It was a joke, for crying out loud!"

Ted laughed. "She also might end up paying me rent the same way. What do you think?"

"I think life just got a whole hell of a lot better!"

Pepper drank her third shot and held up her shot glass. "I want another one."

Ted put the cap back on the bottle. "Not until you eat something." He set the bottle on the floor beside his chair. "I don't want to have to carry you out of here."

"Party pooper."

"If you do move in with us, kiddo, the party is just starting."

"That's the goddamn truth." Butch opened the extra beer and drank it out of the bottle. "Do you have your stuff in your car?"

"No. All I have with me is my purse. Everything else is still at Lois's house."

"How bad was it when you left? Can you go back tonight and get your clothes?"

"I think so. Maybe I'll be lucky and she'll just ignore me."

"I'll go with you."

Ted tapped his fingers on the table. "Butch, I don't think that's a good idea. I'll go."

"Why the hell shouldn't I go? I don't give a shit what Lois thinks of me. My life is none of her goddamned business."

"Lois is already being a bitch to Pepper. If you show up, it'll be even worse."

Pepper agreed. "Butch, Ted's right. Let him help me get my stuff. There's not that much. I sold all my furniture so I could fit everything in my car. Other than my clothes, I only brought back my TV, my stereo, my laptop, and a few boxes of things. Most of it is still packed. I've been living out of my suitcase."

"Damn it, Pepper, it should be me."

"That's what I said ten years ago."

Butch reached into his back pocket and took out his wallet. "Let me show you something." He flipped through his credit cards until he came to the last sleeve. He carefully pulled out a picture he had tucked behind the card and handed it to Pepper.

Pepper stared at an image of herself in a white sundress, her long reddish brown hair framing her face. She remembered the day Ted took the picture. The three of them had gone on a picnic the day after they graduated, in the same field Ted had painted. Ted took his camera. He decided he wanted to paint her in the white sundress. She had posed for him, so he would have shots to work from. Butch asked him for a copy of his favorite.

"You kept this?"

"Of course I did."

"Why?"

Butch shifted in his chair, then took a sip of beer. "You were beautiful that day." He stared at her for a moment. "You still are."

Pepper's eyes filled with tears. "This was the last time . . ." She couldn't continue.

Butch finished her thought. "It was the last time the three of us were together. I found out a week later that Sandy was pregnant, and all hell broke loose."

Pepper squeezed her eyes shut, trying to keep the tears inside. She remembered being with Butch and Ted that day. They had made sure they went to an isolated spot, where no one would see them. She hadn't worn anything under the sundress. Ted had asked her not to, so she would surprise Butch. The three of them made love on a blanket, surrounded by daisies. It was the happiest day of her life.

She hadn't been with either of them since.

1 dead in attic

Chris Rose

Photographs by Charlie Varley

Chris Rose
BOOKS

Portions of the proceeds from every sale of this book will be shared with ARTDOCS and the Tipitina's Foundation – **rebuilding New Orleans, one song at a time**.

ISBN 0-9777715-0-4

Published by Chris Rose Books
6308 Magazine Street
New Orleans, LA 70118

www.chrisrosebooks.com

Webmaster: Fred RedBean Plunkett
Design: Richard Rose
Printing: MOSAIC

Introduction

Writing an introduction to this book almost seems a superfluous notion. My story, emotions, actions and mission are all laid out in the text that follows. I pretty much said everything I had to say.

For now.

The stories that follow comprise most of the columns I wrote for The Times-Picayune between August 29, 2005 and New Years Day, 2006. The order is not chronological, but thematic: the days after Katrina, coping in the Big Uneasy, my family's life in exile, and the tragicomic characters and controversies that burst through.

Newspapering is a pressure business by design and necessity, but never have I felt it more than during those four months. Because of the scope of our disaster, suffering, destruction and death, what we were doing at the newspaper became more than just reporting the news.

Katrina's aftermath transformed The Times-Picayune from a commodity of choice to an essential resource. Everyone, it seems, turned to us and our sister website, nola.com. In the tragic void left by our political leadership, the newspaper and WWL radio became the only voices with any range and power, the only voices of reason, of common sense and of hope.

Before Aug. 29, I spent most of my work day stalking celebrities and reveling in the frivolity of the entertainment industry. That seems like a century ago and it seems unlikely that I'll go back to that life.

After the storm, I just started writing, not attempting to carve out any niche but just to tell the story, however it revealed itself to me.

As I look back, I realize I never thought out or planned a thing, but careened from one episode to the next, absorbing the enormous tragedy and dribs of comedy attendant to the Aftermath and sometimes it hit me so hard that all I could do was curl up on the floor, rock back and forth and howl.

I learned a lot about mental illness in those four months. I have been to the dark recesses. Thank God I could exorcise the pain by writing it. That way, in the morning, I felt better and now it was up to the readers to deal with. Nice therapy if you can get it.

The support from our community and our readership has been overwhelming. By year's end, I had received more than 10,000 emails, about a thousand phone calls and the occasional lost art of a letter.

I tried to answer as many as I could. Many folks poured out their hearts in their correspondence and I just want to say thank you to as many as possible, and acknowledge that their stories have been heard.

For those I missed, thank you. The piles of email I received each morning telling me to keep up the fight were what I needed, in fact, to keep up the fight.

There are hundreds of players involved in the process that got me to the point of putting this book together. I can't name them all. But a few, I must.

Thank you James O'Byrne and Mark Lorando, two editors who support me, save me from myself and understand the concept of literature in a hurry. Thanks to The Times-Picayune for rising to the occasion. I am proud to be part of this team. I will never forget the Warriors of Laurel Street. Brothers, forever.

Thanks Mom and Dad, for taking my family in. You are my heroes. Richard and Diane, John and Ellen, James Ledet and Joe Fontana ... how could we ever begin to repay? David and Gus, Peepaw and Pawpaw, Sandra and Glynn; for shelter from the storm.

Kelly. For the journey this far, and the journey ahead. And Katherine, Jack and James; reasons to get up every day and go forward. When, truth be told, sometimes I really didn't feel like it.

Chris Rose
January 6, 2006

3

Who We Are

Dear America,

I suppose we should introduce ourselves: We're South Louisiana.

We have arrived on your doorstep on short notice and we apologize for that, but we never were much for waiting around for invitations. We're not much on formalities like that.

And we might be staying around your town for a while, enrolling in your schools and looking for jobs, so we wanted to tell you a few things about us. We know you didn't ask for this and neither did we, so we're just going to have to make the best of it.

First of all, we thank you. For your money, your water, your food, your prayers, your boats and buses and the men and women of your National Guards, fire departments, hospitals and everyone else who has come to our rescue.

We're a fiercely proud and independent people, and we don't cotton much to outside interference, but we're not ashamed to accept help when we need it. And right now, we need it.

Just don't get carried away. For instance, once we get around to fishing again, don't try to tell us what kind of lures work best in your waters.

We're not going to listen. We're stubborn that way.

You probably already know that we talk funny and listen to strange music and eat things you'd probably hire an exterminator to get out of your yard.

We dance even if there's no radio. We drink at funerals. We talk too much and laugh too loud and live too large and, frankly, we're suspicious of others who don't.

But we'll try not to judge you while we're in your town.

Everybody loves their home, we know that. But we love South Louisiana with a ferocity that borders on the pathological. Sometimes we bury our dead in LSU sweatshirts.

Often we don't make sense. You may wonder why, for instance — if we could only carry one small bag of belongings with us on our journey to your state — why in God's name did we bring a pair of shrimp boots?

We can't really explain that. It is what it is.

You've probably heard that many of us stayed behind. As bad as it is, many of us cannot fathom a life outside of our border, out in that place we call Elsewhere.

The only way you could understand that is if you have been there, and so many of you have. So you realize that when you strip away all the craziness and bars and parades and music and architecture and all that hooey, really, the best thing about where we come from is us.

We are what made this place a national treasure. We're good people. And don't be afraid to ask us how to pronounce our names. It happens all the time.

When you meet us now and you look into our eyes, you will see the saddest story ever told. Our hearts are broken into a thousand pieces.

But don't pity us. We're gonna make it. We're resilient. After all, we've been rooting for the Saints for 35 years. That's got to count for something.

OK, maybe something else you should know is that we make jokes at inappropriate times.

But what the hell.

And one more thing: In our part of the country, we're used to having visitors. It's our way of life.

So when all this is over and we move back home, we will repay to you the hospitality and generosity of spirit you offer to us in this season of our despair.

That is our promise. That is our faith.

Early Days

Facing the Unknown

I got out.

I'm mystified by the notion that so many people didn't even try, but that's another story for another time.

We left Saturday, my wife, kids and me. We went first to Picayune, Miss., thinking that a Category 3 storm would flood New Orleans and knock out power, but that we'd be dry and relatively comfortable in the piney woods while the city dried out.

Sunday morning, of course, Katrina was a massive red blob on our TV screens — now a Cat 5 — so we packed up and left again.

We left my in-laws behind in Picayune. They wouldn't come with us. Self-sufficient country folk; sometimes you can't tell 'em nothing.

We don't know what happened to them. My wife's dad and her brother and their families: No word. Only hope.

Like so many people around the country wondering what happened to those still unaccounted for; we just don't know. That's the hardest part.

If you take the images you've seen on TV and picked up off the radio and internet, and you try to apply what you know to the people and places you don't know about, well, the mind starts racing, assumptions are made and well … it consumes you.

The kids ask you questions. You don't have answers. Sometimes they look at me and though they don't say it, I can see they're wondering: Daddy, where are you?

My 6-year-old daughter, she's onto this thing. What is she thinking?

We spent Sunday night in a no-tell motel in a forgotten part of downtown Vicksburg; a neighborhood teetering between a familiar antiquated charm and hopeless decay. Truth is, it called to mind my beloved New Orleans.

Most of the folks in the hotel seem to live there permanently and it had a hard-luck feel to it. It was the kind of place where your legs start itching in the bed and you think the worst and you don't want your kids to touch the carpet or the tub and we huddled together and I read them to sleep.

Monday morning, my wife's aunt told us they had a generator in Baton Rouge. As Katrina marched north and east, we bailed on our sullen little hotel and drove down along the western ridge of the storm, mostly alone on the road.

Gas was no problem. We had catfish and pulled pork in a barbeque joint in Natchez and the folks there — everyone we have met along our three-day journey — has said the same thing: Good luck, folks. We love your city. Take care of it for us.

Oh, my city. We have spent hours and hours listening to the radio. Image upon image piling up in your head.

What about school? What about everyone's jobs? Did all our friends get out? Are there still trees on the streetcar line? What will our economy be like with no visitors? How many are dead? Do I have a roof? Have the looters found me yet? When can we go home?

Like I said, it consumes you as you sit helplessly miles from home, unable to help anyone, unable to do anything.

If I could, what I'd do first is hurt the looters. I'd hurt them bad.

But you have to forget all that. You have to focus on what is at hand, what you can reach and when you have three little kids lost at sea, they are what's at hand and what you can reach.

I brought them to a playground in Baton Rouge Tuesday afternoon. They'd been bottled up for days.

Finally unleashed, they ran, they climbed, they fell down, they fought, they cried, they made me laugh, they drove me crazy; they did the things that make them kids.

It grounds you. You take a breath. You count to ten. Maybe — under the circumstances — you go to twenty or thirty this time.

And tonight, we'll just read them to sleep again.

We have several books with us because — and this is rich — we brought on our evacuation all the clothes and things we planned to bring on a long-weekend trip that we were going to take over Labor Day weekend.

To the beach. To Fort Morgan, right at the mouth of Mobile Bay.

Man.

Instead of that, I put on my sun tan lotion and went out in the yard of the house where we're staying in Baton Rouge and I raked a massive pile of leaves and limbs from the yard and swept the driveway.

Doing yard work and hitting the jungle gym on the Day After. Pretending life goes on. Just trying to stay busy. Just trying not to think. Just trying not to fail, really.

Gotta keep moving.

The First Time Back

The first time you see it ... I don't know. Where are the words?

I got to town Monday afternoon. I braced myself, not knowing how it would make me feel, not knowing how much it would make me hurt.

I found out that I am one of the lucky ones. High ground. With that comes gratitude and wonder and guilt. The Higher Powers have handed me my house and all my stuff and now what? What is there?

I live Uptown, where all the fancy-pants houses are and they're all still here. Amid the devastation, they never looked so beautiful. They never looked more like hope. This swath of land is where this city will begin its recovery.

There are still homes and schools, playgrounds, stores, bars and restaurants. Not so many trees, I'm afraid. We'll have to do something about that.

The Circle K near my house was looted, but there are still ample supplies of cigarettes and booze. They just took what they needed. The hardware store and Perlis — the preppy clothing store — same thing.

Someone kicked in the window at Shoefty, a high-end shoe boutique and what good a pair of Manolo Blahnik stilettos is going to do you right now, I don't know.

Idiots.

I myself was escorted out of the local Winn-Dixie by narcotics officers from Rusk County, Texas.

I told them I thought it was OK to take what we need. "And what do you need?" the supervisor asked me. I reached into my bag and held up a bottle of mouthwash.

I told him I will come back to this Winn-Dixie one day and pay for this bottle and I will. I swear it.

Right by the entrance to the store, there is a huge pile of unsold newspapers stacked up from the last day they were delivered, Sunday, Aug. 28.

The Times-Picayune headline screams: KATRINA TAKES AIM.

Ain't that the truth? Funny, though: The people you see here — and there are many who stayed behind — they never speak her name. She is the woman who done us wrong.

I had the strangest dream last night, and this is true: I dreamt I was reading an ad in the paper for a hurricane-relief benefit concert at Zephyr Stadium and the headliner act was Katrina and the Waves.

They had that peppy monster hit back in the '80s, "Walking on Sunshine," the one they play on Claritin ads on TV and that almost seems funny in light of what happened.

Almost.

Riding my bike, I searched out my favorite places, my comfort zones. I found that Tipitina's is still there and that counts for something. Miss Mae's and Dick & Jenny's, ditto.

Domilise's po-boy shop is intact, although the sign fell and shattered but the truth is, that sign needed to be replaced a long time ago.

I saw a dead guy on the front porch of a shotgun double on a working-class street and the only sound was wind chimes.

Everybody here has a dead guy story now. Everybody here will always be different.

I passed by the Valence Street Baptist Church and the façade was ripped away and I walked in and stared at the altar amid broken stained glass and strewn Bibles and I got down on my knees and said thank you but why? why? why? and I'm not even anything close to Baptist.

It just seemed like a place to take shelter from the storm in my head.

The rockers on my neighbor's front porch are undisturbed, like nothing ever happened. At my other neighbor's house — the ones who never take out their trash — a million kitchen bags are still piled in the mound that's always there and I never thought I'd be happy to see garbage, but I am.

Because it reminds me of my home.

I haven't been down in the kill zone yet. I haven't seen the waters. I haven't been where all hope, life and property are lost.

I have only seen what I have seen and we took the hit and it is still here. This is where we'll make our start. This is where we'll make our stand.

And when everything gets back to normal — whenever that may be — I'm going to do what I've been putting off for a very long time and I'm going to walk next door and tell my neighbors that they really do need to start taking out their trash.

Survivors

They're telling the people they have to go. They're going door to door with rifles now.

They came to our little hovel on Laurel Street Uptown — a dozen heavily-armed members of the California National Guard — they pounded on our door and wanted to know who we were.

We told them we were the newspaper, the Big City Daily. I admit, it doesn't look like the newsrooms you see on TV. I suppose if we wore shirts, we'd look more professional.

The Guard moved on, next door, next block.

They're telling people they have to go.

It won't be easy. The people who stayed here have weathered 10 days of unfathomable stench and fear and if they haven't left yet, it seems unlikely that they're going to be willing now.

In a strange way, life just goes on for the remaining. In the dark and fetid Winn-Dixie on Tchoupitoulas, an old woman I passed in the pet food aisle was wearing a house frock and puffy slippers and she just looked at me as she pushed her cart by and said: "How you doin', baby?"

Like it's just another afternoon making groceries.

I love the way strangers call you baby in this town.

Outside the store, there's an old guy who parks his old groaning car by the front door from sunup to sundown. There are extension cords running from his trunk into the store, which still has power — don't ask me how; I have no idea — and he watches TV in his front seat and drinks juice.

That is what he does, all day, every day.

At this point, I just can't see this guy leaving. I don't imagine he has anyplace else in the world but this.

And life goes on. Down on St. Claude Avenue, a tribe of survivors has blossomed at Kajun's Pub where, incredibly, they have cold beer and cigarettes and a stereo playing Elvis and you'd think everything was in standard operating procedure but it is not: The Saturday night karaoke has been indefinitely suspended.

The people here have a touch of Mad Max syndrome; they're using an old blue Cadillac for errands and when parts fall off of it — and many parts have fallen off — they just throw them in the trunk.

Melvin, a bar owner from down the block, had the thing up for sale for $895, but he'll probably take the best offer now.

Melvin's Bar and Kajun's Pub have pooled their inventories to stay in business.

"We've blended our fortunes together," said Renee dePonthieux, a bartender at Melvin's. "We carried everything we could down here, and we'll make the accounting later. What else are you gonna do? In case you haven't heard, Budweiser ain't delivering."

A guy with a long goatee and multiple tattoos was covering a couple of aluminum foil pans of lasagna and carrying them up to the roof to cook them in the sun on the hot slate shingles.

Joann Guidos, the proprietor at Kajun's, called out for a game of bourre and they all dumped their money on a table and sat down and let the cards and liquor flow.

A National Guard truck pulled up and asked if they were ready to leave yet. Two guys standing out on the sidewalk in the company of pit bulls said: "Hell no."

dePonthieux said: "We're the last fort on the edge of the wilderness. My family's been in exile for 300 years; this ain't shit."

I just don't see these people leaving.

Uptown, on what was once a shady street, a tribe is living in a beautiful home owned by a guy named Peanut. There is a seaplane in his driveway, a bass boat in the front yard and generators running the power.

Let's just say they were prepared.

All the men wear pistols in visible holsters. They've got the only manicured lawn in the city. What else is there to do all afternoon, really?

Christine Paternostro is a member of this tribe and she is an out-of-work hair stylist from Supercuts in a city where no one shaves or bathes. Not many prospects for her at this point.

"Everyone will need a haircut when this is over," I offered.

While members of this tribe stood talking on their street, a woman came running out of the house, yelling: "Y'all, come quick. We on WWL! We on WWL!"

Everyone ran in the house and watched a segment about how people are surviving in the city. And these guys are doing just that. (Although I think the airplane in the driveway is a little over the top.)

As I was leaving, the WWL woman said to me: "Are you staying for dinner?"

I was not, but I asked what they were having. "Tuna steaks," she said. "Grilled."

If and when they rebuild this city and we all get to come home, I want to live near people like this. I just can't imagine them ever leaving.

They make me wonder if I ever could.

Life in the Surreal City

You hear the word "surreal" in every report from this city now. There is no better word for it.

If Salvador Dali showed up here, he wouldn't be able to make heads or tails of it. Nobody could paint this.

He did that famous painting of the melting clock, and our clocks melted at 6:45 the morning of Aug. 29. That's what the clocks in the French Quarter still say. That's when time stood still.

The Quarter survived all this; you've probably heard that much. Most of what remains unscathed — and I'm using a very relative term here — is a swath of dry land from the Riverbend through Audubon Park, down St. Charles and Tchoupitoulas to the Quarter and into the Bywater.

It's like a land mass the size of Bermuda, maybe, but with not so many golf courses.

There are other dry outposts in the great beyond — little Key Wests across the city — but I haven't seen them.

The weather is beautiful, I don't mind telling you. But if I wrote you a postcard, it wouldn't say, "Wish You Were Here."

There are still hearty rose bushes blooming on front porches, and there are still birds singing in the park. But the park is a huge National Guard encampment.

There are men and women from other towns living there in tents and who have left their families to come help us and they are in the park clearing out the fallen timber. My fellow Americans.

Every damn one of them tells you they're happy to be here (despite what you've heard, it still beats the hell out of Fallujah), and every time I try to thank them, on behalf of all of us, I just lose it. I absolutely melt down.

There is nothing quite as ignominious as weeping in front of a soldier.

This is no environment for a wuss like me. We reporters go to other places to cover wars and disasters and pestilence and famine. There's no manual to tell you how to do this when it's your own city.

And I'm telling you: It's hard.

It's hard not to get crispy around the edges. It's hard not to cry. It's hard not to be very, very afraid.

My colleagues who are down here are warriors. There are a half-dozen of us living in a small house on a side street Uptown. Everyone else has been cleared out.

We have a generator and water and military food rations and Doritos and smokes and booze. After deadline, the call goes out: "Anyone for some warm brown liquor?" And we sit on the porch in the very, very still of the night and we try to laugh.

Some of these guys lost their houses — everything in them. But they're here, telling our city's story.

And they stink. We all stink. We stink together.

We have a bunch of guns, but it's not clear to me if anyone in this "news bureau" knows how to use them.

The California National Guard came by and wanted an accounting of every weapon in the building and they wrote the serial numbers down and apparently our guns are pretty rad because they were all cooing over the .38s.

I guess that's good to know.

The Guard wanted to know exactly what we had so they would be able to identify, apparently by sound, what guns were in whose hands if anything "went down" after dark here at this house.

That's not so good to know.

They took all our information and bid us a good day and then sauntered off to retrieve a dead guy on a front porch down the street.

Then the California Highway Patrol — the CHiPs! — came and demanded we turn over our weapons.

What are you going to do? We were certainly outnumbered, so we turned over the guns. Then, an hour later, they brought them back. With no explanation.

Whatev. So here we are. Just another day at the office.

Maybe you've seen that Times-Picayune advertising slogan before: "News, Sports and More."

More indeed. You're getting your money's worth today.

Hope

Amid the devastation, you have to look for hope. Forward progress of any kind.

Even the smallest incidents of routine and normalcy become reassuring. For instance, I was driving down Prytania, and at the corner of Felicity, the light turned red.

Out of nowhere, in total desolation, there was a working stoplight. I would have been less surprised to find a Blockbuster Video on Mars.

And the funny thing is, I stopped. I waited for it to turn green, and then I drove slowly on my way, even though there were no other cars anywhere and the likelihood of getting a ticket for running the only traffic signal in town seems very unlikely right now.

Considering.

Also on Prytania, there was a gardener watering the plants on the porch of Nicolas Cage's mansion, and I guess that's a good sign. Life goes on. In very small ways.

The toilets flush now, and I never thought that would be a sound of reassurance. An even better sound was finding out that WWOZ is broadcasting on the Web — radio in exile — laying out their great New Orleans music.

That's important. I have no idea from where they're operating or which disc jockeys are spinning the discs, but I can tell you this: The first time I hear Billy Dell's "Records from the Crypt" on the radio again, I will kiss the dirty ground beneath my feet.

On Friday, you started to see guys with brooms cleaning Canal Street and Convention Center Boulevard. Up until then, any tidying up required either a backhoe, a crane or a Bobcat.

God only knows where they're going to put all this garbage, all this rubble, all these trees, but they're gathering it up all the same.

The streets of the French Quarter, absent the rubble of the CBD, basically look and smell the same as they do the day after Mardi Gras, except with no broken strands of beads in the gutter.

OK, maybe it was a real windy Mardi Gras, but you get the point.

It just needs a little face-lift, a little sweeping up and a good hard rain to wash away ... all the bad stuff.

A counterpoint to that scene would be Uptown on Broadway — Fraternity Row — where the street is actually cleaner than usual, and that's because the fine young men and women of our universities had not yet settled into their early-semester routines of dragging living room furniture out onto their front yards and drinking Red Bull and vodka to while away their youth.

I wonder where all of them are? When this is over, who will go there and who will teach there?

What will happen to us?

One thing's for sure, our story is being told.

The satellite trucks stretch for eight blocks on Canal Street and call to mind an event like the Super Bowl or the Republican Convention.

It's a strange place. Then again, anywhere that more than 10 news reporters gather becomes a strange place by default.

I saw Anderson Cooper interviewing Dr. Phil. And while Cooper's CNN camera crew filmed Dr. Phil, Dr. Phil's camera crew filmed Cooper, and about five or six other camera crews from other shows and networks stood to the side and filmed all of that.

By reporting this scene, I have become the media covering the media covering the media.

It all has the surrealistic air of a Big Event, what with Koppel and Geraldo and all those guys wandering around in their Eddie Bauer hunting vests, and impossibly tall and thin anchorwomen from around the region powdering their faces and teasing their hair so they look good when they file their latest report from hell.

"And today in New Orleans ... blah blah blah."

Today in New Orleans, a traffic light worked. Someone watered flowers. And anyone with the means to get online could have heard Dr. John's voice wafting in the dry wind, a sound of grace, comfort and familiarity here in the saddest and loneliest place in the world.

It's a start.

Rita Takes Aim

The slightest rain fell here Thursday morning.

You know, the kind of New Orleans rain that just gives everything a light coat and sheen, that tamps down the dust of the old shell roads and washes down the oyster stink in the French Quarter gutters and slicks up all the playground equipment and makes New Orleans smell — is it possible? — so fresh. So Southern.

The kind of rain that falls even though the sun is shining. Does that happen in other places?

New Orleans rain has always been like drops of clarity in an otherwise murky habitat, sometimes too much, sometimes too little, but always a marvel to behold. There's always something that needs to be washed down here.

In "A Streetcar Named Desire," Blanche Dubois said it best: "Don't you just love those long rainy afternoons in New Orleans when an hour isn't just an hour, but a little piece of eternity dropped into our hands — and who knows what to do with it?"

Indeed, what to do?

That was the rain that fell Thursday. And we needed it. Because the oyster stink is at noxious levels and the city is stacked with an Apocalyptic vision of dry kindling that requires only one dummy with a discarded cigarette to torch an entire block.

Which raises one of the things that most catches the eye here — the trees. Or the lack thereof. I don't know that anyone will ever be able to count how many trees fell or just plain withered and died under Katrina's fierce hot breath, but I'm sure some expert will tell us in due time. Whatever the raw number, it won't match the impact on the senses.

I can't remember where I read it now, but someone interviewed a New Orleans artist who had returned home last week and this guy — whose very living hinges upon his interpretations of shadow, nuance and color — said the problem with New Orleans now is that there is too much sunlight on the ground.

That changes everything. Because if there was ever a town that couldn't afford to surrender shade, it is this one, where a walk on a summer afternoon can be like sauntering through a blast furnace.

Maybe only the bad golfers will be happy about this development, for their way from tee to green now lies so much more accessible.

It had been three weeks since it rained — since you know when — and that's as unfathomable a notion here as a September without fresh oysters.

Of course, by the time you read this, Friday, rain might not be such a charming enterprise here. And Blanche Dubois' notion of eternity my not be so romantic.

Rita swirls out in the Gulf of Mexico, capriciously choosing its path of destruction and even the slightest brush of wind could take out so many more trees and the slightest rain — the kind that tourists with their Big Ass Beers in hand used to stand under French Quarter balconies and watch with a sense of comic wonder — could wind the clock back three weeks to that piece of eternity we don't ever want to live again.

Under one of those French Quarter balconies, those famous mannequin legs at Big Daddy's strip club improbably swing in and out of a window, an alluring, optimistic or delusional signal that the libertine times will once again return to the Old City. That les bons temps will rouler again some day.

There is no power on that block of Bourbon Street where the legs swing; the owner just thought that the best use of portable power would be to swing those legs.

Swinging in the rain. Drinking a hurricane instead of dodging one. Living in a place where the past and present and future have never collided so chaotically and without rational analysis.

There is no one who can tell us what tomorrow will bring. But, personally, I consider it a very bad sign that the killer hurricane that dances on our television screens and toys with our collective psyche is named after a meter maid.

That can't be good.

The Empty City

It's hard to imagine that it could have felt any lonelier in New Orleans than it has for the past three weeks. But Friday, everything just disappeared.

What little life there was seemed to dissipate into the not-so-thin air of a colossal barometer drop. The Furies, it seems, are aroused.

The wind buffeted cars and put the heavy hand on already weakened trees. Magazine Street boutique signs — most hanging askew by only one chain after Katrina — spun in place like pinwheels. Loose power lines whipped and flapped across Uptown and Lakeview streets like fly fishing rods.

The rain came, misting one minute, blinding the next. Outside of the CBD emergency operations center, anywhere you drove, you saw ... nobody.

The folks who had been trickling into town for the past week or so, checking on homes and businesses, simply ghosted. Police on the outskirts of town blocked all entry. The big National Guard camps in Audubon Park disappeared overnight without a sign that they were ever there.

So much for the repopulation plan. A TV station reported that there were only 500 civilians left in the city as Hurricane Rita set aim on the Cajun Riviera, all those miles away to the West, and you were hard pressed to find any of them.

A passing truck stopped me, and the guys inside asked for directions to the Nashville Wharf and it was good just to talk to someone.

The isolation can be maddening. The car radio just tells you bad things. You just want to find someone, anyone, and say: "How 'bout dem Saints?"

You know those classic New Orleans characters — the cab drivers, bartenders and bitter poets — who buttonhole you and natter on and on forever about tedious and mundane topics that date back to Mayor Schiro's term and when the Pelicans played out on Tulane Avenue? Usually when you're in a hurry somewhere?

I'd give anything to run into one of those guys right now. Go ahead and tell me about the fishing in Crown Point; I'll listen to just about anything you have to say.

I went to Walgreens on Tchoupitoulas, which had been open most of the week, figuring there would be life there, but it had shuttered at noon. There was a sign on the door that said: "Now Hiring" and that's funny.

I guess.

The day before, the store's public address system was stuck in a time warp, a perky female voice reminding shoppers (both of them): "Don't let Halloween sneak up on you; stock up on candy early. You'll find great savings now ... at Walgreens!"

Truth is, there sure was a hell of a lot of candy there. Trick or treat.

As I drove around, the gray sheets of rain pushed around all the stuff in the street and, trust me, there's a lot of stuff in the street. For as far as you looked up and down every avenue, the same blank vistas.

Across town, the water was rising. Again. I suppose there were people there, trying to save our city again, though the cynical might ask: What's to save?

On dry land, the only place I found people gathered was at the fire station on Magazine Street in the Garden District. I went by to drop off some copies of the newspaper for the local guys and found about 60 firefighters from all over the country hanging out in a rec room watching TV and frying burgers.

That was perhaps the strangest sight of all, these guys just sitting around. Stranger in some ways than the desolation.

Because for once, with all this rain soaking the downed trees and rooftops, and nobody around to do something stupid like start a fire, they had nothing to do.

Just sit and watch TV in a haunted city.

God and Strippers

Even at the End of Days, there will be lap dancing.

Over the weekend, while a desolate, desperate city plunged into darkness and the waters rose again in the Rita Aftermath, and while a population spread across the nation watched new horrors with churning guts on TV, a strip club opened on Bourbon Street.

The symbolism of this event can hardly be overstated.

The Saints are gone. The Hornets are gone. Zephyr Field is a staging area for choppers to go find dead people.

No college hoops. No movie theaters, no Swamp Fest, no Voodoo Fest. No horses running at the Fairgrounds. No line for Friday lunch at Galatoire's.

But there are topless women hanging upside down from brass poles at a place called Déjà Vu. Gaudiness, flesh, neon and bad recorded music have returned to one small outpost on the Boulevard of Broken Dreams, and if that's not one small step towards normalcy — at least as that term is defined in the Big Uneasy — then I don't know what is.

There were about 100 guys in there Saturday night, all of them with very, very short hair, which is basically what everyone around here who's not a journalist has these days.

Exactly how a posse of exotic dancers were smuggled into town during the most severe lockdown in this city since the hurricane crises began, well, I don't know.

Inexplicable things seem to be the norm around here these days.

When I walk down the street one day and some rumpled grifter tells me he knows where I got my shoes, then I guess I'll know we're fully on our way home. (Of course, I could be cynical and tasteless and tell the guy: I got them at Wal-Mart on Tchoupitoulas like everyone else, but that would be cynical and tasteless.)

And speaking of tasteless: This is not a topic I want to delve too deeply into, but someone has to call out the demagogic ministers who have used Katrina's destruction to preach the message that God was tired of this city's libertine ways and decided to clean house.

Let me roll at you some snippets of wisdom that have been widely distributed on the Internet from Rev. Bill Shanks, pastor of New Covenant Fellowship in Metairie: "New Orleans now is Mardi Gras free. New Orleans now is free of Southern Decadence and the sodomites, the witchcraft workers, false religion — it's free of all of those things now. God simply, I believe, in His mercy purged all of that stuff out of there — and now we're going to start over again."

Well, almost. It's an interesting interpretation, to be sure, and Shanks is not the only man of the cloth to make such claims. No doubt, it's a good message for the evangelical business.

Of course, try telling some poor sap down in St. Bernard Parish who has never heard of Southern Decadence and who goes to Bible study every Wednesday night that he lost his house and his job and his grandmother died in a flooded nursing home because God was angry at a bunch of bearded guys in dresses over on Dumaine Street.

Collateral damage, I guess. The question that arises, of course, is that if Shanks' prophecy is true, how come Plaquemines, St. Bernard, the East and Lakeview are gone, but the French Quarter is still standing?

I'd suggest that there are those who have confused meteorology with mythology, global warming with just plain hot air, but that might be cynical and tasteless. Might be crass and gaudy.

And I'll try to leave that stuff where it belongs — in the French Quarter, where the craziest patchwork of people ever gathered on this planet are cobbling back together a strange and mind-boggling Twilight Zone of what it once was.

File that one under: Only in New Orleans.

The More Things Change

You hang around New Orleans long enough these days and you begin to absorb what is new and what is different.

For instance, I was sitting on my front stoop and an RTA bus marked MAGAZINE zoomed by. I thought: Well, how about that! That's a good sign.

Never mind that the bus was empty; at least it was running and that's a sign of normalcy. And it was driving way too fast and therein was another harbinger of the same-ol', same-ol'.

Then, about 90 seconds later, another RTA bus marked MAGAZINE whizzed by, shaking my house to its foundation. It, too, was empty, but it was the realization that there were probably only two busses running the entire Magazine Street route and here they were, one right after the other and I thought: We're back!

What could be a better indication of a return to the old ways than the colossal inefficiency of our public transportation system? I don't know about you, but I will sleep better tonight; at least, that is, until an RTA bus blows by the house at midnight at Category 5 speed and does more damage to my plaster ceilings than Katrina did.

Of course, a common joke around here — dire times make for dire humor — is that when the Mayor announced that he was laying off 3,000 workers this week, who would notice? I believe he, or some other public official, called them non-essential employees and I'll let you fill in your own punch line here.

I just hope it's not the two guys who've been assigned to cut the grass on the neutral grounds for the past 10 years; man, things would really be different around here without them.

I have a feeling I just really ticked off 3,000 people, maybe more. But then, that would be another sign of normalcy, wouldn't it? People being angry at the local newspaper: a comfort zone if ever there was one.

A casual drive around town — or at least what remains of it — is also a compelling reminder of the old days. It reminds you how much a simple afternoon drive can be facing danger to its core.

First of all, at least half the city's one-way signs were turned sideways by the wind and now point in the wrong direction. And half the people driving around here are guys from out of state in massive pickup trucks and the National Guard put up temporary stop signs at intersections where traffic lights are now working, so it's all a game of Russian roulette. Or maybe chicken.

A run to the local drug store/gas station/strip club has turned into a not-so-virtual game of Grand Theft Auto.

Every now and then I see some church lady tooling down the road at 7 mph in her cream-colored, four-door Grand Marquis and I can only wonder: Why are you here?

I know it's probably bad taste to kick the city while it's down, but it is interesting/fun/mind-boggling to watch some of the old New Orleans civic quirks work their way back into operation.

For instance, the mayor has urged business owners to come back into town and open up and we residents have been encouraged to patronize them, but neighborhood restaurants and bars are bum-rushed by the authorities every night at 8 p.m. and told to close for curfew.

I'm no restaurateur, but I can imagine it's got to be hard to build up a steady dinner clientele when you close at sunset. Oddly — maybe not so oddly, when I think about it — the strip clubs on Bourbon Street have somehow been exempt from this rule and there are tons of big, beefy guys in town (who drive really big pick-up trucks) with disposable cash who are all too happy to stuff garter belts full of fivers until the sun comes up and then they have to report to work and operate heavy machinery on a one-way street.

Yes, indeed, all is returning to normal. I think there is no better indication of this than the running commentary that has been taking place on the plywood boards mounted over the windows of Sarouk Shop Oriental Rugs down on St. Charles Avenue near Lee Circle.

Early on, in the hairy days of Aftermath, the owner/proprietor/squatter who was living there spray painted (I'm no handwriting analyst, but I'd say it was with some urgency): "Don't try: I am sleeping inside with a big dog, an ugly woman, two shotguns and a claw hammer."

Claw hammer. Nice touch.

Then, in a spray paint posting dated 9/4/05 (talk about meticulous graffiti!), it says: "Still here. Woman left. Cooking a pot of dog gumbo."

Like I said, dire times call for dire humor. Or maybe it wasn't a joke; some strange things have happened around here lately.

Anyway, in a spray painted update, dated 9/24, it says: "Welcome back, y'all. Grin & bear it."

Ain't that the truth? I mean, what are the other choices?

Enough to Feed an Army

I was walking around the French Quarter Saturday, surveying the hurricane clean-up efforts 12 days after the storm, when I came upon Finis Shellnut, who possesses one of the best names I've ever known.

"Come here," he told me. "I'm going to show you something you will never believe."

Shellnut is a real estate wheeler-dealer in the Quarter but is perhaps better known as the (now ex-) husband of Gennifer Flowers. They're originally from the Arkansas power network: He takes credit for introducing the Clintons into the Whitewater deal; she conducted more personalized business with the ex-president.

Together, they opened the Kelsto Club on St. Louis a few years ago and he held court behind the bar while she sang torch songs in the front of the windows that open across the street from the legendary Antoine's restaurant.

But they divorced just weeks before Katrina, which he weathered in the French Quarter. And after the storm passed, he immediately established himself as the go-to guy for goods and services on the street. Lumber, gas, cash, ice, backhoes, clean-up crews, cold champagne: Finis Shellnut can get it all. Within the hour, generally.

"I'm like Mr. Haney from Green Acres," he said. "I can get anything anybody needs." And then he proved it.

He led me around the corner, to an unmarked delivery entrance for Antoine's, where a guy named Wilbert has been reporting to work every day, trying to keep on top of the food situation before it all rots and stinks — and then he trudges "back over to the projects," as he says, to sleep in a tenement with no tenants and no power.

So Wilbert deals with rancid butter and tomatoes that have gone to black. But there's one thing he hasn't had to deal with, and that's what Shellnut wanted to show me.

He positioned me in front of a big storage cooler that is probably about 40 years old and then he pulled the door open and a cloud of frost blew out. Inside, it was cold. Real cold. Not only had the ice inside of Antoine's meat and seafood locker not completely melted — it hadn't even started to melt.

Don't ask me how this is possible. I do not know. And I did not take down the name of the ice company nor the refrigerator manufacturer but I should have, because they've got a good bit of P.R. to capitalize on.

Because together they had saved shelves and shelves of lobster tails and soft shell crabs and tubs of lump crab meat and filets and New York strips and tenderloin tips. Thousands of them.

This wasn't just a big pile of food. This was the overabundant but abandoned inventory of the city's glorious tradition of over-consumption. It was like looking at a small piece of New Orleans history.

And 12 days after the storm, when the city's survivors had long acclimated to diets of looted Doritos, Salvation Army cheeseburgers and pre-packaged MREs from the National Guard ... it made me hungry.

And speaking of the National Guard: We're standing there looking at all this food and Shellnut says to me, "What are we going to do with this?"

He told me he'd been trying to give it to NOPD officers, but they were all too individually stressed out to embrace the concept of fine dining and there was no discernible central command to alert to this situation. And this was one hell of a situation.

I asked Shellnut if he was sure — IF HE WAS POSITIVE — that this was what it looked like: fresh food. I mean, how could it be?

He shrugged. He said this is how they found it, him and Wilbert. So we cut open a filet and we popped a lid on the lump crabmeat and smelled them and they smelled ... beautiful.

So I proposed this: Uptown, where we have been operating an ad hoc "news bureau" by generator from inside a reporter's house, we are under the protective operations of the California National Guard.

They patrol our area and have given us their MREs (the beef ravioli is to die for) and they have generally treated us with more respect, grace and kindness than one has a right to expect under martial law.

Fact is, every one that we have come in contact with — and there are plenty of them — has been a Good Joe.

Back home in California, these men and women are cops and teachers and businessmen who were given about 12 hours notice to tie up any loose ends in their lives and say goodbye to their families and come to New Orleans to bring some serious heat and restore order on our streets.

And they're doing a helluva job and that big pile of meat looked like a real good way to put into action what we've been putting into words for them for two weeks: Thank you.

But first, I figured we better test it. Despite its alluring physical appearance, if it was, in fact, rotten — as every other steak in this city most certainly was at this point — then I did not want to be personally responsible for wiping out an entire unit of the California National Guard.

With all the bad headlines coming out of this town, that's not one I wanted to add to the pile.

So I tested it on my colleagues. I brought home about a dozen massive beef filets and I seasoned and cooked them and they were excellent. (No one would try the crab meat; despite appearances, the implications seemed daunting.)

In the morning, I polled my group of housemates and found no reports of constitutional distress — at least no more distress than usual, considering our fairly unhealthy living conditions. But enough about that.

So Sunday morning I went back to visit Shellnut. "Are you sure it's OK to take these?" I asked, and he assured me he had cleared it with the restaurant and I hope that is the case and if it is not: Mr. or Mrs. Guste — or whoever currently runs that classic culinary landmark — we'll clear this up later. Somehow. I give you my word.

So we packed up 240 filets and tenderloins and I dropped them off at Sophie B. Wright Middle School, where the California Guard unit is stationed.

Then I hustled a few grills off of some front porches in my neighborhood — which is basically in preserved physical condition, so if the worst thing that happened to you in Katrina was losing your old Weber, then I don't want to hear about it.

It went to a good cause.

Then I called in a delivery of 20 bags of charcoal from a colleague in Baton Rouge and we set up at the corner of Prytania and Napoleon, under the oaks (they're still there!) and we had us a Sunday afternoon barbecue.

And when I was informed that 240 steaks were not going to be nearly enough for the 600 Guardsmen and women based at the site, I dispatched a team of them to go down to the Quarter and find Shellnut — which is not hard to do — and they came back with him and also a few hundred more steaks.

The Guard, they went nuts. Absolutely nuts. As platoons came back from patrols, they were greeted by four grills going full steam, a much better smell than our city streets, in these hard times.

At one point, several company cooks returned and were thrilled to have some real cooking to do so they relieved me of duty. That was their prerogative. It is, after all, martial law.

So then I just watched. Shellnut and I leaned against my car and took in the scene and all these guys, they just fell over us with gratitude, like we were the heroes — an absurd notion. But maybe for one afternoon, we did a little bit of good on behalf of our city, our people, and particularly Antoine's world famous restaurant.

And with my story told, I'd just like to add — gently, so as not to sound like I'm complaining — but if we ever have a storm like Katrina headed this way again, if Wilbert or someone else down at Antoine's could toss a few hundred pounds of potato salad into that cooler before it hits, that would be great.

Because it would have been really nice to have some fresh sides with all that meat. Now that would have been something.

Tough Times in the Blue Tarp Town

Blue Roof Blues

The first time I came back to New Orleans after Katrina, I'll admit that the whole specter shook me to my core. After spending eight days reporting in the city, my hands were shaking and I had lost about 10 pounds. It was time to take a break.

As I drove to Baton Rouge to catch a flight, I pulled off at the first interstate exchange with any life to it — Laplace — and went to the McDonald's and got a Big Mac, a fish sandwich, large fries and a large coke.

I inhaled the stuff as a I drove and, two exits later — Sorrento or somewhere like that — I pulled off and went to the McDonald's there and got a Big Mac and a large coke to sustain me for the rest of the drive, my own personal take on "Supersize Me."

Then, after a brief respite with my wife and kids in Maryland, I returned to New Orleans for more. Reporting, that is. Not McDonald's.

The second time I left New Orleans, Armstrong Airport was open and again my hands shook as I drove away from town but when I settled in my seat as we went aloft, my troubles, too, stayed behind on the ground.

I looked down over the region as we rose and — maybe you've seen pictures of this — the sea of blue color beneath me was nothing less than awe-inspiring.

At first I had this vision that I was flying over Beverly Hills until I realized all that blue beneath me was not swimming pools but roof tarps and coverings. It is the color that bonds us in these times, maybe even more than that weird purple hue that Rex, LSU and K&B seemed to conspire to make us love so many years ago.

The Blue Roof Town. Man, there's a great country song in there somewhere.

There are a lot of heartache songs in this whole ordeal, no doubt assisted by the syncopative double-whammy of Rita/Katrina.

Somewhere, right now, someone is writing a song that will make Tim McGraw a million dollars; I just hope that someone is from New Orleans.

On my most recent trip back to New Orleans, earlier this week, I was waiting for my connection in Memphis and listened while the gate agent called the names of standby travelers to come forward: "Passenger Cheramie. Passenger Bettincourt ..."

The gate agent's Tennessee drawl mauled these names but it was a wondrous thing, to hear these beautiful French names being called and to know that our people were coming home.

Settling into their seats, almost everyone turned to the stranger next to them and asked: "Have you seen it yet?"

It. That is our home. That is our place.

Such a haunting quietude consumed the plane as we descended over Lake Pontchartrain. You could tell that most of the people on the plane were coming home for the first time, and instead of the usual world-weary travelers burying their noses in paperbacks or trying to catch a last wink of sleep, everyone craned for looks out the windows to see what "it" looks like now.

It felt like a plane full of kids on their first flights, like they had never seen such a vista from the air before. And, of course, they hadn't.

I wanted to pipe up: Man, you should have seen it a month ago; it was so much worse. Or maybe tell them all: It's not as bad as you think it's going to be.

Or I thought I could harness more practical advice from recent experience and tell them: Whatever you do, DO NOT open your refrigerator. Ever. Again.

But, even though I have one of those profoundly annoying personal compulsions of talking to (at?) strangers all the time — particularly at inappropriate moments — I found myself lingering on some advice whose provenance I have long forgotten (and seldom followed), but which seemed so apt for this anguished moment: "If you cannot improve upon the silence, do not speak."

Words of wisdom, to be sure. At a time like this, a flow of platitudes from a self-absorbed dilettante veteran of the War of 2005 — a dilettante with shaky hands, no less — is not what anybody needs to hear.

So I kept my mouth shut and let the passengers' heads wrap around what was about to happen to them when they got out of the plane and drove to their homes for the first time.

For some, it will be a foul-smelling but mildly comic discovery that they forgot to empty their Diaper Genie before they left. For a friend of mine who accompanied his mother to their home off Paris Avenue in St. Bernard Parish over the weekend, it was the discovery of two tenants in the rental side of her shotgun double — two tenants who had been dead for 33 days.

Wrap your head around that.

For those who return to the area and those who do not and those who never left, these are our collective memories now, our marks of distinction and suffering, small stuff like Aunt Ida's meatloaf sitting in your fridge for five weeks or big stuff like dead people on the other side of your living room wall.

Like our blue tarp rooftops, these are the bonds that we share forever. They are the bonds that will hold us together.

The Smell

New Orleans still unfolds itself to you in a sensual way. That was always her seductive forte, but it is different after the storm.

For instance, in the immediate days after the flood, it was sound: choppers, jets, boats, sirens, big trucks, bigger trucks, chainsaws. And then at night, the damn scariest silence you never heard.

Then it was sight: The impenetrable darkness of the night, punctuated in the distance from time to time by a red or blue cherry top on a slow-rolling cruiser and most likely the driver — a young state trooper from some town in the Midwest suddenly dropped into Fallujah — was as terrified as you.

There were lots of monsters under the bed in those early days.

Then came the blinding sunlight of morning — so much of it unfiltered by tree limbs after Katrina's indiscriminate and not-so-tidy pruning job — just slamming straight into your face and onto the ground.

Now the choppers are gone, and most of that other industrial noise, and at night you hear crickets. And the sunlight, so hellish weeks ago, is getting better with the approach of autumn, and the scary darkness is now sliced apart at night by streetlights and the yellow glow from occasional bedroom windows.

That leaves us the sense of smell. And, wow.

Louisiana balladeer Randy Newman once wrote a song lamenting Baltimore's civic downfall many years ago with the line: "Oh, Baltimore. Man, it's hard just to breathe."

That would be New Orleans now. It stinks here, just flat out stinks. There are random piles of residential and commercial trash just everywhere and even where there is no visible evidence, the slightest wind shift can take you to Puke City.

I mean it; it's rough. Even in places that are cleaned up and open for business, you can still smell the Aftermath. The CVS and Walgreens drug stores are open Uptown and even though the air-conditioning is blasting and they've cleaned the hell out of those places, you can still sense it when you first walk in, just barely taste it.

A friend of mine e-mailed me recently that when she walked into a grocery store, her daughter said to her: "Mom, it smells like ass in here," and I know that's not very appetizing terminology or imagery for a newspaper, but standard operating procedures have changed around here because New Orleans, it smells like, well ... never mind.

I'm just trying to convey what it's like and I can certainly muster no better description than that.

On many streets, refrigerators are duct-taped shut and lined up along the curbside calling to mind nothing so much as the image of empty Mardi Gras parade ladders all in a row. All these structures, just waiting for something to happen.

Only problem is, there are no clean-up crews following these imaginary parades to remove the debris. So they stand, sturdy sentinels, fortress walls.

We should rename the streets around here Whirlpool Way, Amana Avenue and Kenmore Court, because that's what it looks like. The streets are paved in appliances. Where trees once stood, they are sometimes the only shade on a block.

Where are they going to put all these things? I don't suppose that they can be used to buttress our wetlands like they do with discarded Christmas trees every year, huh?

Do we even have any wetlands?

And, problem is, for every person who comes back here, either to reclaim residency or just to gather some valuables and clean up a bit, more garbage accumulates. Pity the folks who had been in the middle of home renovations when this hit, because their dumpsters are now brimming with a primordial stew so nasty that even the rats abandoned it.

Very strange side note here: There are no rats. Everyone talks about this, says the same thing — they haven't seen a rat since Day One. Here on Dry Land, where I live, we thought they'd overrun us. But I don't know.

Anyway, I remember — until it was deemed injudicious by an image-conscious administration — when the city used to measure the success of Mardi Gras by announcing the accumulated tonnage of garbage that was collected during Carnival season. Well, by that measure, Katrina was a very successful hurricane.

Very.

Stink is a situation that TV and radio cannot successfully portray; olfactory being one of the senses not yet conquered by the airwaves or Internet. And until The Times-Picayune can successfully produce a scratch-n-sniff version of the daily newspaper — and this technology still seems to be at least three or four years down the road — then even we can only fail in our efforts to accurately capture the foulness of some of these street corners.

I don't mean to be complaining here, jumping on the gripe train and all that. Compared to losing a loved one, a home or a job, this is civic kibbles and bits. But in terms of livability, it matters. There seem to be 900 guys from Texas who've been trucked into town to cut down trees and limbs; aren't there a dozen guys from River Parish Disposal who can cruise around New Orleans every day picking up stuff?

The whole idea of it makes me very nostalgic, the radio playing in my back yard on autumn Sunday afternoons in New Orleans, after a Saints game, listening to Buddy D pitching River Parish Disposal: "Our business stinks, but it's picking up."

What a great slogan that is.

Buddy D. The Saints. Garbage pick-up. Ah, memories of my old New Orleans.

The Elephant Men

Every night, we gather on my front stoop. We are multiple combinations of jobless, homeless, family-less and sometimes just plain listless.

We sit and some of us drink and some of us smoke and together we solve the problems of the city — since no one in any official capacity seems able or inclined to do so.

We're just one more committee howling at the moon. We are a civic life-support system.

It began with close friends and neighbors, gathering as we trickled back into town, comparing notes and stories and hugs of comfort and welcome home. But the breadth of visitors has widened.

One night, while I was sitting with a couple of friends, a guy pulled up to the curb in an SUV and regarded us carefully. As the passenger side window rolled down, I assumed it was an old friend stopping to say hello, so I stepped up to the door.

Turns out, it was a total stranger. He said: "Displaced dads?" He had a six-pack of Corona on the front seat and he was just driving around randomly, looking for someone to connect with, someone to talk to, something — God help us — something to do.

We nodded. Yeah, we are men without their women. Women without their men. Parents without their children.

But not without beer.

And he got out of the car and he sat with us for hours and we told our stories to each other and asked about each others' families, now spread across the planet, and when it was over we had a new friend. A displaced dad. Just looking for a place we used to call home.

We stoop-sitters tend to get very wry and blend dark humor with our rants against the machine, but sometimes it gets very sad.

We often deal with First Timer Syndrome. As my immediate neighbors trickle back into town, one by one — either just to clean up and move on or to move back in for good — they generally end up on my stoop. And they often cry.

It's the first time they've been back to town and they are shaken to their very core at what they've seen and smelled and we grizzled veterans of this war try to provide shelter from their storm.

They apologize for losing it but we tell them that many tears have been shed here on this stoop and they are ours and it's OK. It happens to all First Timers. Hell, it happens still.

They're easy to spot, the First Timers. They either sob or they sit silent and sullen, the occasional pull on a bottle of beer, with very little to add to the conversation of the night.

The next night, they usually come back, and they are a little better. One day at a time. Ain't that the way of life around here?

We sit around night after night because some of us are unable to sit still in a restaurant for 90 minutes or aren't ready to go back to the bar scene. Many can't concentrate on reading and television seems like an empty gesture so we talk, and we talk about the same damn thing over and over.

We talk about it. The elephant in the room.

I suspect many folks have sat with us and thought, upon going home: You guys need to get a grip. You need to talk about something else. You need to get a life.

That may be, but I, personally, have been unable to focus on anything but the elephant. I have tried to watch TV or read a magazine but when I see or hear phrases like "Tom and Katy" or "World Series" or "Judge Miers," my mind just glazes over and all I hear is the buzz of a fluorescent light. That is the sound of my cerebral cortex now.

I can't hear what they're saying on TV. I don't know what they're talking about. I think: Why aren't they talking about the elephant?

Once, in an out-of-town airport, I searched desperately for something to read about the elephant, but we have been tossed off the front pages by other events. Finally I found a magazine with a blaring headline: "WHAT WENT WRONG" and I thought, finally, something about us.

It turns out, though, it was People magazine and "WHAT WENT WRONG" was not about FEMA or the levees or the flood, but about Renee Zellweger and Kenny Chesney.

And the fluorescent light goes zzzzzz.

One newcomer to the stoop one night said something along the lines of, "Can you believe that call at the end of the White Sox game the other night?" And you would usually think that such a statement made in a group of drinking men would elicit an argument, at least — if not a bare-knuckle brawl — but the fact is we all responded with silence.

We're a porch full of people who don't know who's playing in the World Series and don't know what movies opened this week and don't know how many died in Iraq today.

We are consumed. We would probably bore you to tears. But it is good therapy and we laugh more than we cry, and that's a start, that's a good thing, that's a sign of winning this war, of getting this damn elephant out of our city — out of our sight.

Mad City

It has been said to me, almost a dozen times in exactly the same words: "Everyone here is mentally ill now."

Some who say this are health care professionals voicing the accumulated wisdom of their careers and some are laymen venturing a psychological assessment that just happens to be correct.

With all due respect, we're living in Crazy Town.

The only lines at retail outlets longer than those for lumber and refrigerators are at the pharmacy windows, where fidgety, glassy-eyed neighbors greet each other with the casual inquiries one might expect at a restaurant:

"What are you gonna have? The Valium here is good. But I'm going with the Paxil. Last week I had the Xanax and it didn't agree with me."

We talk about prescription medications now like they're the soft-shell crabs at Clancy's. Suddenly, we've all developed a low-grade expertise in pharmacology.

Everybody's got it, this thing, this affliction, this affinity for forgetfulness, absent-mindedness, confusion, laughing at inappropriate circumstances, crying when the wrong song comes on the radio, behaving in odd and contrary ways.

A friend recounts a recent conversation into which Murphy's Law was injected — the adage that if anything can go wrong, it will.

In perhaps the most succinct characterization of contemporary life in New Orleans I've heard yet, one said to the other: "Murphy's running this town now."

Ain't that the truth?

Here's one for you: Some friends of mine were clearing out their belongings from their home in the Fontainebleau area and were going through the muddle of despair that attends the realization that you were insured out the wazoo for a hurricane but all you got was flood damage and now you're going to get a check for $250,000 to rebuild your $500,000 house.

As they pondered this dismal circumstance in the street, their roof collapsed. Just like that. It must have suffered some sort of structural or rain-related stress from the storm and then, two weeks later, it manifested itself in total collapse.

Now I ask you: What would you do if you watched your home crumble to pieces before your eyes?

What they did was, realizing their home now qualified for a homeowner's claim, they jumped up and down and high-fived each other and yelled: "The roof collapsed! The roof collapsed!"

Our home is destroyed. Oh, happy day. I submit there's something not right there.

I also submit that if you don't have this affliction, if this whole thing hasn't sent you into a vicious spin of acute cognitive dissonance, then you must be crazy and — like I said: We're all whacked.

How could you not be? Consider the sights, sounds and smells you encounter on a daily basis as you drive around a town that has a permanent bathtub ring around it. I mean, could somebody please erase that brown line?

Every day I drive past a building on Magazine Street where there's plywood over the windows with a huge spray-painted message that says: I AM HERE. I HAVE A GUN.

OK, the storm was more than two months ago. You can take the sign down now. You can come out now.

Or maybe the guy's still inside there, in the dark with his canned food, water and a gun, thinking that the whole thing is still going on, like those Japanese soldiers you used to hear about in the '70s and '80s who just randomly wandered out of hiding in the forests on desolate islands in the South Pacific, thinking that World War II was still going on.

The visuals around here prey on you. Driving in from the east the other day, I saw a huge, gray wild boar that had wandered onto the interstate and been shredded by traffic. Several people I know also saw this massive porcine carnage, all torn up and chunky on the side of the road.

It looked like five dead dogs. Directly across the interstate from it was an upside down alligator.

I mean: What the hell? Since when did we have wild boars around here? And when did they decide to lumber out of the wilderness up to the interstate like it's some sort of sacred dying ground for wildebeests?

Just farther up the road a bit are all those car dealerships with rows and rows and rows of new cars that will never be sold, all browned-out like they were soaking in coffee for a week, which I guess they were.

All those lots need are some balloons on a Saturday afternoon and some guy in a bad suit saying: "Let's make a deal!"

Welcome to the Outer Limits. Your hometown. Need a new car?

Speaking of car dealers, no one epitomizes the temporary insanity around here more than Saints owner Tom Benson, who said he feared for his life in a confrontation with a drunk fan and WWL sportscaster Lee Zurik at Tiger Stadium last Sunday.

Admittedly, the shape of Lee Zurik's eyebrows have an oddly discomfiting menace about them, but fearing for your life?

Just get a good set of tweezers and defend yourself, Tom. Get a hold of yourself, man.

Maybe I shouldn't make light of this phenomenon. Maybe I'm exhibiting a form of madness in thinking this is all slightly amusing. Maybe I'm not well, either.

But former city health director Brobson Lutz tells me it's all part of healing.

"It's a part of the human coping mechanism," he said. "Part of the recovery process. I have said from the beginning that the mental health concerns here are far greater than those we can expect from infectious diseases or household injuries."

The U.S. Army brought Lutz onto the USS Iwo Jima a few weeks ago to talk to the troops about how to deal with people suffering from post-traumatic stress.

They were concerned, primarily, with the dazed-out looking folks who wander around the French Quarter all day.

"I told them to leave those guys alone," Lutz said. "They may be crazy, but they survived this thing. They coped. If they were taken out of that environment, then they could really develop problems. Remember that, in the immediate aftermath of all this, the primary psychiatric care in this city was being provided by the bartenders at Johnny White's and Molly's."

Interesting point. I mean, who needs a psychology degree? All anyone around here wants is someone to listen to their stories.

I thanked Lutz for his time and mentioned that our call sounded strange. It was around noon this past Thursday.

"Are you in the bathtub?" I asked him.

"Yes," he said. "And I'm having trouble coming up with sound bites."

Like I said, we're all a little touched by Katrina Fever.

My friend Glenn Collins is living in exile in Alabama and one Sunday afternoon he went to a shopping mall in Birmingham. He went to the Gap and was greeted by a salesclerk with a name tag that said "Katrina."

He left immediately. He went next door to the Coach boutique, where he was greeted by a salesclerk with a name tag that said "Katrina."

He kinda freaked out. He asked the woman something along the lines of: What's with all the Katrinas? And she blurted out: "Oh, you know Katrina at the Gap? She's my friend!"

"I wish I was making this up," he told me. "I mean, what are the odds of this?"

He needed a drink, he said. So he went to a nearby Outback Steakhouse and ordered a beer but the bartender told him they don't sell alcohol on Sundays.

"But I'm from New Orleans!" he pleaded. "Don't you have a special exemption for people from New Orleans? Please?"

They did not. So he drove across three counties to get a drink. He said to me: "The Twilight Zone, it just keeps going on and on and on."

1 Dead in Attic

I live on The Island, where much has the appearance of Life Goes On. Gas stations, bars, pizza joints, joggers, strollers, dogs, churches, shoppers, neighbors, even garage sales.

Sometimes trash and mail service, sometimes not.

It sets to mind a modicum of complacency that maybe everything is all right.

But I have this terrible habit of getting into my car every two or three days and driving into the Valley Down Below, that vast wasteland below sea level that was my city, and it's mind-blowing A) how vast it is and B) how wasted it is.

My wife questions the wisdom of my frequent forays into the massive expanse of blown-apart lives and property that local street maps used to call Gentilly, Lakeview, the East and the Lower 9th. She fears that it contributes to my unhappiness and general instability and I suspect she is right.

Perhaps I should just stay on the stretch of safe, dry land Uptown where we live and try to move on, focus on pleasant things, quit making myself miserable, quit reliving all those terrible things we saw on TV that first week.

That's advice I wish I could follow, but I can't. I am compelled for reasons that are not entirely clear to me. And so I drive.

I drive around and try to figure out those Byzantine markings and symbols that the cops and the National Guard spray-painted on all the houses around here, cryptic communications that tell the story of who or what was or wasn't inside the house when the floodwater rose to the ceiling.

In some cases, there's no interpretation needed. There's one I pass on St. Roch Avenue in the 8th Ward at least once a week. It says: "1 Dead in Attic."

That certainly sums up the situation. No mystery there.

It's spray-painted there on the front of the house and it

probably will remain spray-painted there for weeks, months, maybe years, a perpetual reminder of the untimely passing of a citizen, a resident, a New Orleanian.

One of us.

You'd think some numerical coding could have conveyed this information on this house, so that I — we all — wouldn't have to drive by places like this every day and be reminded: "1 Dead in Attic."

I have seen plenty of houses in worse shape than the one where 1 Dead in Attic used to live, houses in Gentilly and the Lower 9th that yield the most chilling visual displays in town: low-rider shotgun rooftops with holes that were hacked away from the inside with an ax, leaving small, splintered openings through which people sought escape.

Imagine if your life came to that point, and remained there, on display, all over town for us to see, day after day.

Amazingly, those rooftops are the stories with happy endings. I mean, they got out, right?

But where are they now? Do you think they have trouble sleeping at night?

The occasional rooftops still have painted messages: "HELP US." I guess they had paint cans in their attic. And an ax, like Margaret Orr and Aaron Broussard always told us we should have if we weren't going to evacuate.

Some people thought Orr and Broussard were crazy. Alarmists. Extremists. Well, maybe they are crazy. But they were right.

Perhaps 1 Dead in Attic should have heeded this advice. But judging from the ages on the state's official victims list, he or she was probably up in years. And stubborn. And unafraid. And now a statistic.

I wonder who eventually came and took 1 Dead in Attic away. Who knows? Hell, with the way things run around here — I wonder if anyone has come to take 1 Dead in Attic away.

And who claimed him or her? Who grieved over 1 Dead in Attic and who buried 1 Dead in Attic?

Was there anyone with him or her at the end and what was the last thing they said to each other? How did 1 Dead in Attic spend the last weekend in August of the year 2005?

What were their plans? Maybe dinner at Mandich on St. Claude? Maybe a Labor Day family reunion in City Park — one of those raucous picnics where everybody wears matching T-shirts to mark the occasion and they rent a DJ and a SpaceWalk and a couple of guys actually get there the night before to secure a good, shady spot?

I wonder if I ever met 1 Dead in Attic. Maybe in the course of my job or maybe at a Saints game or maybe we once stood next to each other at a Mardi Gras parade or maybe we once flipped each other off in a traffic jam.

1 Dead in Attic could have been my mail carrier, a waitress at my favorite restaurant or the guy who burglarized my house a couple years ago. Who knows?

My wife, she's right. I've got to quit just randomly driving around. This can't be helping anything.

But I can't stop. I return to the Valley Down Below over and over, looking for signs of progress in all that muck, some sign that things are getting better, that things are improving, that we don't all have to live in a state of abeyance forever but — you know what?

I just don't see them there.

I mean, in the 8th Ward, tucked down there behind St. Roch Cemetery, life looks pretty much like it did when the floodwater first receded 10 weeks ago, with lots of cars pointing this way and that, kids' yard toys caked in mire, portraits of despair, desolation and loss. And hatchet holes in rooftops.

But there's something I've discovered about the 8th Ward in this strange exercise of mine: Apparently, a lot of Mardi Gras Indians are from there. Or were from there; I'm not sure what the proper terminology is.

On several desolate streets that I drive down, I see where some folks have returned to a few of the homes and they haven't bothered to put their furniture and appliances out on the curb — what's the point, really? — but they have retrieved their tattered and muddy Indian suits and sequins and feathers and they have nailed them to the fronts of their houses.

The colors of these displays is startling because everything else in the 8th is gray. The streets, the walls, the cars, even the trees. Just gray.

So the oranges and blues and greens of the Indian costumes are something beautiful to behold, like the first flowers to bloom after the fallout. I don't know what the significance of these displays is, but they hold a mystical fascination for me.

They haunt me, almost as much as the spray paint on the front of a house that says 1 Dead in Attic. They look like ghosts hanging there. They are reminders of something. Something very New Orleans.

Do these memorials mean these guys — the Indians — are coming back? I mean, they have to, don't they? Where else could they do what they do?

And — maybe this is a strange time to ask — but who are these guys, anyway? Why do they do what they do with all those feathers and beads that take so much time and money to make? What's with all the Big Chief and Spy Boy role-playing?

As many times as I have reveled in their rhythmic, poetic and sometimes borderline absurd revelry in the streets of our city, I now realize that if you asked me to explain the origins and meaning of the Mardi Gras Indians — I couldn't do it.

I have no clue. And that makes me wish I'd been paying more attention for the past 20 years. I could have learned something.

I could have learned something about a people whose history is now but a sepia mist over back-of-town streets and neighborhoods that nobody's ever heard of and where nobody lives and nothing ever happens anymore; a freeze frame still life in the air, a story of what we once were.

Despair

She had a nice house in Old Metairie, a nice car, a great job, a good man who loved her and a wedding date in October.

A good life.

He was from Atlanta and had moved here to be with her because she is a New Orleans girl and New Orleans girls never live anywhere else and even if they do, they always come back.

That's just the way it is.

For the hurricane, they fled to Atlanta. His city. His people.

Meantime, her house was destroyed, her car was destroyed and within days, she was laid off from her job. And, of course, the wedding here in New Orleans was canceled.

When all settled down, he wanted to stay in Atlanta. But she is a New Orleans girl and you know the rest. Equanimity courses through our blood as much as platelets and nitrogen — it is part of our DNA — so she was determined to return, rebuild, recover.

So they moved back here.

A few weeks ago, they moved into my neighborhood. She arrived first. That afternoon, she came over and joined the group that sits on my stoop every night solving the world's problems.

I introduced her around to the local gang and welcomed her back to the neighborhood; she had been a neighbor many years ago.

Like many Post-Katrina First Timers, she was a wreck on that first night. Didn't say much. Just sat there. Not the girl I used to know. But then, who is?

To add to her troubles that first night, her fiance, who was following her to New Orleans that morning in a rented truck, had gotten a flat tire outside of Mobile and was stranded on the side of the road.

She drove on because she had the pets in her car. He called the rental company for help; it wasn't the kind of vehicle with a tire that just any John Doe can change.

He called the trucking company all day. They kept telling him that they would be there within an hour and that's what he told her so she waited. We all waited.

By 8 p.m., he got fed up with the trucking company and called them and told them he had started the engine and was going to drive to New Orleans on the exposed tire rim. And that's what he did, calling the trucking company every few minutes to give a new location.

When she related this news to us, we all knew right then that we would like this guy.

Naturally, the trucking company showed up within minutes and changed the tire. He arrived late that night. He met all the neighbors and they all knew the story of him driving on the rim and they all thought that was hilarious.

And so their new life began on my block. They were one of us now, the survivors, the determined, the hopeful, the building blocks of the New City. Members of the tribe.

They settled in. I used to see them walking in the park and reading the paper on their front porch and occasionally they sat on my stoop, and life went on.

But I guess things were not going so well. She was always pretty grim — not the girl I used to know — but he seemed jolly enough and we would talk in the 'Hey, how ya doin'?' kind of way.

Turns out, he couldn't stand it here. And, truthfully, if you weren't from here, didn't have a history here, didn't have roux in your blood and a stake in it all: Would you want to be here?

I wouldn't.

But she is a New Orleans girl. To hell with no house, no car, no job, no prospects. This is where she belonged. And her mama lives here. End of discussion.

He moved back to Atlanta. She stayed. He came back. Try again. Work it out. Whatever it takes.

A few nights ago, they drank wine and in some sort of stupid Romeo and Juliet moment, decided that they would kill themselves because all hope was lost and living here amongst the garbage and the rot and the politics and the profound sense of failure was sucking the marrow out of their bones.

Not even love could overcome. Here, in the smoking ruins of Pompeii, sometimes it's hard to see the light.

She told friends later that she didn't really think they would do it. Said they got caught in the moment and let the bad stuff crawl all over their minds. The darkness can be so damn dark and they weren't thinking straight. But she didn't think they were really going to do it.

But he did. Right then, right there.

So he's dead, and a family in Atlanta has lost a son, a brother, a friend. Another notch in Katrina's belt.

My stoop is empty these nights. None of us really knows what to say anymore.

This is the next cycle. Suicide. All the doctors, psychologists and mental health experts tell us the same thing: This is what happens next in a phenomenon like this. But has there ever been a phenomenon like this?

Where are we now in our descent through Dante's nine circles of hell?

God help us.

The most open, joyous, free-wheeling, celebratory city in the country is broken, hurting, down on its knees. Failing. Begging for help.

Somebody turn this movie off; I don't want to watch it anymore. I want a slow news day. I want a no news day.

A friend of mine who used to live here said on the phone from Philadelphia the other day: "I don't know how you guys can even get out of bed in the morning."

Well, obviously, some of us don't.

But we have to try. We have to fight this thing until there is no fight left. This cannot be the way we go out, by our own hands.

My neighbor is in a hospital in another part of the state now, learning how to deal. She talked to friends over the weekend and said she is not going to run away from this. She is a New Orleans girl and this is where she is going to stay and try again. And again. And again.

She told her friends this weekend that she still has hope.

I don't know what flavor of hope that she's got, or how she got it, but if she's got a taste of it in her mouth, then the rest of us can take a little spoonful and try to make it through another day, another week, another lifetime.

It's the least we can do.

The Ties That Bind

My Introduction to New Orleans

I was sitting in Donna's on Rampart Street last Saturday night, shaking my legs to a righteous swing session with the New Orleans Jazz Vipers, when a stunning realization hit me in the face: It was a hurricane, or something very close to it, that brought me to this city in the first place.

It was November 1980. I was in school in Wisconsin, floundering both personally and academically. I had a friend in the same situation. We decided to blow off our classes and head out of town the week of Thanksgiving, pointing South with a tent and two sleeping bags in an attempt to decide whether we wanted to stay in college or find another direction in life.

I had told my parents in Maryland that I had a load of school work and would not be home for the holiday. And off we went, destination: South Padre Island in Texas, where I had gone for spring break the year before and had a gas.

But South Padre was miserable. It was deserted. Oil from a runaway well in Mexico was fouling the beach. And worst of all, the wind was relentless and borderline scary. It blew our tent all over the beach and when we'd party a little and try to play Frisbee, the disc would get caught in the wind and take off 300 yards down the beach.

A state trooper told us there was a mighty storm brewing out in the Gulf of Mexico; that the situation was certainly not going to improve and, in fact, might get a lot worse.

He suggested we leave.

So we packed up and decided to head for the Florida panhandle. Nice beaches, we'd heard. And so we hit the road again, passing through south Louisiana in the middle of the night.

Somewhere out in Acadiana, we stopped at an all-night gas station and the girl at the cash register was wearing a baseball cap that said: "I'm a real Coonass, me."

OK, I'm thinking. I'll take the bait: "What's a Coonass?" I asked her.

"Me," she replied.

I turned to my friend, also named Chris, and said: "Let's get the hell out of this state." Two hours later we were passing the interstate exits to New Orleans.

What did I know about New Orleans at the age of 20? At this point in my life, I was already a Meters, Wild Tchoupitoulas and Neville Brothers fanatic, having been turned onto them by my older brother who had incorporated annual trips to Mardi Gras into his life's journey.

My sum total knowledge of the place was that it was probably a great place for a couple of lost college boys to do some serious partying.

We considered this option but, between us, Chris and I had less than $100 and we hoped to road trip for at least a week or so, and then we'd need gas money back home — 1,000 miles to Madison.

So we bypassed New Orleans, figuring to sleep on the beach in Florida and eat campfire beans, which is what we did. For one night. Then whatever storm had been brewing in the Gulf descended upon us. The same lashing wind sent sand stinging into our legs.

Someone told us the storm had kicked east. It was going to get nasty. For two down-and-out, borderline depressed guys, this trip was simply not working out. We've got to get out of here, we said. New Orleans, we agreed, money or not.

The first New Orleans bar I ever walked into — a rite of passage as meaningful as your first car or your first kiss — was Tujague's on Decatur Street. I'll never forget the impression that the tiles and the sexy lighting and the lazy ceiling fans and slow-moving clientele had on me: What year is it, I thought? This place is gone, man, long ago gone.

We ate dinner at what I believe was Café Sbisa, but I'm not positive, all these years later. All I know is, we could only afford a couple of appetizers and we were surrounded by a busy and talkative staff of tall, thin gay men and this was all very exotic to us.

Next, naturally, we were on Bourbon Street. We put $40 in the glove compartment of our car for gas back to Wisconsin (forty bucks to Wisconsin, imagine that) and we decided we would hang out until we ran out of money.

That took about six hours.

Bourbon Street was jumping. The street was packed. The night before, Sugar Ray Leonard and Roberto Duran had sparred in the Superdome in one of boxing's truly legendary fights. It was the night Duran exclaimed: "No mas!"

We didn't know or care much about that. We just knew that we had never seen anything like this place before.

At the corner of Bourbon and St. Peter, there was a slow jazz band playing and a young black man singing "The Christmas Song." You know: "Chestnuts roasting on an open fire . . ."

The man was beautiful. I had never seen skin quite his color, and I don't think I had ever seen a black man with green eyes before.

And his voice. Wow. It wasn't Aaron Neville or Johnny Adams or even in their league, obviously, but to me it was angelic and new and soul-settling. I just stood there with my mouth open, filling open mouth with much beer, but also just in plain awe.

He didn't use a microphone and everybody in the place was quiet, just hanging onto the moment. I doubt that Bourbon Street has many musical "moments" anymore, having descended over the past few decades into a cacophonous sprawl, but to my young and nearly virgin ears, I had found something.

Something beautiful. Something that would stay with me, it turns out.

We listened to a few more songs and then left. I wanted to stay, but we agreed that this was no place to meet girls — too mellow and refined — and we wanted to meet girls and so we wandered.

The story, at this point, becomes dramatically less poignant and sentimental so I'll run through the details quickly: We were thrown out of three bars on Bourbon Street and were entering a fourth when a police officer took a hold of my collar and said to beat it.

We were the exact same two guys that I now witness from time to time lousing up our streets downtown. I see their immature, careless behavior and think: Idiots. They don't get this town and they never will.

But now I know there is hope for fools like me.

We ended up in Luther Kent's old bar over on Toulouse Street and the band was big and brassy and loud and we met these beautiful Scandinavian girls and the night was so far beyond perfect that I thought I was in heaven.

I drove from New Orleans all the way to Wisconsin on Thanksgiving Day, pausing twice to stop at gas stations and once to eat Thanksgiving dinner at a Denny's in Illinois.

The following Monday, I returned to classes. Chris did not. I started listening to the Neville Brothers more and more. "The Neville Brothers," their 1978 debut record, became my "date" music. I'd play "Washable Ink" and "Vieux Carré Rouge" and "Audience for My Pain" and I thought I was one very cool brother.

For my male friends, I'd play a cassette of the Wild Tchoupitoulas record with "Brother John," "Hey Pocky A-Way" and "Meet de Boys on the Battle Front" and I'd watch them try to figure out what the hell that was all about.

Not that I knew myself. I just knew I dug it. In between all the Springsteen and John Prine and Little Feat that consumed my musical interests back then, there was this deeper appreciation for sublime funk.

I graduated from college with a journalism degree, moved back to Maryland and was working there when a friend who had wound up at The Times-Picayune called me in the spring of 1984 to say there was a job opening here.

"You'd love this city," she told me.

I thought about that music. That six hours of immortality I had once lived here. I thought about that guy singing "Chestnuts" and thought how sexy it all was in New Orleans. "Yes, I'd love that city," I agreed.

And Jesus, what a ride it has been.

I had not thought about that road trip to New Orleans in years and when I was sitting at Donna's the other night, they were singing these great swing tunes without microphones and it was smoky and intimate and it felt like 1952 and it also felt like that moment I had in 1980. And then it hit me: I first came to this city because I was fleeing a storm.

I have spent hours online since I left Donna's the other night, Googling weather sites and other sources of meteorological data, trying to find out what was in the Gulf of Mexico that last week of November 1980.

I found that a moderate hurricane — Jeanne — was in the Gulf about 10 days earlier and Karl was off the southeastern U.S. that week. Neither amounted to much. But I can't find any reference to a severe storm rolling from Texas across the Gulf to the Florida panhandle in those exact days.

Maybe it was just a tropical depression of some kind, or just the turbulence between Jeanne and Karl, but it was wild and windy I evacuated into — not out of — New Orleans for shelter and safety and that's how I discovered the pulse of this magical place.

It's far past irony to reconsider this event. It's almost absurd, now, to realize how I got here. And it's also the best thing that ever happened to me, to have seen, known, loved and lived this place called New Orleans.

The Funky Butt

When I moved to New Orleans 21 years ago, I was — to coin a contemporary phrase — all in. I loved it from the minute I smelled that burning sugar cane spilling from the Celotex factory across the river, a sweet stink I have always found oddly sexy.

But there was always a caveat to my love affair with New Orleans. I stood firm, fast and unbending on one point: I was not going to raise my children here. No how, no way.

My reasons were obvious: school system, crime, litter, racism, politics.

I thought this place was great for getting my ya-yas out in my 20s and 30s, but I was off to Wisconsin when baby-making time came around. And I was going to make sure I found a wife who believed the same.

And I did. Sort of. We were vague about our discussions but talked often about where we might go — Wisconsin included — when the time was right. We both agreed: This is no place for kids.

But Sonny Landreth changed all that. Yes, that nebbish-looking, Ubangi-stomping guitar god from the southwest Louisiana musical stew made me rethink it all.

True story: It was Jazzfest, 1999. My first child, Katherine, was 5 weeks old. Against the advice of our friends who had children, we brought her to the Fair Grounds for an afternoon.

This was less for her, of course, than for us. She was too young for us to leave her with a baby sitter — that new parent protective coating being tough as tungsten — so if Kelly and I wanted to go, then Kate was coming, too.

It was hot. Scary hot, actually, and really humid and that new parent oh-my-God-we're-harming-our-new-baby thing kicked in. Total buzz killer.

But some nearby sage, and I wish I could remember who it was all these years later, comforted me with these words: Five weeks ago your daughter was submerged in 98 degrees and 100 percent humidity. And she did just fine.

Interesting point. I'm sure the American Medical Association would find many flaws with this logic, but it helped for the moment. And we soldiered on.

We were wending our way through the crowd early on, unable to find a good spot to plant and actually listen to some music. Just one or two bands, we thought, then a plate of some wet, brown food and then we'll head home.

So we were up at the big stage — Acura, or whatever it was called then — and the crowd was too thick and we were trying to get through it and away from it when Sonny Landreth came on.

Have you ever heard this guy? He's making the whole thing up: the riffs, the chords, the notes. I'm no musical scholar, but I think he invented some things. I don't know if there is a specific genre to tag on his music, but it is primeval rock 'n' roll of the first element, a lowdown, fuzz-busting romp in the swamp. And we stopped to dig it.

And I looked down, and there, in the stroller, this beautiful child who had basically remained still and expressionless for the duration of her life — as newborns are wont to do — well, she started to move. To wiggle. And I swear to God, she smiled. For the first time.

I was awash. A Eureka moment: What a GREAT place to raise kids. All this funk, the eccentricity, this otherness. Kind of like college, I thought: so much to learn outside of the classroom.

It was a great afternoon. In a very small way, I was changed. As time went on, Kelly and I talked less and less about moving away and we had two more kids and we haven't discussed it in years and that's that.

I'm not making this up, nor is this some romantic, Katrina-induced revisionism; in fact, I told this exact story during a radio interview on WWNO last spring.

Just so you know. The record shows.

Today, my kids, they dance. They dig music, and that is the best gift I could ever give them, the best medicine they'll ever know.

At a school picnic in Maryland this fall, where they live in exile, a deejay was playing some contemporary dance club number of indeterminate provenance, and my two sons, Jack and James, started doing the funky butt.

No one else was moving — kids or adults. Some of them stared at my kids while they bounced their rumps up and down. I couldn't have been prouder.

When we go to Audubon Park on some Sunday afternoons, there'll be some massive and rollicking family cookout going on nearby and Katherine will start to shake her rear in a way I've seen only on music videos and she says to me: "Look, Daddy, I'm dancing like the brown people."

Ain't that something.

So what's the point? The point is, Sonny Landreth is playing tonight at Southport Hall. New Orleans veterans Paula and the Pontiacs are opening the show.

If you need to be reminded why we live here — and sometimes we all do — may I suggest this as a suitable alternative to whiskey, pills, shooting your refrigerator and running naked through the streets.

The Hurricane Kids

I am writing this from the house where I grew up. It's a thousand miles from New Orleans.

Could be a million, really.

I have come to visit my wife and children, who have settled here amongst my family and old friends in a place we know and trust.

My gang, they live what looks like a normal life here now. School. Shopping. Play dates and birthday parties. Next week, my wife says she's going to start going to the gym.

A normal life. Without me.

Life goes on, I guess. But it's hard to bond the disconnect between what life was like before Aug. 29 and what it's like now.

Talk about loose ends.

Don't get me wrong: Chevy Chase is an amazing place. It was a homey, professional-class neighborhood when my parents moved here in 1963 and is now a profoundly wealthy suburb of Washington, D.C., where famous people live.

It took a hurricane to make it happen, but now my family lives in the same ZIP code as George Will.

That's almost funny.

It's impossible not to like it here. It's so clean and everyone is so educated and polite and everyone cleans up after their dogs and we pass three crossing guards on our walk to school.

Although the streets are familiar to me — I've come back many times over the decades. I can't help but feel lost here. Like I'm moving underwater.

After living in the specter of curfews and military troops and arson and desperate squalor, maybe for the first time in my life I get a hint of what post-traumatic stress really is. Low-grade, to be sure, but you feel it.

I don't recognize any of the kids and I don't know who the parents around me are and I suppose this happens to everyone who relocates to another city but I don't think "relocate" is really the word for what we did.

What happened was, our lives and social structures and friendships and classmates and easy routines were blown across the globe on one fateful morning and now everything is different.

Just like that.

My daughter, she runs into the gym for her homeroom exercises and she starts playing one of those crazy hand-clapping games with a little girl I've never seen before and who is that girl? What are they saying to each other?

I used to know the language and rhythm of her school in New Orleans but here, I stumble.

At the entrance to the school, there is a folding table set up where parents can contribute to a fund to buy backpacks and school supplies for the victims of Hurricane Katrina.

Victims. That's the mantle we wear now. And that sucks. In our lives — in all of our lives — the people we want to be are the rescuers in the boat, not the people plucked from the water, but that's what so many of us have become.

At my son's school, I was introduced to the teachers and administrators the other morning. "This is Jack Rose's father," they would say, and you could see it in their eyes right away: Oh, the Hurricane Boy.

Don't get me wrong, they're unbelievably generous and kind to us. In private, I cry when I think about what everyone here is willing to do, how much strangers here — everyone across this country, it seems — wants to help, wants to make us feel welcome.

But still, my son is the Hurricane Boy and that's not going to change overnight. In my hometown, we are the hurricane family. Evacuees, refugees, whatever.

When I am introduced as someone from New Orleans, people sometimes say: "I'm so sorry."

New Orleans. I'm so sorry.

That's not the way it ever was before, not the way it's supposed to be. When people find out you're from New Orleans, they're supposed to tell you about how they got really drunk there once, or fell in love there, or first heard the music there that changed their lives.

At worst, people would say: I've always wanted to go there.

But now, it's just: "I'm sorry."

Man, that kills me. That just kills me.

And by the time this runs in the newspaper, I'll be on my way back to the city, back to Sorry Town. And I'll leave my hurricane family behind here in what you could only call Pleasantville, and somehow I'll find the means to reconcile the two lives, the new and the old, the temporary and the permanent, a thousand miles apart.

It might as well be a million.

Not the biggest tale of hardship you're going to hear from this storm. Far from it. Just one man's journey. One guy wondering what the light at the end of the tunnel looks like.

Wondering where this all will take us. Wondering if any kids will come by our house on Halloween this year. Wondering who will set up their ladders on the corner where we always watch our Mardi Gras parades. Wondering who will be sitting under our shade tree at Jazzfest.

It's not premature to think about these things. They are the familiar — and very special — touchstones of our lives.

They are the city where I live. The city that exists, at this moment, as a fond memory.

Traveling Man

I'm somewhat consumed by the topic of travel because I've done so much of it lately, hopping from one bankrupt airline to the next in an effort to see my relocated family in Maryland as much as possible.

If you're from New Orleans, the likelihood of running into someone you know at even the most random of American airports has dramatically increased since the storm. So many of us seem to be on the move, coming home, leaving home, visiting family, looking for a lost dog, looking for a job ... but where is everyone going?

While changing planes in Memphis recently, I eavesdropped on a guy who was boarding my New Orleans-bound plane. Since he talked so loudly on his cell phone, I considered it to be fair game for columnizing.

Anyway, I don't want to get too far into this particular point, but let's just say this guy was not your run-of-the-mill stud muffin; not a guy you're going to see on the cast of "The Bachelor," for instance.

In fact, he was round. And there's nothing all that wrong with being round; it's a personal choice and I'm not going to judge here. And he was also considerably older than me so we're talking borderline AARP zone here.

And what he was saying into the phone was that he could make $20 an hour in New Orleans hauling trees and debris and then: "All I have to do is pass the physical."

Mind you, the point of this is not to make fun of this guy. The point is: If you have two arms and two legs — or let's just say you've got three out of four — it appears that there's work for you in New Orleans if you want it.

As long as you can pass the physical.

I am so sick of airports. At Reagan National in Washington, I plugged my computer into the wall to power it up so I could write on the flight and it was still in my suitcase and I walked away for a second to chat with a friend. By the time I returned — and we're talking four minutes here — a gate attendant had been notified by an edgy passenger about this and they were pondering the situation and I was no doubt about to be responsible for shutting down all domestic air travel for the day until I sheepishly claimed possession of this menacing tableau.

I do admit — now, looking back on it — that the power cord running into the suitcase might have looked a little suspicious. I think I'll power the thing up at home before I leave next time. Or maybe just sleep on the plane.

My first Katrina-induced travel was, of course, the evacuation. I marvel to this day how my magnificently chaotic family of five managed to straighten up our house, pack our bags, secure our home and belongings and be on the road on three hours notice - and have the clothes that we threw together in such a hurry sustain us for more than two weeks.

I suppose a Category 5 hurricane rearing up your backside is a compelling incentive for effective time management.

In our mundane Pre-K life, it would usually take us four or five agonizing days to (over)pack for a simple long weekend at the beach and on the first night, someone (me) was always bound to complain that they (I) forgot some key element of wardrobe so essential to my relaxation that the vacation was now ruined in its absence.

You think leisure traveling with me is a pain? If you really want some jollies, you should try hurricane evacuating with me to some crack hotel in Vicksburg — the kind of place where the tub in the bathroom has a series of yellow-brown cigarette burns along the edge. Those are family memories for a lifetime; like telling your kids they can't take off their shoes even when they're inside.

"No, James! Put down that dirty needle!"

(If you only knew how little I was exaggerating here.)

And who smokes in the tub anyway? I guess people who stay in crack hotels, I don't know.

But now my children are safe and sound in the very leafy and upscale Chevy Chase, Md. When I was visiting last weekend, there was an aluminum foil display in the newly converted playroom in my parents' house and I asked my wife what it was and she informed me that it was my daughter's science project for her Brownie troop.

"What are they doing?" I asked.

"They're growing mold," my wife said. Growing mold. If my New Orleans daughter doesn't get the blue ribbon for that project — the state prize, in fact — then there is no justice in this world.

Have Barbie, Will Travel

Traveling back and forth to Maryland to visit my family-in-exile has turned into a ritualistic exercise in tragicomedy.

On the lighter side: Before each journey, I check with my kids by phone to see what they need from our house in New Orleans.

Of course, they need everything, they tell me. Every toy, every article of clothing, every piece of furniture, everything that hangs on the walls, every piece of building material down to the studs.

"Itemize," I urge them.

"Barbies," they tell me.

"I can do that," I tell them.

And so my chore began one afternoon, as I crouched and crawled into their secret places in our house — small, dark spaces I have never been, places that are not hospitable to people larger than, say, a dorm refrigerator.

In the process, I discovered that there has been a population of approximately 50 Barbies living under my roof. I did not know this.

An absurd number, I was thinking, but then I remember that I used to collect empty egg cartons when I was a kid and I probably had a couple hundred — a closet full of them — before my mother brought the hammer down on that curious little hobby of mine.

Truth is, I don't recall even the barest notion of why I collected egg cartons nor what I did with them. I just did. So who am I to tell my kids they have too many Barbies?

Let them be, I say. I mean, I turned out OK, right?

Don't answer that.

The other thing about our Barbies is that they are all naked. They lie in heaps and piles of tangled, plastic, not-quite-anatomically correct nakedness — a truly discomfiting sight to a father who hopes to shield his children from any and all dissolute imagery, although I suspect a contemporary child would need to be at least 13 before these tableaux would access the lurid pockets of the imagination.

My kids, they dress and undress their Barbies incessantly, obsessively, compulsively, but — at the end of the day — they are all naked. (The Barbies, not the kids.) They are bare canvasses, so to speak, upon which to begin the next morning's sartorial exercises.

I decided I could fit about 15 or so Barbies into my carry-on bag and began to try to dress them from the mounds of discarded dresses, gowns and fashionable minis that litter my floors.

I found this task about as easy and pleasant as hanging sheetrock. Apparently you need fingers smaller than toothpicks to accomplish this. I gave up the task.

And that's how I ended up recently wandering around several major American airports with a small satchel stuffed full of naked Barbies. All mashed together in a fleshy heap.

No other luggage to speak of. Nothing checked in. No personal clothes or items; I am fully outfitted in Maryland.

Just a laptop computer, a couple of notebooks and a suitcase full of naked Barbies.

If anybody was ever wearing a sign at airport security that screamed FULL BODY CAVITY SEARCH, it was me.

Guns, knives, drugs, explosives and cigarette lighters — that's old hat. A travel bag stocked with Lesbian Orgy by Mattel is a whole 'nother circumstance.

Mercifully, I made it from Point A (New Orleans) to Point B (Maryland) without incident. That's because none of the security screeners would make eye contact with me. Or maybe I was only imagining that.

Maybe the X-ray machines render the plastic components of Barbies almost invisible. Or maybe the imagery was so creepy that no one wanted to deal with this haggard man with a carry-on bag full of naked Barbies.

Pass by, horseman.

And that's my story. Not much there, really. But there comes a point at which I choose to purge myself of the images and of the smell and the dust and the sepia horizons of New Orleans. Of all the doubt.

Sometimes I just want to ponder something else.

Sometimes I just want to travel halfway across the country just to see my kids smile and to crawl under the covers with them at night and listen to their syncopated chorus of snores and nose whistles, wince at their involuntary spasms and howls, and stare at the ceiling and wonder at the wonder of it all.

Prep Boys & Jesuits

If you've done any traveling in the post-Katrina era, you already know this: It follows you.

Not only is The Horror the only thing anyone around here ever talks about anymore, it's also the only thing everyone Out There wants to talk about when they meet you.

I went to my high school's homecoming in Maryland recently and discovered I was practically a celebrity alumnus by virtue of the fact that I live in New Orleans.

We aging, pot-bellied guys shoved our hands in our pockets and rocked on our heels, standing down by the end zone watching the game.

"How is it?" they all ask, and I know they're being kind and really are concerned, but just how the hell do you answer that question in time to get back to the crucial third-and-long situation on the football field?

I mean, really: What can you tell them? Where do you start? Levees? FEMA? Looting? Do you really want to get into it?

So you lie and make it easier for everyone: "We're getting there," you tell them.

My high school is Georgetown Prep. It used to be affiliated with Georgetown University — way back, a century or two ago — but is now a stand-alone institution in the suburbs of Washington, D.C.

It's a coat-and-tie place, all boys, an academic and athletic powerhouse on 90 rolling acres; one heck of a place to spend your formative years. Latin was required when I went there; I'm sure it still is.

It was like living inside that novel, "A Separate Peace," which was also required reading when I was there.

It's composed mostly of day students, but there are a couple of dormitories there for boarders, and when Katrina blew through

New Orleans, the folks at Prep contacted Jesuit High School in New Orleans and offered to take in some kids for the semester. No charge.

That amounts to considerably more than a nice gesture: It costs $25,000 to go there (which is a few more bucks than it was when I was a lad, to be sure).

There actually weren't any vacancies at Prep, so the academic brain trust there came up with a plan: Any undergraduate roommates who agreed to make room for a Jesuit student and make it three-to-a-room would be offered the coveted privileges allowed only to seniors: televisions and refrigerators in their dorm rooms.

Fifteen Jesuit kids wound up at Prep this fall. Maryland is a whole different world for these kids, trying to break into an alien East Coast social scene in midstream: Who are these girls? What are these people talking about? Don't they have any Abita around here?

After the football game, I met Jude Fitzmorris, one of the Jesuit kids. He's Tom Fitzmorris' kid; you know, that "Mr. Food" guy on AM radio.

Jude said he really likes it there. He's fitting in. He plans to stay the full academic school year. Most of the other guys, he said, are homesick as all get out and they want to come back here.

In fact, some already have.

There's just something about New Orleans that way, I guess, even when it's beaten down like a wet three-legged dog. With mange and fleas. That's blind in one eye. And won't hunt.

That's us. The three-legged dog. But a confoundingly lovable cur all the same.

At that homecoming game (we beat St. Alban's by three touchdowns, by the way), I ran into my friend Rory Coakley, who happened to be in New Orleans the weekend that Katrina began her ramrod track up our wazoo.

He had been moving his son, an incoming freshman — and recent Prep grad — into the dorms at Loyola University. In fact, this September, I was scheduled to host a dinner for Rory Jr. and seven other incoming Prep freshmen at Jacques-Imo's Café on Oak Street.

Another local Prep alum and I were going to give the boys a little shrimp and alligator sausage cheesecake just to let them know they're not in Maryland anymore, then do the old-fart routine of welcoming them to the city and rendering our deep fonts of local wisdom and advice.

Of course, that didn't happen.

Rory called me that Friday, Saturday and Sunday before the storm from his room at the downtown Hilton as things were getting scary around here. I kept telling him to get the heck out of Dodge, but he couldn't find a flight. Or a car. Or a train. Or a bus.

I offered him one of our cars — told him to take it all the way to the East Coast; I didn't care. "You really need to get the hell out of here," I told him.

In my signature fashion, however, my car had zero gas in it and at this point there were no gas stations left open around here. So Rory, his wife, his son and two other Prep grads were on their own.

"Godspeed to you, brother," I told him as I split town with my own family. "See you on the other side."

Rory's a creative and intelligent guy — and fairly well off, it turns out. Like I said, we had a pretty good education, so, in thinking-outside-of-the-box fashion, he walked out of the Hilton lobby and up to a cabdriver and offered him a thousand dollars for a ride to Mobile.

In perhaps another characteristic of a typical Prep alum, Rory was delighted to discover that the cabdriver had a six-pack of Heineken in the car, which he threw into the deal as lagniappe.

Rory decided to drink one beer every hour. The six-pack was finished before they'd even made the Mississippi state line. The trip took so long that the cabdriver said he was too tired to continue, so Rory finished out the driving duties, some 16 or 17 hours later.

A few days later, Rory and I were on the phone — he back safely in Maryland, me in Baton Rouge — watching the grim TV images of the Convention Center.

"You know, that would have been you," I told him. "That's the best thousand dollars you ever spent."

Anyway. At the homecoming game, Rory told me he would be back in New Orleans in January. Turns out, Rory Jr. and some of the other Prep guys are re-enrolling at Loyola.

I wanted to tell him: Are you out of your mind? I mean, I think they're plumb crazy to do such a thing when they can comfortably remain in the safe and familiar environs of Georgetown University, where all the other Prep Loyola guys ended up.

But I swear to God, I wanted to kiss Rory when he told me this. It just slays me that there are people Out There who are committing themselves to this city when they have no other need or obligation to, no other reason than they think it's the right thing to do.

They believe in us.

And this is so important. If our universities don't survive this thing, we're in trouble deep. And I will testify to you that a half-dozen boys from Georgetown Prep are a good place to start.

And yeah, sure, they'll probably wind up being among those really annoying shirtless yahoos you see sitting on living room furniture on the littered front lawns of the frat houses on Broadway, but they're also going to be young men who saw what went down here 10 weeks ago and understand what went down here and they and their parents are still willing to stick it out with us.

Without them, we're toast.

And for that I say: Fried Green Tomatoes and Eggplant Pirogues at Jacques-Imo's on me, boys! Just give me a call when you get here in January.

Here to your new home, this crazy little three-legged dog named New Orleans.

Goodbye

Each time I go to Maryland to visit my children-in-exile, my daughter Katherine asks me the same thing: "Daddy, is everything in New Orleans broken?"

My first impulse is to tell her: "Only our hearts, darling. In a million little pieces. But our spirits shall endure."

But Katherine, being 6, isn't much for purple melodrama or lofty sentiment. She just wants to know if her swing set is OK.

So I tell her that a lot of things are, in fact, broken, but that most of her stuff — that's what counts to a child, right? — is fine. Except for the swing set, oddly enough. It's history. But that's a small price, I tell her.

I try to teach my kids that they are the lucky ones, the fortunate few, and they saw all that stuff on TV so I think they get it.

I think.

They see the piles of donated clothes at their schools in Maryland, and the table where students were raising money to buy backpacks for Katrina kids and so they know: There are folks out there a lot worse off than us.

On TV, they saw the images of people sitting in baskets dangling from ropes out of helicopters and they thought that looked pretty scary but pretty fun all the same and they wish they had done that.

"No you don't," I tell them and leave it at that.

Katherine and my son Jack recently asked me for status reports about their favorite places. The zoo: good. The Aquarium: not so good. Creole Creamery: good. This is important. After all, who would want to live in a town without ice cream?

I try to paint a somewhat accurate picture of what life looks like here, filtered through their lenses; I want them to understand, in some small way, what they will come home to one day soon.

They need to know what will be different in their upside-down world. The fewer surprises, my thinking goes, the smoother it will all go down.

They seem to grasp the situation best by an accounting of their friends. Where are their friends, they want to know. Who will be here when they come back to New Orleans?

I tell them that Walker and Olivia and Margot are like us: They're all here and safe and settled in their own homes.

I tell them that Casey, Helen and the twins Sisson and Tappan all lost the first floors of their homes in the flood but that they are going to live upstairs in their houses and they will be in school with us in January.

They think this sounds cool, this living upstairs thing.

"Can we live upstairs?" Jack asks me.

Hmm. "We can pretend," I tell him. "How about we make believe we live upstairs?"

He thinks this sounds like a good game.

Then I tell them that Lexi and Mila have moved away and they won't be coming back. Same for Miles and Cecilia. Ditto Charlie. They're gone.

They don't like this news, but they process it and they have been aware for a while that lots of families are spread around the country like them, living in new places and going to new schools. Hurricane Kids, just like them.

They don't like the idea that they never said goodbye to Lexi and Mila and Miles and Cecilia and Charlie. I tell them we'll find these kids and we will tell them goodbye. I promise them that we will find these kids. So they can say ... goodbye.

Continuing on the list of friends, I tell them that Sean is up in the air but that he will probably be coming back.

"Why is Sean up in the air?" Jack asks me. He's 4. I try to picture what he is picturing. Sean. Up in the air.

That sounds even cooler than living upstairs. I guess it sounds like he's dangling under a helicopter. I don't know. Sometimes I wonder how we're able to communicate with our children at all.

Katherine asks me about the specific fates of two other friends, Juliet and Nadia. I tell her that, truth is, I have no idea what happened to Juliet and Nadia. Not a clue. Vanished. They're just gone and we don't know where to or for how long and maybe we'll see them again and maybe we won't.

I don't know.

Kids don't work so well with uncertainties.

"Will you find Nadia for me?" Katherine asks.

I tell her yes, I will find Nadia. But I don't know where Nadia is. I can't even find my barber; how am I going to find some kid who has been cast to the fates?

Where did everybody go?

Man, it's a hell of a thing that went down here.

Juliet, Nadia are you out there? Somewhere? Anywhere?

If you are, Katherine says hello.

And goodbye.

Groundhog Day

We have been waking up with Groundhog Day Syndrome for a long time now, dragging ourselves out of bed with a sense of dread that the clock has stopped, the calendar pages don't turn and nothing is changing.

We're Bill Murray. We're Sisyphus pushing the boulder up the mountain. We're trapped in an Escher print, walking down steps that actually lead up, down straight paths that lead us full circle.

OK, for the four of you still reading, I'll stop with the cultural metaphors. You get the point. I get the point. We all get the point.

The point is: It's 14 days until January.

Wait until January, people in New Orleans say. You hear it all the time. Things will get better in January.

It's our mantra of hope, optimism, faith.

Or maybe delusion.

Maybe because we've been Saints fans for so long we are willing to buy futures when the market is flat. So eager to accept promises we don't really believe.

It's always been "wait until next year," and we buy our season tickets and jerseys with the name and number of our new star player — the guy who's going to take us all the way! — and, like Charlie Brown, we keep running to kick the football and Lucy pulls it away.

Again and again. Wait until next year.

But there is merit to the current theory of an impending turn of events for the positive, empirical evidence to shore it up. For New Orleans, that is; the Saints, I'm afraid, are a lost cause and they don't make levees big enough to plug that breach.

But January holds the promise of a sound that has been missing from our city for too long: the music of children. Lots of children.

Sure, there has been a refreshing repopulation of the little critters in recent weeks as schools opened and families trickled home, but the playgrounds still look pretty desolate and there's hardly ever a line for sugar cones at the Creole Creamery.

But there are legions of rugrats coming home this week or next or next, when the school semesters elsewhere end and when the holidays are over.

True, my son Jack's nursery school class will only have 12 of the original 20 kids who were enrolled last September, but I guess that's a decent rate of return. A start.

And I think it will grow. The kid quotient goes up by at least three today.

My family is coming home.

This is wonderful news from a personal standpoint, but I am also filled with anxiety about this, and immeasurable . . . I guess I can say it: Doubt.

Is it safe? Will they pick up on the air of despondency that seems to have engulfed three-quarters of the adult population here? Will they be upset that they don't have a blue roof like everyone else?

These are the questions that nag me.

But I think my friend, the barber Aidan Gill, has summed it up best: "A time will come when someone asks you: 'What were you doing about it?' You can't tell them: 'I was just watching it. I was just an innocent bystander.' Let me tell you something: There are no innocent bystanders in this."

My own call to arms has been that you're either part of the solution or you're part of the problem and it's time we become part of the problem because the solution, whatever it's been up to now, ain't workin'.

So I'm Charlie Brown now. New Orleans is Lucy. And I'm gonna kick that ball a country mile.

Come January, everything gets better. If not, then we wait for Feb. 2.

That's Groundhog Day.

Coming Home

On Aug. 27, my family left our home in New Orleans with a duffel bag full of beach clothes, three sleeping bags, three teddy bears and a basketball.

I always travel with a basketball. It's my security blanket. I never knew how much I'd need one on this trip.

There was a hurricane coming to town and, well . . . you know the rest of that story. I returned to New Orleans a week later. My family wound up in Maryland, in the town of Somerset, just on the D.C. border, in the house where I grew up.

There has always been much hand-wringing over what you were supposed to call people like us — refugees, evacuees, etc. — but the terminology I prefer is that my kids were "embedded" at their grandparents' house. They became mini-celebrities in my hometown. Katrina Kids. A name recognized the world over.

When I went to visit, it seemed like everyone knew who we were. Several times, while trick-or-treating on Halloween, other parents stopped me and said, "We've heard about you." People gave us clothes and toys and tuition (thank you, Concord Hill School) and such an outpouring of generosity that it boggles the mind to realize just how kind strangers can be. My sister loaned us her car for four months, and if that's not love, I don't know what is.

My wife and kids used to spend weekends at my brother's house in Poolesville, Md. — 45 minutes away — and one morning, three bicycles appeared on the front lawn.

No note. No explanation. Just like that.

They'd heard about us.

We made the Somerset town newsletter, but not the local daily like some of our friends did in smaller towns across America. That's the price you pay when you become Katrina Kids in The Washington Post distribution area; you have to fight with Tom DeLay and Saddam Hussein for front-page space.

On the other hand, the crew at the local Starbucks wouldn't let my wife pay for coffee when they found out she was from New Orleans, so it was a two-way street, the good and the bad.

My wife and daughter became social mavens in town; the women of Somerset smothered them with attention and invitations. They thrived. It is a great place, that old town. But the gig is up.

We said goodbye to our extended family and new friends last week, and here's the thing about that — from the Can't Catch a Break files: What should have been the happiest day of the year for us — our homecoming — was actually Teardrop City, saying goodbye to my sister, my brother, their families and, worst of all, my parents, who let us turn their house and their lives upside down and asked in return only that we not break the frail staircase banister or destroy my mother's favorite old sofa and, naturally, we did both.

My parents are heroes. Among the tens of thousands of people who allowed their lives to be jolted by those of us who came seeking shelter from the storm. I felt like we broke their hearts when we left.

But my kids got to know them, and if there's one thing I can thank Katrina for, it's that. And also, my kids got to see snow, make a snowman, throw a snowball, catch flakes on their tongues.

That was a nice finishing touch.

But I'm tired of spending all my life surrounded by goodbyes. That's a lyric by Fred LeBlanc, the Cowboy Mouth drummer, but it captures my core right now. Every day, it seems, it's goodbye to somebody.

But bringing my family home also brought with it the very welcome sound of hello. It was a sound I needed to hear. Hello to all — well, some — of our old New Orleans friends and neighbors.

And it's funny: It wasn't until my wife and kids walked into our house that I realized I had been living with a bunker mentality for a long time.

For instance, I had cleaned out our refrigerator months ago, but the shelves were still in the back yard. My back deck was still a repository for seven red gas cans, even though I hadn't run a generator since September.

My closet and drawers were almost exactly as they had been the day we evacuated; I have worn two sets of clothes since everything went down. Jeans, T-shirts. I look at the suits hanging in my closet and wonder what use I'll ever have for them again.

What did I used to do?

Some folks say it's insane to bring children into this environment, this beaten-down town, and certainly there is merit to that argument.

Is it depressing here? Yes. Is it dangerous? Maybe. The water, the air, the soil . . . I don't know.

And there's little doubt that the kids have picked up the vibe. My 6-year-old daughter started writing a book this week — a writer in the family! — and she has a page about the hurricane in it and it says: "A lot of people died. Some of them were kids."

Mercy. God in heaven, what lives are we handing to these children of the storm?

Then again, there is much about the aftermath that amuses them greatly. For example, where adults see rows and rows of spoiling refrigerators fouling the side of the road, children see mountains of empty appliance boxes to replace them.

It used to be that, when a neighbor on the block bought a major appliance — a once-a-year event — we would commandeer the box and make four or five days of fun out of it. A fort. A playhouse. A cave.

With all these empty boxes around, I thought it would be nearly criminal not to make some lemonade out of all these lemons bestowed upon us, so I borrowed a friend's truck and brought six refrigerator boxes home and built a Christmas village for the kids.

They disappear for hours. In all the muck, you gotta dig for the magic.

When we drove to City Park the other night to look at the holiday lights, we plowed through blighted streets, total darkness, total loss and devastation on the sides of the road.

"Ooh, scary!" was all my son could muster. They thought it was pretty cool, actually, and I'm not going to call them out on that and tell them that, in fact, it's not. In due time, they will find out.

They will learn what went down in this town.

They see the ubiquitous brown stain that marks where the floodwaters settled for three weeks, and they see — not the criminal failure of the Army Corps of Engineers but ... a bathtub ring around the city.

What other place has that?

They love this town, my kids. They had a blast in Maryland, but they all said they wanted to come home and they've not spoken otherwise since they got here.

They know that Al Copeland's house is all lit up for the holidays like some crazy Disney castle and they know we'll go check it out this week, and that alone, for them, is a reason to live here.

They'll go back to their schools in January and we will move on.

It's a big deal, what's happened here and what lies ahead. Rebuilding this city is history in the making, and my family — as we're fond of singing around here — is going to be in that number.

This is not just Anywhere USA we're talking about. This is New Orleans. This is our home. Our future.

It's a hard-luck city right now, and you can look at it as a half-empty, half-full conundrum, although, in New Orleans, the truth is, the glass is shattered.

But we're going to help pick up the pieces. Starting today.

Life in the Refrigerator City

Civil Unrest

Refrigerators are poignant symbols of our city's destruction and our government's inertia — many are now painted with political slogans.

The refrigerators of New Orleans are also the weapons of choice in the rapid deterioration of civility Uptown. Weapons of our Mass Destruction — literally.

It's all a part of NIMBY syndrome — Not In My Backyard — the bane of political processes nationwide (Think Wal-Mart, landfills and halfway houses), but these are particularly wicked and stinky cases.

A small instance would be the case of the jerk who loaded his dead and smelly fridge into his pickup truck one night and drove around Uptown looking for a place to get rid of it, rather than putting it on his curbside like the rest of us and taking his chances on the latest gambling craze sweeping our town: FEMA Garbage Pickup Lotto.

And did he dump it in the river or on some abandoned lot on Tchoupitoulas? No, this pillar of society chose Audubon Park — at the corner of Laurel Street and West Drive — to dump his offensive icebox. Smooth move. What a prince.

There's one oasis for miles in this community that has been cleaned and groomed for repopulation (Thank you, Oklahoma National Guard) — a place to bring kids and pets and grandmothers and see what little remains of nature in this godforsaken wasteland — and somebody dumps a fridge on the corner and drives off into the night.

This kind of crap makes me hubcap-stealing angry. But this was just a skirmish in what has become the Uptown Refrigerator Wars.

Refrigerator clusters have started appearing all over the area, as one guy dumps his fridge on a corner away from his house and then — like iron shavings drawn to a magnet — suddenly there are five appliances on the corner, then 10, then 15.

But it gets worse. It gets personal. The above crimes are random and anonymous. The two I shall now describe involve direct confrontations followed by covert actions and now, no doubt, smoldering resentments among neighbors.

Full disclosure: I was involved in one of these episodes. I'm sure this comes as a great shock to, say, my wife and close friends, to hear that I interjected myself into a petty and juvenile refrigerator dispute but, hey: Like everyone else, I'm mad as hell, and I'm not gonna take it anymore.

To wit: On Friday night, the garbage crews rolled onto my street — huge dump trucks and backhoes and cranes and Bobcats. It was the closest to a parade that we've seen in a while, and we all poured out of our houses to cheer them on. Finally, our 6-foot wall of debris, stretching from one end of the block to the other, was going to be hauled off, and we could begin to try to forget what has happened here.

But while the hard-hatted cleanup crews did their massive sweep-up, a guy from around the corner drove up in his pickup truck and dumped a fridge on the corner.

My neighbor Franke jumped off his stoop and ran over to explain that the refrigerators and other hazardous waste had already been cleaned from this block; that these guys on Friday night were just picking up trees, branches, household debris and regular old garbage.

The guy insisted that the trucks would take his fridge, too, and then he drove off, even as we told him: Don't leave this here.

Well, it took an hour, but the federal contractors got my block clear. We could see our curbs and sidewalks for the first time since the hurricane. The place was swept spotless. It was a time for celebration.

Except for that damn smelly fridge they left on the corner, just like we said they would.

Man, that really chapped me. So, in the middle of the night, I borrowed a friend's dolly and I loaded up the fridge and I dragged it back to the offender's house and unloaded it at his front steps. Since they hadn't picked it up, I was sure he was going to want to do the neighborly thing and take it back.

Now, I ask you: Was I wrong to do this?

Don't answer that. First, let me tell you another story, as reported to me by a very reliable source who shall remain nameless for his own protection. (Me, I'm not circumspect enough to perform my urban civic warfare anonymously.)

Anyway, over in another part of Uptown, several neighbors were working together to roll out their refrigerators to the curb. Everyone explicitly agreed to tape them shut to lock in the stink and foulness therein and take the necessary precautions to prevent widespread dysentery.

Often, as you probably know, getting the full refrigerators out to the curb takes a couple of people, but one guy got restless and refused to wait and he wrestled out his appliance to his driveway alone. He had attempted to tape it shut but had done an obviously inferior job and he wouldn't wait for help.

Then he tied the dang thing to his car to drag it down to the curb. And it fell open. And your mama's seven-week-old casserole spilled out. And it stunk. And he left it there, an open and stinking invitation to all manner of biblical-proportion infestations and plagues.

Naturally, everyone on the block got ticked off. And then one got even.

When a contractor was driving by later that day, a guy on the block offered him $20 to use his Bobcat to grab a hold of the offending refrigerator and move it into the middle of the offender's driveway and drop it — thereby blocking ingress and egress to said driveway.

The contractor accepted the offer and moved the fridge into blockade position. And now the neighbors all eye each other suspiciously and goodwill is withdrawn and there you have it. This is what it has come to.

Now, I know what a lot of you are thinking: There are people in this town who lost EVERYTHING. Their loved ones, their homes, their jobs, their pets, their precious photos and memories.

And their refrigerators.

And all that you rich and idle Uptowners on dry land can find within your hearts to do is bicker over appliances?

You're thinking: You people didn't have a right to survive this storm.

And maybe you're right. Maybe we should go back to fighting each other over Wal-Mart and Whole Foods and college bars. But consider this:

Maybe this signals a return to normalcy. Maybe this is even a healthy sign of the human spirit.

Or maybe we're all just a bunch of petty ingrates.

Really, it's not for me to decide. I am merely the chronicler of events and, OK, a minor participant in the civic unrest.

I am willing to share the blame. But I also view this story as a cautionary tale, a call for civility, a cry of help to the community-at-large, before we tear ourselves apart.

And while we're talking about civility, one more thing:

KEEP YOUR STINKING FRIDGE TO YOURSELF.

Refrigerator Town

In Refrigerator Town there was a Council Full of Clowns
And a tall and savvy King as bald as Cupid.
In Refrigerator Town, while all the poor folks drowned
FEMA and Mike Brown were stuck on stupid.
In Refrigerator Dome, which was temporary home
To the terrified and downtrodden masses;
In Refrigerator Dome, the people waited all alone
While the buses showed up slower than molasses.
In Refrigerator Village, some coppers loot and pillage
And we still don't know how many won't come back.
In Refrigerator Village, they'll have to pass a millage
Just to pay for all those stolen Cadillacs.
In Refrigerator Town, not a child can be found
And the classrooms are as empty as the Dome.
In Refrigerator Town, School Board antics still abound
And you wonder why you'd ever move back home.
In Refrigerator Void, all the houses were destroyed
And you get a sense of widespread fear and panic.
In Refrigerator Void, all the folks are unemployed
And everyone you meet is taking Xanax.
In Refrigerator City, Congress seems to take no pity
On the businesses that cease to operate.

In Refrigerator City, there's a VIP committee

To which nobody can possibly relate.

In Refrigerator Parish, the bickering is garish

And the politicians seem to have no clue.

In Refrigerator Parish, it really got nightmarish

When the sharks showed up on Cleary Avenue.

In Refrigerator 'burbs, the trash is piled up on the curbs

And the neighborhoods are ugly and they smell.

In Refrigerator 'burbs, folks are getting quite disturbed

That their quality of life has gone to hell.

In Refrigerator Land, we have no leg on which to stand

While the politicos can't seem to do a thing.

In Refrigerator Land, it seems the only helping hand

Is the signing bonus at the Burger King.

On Refrigerator Planet, if you can't bag or box or can it,

Just push it out your door onto the street.

On Refrigerator Planet, pick up the garbage, dammit!

'Cause the whole place smells like fetid, rotten meat.

In Refrigerator Wasteland, you have to dress up like a spaceman

Just to rescue your old family photographs.

In Refrigerator Wasteland, stretched from Chalmette clear to Raceland

We're in misery while Halliburton laughs.

From the Refrigerator Pulpits, the preachers said the culprits

For the storm were all the lesbians and queers.

But Refrigerator Church was left in quite a lurch
When it turned out to be the Corps of Engineers.
In Refrigerator Dome, the Saints no longer call it home
No more runs or kicks or punts or touchdown passes.
In Refrigerator Dome, no more famous cups of foam
And Tom Benson's heart's as cold as Minneapolis.
In Refrigerator Land, the levees all are made of sand
And there's no gas, no food, no water and no sewage.
But in Refrigerator Land, we will make our final stand
Because anything beats rush hour in Baton Rouge.

Lurching Towards Babylon

People ask me: What do you cover now that the entertainment industry has fizzled away? After all, for the past 10 years, that was my beat.

My answer: Basically, I spend my days like everyone else, lurching from one "episode" to the next, just trying to live, just trying to survive, just trying not to crack up and publicly embarrass myself, my family and my newspaper.

It's hard, man. It's hard, just to live. I don't mean to be overly confessional here, but sometimes I feel I am no longer fit for public consumption, no longer fit for publication and definitely no longer fit to operate heavy machinery.

I was at my local Circle K the other day, sitting in my car in a borderline catatonic state when I witnessed a guy in a truck in the parking lot wadding up a ball of trash and throwing it out his window.

I have silently witnessed this sight a million times over the past 20 years. On Broad Street, on Magazine Street, in the French Quarter, everywhere. We all have. It's almost like litter is a part of our heritage.

Well, I snapped. I got out of my car and approached the offending vehicle and I tapped on the guy's window.

During my walk to said vehicle, a very loud voice inside my head said to me: Don't do this. You are not well. It's none of your business.

But there are lots of voices in my head these days. You can probably relate. So I wrote this cautionary device off as just so much cacophony and decided: It is your business. The guy rolled down his window and I said, "Are you from here?"

I expected him to say no, and I had this thing in my mind that I was going to tell him, this thing about the sanctity of my city, about the care he needs to take, about how delicate our balance is right now.

But he said yes. And I lost it. Completely. Stark raving mad, if you must know the truth. "You can't do this anymore," I said to him in a voice that wasn't particularly loud, but in a tone I hardly recognized from myself and which was probably laced with just enough tonic to catch his attention.

We looked at each other. And then I said — or maybe I screamed: "You can't do this anymore!"

I'm not sure who was more frightened, him or me, but I kept going. I said: "You can't just throw stuff out of your car window anymore. I realize that there is garbage everywhere — all over our streets — but, still, you can't just throw stuff out your window like it doesn't matter. IT MATTERS!"

The guy was frozen in his seat. He was no doubt wishing he had gone to Winn-Dixie or the Stop-and-Go or anyplace else but this Circle K. But here we were. I laid it out on this poor sap. I said, "We've got to change. We can't go back to the way we were and the way we were was people just throwing crap in the streets like it doesn't matter. We need to do better. We need to change.

"IT MATTERS!" I said again — like he didn't hear me the first time — and then I just stood there in a forwardly lurched position and can I tell you: I'm tired of lurching. I want to stop lurching. But I can't stop lurching.

Needless to say, I freaked the guy out. His eyes got wide and I think he wanted to answer me but no words came. He mumbled something like, "All right," and then his arm got busy rolling his window up and he nodded to me in a fashion that said something between "Don't kill me" and "Seek professional help" and he backed out of the parking lot.

Slowly.

And he was gone. And I was standing there.

Lurched.

He probably got on his cell phone to his wife and said: "We're moving to Houston."

I don't know. I don't mean to push my existential dread on complete strangers but there I stood, now in an empty Circle K parking lot, thinking: What the hell are you doing? I lurched back to my car. I lurched home. And I'm sitting here at my desk — lurched, I might add — wondering where all this comes from.

There is no lesson here. No moral. Other than we have to erase all the bad things we used to do around here — big and small — if we want to survive. We need to be civil. We need to be clean. We need to change. We need to respect ourselves and our city.

Otherwise, some disengaged crazy guy is going to accost you in a parking lot someday and make you wish you'd never gotten out of bed that morning. It will leave you in one serious lurch, my friend.

The Cat Lady

Ellen Montgomery's house near Audubon Park was already almost invisible from the street before Hurricane Katrina shattered the massive cedar tree in her front yard and left a tangled, camouflaged mess that now obliterates the view of just about everything.

If anything, that helped her hide from the National Guard during the tense days — now ancient weeks ago — when word came that they were forcing those who had remained in New Orleans to leave.

"If I was out walking in the neighborhood and I heard the Hummers coming, I would duck down behind a porch or some broken shutters," she said. "I felt like a Confederate spy in enemy territory."

Montgomery was a holdout. A straggler. The resistance.

She stayed behind without power or running water or even a generator. The simple reason: "My babies," she says. Thirty-four cats. (It was 33 for several weeks, until one that had gone missing returned home last Saturday night, "to say hello," Montgomery says.)

She knows what you're thinking. It used to bug her but not anymore.

"Years ago, I said to my vet: 'But I don't WANT to be a cat lady!'" Montgomery recalls. "And he says to me: 'But you ARE a cat lady.' So there you are."

And so, for 30 days, what has she done?

"Well," she pauses. "I sleep late. Let's see ... and then I feed the cats. I read 'The Journal of Beatrix Potter.' It's a lovely book. And then I have my cup of coffee. And that usually lasts a couple of hours. And then I paint and — I don't know. The days just fly by.

"I'm in another world here. I don't feel the heat. I don't feel anything. I am very able to exist on my own. I just paint and that's what keeps me from going bonkers. That's my therapy."

Montgomery has been painting since 1977, when she read the book of Vincent Van Gogh's correspondence, "Letters to Theo."

"I read it and I said: I want to do that," she says. "So I got down and did that and have been doing it ever since."

Indeed. She sits on the floor in the front room of her house — it would be a stretch to call it a "studio" — and she fills canvas after canvas, board after board, paper after paper. If you stood still in front of her for long enough, she'd probably paint you.

Her home is filled with thousands of paintings she has made over the past three decades. She admittedly has sold few works, so mostly they line her walls, floor-to-ceiling in every room, and then they fill stacks and piles randomly assigned through her cluttered 1890s cottage.

And, having recently run out of canvases to work on, she is now working a medium that only a hurricane could provide: She has gathered scores of slate roofing tiles that were scattered off the roofs of her neighbors' homes into the street, and now she paints them.

"They're so beautiful," she says. "I couldn't bear the thought of the National Guardsmen or some contractors trampling over them, so I collected them. I won't have enough time in my life to paint them all."

Over the years, she has painted various abstracts and florals and faces and landscapes, but now her work is fairly dark and muddied and swirly, work clearly influenced by the monstrous forces that have visited upon her life this past month.

Funny thing is, in the beginning, she didn't really know what had happened.

Montgomery has been living the consummate, isolated cat lady existence for years and she was only vaguely aware that a storm was even coming.

The shattered cedar tree and the loss of power, water and phone — and the disappearance of all her neighbors — told her it was something big.

"I went to church that Sunday morning before the storm and a sign on the door said, 'Services canceled,' so I bought a paper and that was the last news I heard," she says.

"There were four or five days where I had absolutely no idea what had happened. But I was safe, the cats were safe, so I thought: why be scared? I firmly believe in God and prayer. I knew I would just ride it out. I am probably more prepared than anyone else in the world to spend time alone."

It wasn't until several days later, when a neighbor returning to retrieve some items loaned her a radio — and stocked her with food and water before leaving again — that the magnitude of the event settled upon her.

"I try to listen to the news a couple of hours a day and it's unimaginable, really," she says. But she has seen no images of it all; has not seen that more than half the city was underwater and has not seen the human misery that filled the Superdome and Convention Center, sights that are now burned into the American consciousness.

"At first, actually, it was kind of nice around here," she says. "The birds came back and the squirrels would come deliver me the news. It's all been so peaceful, really. But it's nice to have the thought of people coming back. I suppose there'll be lots of chainsaws and hammers and all that, so I might miss the silence. But, the truth is, I'm just about out of candles."

Caving In

It's not hard to identify the point at which, during my second tour of press duty here, it was time to get out.

That would be when, in the course of accompanying a photographer to shoot pictures for a feature I was writing, I stood up, blacked out, pitched face-forward into a tree and lay in the grass drifting in and out of consciousness for the next couple of hours.

It was during those "in" points of my in-and-out consciousness, looking up into a profoundly beautiful blue New Orleans sky, that I thought: Maybe I need to eat more. Maybe I need a break. I wonder what my kids are doing today? I wonder if there are any job openings in the Midwest?

There I was, a body lying face up in the grass on the side of the road for several hours in a once-major metropolitan city, a sizeable gash across my forehead, one that — as I study it in a mirror — actually seems to be in the shape of the letter K, which seems a fitting lifetime reminder of what has happened here.

A little more authentic than a tattoo, no?

I was also thinking: Isn't anyone going to come get me? Several notions came to mind:

First of all, even before Katrina (Pre-K, let's call it), a man passed out on the side of the road in New Orleans was not a uniquely alarming sight. But that's usually a vision reserved for the tourist areas, not under the shady streets of Uptown where my meltdown occurred.

Secondly — and I don't mean to be too macabre here — but in the days since Katrina, a body laying anywhere on the street around here has not been a completely unusual circumstance.

You may ask: Why didn't the photographer get me out of there? But he was the only shooter we seemed to have in the city that day and the police chief was about to resign and he had to go get the picture and so I waved him off: "Go ahead," I said. "I'll be fine."

The story is important, I was thinking. Go get the story.

That was about 3:30 in the afternoon. I heard birds singing and every now and then, I could hear the woman we had come to photograph — a Katrina holdout and survivor — cooing to her cats in the distance.

It was not altogether unpleasant, the parts where I was awake. I had some shade. But it occurred to me that this environment is no place for the over-emotional and faint of heart.

If you cry when you watch "Terms of Endearment," then you don't need to be here. Problem is, I even cry at the end of "When Harry Met Sally," so this whole experience is Stress City.

Though people are trickling back into town and businesses are starting to light up, it's still an impossible vista, this whole damn city, where Lakeview looks like a nuclear wasteland with automobile trunks, doors and windows imploded from being underwater and so many things lying upside down in the street that shouldn't be upside down.

Including reporters.

There's a car down the street from my house that careened over a concrete retainer wall and through an iron fence and crashed into the front porch of the Café Luna coffee shop and I've actually gotten used to the sight, after all these weeks.

This little tableau is so far down on the list of priorities around here that it could be four more weeks until somebody thinks to drag that thing away.

Those are things you think about while lying on the side of the road, stuck somewhere between Armageddon and the Dawn of a New Day.

Nobody drove by. Nobody walked their dog past me. No kid rode up on a bicycle and said: "Are you OK, mister?"

When I noticed it was starting to get dark, I got up, a little more than wobbly, and I wandered to my car and drove to the Sheraton Hotel downtown where I am staying and in the morning I wrote the story about the cat lady we were photographing Uptown by the tree that now bears an imprint of my head.

Because the story is important. We've got to get the stories. This is an assignment bigger than any of us. It's history in a hurry.

But, if it's OK with you, I think I'm gonna take a few days off.

The Magnet Man

With a measure of modesty you don't often find among the creative class, Chris Cressionnie describes his vocation thus:

"I used to be an artist who waited tables. Truthfully, now I'm more of a waiter who happens to paint pictures. But, since the hurricane, I really don't do a damn thing."

Cressionnie's employer, Gautreau's restaurant, has not reopened yet. And he hasn't found the muse or concentration to stand at a canvas and paint. Thus, after nature's furious upheaval, a man is reduced to his fundamental primeval nature: hunter and gatherer.

And that's how Cressionnie has created one of the most stirring and amusing post-Katrina visual displays: His 1994 Chevy Blazer is covered with, of all things, refrigerator magnets.

And not just any old souvenir magnets you pick up at a gift shop. In fact, these are your magnets. And my magnets. And everybody else's magnets.

For weeks, Cressionnie has been collecting these delicate little tokens, at once so frivolous and common, but which tell a story of our city. They say where we go to school, what teams we root for, where we order pizza, what gods we pray to, what veterinarians we take our pets to, when our next dentist appointment is, where we like to go on vacation and — this part stays with you — who we love.

At risk to life and limb (sudden stops of the car) and at risk to his senses (he gets into some seriously stinky situations), Cressionnie drives our streets by day — in the dead hours between dropping off and picking up his son at school — and he gathers mementos off discarded refrigerators and, in the process, has created a rolling art installation that is a snapshot of our culture.

American flags. Jesus. Mother Teresa. Daffy Duck. Saints schedules dating back to 2001. Fruits. WWOZ. Tulane. Elysian Fields, spelled out in those classic street tile replicas. Hollywood. Country Day. California. St. Francisville.

I (HEART) New Orleans. All those Harry Lee magnets that the sheriff throws off Mardi Gras floats every winter; each year a different design. Dozens of insurance agents. The same for veterinarians. A photo of two young lovers standing on the Great Wall of China.

Who are they?

On March 27, someone has a doctor's appointment at 9:15 a.m. on Napoleon Avenue. Will they remember? There is a white magnet with wedding bells on it that commemorates the marriage of Essence Allen and Wright Ellie Wright, Nov. 11, 2003.

And there are the children: All these discarded pictures of someone's kids staring out at you from the side of Cressionnie's car. There's one that says: "Happy 1st Birthday Micah. March 12, 2003. Little Fingers, Little Toes. Today you're one. And everybody knows."

There is something maudlin — maybe even mildly predatory — about picking over the remains of our devastation. But there is also something noble about archiving the personal details of our citizenry, particularly when those details were otherwise bound for the dump.

"In many ways, this is kind of sad," Cressionnie said one day while combing the Mid-City and Pigeon Town neighborhoods. "They're like little trophies of people's lives. Keepsakes. But it also seems significant. In my art, I've always tried to make light of things; I've always been a bit of a thorn in the side."

Indeed. As he climbs through piles of waste and abandoned appliances, he receives many odd stares. "People kind of check you out when you stop in front of their house," he said. "You just give them a little wave and everything's OK."

Not all are so friendly, though. Once, when a guy figured out what he was doing, he barked at Cressionnie, telling him to just come inside his destroyed house and take whatever he wanted. Just take it all, the man said.

That's why Cressionnie travels with his boxer, Mika. "Just in case anything happens," he said.

But nothing does. It all settles. And, truth is, Mika seems pretty bored with the project after all these weeks. "She doesn't even try to get out of the car anymore," he said.

The job of an artist is never easy. Sometimes he has to wrestle with duct tape that has pinned down a particularly attractive magnet — maybe a religious icon or a good Disney character.

And then there are the maggots to deal with. Maggots on Magnets. Now there's a great name for a punk band if I ever heard one.

To be sure, he tries the patience of anyone who happens to be driving behind him. "I slow down everywhere," he said. "It's become an addiction, almost. The hunt for the hunt's sake."

On Colapissa Street one day, Cressionnie asked resident Donald Murray if it was all right to grab the magnets off his fridge by the sidewalk. Murray said sure, and called over to some friends to witness the event in a sort of check-this-dude-out kind of way.

"That's nice," said Murray, an African-American, hands on hips, inspecting the car. "Real nice. But I'm going to tell you this to your face: Only a white guy would think of something like this."

They all laughed. A lot and loud. Then Murray and his friends stared in silence and wonder again. Then Murray said: "You're going to need a bigger truck."

The Last Ride

In the trail of tears left by Katrina and Rita, blanketing an entire region of American geography, culture, history and memories, it will be years, maybe decades, until we've compiled the compendium of what we've lost.

There are a million small stories to be told after the hurricanes; stories about corner stores, neighborhood bars, barbershops, local bands, local characters, influential teachers and football coaches, roadside attractions and local institutions.

So much of this stuff, gone now, ingloriously surrendered or disappeared in the wake of the storms.

On Aug. 29, many of these stories ran their final chapter with no two-weeks notice given. No going-out-of-business sale, farewell performance or going-away party. Not even goodbye and thanks for the memories.

The Circle G Riding Stable in Picayune, Miss., is one of these stories.

If you are from southeastern Louisiana or Mississippi and ever rented a horse for a day ride in the country, you probably found yourself at one time or another at the Circle G.

For 35 years, it was a destination for summer campers and church groups, young lovers, city slickers, family picnics, office parties, conventioneers and the plain old looking-for-something-to-do weekend adventurers.

And reporters; the Circle G amassed an impressive portfolio of regional press clippings over the decades, including at least a half-dozen features and profiles in this newspaper alone.

That's because you generally got more than just a horse ride for your money at Circle G. With it you got an education in country living and plain speak from the proprietor, a master raconteur named David Gluth, a former shirt-and-tie New Orleans businessman who moved to Picayune in 1969 — at age 27 — and transformed himself into a rural wag with a large and loyal New Orleans clientele.

He is also my father-in-law.

Picayune is where my family first evacuated for Katrina, figuring on getting out of New Orleans for a few days to avoid the predictable street flooding and power outages.

As the storm grew bigger and turned its eye toward the Mississippi Coast, the tall, tall pines of Picayune — and its relative isolation 15 miles inland — made me think it was no place for my wife and three city kids to ride out a major storm. I was right. On the western edge of the eye, Picayune got hammered.

"I had never really been concerned about hurricanes before," David told me later. "I had weathered them my whole life. But the morning it came in, I was out on our deck and I was watching as 60-foot trees came out of the ground and just flew across the property.

"Huge oaks and tremendous pines — 10 feet around — were just falling all over us. There were tornadoes everywhere and that freight train sound. I started to worry that the roof might blow off, the windows would blow in and the house would collapse. And for the first time in my life, I felt fear."

When it was over, the arboreal devastation was nearly complete. Katrina simply cleared the place out, a once tree-canopied paradise laid open to bare sunlight. Miraculously, the house — and the horses, 30 of them — survived.

"Animals know how to take care of themselves," David said. "They've been dealing with storms for thousands of years; that's how they have survived. In a storm like this, horses just put their butts to the wind, their heads down and their ears forward — and they say their horse prayers." Nevertheless, by that Monday afternoon, it was clear that the Circle G had hosted its last rider.

The deep, slow-rolling, 14-mile path through the woods was a litter of fallen trees. All access to Catahoula Creek, where riders stop for picnics on a long, sandy white beach, was blocked; the trail, carved out by over 35 years of riding, was, in a word, obliterated.

In a matter of hours, a beloved local business was wiped off the books.

Aside from the massive cost and time to rebuild and clear the trails — and fix the barn — there were other concerns.

"I realized that the majority of my customer base was probably gone and those who remained would be involved for a long time in other pursuits that don't include horseback riding," David said.

And so he folded his hand. Over the past few weeks, David tore down the barn and sold the horses, kissing each one goodbye before they were led away. "I've cried more than a few times," he said.

"We get calls every day now from our old customers," he said. "Some are ready to come back, and they get very upset when we tell them what has happened. They say: "No! I rode there when I was a kid and now I ride there with my granddaughter. It's our tradition. You can't do this!' "

Some folks even offer to bring their own chain saws to help clear the place out, but they don't realize the enormity and futility of the task at hand. The Circle G — it's toast. Another notch in Katrina's belt.

"I'm too old to start over," David said. "This has been my life for 35 years, but I'm ready for Page 2 of my life — or Page 3 or 4 or whatever page I'm on now."

But it was a good run. Over three-and-a-half decades, David was joined in the business by his parents, his son David Jr. and his family, and eventually, his fourth wife, Augusta.

Quite the family affair they built, from taking phone reservations in the morning to laying out the hay in the evening and everything in between; a small, self-contained private paradise in the woods.

"When I was a little boy, 6 or 7 or 8 years old, I always wanted to be a horse farmer," David remembers. "I wanted to move to Montana or Wyoming and own a ranch. Well, I never made it to Wyoming but I got to make tens of thousands of people happy, and I guess that's the best thing.

"I never had to work for a boss, and I wish I had saved more money, but I guess you could say I was a little kid whose dream came true."

Lights in the City

At this time of year, many of us are asked to ponder the true meaning of Christmas as some way of recalibrating our actions, lifestyles and character.

Tooling around the Fountainbleau neighborhood the other day, I came across a wasted yard in front of a wasted house in the middle of a wasted neighborhood with trash, debris and the specter of loss everywhere and there, on the corner of this pathetic lot, was a wasted little brown tree wrapped in a single strand of white Christmas lights.

One might ask: What is the point? What are they trying to prove? Are we even on Santa's itinerary this year? Or will he write off New Orleans, grab a quick bite at Ruth's Chris in Baton Rouge and venture off to cities that have Fortune 500-based companies, there to stuff their CEOs' stockings full of FEMA contracts?

Besides, all our chimneys either fell down or are covered with blue tarps. What's a jolly old elf to do?

Whether this small effort — this one pathetic little Charlie Brown Christmas tree in a town full of Charlie Brown Christmas trees — represents hope, delusion or faith, I am not sure. I suppose time, God and the Corps of Engineers will be the ultimate judges of that, and not necessarily in that order.

But tradition marches on and so it must be. Out in a Kenner neighborhood where I often take my kids to look at spectacular holiday light displays put on by the rich folks, many of the houses are gutted. But the FEMA trailers parked in the front yards are decorated with twinkling white lights instead.

It is both the saddest and most beautiful thing you ever saw.

And in places with no trailers, some folks have just decorated their curbside refrigerators and left it at that. Merry stinking Christmas to you, Uncle Sam.

Never mind that Entergy is going to bill you $800 for the use of a single strand of lights this month ($1,400 if you blink those suckers), the weird and oddly celebratory manifestations of the holidays around here are just another sign that: YOU CAN'T STOP US.

Sure, you can slow us down, pare our ranks, tear at our foundations until we cry for mercy. But YOU CAN'T STOP US.

Perhaps no civic organization has shown its resilience in the face of all odds more than the Drunken Santas, a tight-knit group of New Orleanians who, after a round of drinking games at Madigan's bar one night in 1998, decided to take an activist role in the holidays rather than sit around getting soused by themselves.

So they decided to get soused with others. Spreading the cheer is their message. So they dress up in Santa costumes (or skimpier facsimiles thereof for the female members of this organization, the Ho-Ho-Hos) and they charter a fleet of limos and they pub crawl.

These guys are right up there with the Salvation Army and Rex when it comes to giving back to the community this time of year. As Ho-Ho-Ho Natasha Daniel put it: "We have a good time. We push people into garbage piles. Make them take shots with us. You know: all the Reindeer Games."

Now, I realize at this point in the story that the eyes of the righteous are rolling. Wait until they hear about this in Congress, I hear you saying. Now they're NEVER going to give us that $2 billion we need to rebuild New Orleans.

Well, frankly, Congress can go Scrooge itself. And so can the eye-rollers, holy rollers and professional bowlers. (Sorry, I need a third entity to make the rhythm work in that last phrase and I couldn't come up with a damn thing.)

They'll never understand the hardships the Drunken Santas have been forced to endure: From 92 participants and 12 limos last year, their ranks were devastated by Katrina to the tune of just 22 riders this year — only three of them Ho-Ho-Hos, perhaps the worst part of this whole tragedy.

One fellow named Jonathan drove in from Baton Rouge for the event Thursday night only to find that the tree that fell through his roof had caused significant water damage to his auxiliary closet (or whatever you call the closet where you keep things like Santa suits) and had destroyed his costume.

He was forced to participate in street clothes. When will the horror stop! How much more can we take!

Anyway. Shrunken Santas might have been a more appropriate name for the group this year. But they endured. "We love this city and we love this tradition and we want normalcy and we're not going to be stopped," said Drunken Santa Matthew Dwyer, as the group filtered out of the Monkey Hill Bar toward their limos and into a night of destinations unknown.

The Drunken Santas did what they do for no other reason than it was something to break pattern in this wretched little city and — as distasteful as this behavior may strike some — truthfully: It's nobody else's concern. They rented limos to take everybody home so no one crashed into your house so let it be.

Actually, if they had crashed into your house, that might have helped out with the lousy insurance check you're going to get, but that's a cause I'm somewhat hesitant to get behind: MORE DRUNK DRIVERS!

Now, the more astute of you readers out there may have sensed a metaphorical undercurrent here in this sordid tale of debauchery and weirdness.

Yes, I'm talking about Mardi Gras. And why we can't even think about canceling it. And I was going to go into that in far greater detail in this story but I'm out of room here and sometimes even I get tired of reading me so I'll pick up that thought in my next column and I'll let you go after one more thing:

Christmas is a mangled institution and taken all out of context by crass commercialism, awkward passes at co-workers at the office party and a cacophony of maudlin Christmas carols by Dolly Parton.

But does anyone say: THAT SENDS THE WRONG MESSAGE! CANCEL IT!

Do what you do. This Christmas, Hanukkah, Kwanzaa, New Year's Eve, Twelfth Night, Valentine's Day, Mardi Gras, St. Patty's Day and every day henceforth. Just do what you do. Live out your life and your traditions on your own terms.

If it offends others, so be it. That's their problem.

Personally, I think blinking white lights on those stark white FEMA trailers is all wrong, totally missing the point, but I'm not going to knock on your door and tell you that you've got your priorities messed up and that you're sending the wrong message and that the Senate Finance Committee is going to kill the appropriations bill that could save us all because of your stupid trailer.

No, instead, when I drive by your house with my kids next week, I'm sure we'll all agree in the privacy of our car that a subtler combination of red and green — non-blinking, I might add — would have looked much better.

Now, about that inflatable snow globe . . .

Let the Good Times Roll

The Mardi Gras thing. It's not on the table. It's not a point of negotiation or a bargaining chip.

We're going to have it and that's that. End of discussion.

Folks in faraway places are going to feel the misery of missing it, and that is a terrible thing. In the past, I have missed the season a couple of times because of story assignments elsewhere, and it sucked to be away from the center of the universe and not be a part of this city's fundamental, quintessential and indelible cultural landmark.

But we can't turn off the lights and keep the costumes in storage and ladders in the shed for another year just because we are beaten and broken and because so many of us are not here.

In fact, we have to do this because we are beaten and broken and so many of us are not here.

Katrina has proved, more than ever, that we are resilient. We are tougher than dirt. Certainly tougher than the dirt beneath our levees.

The social and celebratory nature of this event defines this city, and this is no time to lose definition. The edges are too blurry already.

Some folks say it sends the wrong message, but here's the thing about that: New Orleans is in a very complicated situation as far as "sending a message" goes these days. It's a tricky two-way street.

On one hand, it is vital to our very survival that the world outside of here understands just how profoundly and completely destroyed this city is right now, with desolate power grids and hundreds of thousands of residents living elsewhere and in limbo.

Jobs, businesses and the public spirit are all about as safely shored as the 17th Street Canal floodwall. We're leaking. And we could very well breach in the coming year or two.

We very well could.

On the other hand, we need to send a message that we are still New Orleans. We are the soul of America. We embody the triumph of the human spirit. Hell, we ARE Mardi Gras.

And Zulu can say they're only playing if they get it their way and Rex can say nothing at all and the mayor — our fallen and befuddled rock star — can say that he wants it one day and he doesn't want it the next day, but the truth is: It's not up to any of them.

It's up to me now. And we're having it.

And here's a simple, not-so-eloquent reason why: If we don't have Mardi Gras, then the terrorists win. The last thing we need right now is to divide ourselves over our most cherished event.

If the national news wants to show people puking on Bourbon Street as a metaphor for some sort of displaced priorities in this town, so be it. The only puking I've seen at Mardi Gras in the past 10 years is little babies throwing up on their mothers' shoulders after a bottle.

To encapsulate the notion of Mardi Gras as nothing more than a big drunk is to take the simple and stupid way out, and I, for one, am getting tired of staying stuck on simple and stupid.

Mardi Gras is not a parade. Mardi Gras is not girls flashing on French Quarter balconies. Mardi Gras is not an alcoholic binge.

Mardi Gras is bars and restaurants changing out all the CDs in their jukeboxes to Professor Longhair and the Neville Brothers, and it is annual front-porch crawfish boils hours before the parades so your stomach and attitude reach a state of grace, and it is returning to the same street corner, year after year, and standing next to the same people, year after year — people whose names you may or may not even know but you've watched their kids grow up in this public tableau and when they're not there, you wonder: Where are those guys this year?

It is dressing your dog in a stupid costume and cheering when the marching bands go crazy and clapping and saluting the military bands when they crisply snap to.

Now, that part, more than ever.

144

It's mad piano professors converging on our city from all over the world and banging the 88s until dawn and laughing at the hairy-shouldered men in dresses too tight and stalking the Indians under the Claiborne overpass and thrilling on the years you find them and lamenting the years you don't and promising yourself you will next year.

It's wearing frightful color combinations in public and rolling your eyes at the guy in your office who — like clockwork, year after year — denies that he got the baby in the king cake and now someone else has to pony up the 10 bucks for the next one.

Mardi Gras is the love of life. It is the harmonic convergence of our food, our music, our creativity, our eccentricity, our neighborhoods and our joy of living. All at once.

And it doesn't really matter if there are superparades or even any parades at all this year. Because some group of horn players will grab their instruments and they will march Down the Avenue because that's what they do, and I, for one, will follow.

If there are no parades, I'm hitching a boombox to a wagon, putting James Booker on the CD player and pulling my kids Down the Avenue and you're welcome to come along with me and where more than two tribes gather, there is a parade.

We are the parade. We are Mardi Gras. We're Whoville, man — you can take away the beads and the floats and all that crazy stuff, but we're still coming out into the street. Cops or no cops. Post-parade garbage pick-up or no garbage pick-up — like anyone could tell the friggin' difference!

If you are stuck somewhere else, in some other town, then bring it to them. If you've got a job somewhere else now, take off that Tuesday and get all the New Orleanians you know and gather in a park somewhere and cook up a mass of food and put some music on a box and raise a little hell.

And raise a glass to us, brothers and sisters, because we're in here fighting this fight and we'll raise a glass to you because you cannot be here with us and we know you want to. Let the whole damn country hear Al Johnson yelling "It's Carnival Time" and let them know we're not dead and if we are dying, we're going to pretend like we're not.

Fly the flag. Be in that number. This is our battle to win or lose. Hopefully, of one mind and one message. That we are still here. And that we are still New Orleans.

Our Katrina Christmas

To call this a Christmas like no other would be stating the obvious, I suppose. What an upside-down world we've found ourselves in here at the bottom of America.

In the Big Picture, maybe that helps one focus on the True Meaning of Christmas. Which is shopping, of course, but here's the thing: My local Pier One didn't sell wrapping paper this year and the Elmwood Wal-Mart didn't have strings of Christmas lights and — as I write this story — my family had been unable to find a lot around here that still had Christmas trees in stock.

Just how were we to engage in the most holy and traditional of holiday sounds — the cash register printing out debit card receipts — without purchasing all the physical trappings that mark the birth of Jesus?

Without that, all we've got is Jose Feliciano singing "Feliz Navidad" on the radio.

Man, that song drives me crazy ... er, loco.

As unfathomable as it seems, my kids might not have a tree to congregate around this morning — although, as my deadline looms, my wife tells me she's making one last, desperate sweep through Metairie to find one, which worries me because I don't know if she'll make it back home before, say, Tuesday.

What about my dinner?

Which brings up this point: How is it that we lost 80 percent of our residents around here, but traffic got worse? Can somebody explain that? How is it that bars close earlier but people drink more? Ah, don't get me started.

Under the circumstances, it's pretty hard to get worked up about it. It's pretty hard to get worked up about any of life's little inconveniences these days; odd, since there are more inconveniences than ever before and some of them aren't so little.

We've got a house. I've got a job. We're way ahead of the game. We're like royalty in one of those old Monty Python movies; we've got clean clothes.

But my daughter fell to pieces about the tree thing. I thought it was the sentimentalist in her, driven to despair because a part of our revered process might be missing this year, part of our seasonal custom gone to seed.

In fact, it was because she told me that Santa wouldn't have anywhere to put her presents. Good to know that she's got her priorities together.

So I told her Santa is not about trees, he's about kids, and we've been through this before anyway, when she discovered a few years ago that we don't have a chimney either. Man, those old storybook legends make it a hard go-round for parents in the 21st century.

I mean, if Santa rode a Humvee pulled by, say, a bunch of potbellied pigs, this whole Christmas thing would be an easier sell. (Funny, though, my kids never cry out for Old World porridge; they're cafeteria traditionalists, picking those they like and dispensing with the rest.)

Anyway, I wound up pulling that old parenting trick of instilling sadness and guilt in children to make them come around to your point of view.

"You know, some of our friends don't even have houses to put trees in this year," I told them, and, unlike when my parents used to invoke starving children in Africa as a reason to finish my dinner — an oblique reference at best to a 6-year-old — the fact is, they understand what it's like to be homeless.

For the past four months, they have been living a thousand miles away with hand-me-down clothes and borrowed toys.

But now they are home. And I wanted to wait until they were here so we could get the tree together, but maybe I waited too long and so it goes.

A Christmas like no other.

I suppose one positive aspect of the circumstances is that my family didn't receive any holiday photo cards with pictures of our friends' pets wearing Santa hats this year.

And we received no tiresome family newsletters from faraway friends whose children are way above average, sweeping everything from the gold medal in the 400-meter back stroke to the Blue Ribbon for animal husbandry at the Iowa 4-H fair this summer.

But this is small recompense. Truth is, we didn't get any Christmas cards at all this year. That has never happened. I suppose they'll show up in June. With our Christmas catalogs, no doubt. And my Newsweeks from October.

Funny how you recalibrate your priorities in life: No mail, no problem. Whatever.

That's Christmas in New Orleans this year. Shape-shifting. Adapting. Getting along and getting by. Pondering the heretofore unknown dilemma: what to get for that special someone on your list who has . . . nothing.

Today it will be my family and my in-laws from Baton Rouge and Mississippi coming to join us in our winter homecoming, to celebrate over a warm meal and probably a few tears and a lot of laughter.

Kind of a simple formula, really. A chance to eat, breathe, forget and remember. One more day to just be alive and be thankful for that and to carry on and up.

And Jose Feliciano on the radio. Singing that dang song.

Tears, Fears and a New Year

When I look back on the year 2005, nothing comes to mind more than the opening line of Dickens' "A Tale of Two Cities."

"It was the best of times, it was the worst of times."

Except for that "best of times" part, it describes New Orleans perfectly.

How did we get here? What happened to my tough-lovin', hard-luck, good-timin' town?

Mercy.

I have cowered in fear this year from the real and the imagined. The fear of injury, the fear of disease, the fear of death, the fear of abandonment, isolation and insanity.

I have had seared into my olfactory lockbox the smell of gasoline and dead people. And your leftovers.

I have feared the phantom notions of sharks swimming in our streets and bands of armed men coming for me in the night to steal my generator and water and then maybe rape me or cut my throat just for the hell of it.

I have wept, for hours on end, days on end.

The crying jags. I guess they're therapeutic, but give me a break.

The first time I went to the Winn-Dixie after it reopened, I had all my purchases on the conveyer belt, plus a bottle of mouthwash. During the Days of Horror following the decimation of this city, I had gone into the foul and darkened store and lifted a bottle.

I was operating under the "take only what you need" clause that the strays who remained behind in this godforsaken place invoked in the early days.

My thinking was that it was in everyone's best interest if I had a bottle of mouthwash.

When the cashier rang up my groceries all those weeks later, I tried, as subtly as possible, to hand her the bottle and ask her if she could see that it was put back on the shelf. She was confused by my action and offered to void the purchase if I didn't want the bottle.

I told her it's not that I didn't want it, but that I wished to pay for it and could she please see that it was put back on the shelf. More confusion ensued and the line behind me got longer and it felt very hot and crowded all of a sudden and I tried to tell her: "Look, when the store was closed . . . you know . . . after the thing . . . I took . . . ."

The words wouldn't come. Only the tears.

The people in line behind me stood stoic and patient, public meltdowns being as common as discarded kitchen appliances in this town.

What's that over there? Oh, it's just some dude crying his ass off. Nothing new here. Show's over people, move along.

The cashier, an older woman, finally grasped my pathetic gesture, my lowly attempt to make amends, my fulfillment to a promise I made to myself to repay anyone I had stolen from.

"I get it, baby," she said, and she gently took the bottle from my hands and I gathered my groceries and walked sobbing from the store.

She was kind to me. I probably will never see her again, but I will never forget her. That bottle. That store. All the fury that prevailed. The fear.

A friend of mine, a photojournalist, recently went to a funeral to take pictures. There had been an elderly couple trapped in a house. He had a heart attack and slipped into the water. She held onto a gutter for two days before being rescued.

It was seven weeks before the man's body was found in the house, then another six weeks before the remains were released from the St. Gabriel morgue for burial.

"Tell me a story I haven't heard," I told my friend. Go ahead. Shock me.

When my father and I were trading dark humor one night and he was offering advice on how to begin my year in review, he cracked himself up, proposing: "It was a dark and stormy night."

That's close, but not quite it. "It was a dark and stormy morning" would be closer to the truth.

What a morning it was.

I was in Vicksburg. I had just left the miserable hotel crackhouse to which my family had evacuated — it must have been the last vacant room in the South — and was looking for breakfast for my kids.

But the streets and businesses were abandoned and a slight but stinging rain was falling, the wind surging and warm, and while my kids played on a little riverfront playground, I got through on my cell phone to The Times-Picayune newsroom, where scores of TP families had taken refuge, and I remember saying to the clerk who answered the phone:

"Man, that was a close one, huh? Looks like we dodged another bullet."

I suppose around a million people were saying exactly the same thing at exactly the same time. What I would have given to be right. Just that one time.

I was trying to get through to my editor to ask: "What's the plan?"

By late afternoon, that's what everyone in the Gulf region was asking.

Of course, it turns out there wasn't a plan. Anywhere. Who could have known?

The newspaper was just like everyone else at that point: As a legion of employees and their families piled into delivery trucks and fled the newspaper building as the waters rose around them, we shifted into the same operational mode as everyone else:

Survive. Wing it. Do good work. Save someone or something. And call your mother and tell her you're all right.

Unless, of course, your mother was in Lakeview or the Lower 9th or Chalmette or . . . well, I've had enough of those horror stories for now. I don't even want to visit that place today.

This was the year that defines our city, our lives, our destiny. Nothing comparable has ever happened in modern times in America, and there is no blueprint for how we do this.

We just wing it. Do good work. Save someone or something.

You'd have to be crazy to want to live here. You'd have to be plumb out of reasonable options elsewhere.

Then again, I have discovered that the only thing worse than being in New Orleans these days is not being in New Orleans.

It's a siren calling us home. It cannot be explained.

"They don't get us," is the common refrain you hear from frustrated residents who think the government and the nation have turned a blind eye to us in our time of need. Then again, if they did get us, if we were easily boxed and labeled, I suppose we'd be just Anyplace, USA.

And that won't do.

We have a job to do here, and that is to entertain the masses and I don't mean the tourists. They're part of it, of course, but what we do best down here — have done for decades — is create a lifestyle that others out there in the Great Elsewhere envy and emulate.

Our music, our food, yada, yada, yada. It's a tale so often told that it borders on platitude but it is also the searing truth: We are the music. We are the food. We are the dance. We are the tolerance. We are the spirit.

And one day, they'll get it.

As a woman named Judy Deck e-mailed to me, in a moment of inspiration: "If there was no New Orleans, America would just be a bunch of free people dying of boredom."

Yeah, you write.

That, people, is the final word on 2005.

photo by RedBean

Chris Rose, a native of Chevy Chase, Md., graduated with a journalism degree from the University of Wisconsin in 1982. After a stint as a staff writer at The Washington Post, he joined The Times-Picayune as a crime reporter in 1984. Over the years, he has covered national politics, economics, Southern regionalism, pop culture and New Orleans nightlife, traditions, lifestyles and entertainment. On Aug. 29, 2005, he became a war correspondent.

He is an occasional commentator for National Public Radio's "Morning Edition," and a contributing essayist to The Lehrer Report on PBS.

He is married to Kelly Gluth Rose, a New Orleans girl. They have three children, Katherine, Jack and James, and were recently joined by a dog left homeless by Hurricane Rita. They named her Luna Biscuit, which is French for Moon Pie, sort of.

Charlie Varley is a British freelance photo journalist who has traveled the world, documenting the sublime to the surreal, from celebrities and presidents to war and peace. He has lived in America for the past decade, spending three of those years chronicling daily life in 48 states from the front seat of a battered Ford Mustang before arriving in New Orleans for good.

This was, of course, a life-altering decision: "I was in the Hyatt when the glass came out," Varley says. "I was standing next to the Mayor as the radios crackled with the news of collapsing levees. I was in the 9th ward as the waters rose. I waded through fetid water strewn with debris and corpses.

"I witnessed the destruction of one of the finest cities in America, her soul bared and exposed, her inequality and inefficiency laid out for all to see. And through it all I saw the grace, courage and dignity of her citizens, forced to flee their homes, their lives, their city, their history.

"I trust her soul will be repaired. May we never forget the displaced and those who perished."

His images of Katrina can be viewed at www.varleypix.com.

Tipitina's Foundation

Tipitina's nightclub is perhaps New Orleans' most treasured nightclub, the former home base of such musical icons as Professor Longhair, James Booker, the Neville Brothers and Dr. John.

The Tipitina's Foundation hosts the Tipitina's Internship Program, which teaches high school students all aspects of the music business and Instrument's A Comin', which provides musical instruments to the New Orleans public school system.

Since Hurricane Katrina, the foundation now works to relocate evacuated musicians back home, repair flood-damaged homes and replace lost and damaged instruments and sound gear.

The foundation website hosts a database containing housing options specifically earmarked for New Orleans artists and the nightclub houses the Music Co-op Office, which has 11 computer workstations for use by musicians and offers free legal aid, health care consultations and more.

The foundation is boosting the Mardi Gras Indian community by handing out grants to tribes to purchase feathers, plumes and other supplies needed for new suits and the club hosts Mardi Gras Indian practice every Sunday night, preserving one of New Orleans' most sacred and mysterious cultural traditions.

The Tipitina's Foundation is a registered 501(c)(3) organization. For more information, please go to www.tipitinasfoundation.org.

ARTDOCS

ARTDOCS was founded in 1998 by New Orleans gallery owner Jonathan Ferrera and physician Vincent Morelli. Its mission is to meet the health care needs of New Orleans artists without health insurance. All writers, poets, musicians, visual artists and performing artists are eligible for services. It is the first program of its kind in the nation.

ARTDOCS sees up to 300 patients per year. Medical visits are free of charge and lab tests, X-rays and other procedures are covered by funds raised in a yearly benefit/art auction and by private donations.

Since Hurricane Katrina, ARTDOCS has expanded its mission to providing grants to help local artists rebuild ravaged studios, replace lost materials and simply to relocate back to New Orleans.

ARTDOCS is helping revive the soul of the city.

ARTDOCS is a registered 501(c)(3) organization.
For more information, please go to www.artdocs.com.